TWO GIRLS DOWN

Praise for TWO GIRLS DOWN and Louisa Luna

'Opening this book is like arming a bomb—
the suspense is relentless and the payoff is spectacular.
Lead character Alice Vega is sensational—I want to see
lots more of her.' Lee Child, #1 *New York Times*
bestselling author of *The Midnight Line*

'From its haunting opening to the pulse-pounding
final sequences, *Two Girls Down* delivers a gripping
read. Alice Vega and Max Caplan are characters I'd follow
anywhere, and Louisa Luna is a writer to watch. Highly
recommended.' Michael Koryta, *New York Times*
bestselling author of *Those Who Wish Me Dead*

'This is such a terrific read. High stakes, relationship-
driven, perfectly paced. *Two Girls Down* has something else
worth noting: three-dimensional female characters. Alice
Vega could give Jack Reacher a run for his money. Maybe
Louisa Luna should write all the thrillers.' Chelsea Cain,
New York Times bestselling author of *Heartsick*

'A knockout, read-it-in-one-sitting novel…Gripping,
emotional, and tautly written, with a wonderful cast
of memorable characters.' Jeff Abbott, *New York
Times* bestselling author of *Adrenaline*

'Louisa Luna is an incredibly talented writer with a
bewitching gift for storytelling, and *Two Girls Down* fairly
crackles with energy and suspense from the first page to the
last. I can't ever recall a time before now that I lost sleep as
a result of reading a crime thriller. This one, I just could
not put down.' Donald Ray Pollock, author of *The Devil
All the Time* and *The Heavenly Table*

'Sensational…One of the book's great pleasures is seeing Caplan and Vega's initially testy entanglement develop into a true partnership. But there are many other aspects in Ms. Luna's story to savor as well: a host of sharply sketched characters, from spaced-out dopers to distraught parents and grandparents; action sequences startling in their sudden violence; and quick psychological revelations that pierce the heart.' *Wall Street Journal*

'I'm always looking for a good thriller, and this just was perfect. It's exactly the kind of thriller that I most enjoy… You really want to spend time with these two main characters. It was one of those things where the plot was great and it was complex enough to keep me interested, but what I loved most was the way these two very, very different characters— complicated with complicated lives—interact.' NPR

'To the pantheon of unforgettable noir detectives, add Louisa Luna's bounty hunter Alice Vega and her partner, PI Max Caplan, one of the best and most original duos to grace crime fiction in many years. *Two Girls Down* is a breathlessly gripping journey into the dark heart of America: I couldn't put it down.' Elizabeth Hand, author of *Generation Loss* and *Hard Light*

'A real nail-biter…The brisk plot combines psychological suspense with solid action, while providing a realistic look at a family under siege, as it builds to a shocking finale.' *Publishers Weekly*, starred review

'An outstanding neo-noir, introducing enigmatic bounty hunter Alice Vega, a perfect female incarnation of Jack Reacher…Vega springs to life in the hands of this immensely talented writer…This is a must-read for fans of strong female protagonists.' *Booklist*, starred review

'This one is a beaut, not only suspenseful but with some real embedded truths about how hard it is to be a mother.' Anna Quindlen, author of *One True Thing*

Louisa Luna is the author of the novels *Brave New Girl*, *Crooked*, and *Serious as a Heart Attack*. She was born and raised in San Francisco and lives in Brooklyn with her husband and daughter.

TWO GIRLS DOWN

LOUISA LUNA

TEXT PUBLISHING MELBOURNE AUSTRALIA

textpublishing.com.au
textpublishing.co.uk

The Text Publishing Company
Swann House, 22 William Street, Melbourne, Victoria 3000, Australia

The Text Publishing Company (UK) Ltd
130 Wood Street, London EC2V 6DL, United Kingdom

First published by Doubleday, an imprint of Penguin Random House US, in 2018
This edition published by the Text Publishing Company in 2019

Cover design by Text, based on the original by John Fontana
Cover images by Jane Fulton Alt/Gallery Stock

Printed in Australia by Griffin Press, an accredited ISO/NZS 14001:2004 Environmental Management System printer

ISBN: 9781925773644 (paperback)
ISBN: 9781925774436 (ebook)

A catalogue record for this book is available from the National Library of Australia

For John Belluso

1

JAMIE BRANDT WAS NOT A BAD MOTHER. LATER SHE WOULD TELL that to anyone who would listen: police, reporters, lawyers, her parents, her boyfriend, her dealer, the new bartender with the knuckle tattoos at Schultz's, the investigator from California and her partner, and her own reflection in the bathroom mirror, right before cracking her forehead on the sink's edge and passing out from the cocktail of pain, grief, and fear.

She was not a bad mother, even though she'd yelled at them that morning. It was Saturday, finally, and Jamie was embarrassed to say sometimes she liked the weekdays more, the predictable rhythm of her aunt Maggie's real estate office where she was the receptionist, the chance to drink coffee and read *Us* magazine online, thinking of the girls in school, which they actually liked for the most part. Kylie, the ten-year-old, might piss and moan over homework, but she loved the day-to-day operations of school—the hurricane of note passing and gossip. She was already popular, had already stolen makeup from Jamie's top dresser drawer and sent texts to boys from Jamie's phone. Bailey, eight, was just as sassy but loved school for the school part, reading and writing—especially vocabulary, the way words sounded and the rules that went with them.

The weekends were hectic, a blur of soccer games and ballet practice, playdates and every last minute crammed with errands: groceries, cooking, pharmacy (Kylie's allergies, Bailey's asthma), cleaning the apartment, dusting and Swiffering every surface to avoid allergies and asthma. And then meltdowns and screaming protests about the rules: one hour on the computer for non-school-related activities, half an hour of video games, one hour of TV, all of which would be broken by Sunday night. Jamie would have to beg them to go to the housing complex playground, which the girls claimed was old, dirty, with two out of five swings broken and a sandbox that smelled like pee.

All Jamie wanted was to get to Saturday night. Then Darrell would come over and maybe the girls would go somewhere for a sleepover, or to Nana and Papa's. Maybe Jamie would let them play video games for a bonus hour in their room and take pictures with her phone just so she and Darrell could drink some beers and watch a movie that didn't feature a chipmunk or a princess. And if the girls weren't there, maybe they'd smoke a joint; maybe his hand would slide up her shirt and they'd end up naked on the couch, Jamie looking at him on top, thinking he is not perfect, he has funny teeth and always wears that leather jacket with the hole in the pit, but there are a few good qualities here. One large good quality: she would think and then she'd laugh, and Darrell would say, "What?" but then he'd laugh too.

But first, errands and then a birthday party for all of them. It was for a girl in Kylie's class, but it was one of those parties to which everyone was invited—siblings and parents for pizza, games, and cake in the family's big ranch-style house in a new development called The Knolls. Jamie didn't like the trend, these big free-for-all events, was worried because Kylie's birthday was in June and maybe she'd want the same thing. Jamie saw the problems coming at her like headlights: their apartment was too small for a party, her mother would never let her hear the end of it if she asked to have it at her parents' place, and the money, all that money, for that many pizzas plus gifts plus a new dress for Kylie and the new dress Bailey would have to have too.

"Why do you guys even have to come in?" said Kylie from the passenger side, eyebrows wrinkled up over her big hot-cocoa eyes, a sneer in her angel lips.

"Fine, we'll wait outside in the car," said Jamie.

"Everyone will see us," said Bailey from the backseat, anxious.

Jamie looked in the rearview, taking in Bailey's face, a palette of worry. How can she care so much about what other people think already? thought Jamie. She didn't want the girls to care; she missed the days when they were too little to worry about appearances or be embarrassed, back when they would streak like hippies before jumping into the tub.

"We're not waiting in the car, Kylie," said Jamie. "Hey—won't Stella Piper be there with her family? Bailey can play with Owen."

From the corner of her eye Jamie saw her shrug, and felt the weight of it.

"They're not friends anymore," said Bailey.

"They're not?" Jamie said to Bailey. "You're not?" she said to Kylie.

"Why can't you shut up?" Kylie said, craning her head around the seat to glare at her sister.

"Mom!" shouted Bailey, pointing.

"I heard it, Bailey." To Kylie: "Don't talk like that to your sister. Why aren't you friends with Stella Piper anymore?"

Another shrug.

"She thinks Stella's dumb. And her glasses are funny," Bailey reported. "She says they make her look like a creature."

"She's been your friend forever, since you were in kindergarten," said Jamie.

"I know," said Kylie, hushed and hissing.

Jamie stopped third in a trail of cars at a light and said, "You shouldn't be mean to someone just because they look funny."

Kylie stared out the window.

"Someday someone might think you look funny, and then how'll you like it?"

Kylie kept staring.

"Well?" Jamie took Kylie's chin in her hand and turned her head. "Well?"

"I won't like it."

Jamie let go and looked up to see a policeman directing all the cars in her lane to the left.

"What's this now?" said Jamie.

Bailey looked up over the seat.

"What is it? What's happening?"

"I don't know, for God's sake," said Jamie.

She pulled up even with the cop and rolled down the window.

"I need to go straight ahead to the Gulf on Branford."

"Branford? That side of the highway's closed for the parade, Miss," said the cop.

"Fuck me," Jamie said, remembering.

Spring Fest. The town's annual parade of toilet-paper-covered floats and high school bands slogging their way through "My Girl."

"Mom!" the kids shouted, embarrassed.

"Well, Officer, I'm about to run outta gas, so what do you recommend?"

The cop leaned into her window.

"Tell you what, I'll wave you through to St. Cloud; then you can take a right to Route 1080 and you can get to the Hess over that way."

Jamie pictured the route in her head and nodded. "That'd be just great, thanks."

"No problem, ma'am," said the cop, tapping the roof of the car.

Jamie drove the path laid out for her by the cop.

"I can't believe you said the f-curse to the police," said Kylie, a look of quiet shame on her face.

"I'm full of surprises," said Jamie.

"Can we go past the parade? Miss Ferno's on a float from her church," said Bailey.

"What? No, we're already late for this thing," said Jamie.

She glanced at both of them. They stared out the window. Someday you'll think I'm funny, she thought. Someday you'll tell your friends, No, my mom's cool. Once she said "Fuck me" right in front of a cop.

Finally, when they got to the Hess, Kylie asked, "Can we split a Reese's?"

She had yet to outgrow an unwavering devotion to sugar—she would pour maple syrup over Frosted Flakes if you turned your head the other way.

"No, you're going to have all kinds of crap at this party; you don't need a Reese's."

Then the wailing began—you'd think someone was pricking their cuticles with sewing needles. Jamie held her head and leaned over the wheel, thinking she should have smoked the very last bit of resin in the pipe this morning. She didn't like to drive stoned, but there wasn't enough in there to mess her up proper, just enough to help her push through, get to the party where it might be acceptable to have a light beer at noon.

"Enough, stop it!" yelled Jamie, feeling her voice crack, the muscles in her neck tense up. "Fine, go get a goddamn Reese's. Get me a coffee with a Splenda, please."

She threw a five in Kylie's lap.

"Go before I change my mind," she said.

The girls unbuckled their seat belts and scrambled out of the car. Jamie watched them run into the mini-mart, heard the clicks of their dress-up shoes. She checked her makeup in the mirror and shook her head at herself, then went out to the pumps.

She continued to shake her head, thought, Jesus Christ, do I ever sound like her—her own mother, Gail—"Before I change my mind" and all those threats. First you swear you'll never be like your mother; then you find yourself sending them to their room and grounding them, and occasionally, once in a while, you hit them once or twice too hard on the back after they say something rude.

Jamie got back in the car and blew air into her hands. Spring Fest my ass, she thought. It was the end of March and still freezing in the mornings and at night, although they'd had more than a few hazy warm days the past two months that fooled everyone into thinking spring was really here; even the black cherry trees were confused—fruit had prematurely formed on the branches, then iced over and broke off the next week in a storm.

The girls had been in the store a long time.

Jamie looked at the time on her phone. 11:32 a.m. They still had to go to Kmart for a gift for Kylie's friend, which meant they would argue about the under-ten-dollar rule, then engage in negotiations until they got to an under-ten-dollar-without-tax agreement. If there was time, maybe Jamie could browse for something for her aunt Maggie, whose birthday was coming up. Maggie was fond of her, and Jamie didn't really know why—maybe because she admired Jamie's pluck, maybe because she'd been a single mother herself after Uncle Stu had left her for a girl in a massage parlor twenty years ago, and she knew how rough it was. Maybe because it was a way to piss off her sister, Jamie's mother, which she enjoyed doing for a list of reasons either one would tell you all about if you asked them. Jamie ultimately didn't care about the details since Aunt Maggie had cleaned up in the divorce and got her real estate agent's license in short order, owned half a dozen homes in the Poconos that she rented out to vacationers, and brokered deals between buyers and the new developments surrounding Denville.

"Goddammit," said Jamie.

She got out of the car and jogged into the mini-mart, scanned the inside quickly and saw only one other person—a man, looking at a porn magazine.

"Hey," she said to the fat boy behind the counter. He seemed too old for the braces on his teeth.

He jumped.

"You see two girls in here?"

"Yeah. They went to the bathroom in back."

Jamie did not say thank you, walked past the guy with the porn and out the back door. She saw Kylie leaning against the cinder block wall, holding a Reese's cup between her thumb and forefinger like a teacup.

"What the hell, Kylie?" said Jamie.

"She had to pee. She said it was an emergency."

Jamie stormed past, rapped on the bathroom door and said, "Bailey, come on, let's move it."

"I'm washing my hands," said Bailey from inside.

"You're done. Let's go."

"I'm trying not to touch anything."

Jamie almost smiled. She had been trying to teach them to line the toilet seat with paper towels, hover above the bowl, and turn the faucets on and off with their elbows in public bathrooms.

"I have Purell in the car. Come on."

The door opened and Bailey came out. She looked at her mother and covered her mouth with her hands.

"We forgot the coffee!"

"It's okay," said Jamie. "Let's go."

They went back to the car and drove to the Ridgewood Mall without speaking, Kylie staring out the window, Bailey reading her school workbook. Jamie glanced at both of them and thought they looked nice. Bailey in a pink princess dress, Kylie in a black dress with a purple flower print and the sweetheart neckline that was a little too old for her, Jamie thought, but since it was a hand-me-down from her cousin, she could not complain. They are both so big, she thought, which makes me so old.

The parking lot was surprisingly not crowded, the first three or four rows of the grid full but that was it. God bless Spring Fest, Jamie thought.

"So what does Arianna want?"

"Aren't we coming in?" said Kylie, shocked.

"No way. I'm going in and out."

"Come on. That's so unfair!" they both said.

"Deal with it," said Jamie. "What does she like?"

Kylie sighed. "She wants a sleeping bag."

"I'm not buying her a sleeping bag. Does she like jewelry?"

Kylie nodded.

"Great. I'll get her some bracelets."

Jamie looked through her purse for her phone and her wallet, left the key in the ignition so the heat would stay on.

"Can we at least listen to music?" said Kylie.

"Yes, you can. I'll be back in five minutes."

Jamie got out and was about to slam the door when Bailey said, "Mom?"

"What?"

She looked up from her book and said, "Do you know you call a group of lions a pride, not a pack?"

Jamie stared at her, then at Kylie, who rolled her eyes.

"No, baby, I didn't know that."

She shut the door and left them.

Into the calm, controlled air of Kmart, pop music from ten years ago in her ears, she forced herself to stay focused. If she didn't have a list, she had trouble concentrating in big box stores, got distracted by displays and sales. That was the point, wasn't it, she thought, to turn you into a kid again who sees something shiny and wants it. When the girls were with her, a ten-minute trip turned into thirty minutes easily, everyone leaving with candy and gum and a tank top.

Jamie went to the toy aisles, skimmed over the bright boxes and tubes and balls to the girls section, Make-Your-Own-Headband, Home Manicure Kit, Bead-a-Necklace—she picked that one up; it was $9.99. You got lucky today, Arianna.

She made her way to the cards and wrapping paper, grabbed a pink gift bag with tissue paper already lined inside and a white card dangling from the handle.

Then on her way to the checkout she stopped when she saw a sheer cowl-necked sweater on a sale rack. The tag read $21.99. Nope.

At the register, she checked her phone (11:55). Oh who cares, she thought. It doesn't matter if you're late to this kind of thing; it's an open house. Suddenly she felt relaxed, realized her hands were in fists, holding the strings of the gift bag hostage in her fingers. The day opened up in front of her. The party would eat up a couple of hours, then maybe they'd stop by her parents' place, then she could pick up McDonald's for dinner, and then they could waste time until Darrell came over and she could send them to her room and let them watch TV in her bed.

It didn't seem that bad when she thought of it that way. Just some hours to fill.

She paid, picked up her bag, and left. Into the parking lot, back to her car, she sped up. Confused at first, she thought, This is my car. Checked the dent in the fender, the plate. No girls.

I'm going to kill them, she thought, took a breath too quickly and coughed, started talking to them in her head. Don't even tell me you can't tie it in a knot till we get to the fucking party, Bailey. Or you, was this your idea? she thought, picturing Kylie's face. You and your sweet tooth, looking for free samples.

Jamie looked around at the stores: Reno's Coffee, Morgan Housewares, StoneField Ice Cream. She ran to the latter, coughing like she was a smoker, entered through the doors. It was quiet and cold inside. A woman and two little boys and a baby in a car seat sat in a booth. The girl behind the counter had a ring in her lip.

"You see two girls come in here?" said Jamie.

"Yeah, they were just in here."

For a second they stared at each other.

"So where are they?" said Jamie.

Lip Ring shrugged.

"How should I know? They left a few minutes ago."

Jamie could feel the blood rush in her chest. She started to leave, then turned back and said, "Lemme ask you something: How the fuck do you eat with that thing in your face?"

She left and slammed the door before she could hear the answer.

Then Reno's Coffee—a couple, a man post-workout, everyone on his phone.

"Did you see two girls in party dresses?" she asked the people behind the counter. "Eight and ten years old. Did they come in to use the bathroom?" Then to the couple and the man: "Did you see two girls?"

They all said no.

She left, looked back at her car, still empty.

Then Morgan Housewares, Global Market, Eastern Sports. By the time she got back to Kmart it was 12:11, and the fear had become a rock in her throat.

"I can't find my girls," she said to the security guard. She put her hand to her lips after she said it, like she was trying to get the words back.

"Did you lose them in the store, ma'am?" he said. His double chin was strangled by his uniform shirt.

"No, they were in the car. I was in here. Now they're gone."

"We can page them in the store," he said.

"They're not in the store. I was in the store."

"Maybe they came in to look for you," he said.

"Yeah, okay. Yes, please, page them."

She was standing in Customer Service with Geri the Customer Service Liaison and two other security guards when she heard the guard with the double chin's voice say her daughters' names: "Kylie Brandt, Bailey Brandt, please come to the Customer Service Center."

Jamie watched people emerge from the aisles, calm, bored. It was not their daughters' names in the air.

"You have bathrooms? Where are the bathrooms?" she said.

Geri pointed to the left.

"You can hear the loudspeaker in there too," she said. Jamie couldn't even see this woman; her face was a smudge with dull gray spots in the middle.

Jamie ran now through the white aisles, hearing the sound of her own wheezing and rationalizations as she talked to herself, "She had to pee, Bailey had to pee. Maybe one of them got sick from that Reese's."

She threw herself onto the door and into the bathroom, knocked on and pushed open every stall. A woman with a walker and a younger woman stood at the sinks.

"Did you see two girls? I can't find my girls."

The woman with the walker appeared not to understand. The younger woman said, "No, what did they look like?"

"They're wearing dresses," Jamie said, and ran out again, to the front of the store.

She passed the security guards and Geri, and now a small crowd of people looking and talking, to the front doors where she exited, ran into the parking lot, back to her car, which was still empty. She hit the hood with her hand and ran back to the store, where more people stood, watching her.

The face of a man with a mustache blurred in front of her, next to the guard with the double chin.

"Ma'am, I put out a Code Adam alert for the entire mall and called the police. Do you want to sit down?"

Jamie didn't understand the words he said. He held out his hand, to guide her inside to a cushioned folding chair, where someone would bring her a glass of water.

Jamie didn't take it. She dug her fingernails into her scalp and whispered, "My girls . . . my girls."

They always think they won't get caught, thought Cap. They want to get caught, Nell said to him once. Otherwise why do it? And Cap said, No one wants to get caught, not even the ones who feel guilty, and that is actually most of them. Not even Catholics. And you need a little bit of ego to think you're the one who's not going to get caught. That you're the one guy who'll fool his wife forever; you're the one woman whose husband never asks too many questions. Maybe you are. Maybe you get to have it all—a sweet home life and something breathless and dramatic on the side. Maybe you deserve it, too. Maybe she's a bitch and you never wanted to marry her in the first place. Maybe you never wanted to work this job in this trashy old town and drive this piece-of-shit car and have these screaming kids with cheese curl dust on their fingers. Maybe the only way it gets better is to have an hour with the waitress from the diner or the fresh young babysitter in a motel room or your car with the backseat folded into the trunk.

Maybe you're just an asshole.

Cap had stopped flipping through the possibilities a long time ago. The truth was he didn't care why they did it; it was just his job to catch them. A pocket-sized DVR tucked into a cigarette box, one full water bottle, and one empty, black coffee in a thermos. Beaded seat cushion like the cabbies used to have back in Brooklyn when he grew up. Sometimes reading material but not for this kind of active surveillance, which usually took place over lunchtime or a coffee break. Passion doesn't take long.

His phone buzzed. It was a text from Nell: "Do u have anything 4 din in the house???"

Cap wrote back: "Let's order Justino's."

Nell wrote: "Sick of pizza. Chinese. I'll get mu shu."

Cap wrote: "Great."

Nell wrote: ":)"

Sideways happy face. People are going to start putting sideways happy faces on their headstones, he thought. Here lies Max Caplan: Father, Ex-husband, Private Investigator, Disgraced Cop, :). Sideways happy face.

Definitely "Father" first on the headstone. Leave it to his daughter, Nell, he thought, to think of dinner at 5 p.m., not because she was hungry but because she knew he would have a bowl of cereal unless she took care of it. He told her not to worry because he was basically okay. He never went into how much he drank on nights when he wasn't working or when she was at her mother's, how he woke up in the middle of the night after passing out on the couch with the TV blaring.

The door to room 7 opened, and Cap propped the cigarette box up on the side mirror and tapped Record on the DVR. A man and a woman came out. The man had a belly that seemed to go all the way around his waist, like a life preserver, over his belt. The woman was, unfortunately, blond and trashy-looking, tight jeans and a spray tan. You couldn't fight the stereotype a little, lady? Cap thought as he watched it all through the screen. He zoomed in as much as he could on the couple, getting their entire bodies in the frame. You wanted to see the body language as much as the face, he'd found. Hands and hips and feet. If they didn't kiss you wanted to see how they touched, and if they didn't touch, if you could see every part of them, it was easier to see if they wanted to.

These two touched. The man had his hand on her elbow, her arm was around the life preserver, both of them talking with their mouths downward, whispering, thought Cap. The man said something, and the woman laughed and then put her fingers to his lips, like she was shushing him. Playful, intimate. Then the woman got in her car and drove away, and the man watched her go. He walked across the lot to his car, and then sat in the driver's seat for a couple of minutes. He sat, and Cap sat. Cap watched him rub his face with the heels of the hands and then the fingers. Guilty, big guy? Then the man drove away. Cap tapped Pause.

"Oh, Mr. Svetich," he said.

Watching another man cheat on his wife was exhausting. Cheating was one thing Jules could never accuse him of when they were married. He worked too much, drank too much, smoked too much (which was really hardly at all, but too much for her); he was emotionally unavailable and never wanted to talk about things. He was vaguely resentful and angry at Jules for bringing him not even to Philly but to a part of Pennsylvania where he was the only Jew in the room at any given function. Then he lost his job, and there was nothing vague at all about how resentful and angry he was.

Once he threw a beer bottle at the bathroom door when Jules was in there and wouldn't come out. He was always too tired. He didn't spend enough time with Nell. He snored and twitched when he slept. His pee aim was poor in the middle of the night. He had dandruff sometimes and rarely clipped his toenails. But he never cheated on her.

Cap put the camera in his pocket and drove away, heading home, to Denville. He stopped at the beer distributors close to his house, picked up a case of Yuengling for him and club soda for Nell. In the parking lot he walked past a guy who looked familiar, but in a town of fifteen thousand everyone looked familiar. At the grocery store you ran into the guy who cut your hair and the woman who'd served you an Irish Car Bomb on the house last weekend. At your kid's soccer game you saw the postman and the city councilman and the gal who handed out free samples in front of StoneField Ice Cream. The longer he was a cop, the more Cap thought this was not such a nice thing. He hated knowing people. The Iraq War vet who he used to shake hands with at bars eventually holed up in his house with a jug of vodka and a gun. The flirty waitress at Applebee's who left her newborn in the garbage in the restaurant bathroom. The former high school football star who OD'd on oxy and Heineken. Keep your small towns, thought Cap. Give me a city where I don't recognize the corpse.

"Hey, Cap, right?" the guy in the beer distributors parking lot said.

Place him, place him, thought Cap. You've known him for a while because he looks older and fatter and redder now than he used to.

"It's me, Chris. Chris Morris."

School, parent-teacher conference a few years back. His daughter was the same age as Nell.

"Chris. How's it going? How's your daughter . . ?"

Cap paused, struggled.

"Ruthie," said Chris, unoffended. "Yours is Nell, right?"

"Yeah, Nell."

"Mine's giving me a heart attack. Literally. I go for a checkup last week, my blood pressure's 140 over 90. He asks do I have more stress at work, am I eating more salt? I say no, I got a sixteen-year-old girl at home. He goes, that's it, then."

Cap nodded and smiled and did the man commiseration thing. He pictured himself and Nell playing Texas Hold'em at the kitchen table last Saturday night.

"Everything's a fight too. Tonight she's going to that dance, and it's like negotiating with the goddamn UN trying to get her home at a decent time."

Cap stopped him, held out two calm fingers.

"There's a dance tonight?"

"Yeah, over at St. Paul's. Nell's not going?"

"I don't know. Maybe she forgot to tell me."

"Watch that, brother. It's very convenient what they forget."

Chris kept talking until Cap said he was running late. They shook hands again. Cap put the beer in his trunk and drove away. Why hadn't Nell told him about the dance? The real question was, why wasn't she going? The even more real question: Why didn't she want to go?

It wasn't like she didn't have friends. Sophie Kenton and Carrie Pratt were always around, and now that guy, Nick, who was definitely gay even if he wasn't telling people yet. Why wouldn't they all go together?

She ran cross-country in the fall, played soccer in the spring, got mostly A's, played tenor drum in the marching band, organized student trips to the local soup kitchen and the children's wing of the hospital. Cap thought she was beautiful, but she had inherited Jules's dramatic features, a long, distinguished face and nose. Jules, a Women's Studies professor at Lehigh, said Nell resembled a young Virginia Woolf. Cap knew teenage girls did not want to look like Virginia Woolf; they wanted to look like red-carpet movie stars, all lips and breasts and curved tan backs.

Cap was sure it was his fault, certain that the divorce four years ago had permanently damaged his daughter's self-esteem. They'd done the right things, sent Nell to a therapist; both he and Jules were careful to tell her it wasn't her fault, but still, always, shit got through. Cap truly believed there was nothing harder than being a kid. You were always an alien trying to learn the earth rules.

He pulled up to the house and sighed. It still made him sigh and sometimes laugh that he had gotten the house with all the ghosts. Jules got to move to a new condo with white carpeting and vertical blinds.

The place had come in handy when he started his business, though. He'd converted the mudroom and the den into a small office and had his clients come through the side door.

And more important, Nell liked it—she liked the three narrow floors and the bathroom fixtures modeled after the original ones that were installed when the house was built in the '20s, the dusty living room set and the small grave markers in the backyard for Elmer the parakeet and Nigel the goldfish. She even loved their crazy neighbor Bosch and his crazier mother, Iris. So every time Cap felt like putting his fist through the crooked kitchen doorframe and the sunken bottom stair, he thought of Nell under an old blanket, reading a book in the chair by the window while it rained outside.

He came through the front door and saw her in the kitchen, taking the lids off takeout containers.

"Hey," she called.

"Hey."

She examined the food with her arms crossed, reviewing the evidence.

"They forgot duck sauce, I think," she said.

"Christmas is ruined," said Cap.

Nell chuckled. It was an old joke.

"Got enough beer there, Dad?" she said, sitting down, picking out orange chicken bits with chopsticks.

"I'm not drinking it all tonight, Bug."

He opened the fridge and heaved the case in. Took one out and opened it.

"How'd the stakeout go?"

"Good for me. Bad for Mr. and Mrs. Svetich."

"That's sad. Isn't it sad?"

"Yeah, it is, of course it is," said Cap. "Just the job, though."

"What about the deadbeat dad?"

"Slippery guy. Hasn't used a credit card or had a bank account in eight months."

"Dirtbag," said Nell.

"Generous word for it," said Cap. "How was the parade?"

"Drumline's solid," she said, making a fist. "The flutes were all over the place—whatever. Try this," she said, sliding a foil bag across the table.

Cap opened it and pulled out what looked like fried fish sticks.

"Mrs. Paul's," he said, taking a bite. "Shrimp, right? Is it shrimp toast?"

"Yeah, isn't it good? I had it at Carrie's house. Her parents are doing this pescatarian thing."

"Pescatarian?"

"You know, just fish and vegetables, no meat."

"Sounds boring," said Cap.

Nell shrugged. "Who knows. They read some article."

He watched her eat, use the chopsticks like a professional like he taught her. Jules with all her intellect couldn't do it, tried until she got splinters in her fingers. There was a time toward the end of the marriage when Cap showed Nell how to pick up ice cubes with chopsticks, just so Jules would feel left out. How desperate and stupid, he thought later. If he were to title the last year of their marriage, it would be "Desperate and Stupid."

"What're Carrie and Soph up to tonight?" he asked.

Nell didn't look at him, pushed her food around with the sticks. About to lie, Cap thought.

"Ridgewood, maybe," she said.

She didn't elaborate. She was good. Answer only the question asked. No additional information.

"I ran into Chris Morris at Valley," he said. "Ruthie Morris's dad."

Nell laughed and pointed at him.

"I totally made you, Caplan."

"What?" said Cap.

"Let's go over the scenario," she said, drawing an invisible chart on the table. "You run into Chris Morris, exchange hi-how-are-you's; the conversation turns to your daughters, and somehow the subject of a dance at St. Paul's comes up. He says, Ruthie's going, isn't Nell going too, and you act cool like, Oh maybe she just forgot to tell me about it. But you want to be subtle, and you figure I'll crack if you ask about Carrie and Sophie's whereabouts, because chances are they'll be at the dance. Yes?"

Cap leaned back in his chair and smiled. How could you not love the critical mind of this girl? She was literally the best of him and Jules— smart, funny, honest, kind. How could she not have twenty boyfriends? His answer was that she was too good for them. Her answer, if she would ever share that with him, would be considerably more frustrating: that those little Proactiv-smearing, dubstep-listening, malt-liquor-drinking punks at school weren't interested.

"What am I going to say next?" he said.

Nell thought about it.

"Why aren't you at the dance, Nell?" she said.

"Pretty good."

"So," she said, leaning back like he was. "What do *I* say now?"

He shook his head. "You're better at this than I am, Bug. I don't know what you say."

Now that the game was over, Nell suddenly seemed tired. They both started eating again.

"I didn't feel like it. St. Paul's guys are pretty dumb."

"Dumber than DW guys?"

"No, but the St. Paul's guys act like animals around girls. Actually, that's doing animals a disservice. The St. Paul's guys are totally socially disabled."

"But Carrie and Sophie still went, right? They're probably standing in a corner making fun of people. You could be doing that, too. You're really good at that," said Cap.

"Okay, here's the thing—they might be standing in a corner making fun of people, but deep down they really want one of those guys to come over and talk to them, and they make fun of them so they can counteract the possibility that no one will come over and talk to them. So I didn't want to do that. It's depressing."

She had apparently thought this through. She did not seem sad.

"What about Ruthie Morris, does she stand in the corner too?" said Cap.

"Uh, no. Ruthie's on the dance floor, probably drunk, not wearing a bra."

"Really? Little Ruthie Morris?"

"Dad, she's not little anymore. She's not the brightest bulb on the tree. And there's a rumor she's into autoerotic asphyxiation."

Cap choked on a bite of spring roll and coughed, felt the air squeak around the blockage in his throat.

Nell found this hilarious and laughed. "Do you need the Heimlich?" she said.

Cap shook his head, drank half his beer in one sip, and recovered.

"I'm sorry, what was that?" he said.

"Autoerotic asphyxiation," she said, matter-of-factly. "When someone likes to get choked during sex."

"I know what it is," Cap said, holding his hand up like he was stopping traffic. "How do *you* know what it is?"

"I saw a *Dateline* about it."

"Really? A *Dateline*?"

"Yes, Dad, not a big deal."

Not a big deal. Cap didn't ask any more about the dance, or about braless Ruthie Morris. He pictured poor Chris Morris's face when and if he ever found out his little girl was into the rough stuff. Then he looked at Nell and was thankful.

Soon they finished eating. Nell put the plates in the dishwasher and went to the living room. Cap wrapped up leftovers, started another beer.

"What movie do you want to watch?" she called to him.

"How about one where someone crosses a mild-mannered guy and then he goes nuts and seeks revenge?"

"Okay."

Cap put the containers in the fridge and heard the news coming from the other room.

"That doesn't sound like a mild-mannered guy seeking revenge," he said.

"There's Junior," said Nell.

Now he felt obligated to watch. He stood in front of the TV and saw his old boss on the screen: "All we have to say right now is that these two girls are missing, and if you have any information, call us, email us. You can remain anonymous."

"What happened?" said Cap.

"Two sisters from Black Creek were kidnapped," said Nell. She stared at the screen and moved her eyes back and forth like she was reading text. Cap knew her mind was spinning with possibilities.

"Have we seen the parents yet?"

"They showed the mother."

"Custody dispute. I'm sure daddy has them. That's what most of these are, Bug. They're not even putting out an AMBER Alert yet."

He took the clicker from her and changed the channel. He didn't want his former boss and co-workers and two kidnapped girls and their devastated mother in his quiet house. He wanted his daughter and his can of beer and a mild-mannered guy seeking revenge. Case closed.

In a room in a house in Central California, a girl stood on her hands. She was too old to be called a girl anymore, thirty-three, but she still felt like one. Not in the good way of having her whole life in front of her. In the bad way of being able to see only the edges of things, to peek around the corners when what you wanted was a city planner's blueprints of the whole block seen from above.

Her old boss in fugitive recovery, Perry, used to call it Little Bad and Big Bad. Little Bad was the teenager on the front porch with a Phillips screwdriver tucked into his pants. Big Bad was his daddy waiting inside with a loaded .38 and a pissed-off pit bull. There was always a worse thing that you couldn't see, and it was closer than you thought.

She breathed through her nose the way they taught her when she took three months of yoga. She'd quit because she couldn't do what they asked. Focus on your breathing, they said, stare at a point on the wall, picture a string floating up from the top of your head and your chakras glowing blah blah blah. She got sick quickly of the instructor's monologue, of the incense, of the women and their personalized mats. At the end when they all would lie on the floor in the corpse pose, she would look at the women around her, mouths open like fish, some actually sleeping with dumb smiles on their relaxed faces. Of the corpses she'd seen, none had looked so peaceful.

The dead were contorted like zombies; they had holes in their heads; they were kids with limp limbs.

So she quit, bought a book and learned on her own. Moved through the poses but didn't do them all. Practiced the handstand until she could do it. First against the wall, then in the middle of the room. First for two minutes, then five, then ten. Now fifteen minutes in the middle of the room at four or five in the morning when she woke up. Her head was not exactly empty, but this was the time when she felt the most pleasant, the most like the way people on the street looked, she thought. People she saw in the grocery store or the gas station. Pushing babies in strollers or walking in a pair, or just alone hurrying to their cars, tapping away on their phones. Even if they weren't smiling, even if they were yelling at their kids or worried about being late to work, she thought they had something on her, and she was never going to get it back.

She scissored her legs down and stood up straight. Rolled her head around. She checked the time on her phone. It was 4:28. The sky was navy blue outside. She could hear some birds.

She sat at her desk and opened her laptop, saw she had some new messages. Two junk, a message from her brother, and something she didn't recognize.

From mshambley@denvilleareareaylty.com. Subject: Missing Person Inquiry. The message read, "Hello Miss Vega, I read about you in regards to the Ethan Moreno case. I would like to speak to you about your services. My niece's daughters have disappeared. Please find my contact information below and let me know when is a good time. Sincerely, Maggie Shambley."

She looked at the street address and went online, typed "girls missing denville pa" and read three articles, saw half a dozen pictures of the missing girls, their mother, the parking lot where they were last seen.

She wrote: "Ms. Shambley, I am available now. Please call 916-567-1194. Best, Alice Vega."

She left her laptop, took a shower, got dressed. She pulled a travel bag down from her closet and set it on the floor. She packed it with clothes and a small pouch with a toothbrush and floss. She opened the lockbox where she kept her Springfield and placed it in a foam-lined hard case along with two magazines of twenty rounds each.

Then she sat in the one chair at the kitchen table with her laptop and phone in front of her, her bag and the gun case at her feet. When Maggie Shambley asked how soon she could be there, she would say, "Tonight."

She felt the muscles in her arms twitch from the handstand. The idea is you close your eyes and empty your head until you feel the life in everything, in the trees and the birds and the man you hate. Until you feel the peace. For Alice Vega there was never peace when she shut her eyes. There was always, always a fight.

2

SHE ARRIVED AT JAMIE BRANDT'S PARENTS' HOUSE AROUND 9 P.M. local time. There were five news vans at the curb with their networks' names and numbers splashed across the doors. Vega parked on the opposite side of the street along a copse of trees and saw a dark sedan down the block that looked like an unmarked police car, thought she could make out a figure inside it. She got out and crossed the street, watched as all five of the van doors slid open and people jumped out.

Vega actually didn't mind reporters or the twenty-four-hour cycle. In the best circumstances they helped her and the cops she worked with, circulated names and photos of the missing so often that a viable tip was bound to come through. It didn't matter that she was only one person—there were a hundred senior citizens and amateur detectives online who were happy to help catch a pervert or a criminal. But news outfits could also clog up good leads, spread bad information, start witch hunts. Then they were just dumb dogs ripping up a nice lawn, and Vega knew not to tempt them in the first place.

About ten of them came toward her, all wearing jeans and fleece or windbreakers, except one of the women with a suit, neatly highlighted blond hair, and a mask of makeup that suggested she was the on-location correspondent. The rest Vega suspected were producers, looking for a peek into the house, or at least an emotional sound bite from a family friend. They started asking her questions, but Vega moved along and didn't even look at them.

"Excuse me, Miss . . . Ma'am—"

"Are you a friend of Jamie Brandt's?"

"This could help Kylie and Bailey—"

As soon as Vega hit the curb she left them behind since they couldn't cross the property line; she walked up the drive to the house, a ranch-style place in some disrepair surrounded by a brown lawn. Motion lights came on as she approached the door and rang the bell.

A woman answered, in her seventies, well-dressed with gold jewelry and tasteful makeup, her white hair cut short and styled into a wave. The news crews started babbling as soon as they saw her.

"Miss Shambley, a statement for the eleven o'clock—"

"Can we talk to Jamie—"

"What's the latest, Maggie?"

The woman, Jamie's aunt, Maggie Shambley, was nervous, didn't know where her eyes should land as they jumped from the reporters back to Vega.

"I'm Alice Vega," Vega said, taking the older woman's soft hand and shaking it, trying to hitch her attention.

"Hi, Maggie Shambley. Come in, quick."

Maggie stepped aside.

Vega followed her inside and shut the front door, saw beige carpeting and tan walls, plaid-patterned living room furniture, smelled the stale smell of cigarettes and pizza hanging in the air.

There was a man sitting in a recliner, balding, overweight, who blinked at Vega like he couldn't quite see her. Then his eyes went back to the television screen, to a basketball game with the sound off. A woman came from another room, tall but hunched over, wearing a pinkish tracksuit. She looked to be the same age as Maggie Shambley but had not turned out as well. She was like the Maggie Shambley that had been left out in the sun.

"Those idiots still out there?" the tall woman said.

"This is Alice Vega," said Maggie, ignoring her question. "This is my sister, Gail, and her husband, Arlen White, Jamie's parents. Jamie's staying here for the time being."

Vega shook their hands. Arlen White did not stand, so she hovered over his recliner.

"You want something to drink, kitchen's right through there," said Gail White.

"I'm fine, thanks."

"Let's sit," said Maggie.

She and Gail White sat on the couch. Vega sat on the ottoman, facing the three of them.

"You'll forgive my manners," said Gail. "Or lack thereto. I am beat down tired."

She picked up a pack of cigarettes from the end table and lit one.

"It's been a hard couple days for everyone," said Maggie.

"I'm sure," said Vega.

"Thanks for coming so quickly," said Maggie.

"Which one is this again?" Arlen asked Maggie.

"This is Alice Vega. She finds missing persons."

"We talked to a lot of police already," said Gail.

"I'm not with the police," said Vega.

"Who are you with?"

"She's a private investigator," Maggie said to Gail, the tiniest edge in her voice, which made Vega think of a florist snipping a bud off a stem. "She has an excellent reputation."

"Well, great," said Gail. "There's been a lot of police, and they haven't done a damn thing."

"I understand. Could I please speak to Jamie?"

"She's in the shower," said Gail, pissed.

"She'll be out in a minute," said Maggie, talking over her sister. "We didn't know when you'd be here exactly—"

Gail stood and went to the kitchen, which Vega could see from the living room over a countertop covered with papers. Vega watched Gail make a drink. Vodka from the freezer and Fresca from the fridge.

"She doesn't need to answer more questions," Gail said. "What's the use of that, exactly?"

"You're not with the police?" Arlen said from the recliner.

"No, she's not with the goddamn police, Arlen," Gail snapped. She came back into the living room. Vega could hear the ice cubes knocking the edge of her glass. "She's a detective."

A phone rang.

"Get it, Arlen," said Gail.

Arlen picked up a cordless phone from his lap and began talking into it.

"I don't see what she can do that no one else can," said Gail.

"She's here to help us, Gail," said Maggie. "Could you please keep an open mind?"

"Right, sure, everyone's here to help. Two days and no babies. Those cops couldn't find their asshole with a mirror and a flashlight."

Gail stared at Vega, fueled by her drink and two days of anguish plus a lifetime of petty frustrations, Vega assumed.

Arlen hung up the phone, and all the women looked at him.

"Sam again. She says Jamie can make another statement tomorrow."

"Sam's my lawyer," said Maggie to Vega. "She's handling the press and setting up a call center from my office."

Vega nodded, and they were quiet again. Gail began to pace.

"So you find missing people, that right? How many you found so far?"

"Eighteen."

"How many times you been hired is the real question?"

"Eighteen."

This pushed Gail back for just a second. She took a sip of her drink and prepared to say something else.

Then there was another voice, high and hoarse:

"How many of them were kids?"

Vega turned her head and saw Jamie Brandt emerging slowly from a dim hallway.

Her face was pale, her eyes looked like dark cutouts in a white mask. Her hair was wet and straw blond. She wore sweatpants and a cropped T-shirt. Vega thought she couldn't have been older than thirty.

Vega stood up and said, "Most of them."

"When you found them, were they alive, or what?"

Vega looked her right in the eyes and said, "Sixteen alive. One dead. And one alive but"—she tapped her head—"dead."

Jamie nodded, stepped forward.

"What do you want to know?"

"You don't have to do this," Gail said to her.

"No, I want to talk now," she said, sitting on the couch. "Maggie thinks you can help, great." She took a cigarette from her mother's pack, lit it, and said, "So fucking help."

Vega sat back down and stared straight at Jamie as if they were the only two people in the room.

"Is there anyone who you think might want to kidnap your daughters?"

"No," Jamie said, exhaling smoke. "No one."

"Where is the girls' father?"

"I don't know. Cops are looking for him. He took off after Bailey was born. I haven't seen him since then."

Jamie's eyes had a glazed look. Vega suspected she'd said it all to the police.

"What kind of a man was he?"

This made Gail and Jamie both laugh harshly and shake their heads.

"What kinda man leaves a wife and two little girls?" said Gail.

Vega ignored her and kept talking to Jamie.

"Was he a drinker?" said Vega.

Jamie shrugged one shoulder.

"Sure," she said.

"Was he a drunk?"

"Not like, professionally, if that's what you mean. Hey, you know, he didn't take them. He's the cops' first idea too, but I told them, if he didn't want them then, he sure as shit wouldn't want 'em now when they're just about to be teenagers."

"What else can you tell me about him?" said Vega, her voice steady.

Jamie sighed. "He couldn't hold down a job, and he liked girls with big tits. Any girl with big tits. They could look like Oscar the Grouch in the face, but as long as they had big tits, he liked them."

Maggie Shambley pressed her fingers to her forehead as if she had a headache.

"Is there anyone else you know who would have something to gain by taking the girls?" said Vega.

"No, no," Jamie said, shaking her head.

"Is there anyone who has shown an interest in the girls that struck you as strange?"

"No."

"Anyone at school?"

"No."

"You have any enemies you're aware of?"

Jamie's eyes flickered, combative.

"I'm not a saint, you know, but does someone hate me so much they'd take my kids? No. Cops asked me all this."

"You owe anyone money, for gambling or drugs?"

"Je-sus Christ," said Gail, standing up. "She's the victim here, you know."

"Mom, sit down," said Jamie. Her jaw was tight, the bottom row of teeth jutting out in a stiff underbite. "I buy a dime of pot every three weeks from a guy named Rocky Tibbs. I pay him up front every time. I told the cops all about it. Rocky's got six kids or something; he doesn't need mine. You got any more fucking questions?"

They were all quiet. The only sound was Arlen's labored breathing.

Then Vega said, "Why did you keep his name?"

"Huh?" Jamie said.

"Your ex-husband's. He sounds like someone you're glad to be rid of. Why did you keep his name?"

Jamie paused. Everything up until now, Vega knew, the police had asked her. Maybe not this.

"'Cause it's their name. The girls'. It's on their birth certificates."

Jamie stamped the cigarette into an ashtray on the coffee table. She touched her lips.

"I wanted people, all their little friends and their parents, to know I'm their mother, me."

She pointed to herself and started tapping her foot, moving her whole leg like she was pressing the pedal on an old sewing machine.

Vega left with Maggie Shambley close to eleven. The temperature had dropped. Vega felt cold wet air on her neck and ears.

"You have to forgive my sister," said Maggie. "All of them. I know they don't show it right now, but they're all very glad you're here."

"Sure," said Vega.

"That's me," said Maggie, pointing to a Lexus across the street. Then, "Oh, here."

She handed Vega a business card that read "The Old American Inn" in curly script.

"A friend of mine runs it. She and I have an arrangement. It's the best bed-and-breakfast in the area. I brokered the deal for the place myself."

Vega took the card and stared at it.

"I'll really be fine in a hotel. Like a Best Western or something."

"Oh no," said Maggie. "This place is so much better."

"I don't really eat breakfast," said Vega.

Now Maggie smiled like a grandmother and said, "Breakfast is entirely optional. It's cleaner and quieter than any motel, you'll see. And there are bedbugs in all those motel chains. Have you heard about that?"

She pulled her keys out of her purse, nodded to the house, and said, "What do you think?"

"Hard to say right now. I have to do some research."

"Will you be talking to the police?" said Maggie.

"Yes, tomorrow. I'll need to speak with Jamie afterward."

"I'm sure she'll be more amenable," said Maggie.

Vega was not at all sure of this.

"I will speak with you soon, Miss Vega. Thank you for coming."

They shook hands again, and Maggie got into her car and drove off. Vega looked down the road at the unmarked car. She wasn't sure but thought she could see the shadow of a man at the wheel. The man didn't move and didn't seem bothered by her seeing him. Vega stood up straight and stared at him for another minute. She wasn't bothered either.

Later, in her room at the inn, Vega emptied her head in an email to the Bastard.

TO: OMGBastard@thebastard.com

FROM: Alice Vega

RE: Info

I'm near Phila working a case. Could you look up the following for me:

- Whereabouts of Kevin Michael Brandt, dob: 12/19/81, ss: 199-75-8225. Start with PA, NY, OH, WV, MD, DE, then expand to all US. Any other relevant information.
- Ridgewood Mall on Sterling Road E—can you get me security camera feed from around the Kmart from last Sat until 1pm? Also all parking lot exits/entrances.
- Hess Gas on Township Hwy 148—security camera feed from last Sat morning.

- Staff and faculty at Starfield Middle School and Denville
  East Elementary—look for anything that stands out.
  Asap.

She looked up the police blotter from the past two months on the *Denville Daily Tribune* website—domestic violence, shoplifting, and minor drug busts, all for oxycodone, Vicodin, Percocet, heroin. And more oxy and more heroin. She went back a year or two, looking for times when the Denville Police Department had made the news. In 2013, budget cuts required reduction of the department by five officers. In 2014, a scandal—a former high school football star overdosed on oxy in the holding cell where he was awaiting processing.

Vega scanned the photos; she paused on the detective who had resigned to avoid further attention from the Schuylkill County district attorney. The photo was from a better day, the detective smiling and standing with another man, shutting one eye into the sun, both of them holding thin silver fish on lines. She felt like she recognized him, his smile and curly brown hair, but maybe he had one of those faces.

She checked the time in the corner of her screen: 2:42 a.m. She was not the least bit tired.

Downtown Denville was made up entirely of shabby storefronts on narrow streets and neighborhoods with weighty American names from a more industrious time, evoking coal mines and lumberyards: Bullrush, Rockland, Black Creek.

Vega didn't see one black or Hispanic or Asian person. Everyone was white, and smoked cigarettes and drove cars with dents. At an intersection there was a man in a hospital gown and flip-flops, hitch-hiking. His face was unshaven, gaunt, calm. Vega drove closely past him but did not stop.

The police department was an unadorned three-story beige building on a corner. Vega parked her rental on the street and saw three or four news vans in the parking lot; she recognized Channel 12 from the night before at Gail and Arlen White's house.

Inside, the station smelled like every other one she'd ever been in, half government facility and half men's locker room: astringent, with the smell of old shoes and sweat.

The lobby was full of people, sitting in the folding chairs against the walls, standing, talking to each other or on phones. Behind the reception counter were two women, one fat, one thin. The fat one wore a cop's uniform and was explaining a form on a clipboard to a man who kept saying, "Do I need a lawyer? Should I call a lawyer?" The thin one was not a cop, wore wide-rimmed glasses and an oversized sweater.

Vega stood in line for forty minutes and listened as the women behind the counter gave out forms and phone numbers, telling everyone they had to talk to someone else or wait or come back later. Vega eventually stepped up to the front of the line and faced the thin woman with the glasses.

"Can I help you?" she said to Vega.

"I'd like to speak to Captain Hollows."

The thin woman wasn't happy to hear this.

"What's your name?" she said.

"Alice Vega."

"What's that?"

"Alice Vega. V-E-G-A."

Vega watched the woman write on a pad, "Alice Veja."

"Does he know what this is in regards to?"

"I have some information about the Brandt girls."

Vega watched the woman's eyes go wide but only a little. She picked up the phone and dialed three numbers. She cupped her hand around the receiver to create a little shield.

"Alice Vay-zha is here to see you. She has information about the Brandt girls? Yeah, okay."

She hung up and said, "Someone's going to come down for you."

"Thanks."

Vega waited. Clock on the wall said 9:17.

A cop with a shaved head and heavy eyes came down the stairs. Plainclothes, white shirt and brown pants, comfortable shoes. A look of either apathy or exhaustion. Around six feet tall. Vega could have picked him out as a cop in a dark movie theater.

"You here for the Captain?"

"Yes."

He turned around and started walking back the way he had come, up the stairs.

"You in town for long?" he said, still facing forward.

"A little while," said Vega.

"How long, do you know?"

It didn't exactly sound like he was accusing her of something, but that he might be starting soon.

"Not sure yet," she said.

"Oh yeah?" he said, a little dare.

Vega guessed he wasn't crazy about the idea of her being in town at all. She was a quarter Mexican with dark hair and light eyes, her skin fair but easily tanned; she looked more ethnic depending on the day. Maybe this was one of those days, and maybe he didn't like that.

Or maybe he just didn't like strangers.

They came to the second floor, full of cubicles and cops, plainclothes and uniforms, phones ringing, one man yelling over another to be heard, a snap of laughter.

"It's a nice place," the cop said. "You'll enjoy it more than you think."

"Sure."

They stopped in front of a glass door, and the cop opened it and showed Vega in.

The man behind the desk was on the phone. He said, "I'll call you back," and hung up.

"Hi, Miss Vega, right?" he said, coming toward her. "Greg Hollows. Everyone calls me Junior."

He shook her hand, then pointed at the cop who had brought her. "You've met Detective Ralz."

"Sure."

Ralz left without a sound.

"Please, have a seat."

Vega sat in a chair opposite the desk. She glanced up at the ceiling, peeling paint in the corners. The radiator under the one window made crackling noises.

Hollows did not sit. He leaned backward against his desk so he was standing over her. He had a boyish face, big blue eyes and hair a little long in the front that she suspected he would have to constantly push back from his forehead, boyishly.

He smiled at her.

"When you get into town?"

He asked like he was an old friend, someone she had run into at a high school reunion, making chitchat over a beer.

"Last night."

"What do you think of Denville?"

"It's fine."

"It's a nice place to live."

"That's what I hear."

"Planning on staying long?"

"A few days."

"That's all it'll take, huh?"

"That's all what will take?"

Hollows scratched his chin and then laughed gently. He leaned down so his face was close to her ear.

"I know who you are, Miss Vega. And I know why you're here."

Then he went back behind his desk, sat down.

"I had a chat with Maggie Shambley this morning. She's a nice lady."

Vega said nothing.

"I know she hired you to find the Brandt girls."

They stared at each other. They waited.

He rubbed his eyes and said, "I'm glad you came to see me. Because I would've come to see you this afternoon. I have every man in my shop working the Brandt case around the clock. They are capable, professional, and determined, and they will find these girls. We have no need for a private detective here."

He paused.

"I realize you have special skills."

He turned to his computer and tapped a key, then swiveled the screen toward Vega. She saw an old photo alongside an article. It was her and Sheriff Colson with Ethan Moreno and his parents.

"You're pretty famous out in California, huh?"

Hollows glanced at the article.

"Big hero. The bounty hunter who found Ethan Moreno."

Vega looked back at him and stopped smiling.

"You're still not a cop. You're a girl with a gun who's watched too much Buffy. So I'm asking as nicely as I can here, with all respect to you, that you tell Maggie Shambley you quit and that you stay out of the way. We don't need civilian assistance in this matter, Miss Vega."

She let that sit for a moment. She waited until Hollows opened his mouth to say something else and then she spoke instead:

"You have twenty-nine police here, not counting yourself and your chief, right?"

Hollows was surprised but recovered quickly.

"I know that doesn't sound like a lot—"

"I figure you're probably the only captain in a town this size, maybe two lieutenants, two sergeants, on management and strategy, right? You seem to have had a bit of an oxy-heroin problem here for the last five years or so, so you probably have at least two teams of detectives on narcotics. Which leaves one team for homicides, one for sex crimes, one for robberies and burglaries. Which leaves fourteen patrol cops who answer the rest of the calls: domestic violence, shoplifting, assault and battery, vandalism. And in their spare time they do traffic control. You've had your funds cut three years in a row, and you can afford only one additional secretary at reception, so it's very possible that you don't divvy up the jobs at all and it's more of a first come, first served or 'clusterfuck' type of situation. Which, judging by the age of that machine you're typing on and the disrepair of this office in general, I tend to believe."

Hollows paused briefly. Vega was not close enough to see if his eyes were dilated, but she bet they were. Thinking hard. He leaned back in his seat and threw up his hands gently into little finger fireworks.

"So you know how to use the Internet. I guess that's supposed to impress me?"

"I'm sure you know how to use the Internet too. I'm sure you know about David Haber, who lives two blocks from the Brandts, convicted of statutory rape in 2004. And Robert Vilinsky who lives half a mile from the girls' grandparents' house, pleaded no contest to trafficking in child pornography in 2012."

"I couldn't confirm or deny either as it would compromise the confidentiality of an ongoing investigation," said Hollows.

"Sure," said Vega. "Do you know the name Warren Pearson?"

"Should I?"

"He was arrested for assault five years ago in Philly. Bar fight, slammed his opponent's face into a pinball machine. Spent sixty days in County. His bunkmate was a guy named Jay Nunez who, in addition to being arrested for possession of crack and heroin, was awaiting trial for molestation of his four-year-old stepson."

"I have a feeling you're going to tell me how this relates to my case."

"Last year Pearson got a job with a company called Diego Tree Service and Maintenance, the landscapers for most of Schuylkill County's public schools, including Starfield Middle School and Denville East Elementary, where Kylie and Bailey Brandt attend, respectively."

"So you think Warren Pearson kidnapped the Brandt girls to give them to a pervert he met in County?" said Hollows. He moved his tongue to the front of his teeth, cleaning out the space.

"Not particularly. But you had never heard of those men before I just told you about them. I'm not looking to impress you. And, with all respect, I think you need all the civilian assistance you can get."

"To chase dead ends?"

"To shake out every rug in this trash heap town until you find those girls. It has been almost forty-eight hours. You don't even have the time to be arguing with me right now."

Hollows smiled and folded his hands together. This is the church, here's the steeple.

Vega knew she was losing and kept calm. Her eyes combed Hollows's desk—stapler, letter opener, a cup filled with pens. No scissors that she could see. Not yet, she thought. Not just yet. No sense breaking down the front door if you can pick the lock in the back, Perry would say. She wrote the email to the Bastard in her head: Captain Greg "Junior" Hollows. Give me everything you got.

Mrs. Svetich sat across from Cap in his office and watched the images on his laptop. Cap glanced back and forth between her face and the screen. She was an attractive woman, maybe not as young as the woman her husband was sleeping with, but she had nice eyes and smooth skin, and long brown hair tied up in a knot on top of her head like some Italian actress. Cap tried to see it from Mr. Svetich's point of view. Gray hair at the roots, thin lips pressed together when she was upset, ruler-thin body but not from working out—naturally bony, thin wrists and thick hands.

She shook her head gently and said, "Okay, that's enough."

Cap pressed Stop and faced her. This was not an unfamiliar moment for him. When women thought their husbands were cheating, they were usually right, and he had had plenty of them as clients. He could typically tell how they were going to act—which were the sobbers and which were the plate throwers. Mrs. Svetich, though, could go either way.

"So," she said. "What now?"

"Well," said Cap. "That's up to you."

"I know," she said, annoyed. "I was thinking out loud. I know *you* don't know what now, I was asking myself that."

"Of course."

She laughed a curt little laugh.

"You know what, though, Mr. Caplan?"

"What?"

"I think this would almost be easier if he was a nice guy, but he's not. He was when we got married a million years ago, but he's been a jerk for a long time. We had a fight two weeks ago, and he called me an asshole. Who talks to their wife like that?"

She seemed to wait for Cap to respond, so he said, "It's very disrespectful."

"Yes, it is. And now, it's like, okay, I'm free. I get whatever I want because I have this tape. I get the kids. I win. Who cares."

Pause, thought Cap. Let her breathe.

"You married?" she asked.

"Divorced."

Mrs. Svetich nodded.

"I'm sure you don't have anything to tell me that makes this moment easier."

There was, actually, a great deal Cap could tell her. What he really would like to say was, Two years. You'll be a basket case for two years. Then you'll start feeling like a normal person again. You'll start enjoying the taste of coffee and watching your kid's school play. But for two years you will be a schizophrenic. Angry, guilty, sad.

Instead he shook his head.

"Yeah, I thought as much," said Mrs. Svetich. "Yes. So. Your bill," she said, opening her purse.

"I can send you an invoice."

"No, thanks. Please don't take this the wrong way, but I'd like to pay now so I can never think about you again."

Cap nodded and handed her the invoice. She pulled out a checkbook and a pen and scribbled the numbers and words, ripped the check out, and held it out for Cap to take, the paper shaking in her hand. Cap took it from her, and Mrs. Svetich stood up to leave, so Cap did too.

He tried to think of something else he could say.

"Don't worry," said Mrs. Svetich. "There's nothing you can say."

She laughed again, but oh, her eyes. He could see drops hanging off the lower lids. One blink would make them roll. He walked with her to the door.

"Thanks, Mr. Caplan," she said in a strange high voice. She didn't blink and didn't look at him as she left.

Cap shut the door, rolled his shoulders back, and made a sound like "Gah." He checked his watch, 12:15. Really too early for a beer. He sat back in his chair and scrolled through his emails.

He clicked on one with the subject line "Inquiry" from an address he didn't recognize:

Mr. Caplan,

I am interested in retaining your services. Please write me back at this address and let me know your availability for a conversation.

Thanks,

A. Vega

New business is good, he thought. What had just happened with Mrs. Svetich was the hardest part of the job. Everything else: tracking down people who weren't candidates for Mensa to begin with, filling out paperwork for the retail outfits that hired him, making his own hours, leaving his old Sig in a MicroVault in the closet, not waking up with his jaw locked from tension—this was all the good part.

So he wrote back:

Hello,

I am available to speak now until 2:30 p.m. this afternoon or otherwise after 7 p.m. tonight. Also I am free tomorrow between 9 a.m. and noon. If those windows don't work for you, please let me know what times might.

Thanks for your interest,

Max Caplan

He hit Send and leaned back. Sipped his cold coffee and opened the folder for the skip. He flipped through the pages: the driver's license photo of Brandon Haas, last known street address. Trouble finding this one. Didn't want to pay child support for his two-year-old twin boys, so he moved out of his apartment and ditched his cell. Only after he'd insisted on a paternity test because he told the mother of his children, "Can't be mine, they look colored." The mother had said to Cap that Brandon was full of shit because he knows she would never sleep with a black guy. Good, good people.

And now he heard the doorbell from the front of the house and figured it was UPS. He found himself feeling relieved that he could step out of Brandon Haas's life for a moment as he went through the door that led to the rest of the house. Through the hallway and living room and to the front door. He glanced through the window and saw a woman there, no one he recognized. He opened the door and there she was. She was slender but not small, big eyes taking up most of her round doll-like face, little makeup, brown hair pulled back. Pretty in an unadorned way.

"Max Caplan?" she said.

"Yes?"

"I'm Alice Vega. You just sent me an email."

Cap looked around.

"You got here pretty quickly."

"I was close by."

Cap tried to read her. Clothes were a giveaway for the type. Mrs.

Svetich's blouse with the boat neckline and khaki pants showed that she had dressed up, that she had maybe once held a job where she wore these clothes, even if she was a stay-at-home mom now. The mother of Brandon Haas's children, Hayley, wore stained jeans and an extra-small T-shirt.

Then there was the face and body: eyes, lips, hands. That will tell you the state of mind. Mrs. Svetich was all tight neck muscles and pleading eyes—desperate, sad, tense. Hayley Haas twitched and ran her words together and screwed her lips up into crazy angles—angry, unpredictable, drunk.

Alice Vega wore black, all black. Black pants, black blouse, black boots, black canvas jacket. Her face had no discernible expression, but there was emotion there; Cap just couldn't make it out.

"Is this still a good time for you?" she said.

"Yeah. It is. Let's go around to my office."

She nodded and smiled politely. Cap turned the lock on the doorknob and closed the front door, walked across the parched lawn to the driveway.

"You from around here?" he said over his shoulder.

"No," she answered, and that was all.

Okay, Cap thought. Not a talker.

They walked up the concrete path alongside the house, Vega still behind him a step. Cap opened the door to his office and held it open.

"Where are you in from?" he said.

She stepped inside. He watched her eyes cover the room like headlights, and he suddenly felt embarrassed about the space. The IKEA furniture seemed old and shabby; the stained wood floor did not seem part of the house's old-school charm; it just looked cheap.

"California," she said.

"Wow, long way," he said. "Would you like coffee?" he asked, pointing to the Krups in the corner.

"No, thanks."

"Please sit."

She sat on the edge of the chair, like she was ready to leave suddenly. Cap sat behind his desk and realized how messy it was, covered in folders.

"What can I do for you, Ms. Vega?" he said.

"I've been hired by the Brandt family. I understand you used to be a detective with the Denville Police. I need your help."

Cap's professional smile disappeared.

"Are you a PI?" he asked.

"I find missing persons."

Cap nodded.

"I'm not sure how I can help you."

"I met with Greg Hollows this morning."

Cap moved the Brandon Haas folder on his desk an inch to the left. "And how is he?"

"Reluctant. He doesn't want my help. Says he doesn't need it."

"I doubt that."

"So do I," said Vega. "It's easier if I do this with the police. I'm sure you understand."

"Yeah," said Cap. "Easier, cheaper, quicker. I'm still not sure how I fit in here. You know I'm no longer with the police."

"I do. Most information I can get. I have a guy who can get it for me. I don't need to know how to find the girls' father, or get video feeds—I have the full cooperation of Jamie Brandt and her family as of now. But there's a piece I can't get to."

"Witness statements," said Cap.

"Yes. I could get employees from local businesses, but the people in the parking lot, passersby; there's no way I could get them all."

She paused. Cap watched her eyes travel quickly to the corner of the room as she thought.

"I *could* get them. It would just take time."

"Which you don't have," said Cap.

"Which I don't have," said Vega.

Cap smiled and tried to look casual. He sipped his cold coffee casually, to show Vega how much he didn't care about the Brandt girls or the police department.

"Okay," he said. "You seem like a resourceful person who's done her homework. So you know all about me, right?"

"Some."

"So you know that I ended my relationship with the Denville PD two and a half years ago, and it was not exactly what you'd call an amicable breakup."

Cap waited for Vega to say something. Her face again a blank sheet.

"I don't have witness statements, Ms. Vega," said Cap. "I don't have access to witness statements. I literally can't walk into the station or else I violate the terms of my agreement with them, okay? What I'm telling you is you have a broken arm and you need a paramedic, not a guy in an alley with a box of Band-Aids."

They were quiet. Vega cocked her head a small bit to the side and then reached for an inside pocket. Just for a second Cap felt his legs tense up, the back of his head tingle. Old reflex.

She pulled out a sheet of paper folded into quarters and unfolded it. She leaned forward on the tip of her chair and placed the paper on Cap's desk so he could read it. It was a printed copy of one of the articles from the *Trib*. Cap forced a laugh.

"You know, I've made a great effort not to look at this stuff. I know you just met me, Ms. Vega, and I know you'd never guess this about me, but I don't have the greatest self-esteem to begin with, and this just makes me feel bad about myself."

Vega held her hand over the paper like it was a Ouija board.

"This says that you resigned less than twenty-four hours after this kid, Ron Samuels, died in police custody. Less than twenty-four hours. That makes me think you did it quick to make it go away, to avoid criminal or civil litigation. It says you were on track to become sergeant. In less than twenty-four hours, you decided to crash the career you'd been building your whole life without a fight. There's only one reason anyone does that."

"Why's that?" said Cap.

"To protect someone. Probably a friend, colleague. Probably someone else was in the room when Ron Samuels died. Someone who made the wrong call, didn't call an ambulance when he should have. Maybe there was negligence, maybe not. Sounds like the kid had a drug problem. But something happened in that room. If you were culpable, maybe you would have tried to negotiate at least to get some part of your pension, something. But you didn't. Because you were protecting someone else."

Vega was so calm when she spoke that Cap couldn't quite be angry. Hearing her recount the experience just made him tired.

"Hey, what do you want?" he said.

"Witness statements."

Cap held out his arms to show how empty they were. No witness statements here.

"I don't have them. I don't know what to tell you."

"Someone in the Denville Police owes you a favor. I propose you call it in. I will give you half of whatever I make from this. Jamie Brandt's aunt has a lot of money, and I don't work cheap. If I work a month on this case, your half could be upwards of twenty-five K."

Who the fuck *are* you? Cap thought. Where did you come from? He tried not to imagine putting twenty-five thousand dollars into his anemic share of Nell's college fund. Which would probably cover book costs, but it was a start.

"What if I said I don't care about the money?" he said.

"I don't care," said Vega. "I don't care about you and your personal needs and wants. I don't care that you feel bad about yourself or that you have or haven't come to terms with your former career—I don't care. I am looking for these two girls, just a little younger than your daughter, Mr. Caplan, and you could help me do that. You have the capacity to do that. So why wouldn't you do that?"

Her eyes searched his face. He felt like he was in a dream state, like he would look down and suddenly realize he had the body of a horse.

"I don't do police work anymore, Ms. Vega," he said. "I don't associate with police. I have my own business, my own clients. I'm working on something right now," he said, tapping the Brandon Haas folder. "I'm sorry, I can't help you."

They stared at each other for what felt to Cap to be about thirty minutes. Then Vega nodded and finally took her eyes off him. She looked at the floor.

"Okay," she said quietly.

She finally sat back in the chair, and Cap relaxed his neck and exhaled. She looked up at him and smiled. It was not what he would call genuine but it was respectful. It made him want to tell her more.

"I'm sorry," he said again. "I admit the things I work on are not as serious as this."

"Skips and cheaters?" she said.

"Skips and cheaters," he said.

"So if this one," she said, pointing to the Brandon Haas folder, "were out of your way, just disappeared, you would reconsider?"

Cap laughed. "I don't know. I'd love to say to you, No way, but I'm getting that you probably don't hear that a lot."

Cap's cell buzzed on his desk; the photo of a pug dog came up, the one that Nell had set as her profile picture.

"I'm sorry," he said, holding the phone. "Will you excuse me?"

"Yes, please," said Vega.

Cap tapped Accept and headed out of the office, through the door into the hallway of the house.

"Hey, what's wrong?"

"Dad, nothing's wrong. Don't panic," said Nell.

"Worst possible thing you could say to a parent. What's up?"

"Mom's car broke down at her work, and she was going to pick me up from practice, but now she's got a class this afternoon, and then she has to wait for the tow, so could you pick me up and take me to Carrie's?"

"Sure, what time?"

"Like five-fifteen-ish."

"Yeah, that's fine. How are you getting from Carrie's house to Mom's if Mom has no car?"

"Carrie's mom can take me." Then Nell whispered, "After we eat quinoa cakes and barley salad."

Cap smiled.

"Thanks, Dad."

"No prob, Bug. Hey, does your mom need . . . is she okay?"

She's not okay, Dad; she needs you to save her. And she says she's sorry about all the fights that you had at the end and that nasty voice mail she left you that time, and she's really grateful you never called her an asshole. And she wants you back and wants us to be a family like we were, three against the world.

"She's fine; she has Triple A. I gotta go. See you later. Thanks, Dad, I love you."

"Love you too," said Cap.

He hung up and went back into the office. Vega was sitting where he had left her, hands in her lap.

"I'm sorry about that. It was my daughter. And you know, if she calls instead of texts, I know something's up."

"Of course, it's no problem."

"Where were we?"

"You don't want the job," she said. She was not angry.

"Right," Cap said. "I've just got too much on my plate right now."

Vega nodded. They were quiet for a moment. Then she stood.

"Sorry to bother you."

"Not at all, thank you for coming by. I hope everything works out."

Cap walked her to the door.

"Nice to meet you," he said, extending his hand.

"You as well," she said, shaking it.

He opened the door for her, and she stepped out.

"Hey, Ms. Vega?"

She turned.

"How did you know I had a daughter? It wasn't in any of the articles about me—I went through a lot of trouble to keep it out."

Her eyebrows raised up just a little bit, in a tiny arch, charmed.

"I saw her shoes when you opened the front door. Female athletic shoes."

Now Cap smiled, both of them caught in the joke.

"I see," he said. "So how'd you pin her age?"

"You have a copy of *Othello* on the dashboard of the car in your driveway."

"How do you know it's not mine?" he said. "Maybe I live for Shakespeare."

"Just a hunch," she said, shrugging, looking down.

Was she looking down shyly? Was this flirting? Cap couldn't tell. He hadn't been on a date in so long he'd forgotten what it felt like.

"Thanks for your time," said Vega, and then she left.

Cap watched her go, fairly certain he saw the lines of a holster crossing her back under her jacket.

3

IN THE CAR, VEGA SCROLLED ON HER PHONE TO THE PHOTOS SHE
had taken of Caplan's file while he'd been on the phone in the other
room. She stared at the photo of Brandon Haas, looked over his stats,
and tapped out another email to the Bastard on the screen.

Later in her room at the inn, she was studying footage from the
Kmart parking lot when the message from the Bastard came in:

"Got a Brandon Hass with same birthday as your Haas from ADP
paycheck dated 3/15, Luke Construction out of New Castle, PA. Also
leases, driver license, but all old.

Also Junior Hollows is boring as shit but his wife has two Facebook
pages, and you'll get a kick out of one of them."

Vega sniffed in approval at the Bastard's ingenuity and stopped reading, closed up her email, and went online to find a number for Luke
Construction.

Vega was on her way out the front door, patchouli and lemon still in her
nose from the sitting room, a slip of paper in her hand with an address
on it.

"Ms. Vega?"

She turned. It was Elaine, the owner of the inn. She was a slender
woman in her seventies with long hair. She wore a lot of scarves and
beads and was holding a basket of fruit.

"Hi," said Vega.

"This is for you," Elaine said, presenting the fruit.

Vega stared at it.

"It's your welcome basket," Elaine added. "Usually I have it waiting in folks' rooms, but this all happened so quickly I didn't have a chance."

"Thanks," muttered Vega. "It's really not necessary."

Now Elaine gave her a bit of the side eye, wagging a teasing finger.

"Now you strike me as the kind of person who doesn't eat unless she's reminded, right?"

Vega made herself smile. She felt about ten years old.

"So you take it with you. These are all organic. I'd like to tell you they're local, but this isn't the best time of year for fruit around here."

Vega took the fruit. It was unexpectedly weighty.

"I'll get the door for you," said Elaine.

"Thanks."

Elaine opened the passenger side door, and Vega dropped the fruit basket on the seat.

"Cheese and wine at six if you like," said Elaine.

Vega continued to smile, and then Elaine was off, down the front path, her skirt swishing around her. Vega got into the car, started the engine, and plugged the address from the slip of paper into the GPS.

"Head northwest on Market Street," it said.

She checked her mirror and made herself smile again, just to see what it looked like.

Vega parked on the vacant west side of the lot of New Town Mall, where a Real Food Market was being built. It didn't look like much of anything yet, a crevasse where whatever had been there before had been recently gutted, and dumpsters of debris.

She sat in the car for a few minutes and watched construction workers walking around, talking in groups. There were only about ten of them. She figured most had quit for the day. It was just after five. She glanced around at the other stores.

She got out and went to a Home Depot, up and down the aisles to Tools and Hardware.

At the register, a man with a ponytail and yellow teeth said, "You find everything okay today?"

Vega watched the items show up on the digital screen:

Straight Link Chain, 5 ft
EZ Bungee cord, 2 ct
Iron Tough Pipe Wrench

She said, "Yeah, thanks. Do you know where I can get a hot tea?"

Vega walked from her car to the construction site, about forty feet. The tea spilled over the sides of the open cup, ripping hot streams down her fingers. Two groups of men, one of three, one of five. She went up to the three-man group.

"Hey, baby," said the one on the left. "You bring me coffee?"

She said to the one in the middle, about five-ten, crew cut and a forehead hanging over his eyes like an awning, "Brandon Haas?"

"Yeah?" he said. Amused, excited. The others shouted and laughed.

Vega started by throwing the hot tea at his crotch. He screamed and crumpled to the ground. The comedian on the left went for her and she cracked him across the nose with the pipe wrench. The one on the right came half a second later, and she punched him, an uppercut to the jaw with the chain wrapped around her fist. All three down.

Then came the other five. Vega squatted and pulled her jacket back so they could see the gun.

"Just don't," she said.

She wound the chain around Haas's neck and cinched it like a leash. He coughed and choked. The two on the ground stirred and moaned.

"Fuck you, bitch," said one of the five, coming at her.

"I'm telling you, don't," she said, her right hand on the gun, her left pulling the chain choking Haas at her feet. "You want to die for a guy you met a couple of months ago?"

He stayed where he was.

She started to pull Haas across the lot. At first he coughed and sputtered, pried his fingers underneath the chain to distance it from his neck, his legs twisted up over his crotch.

"Kick your legs," she said.

Haas grunted and tried to ball up.

Vega yanked the chain and leaned her head over him.

"Kick your legs; I can't pull you on your ass the whole way."

He kicked, crab walking, still trying to pull at the chain. Vega saw it was starting to tear the skin on his neck. She didn't stop moving until she got to her car, and then she dropped him on the pavement.

Haas coughed and fell flat on his back, squirming. Vega examined her key chain to find the little icon of the open trunk and pressed it. Haas lifted his head and tried to speak. Vega straddled him.

"Don't say anything," she said.

She wrapped a bungee cord quickly around his wrists and tried to pull him up.

"Stand. Stand now," she said.

His limbs were gummy, and he kept folding down to his knees. Shock, she thought.

Vega hoisted him up under the arms and pushed him into the trunk, then lifted his legs in. He started to breathe deeply, the color coming back into his face from being choked.

"Who are you, who the fuck are you?" he said.

She thought of what Perry would say, what he always said when some deadbeat skip asked him who he was, but she was too preoccupied to deliver the line, to really give it the nice spin Perry used to. She slammed the trunk closed. She got in the driver's seat and heard him screaming.

"Fucking bitch! I'm-a fuckin' kill you! Let me out!"

She looked at the fruit basket on the seat next to her.

Alice Vega had left Cap in a strange mood. He'd written another email to Brandon Haas's brother and talked to his former landlady, who said he'd left no forwarding address but that he had left the bathroom filthy. Cap had quit soon afterward and found himself reading up on the Brandt girls. Disappeared from a car in a parking lot. Police were talking with witnesses who thought they may have seen the girls get into a car across the street from the mall, but the articles had no further detail.

He watched a few clips from the news; they were all variations on the same story; even the on-location anchorpeople looked the same in bland suits and product-sculpted hair. The mother had given a statement. She looked familiar to Cap even though he was sure they'd never met. She looked like folks around Denville, especially Black Creek, not a terrible neighborhood but one where you wouldn't be surprised to see people doing the extended handshake of a drug deal on the sidewalk.

In the clip she wore pink lipstick and eyeshadow, as if she could attract more attention to the case by being brightly made-up. A white blouse that was too small, stretching at the buttons between her breasts.

"I just ask you to please call the police if you know anything about my girls," she said, her voice shaking. "And if you got them, just drop them off where they can make a phone call and you can, you can go about your business."

She paused and looked down. An older woman behind her put her hand on her shoulder.

The mother looked back up with tears spilling down her face, trailing lines of gray mascara, and said, "Bailey has asthma and needs her sprays."

Cap hit Pause and closed his laptop. If I am not looking at it, it does not exist.

After a moment he opened the laptop again, this time typing "Alice Vega California" into Google.

A ton of hits, news items from three years ago popped up. The *Sacramento Bee* in California:

> 11-year-old Ethan Moreno of Modesto was found alive three weeks after he had been abducted, chained to a sink in a West Halsey home.
>
> Central California–based bounty hunter Alice Vega discovered the boy and apprehended one of his captors, 27-year-old Quincy-Ray Day. Vega stands to collect the $100,000 reward from the FBI as well as an undisclosed sum from Moreno's family.

He skimmed through other articles: how she found a teenage girl who'd run away from her rich parents to marry her boyfriend in Reno. A few more: just the mention of her name; she'd been brought in to assist police representing private clients in San Francisco, Los Angeles, Phoenix, Chicago, New York. Not a kid she couldn't find.

Cap smiled, filled with an unnamable excitement. He couldn't place the feeling, except he remembered once walking with his mother in

Greenwich Village when she'd dropped her keys, and a short, dark-haired man picked them up and handed them to her. She thanked him and he nodded, kept on his way, and she stopped and faced Cap and said, suddenly breathless, "Was that Al Pacino? Did you see him, Maxie? Was that him? I think that was him."

Nell got into the car with four backpacks and duffel bags and threw them into the backseat.

"Hey, Dad," she said, stretching across to kiss him on the cheek.

Cap could feel sweat underneath her lip and heat coming off her forehead. He had an urge to take a deep breath. It reminded him of when she was little and would come out of the tub smelling like a wet cat.

"Good practice?" he said, pulling out of the lot.

She shrugged.

"Okay. Just drills and, like, one or two new plays, but we need more if we're up against Valley."

"You say Steves knows what he's doing."

"I think so. He doesn't want anyone's opinion though, you know. And he's only, like, five years older than us."

"Boys in their twenties like to think they're grown-ups," said Cap.

Nell said, "Huh," then began to text.

"So, they still haven't found those girls," he said, tentative, watching her from the side.

She stopped texting.

"I know, it's awful. They can't find the dad either; he ran out on them when they were babies. So my question is, why would he want them now?"

She was engaged, gesturing as she spoke, holding her hands out to an invisible crowd. Cap felt guilty; the kid didn't think he wanted to talk about it so she hadn't said anything since he had turned off the TV on Saturday. But she'd been doing the due diligence in her head; it was like when Cap was working a case he couldn't shake off the brain. You find yourself awake at three a.m.—was it because you had to pee or because your subconscious was giving you clues?

"And why would he take them from a Kmart parking lot? How would he know they were going to be there? Was he tailing them?"

"These are all valid questions," said Cap.

"I don't like the dad for this," she said definitively. "Doesn't add up."

"Who do you like then?"

"I don't know," she said, exasperated. "I don't have any real details, just the news and you know how they mess it all up."

Cap nodded. They were quiet.

"I watched an interview with the mom," he said.

"Was it the one where she said the younger one needs her asthma medication? Wasn't that awful," said Nell. Then, quietly, she repeated, "Awful."

He watched her as she picked at the skin around a fingernail.

"So," said Cap, trying to sound casual, "I met with this woman today; she's working on the case."

"What do you mean?" said Nell in her interrogation voice.

Cap coughed into his fist.

"A woman came to see me who's working the case. She's been hired by family—"

"The private investigator from California?" said Nell.

"Yeah, how'd you know that?"

"It was on TV, Dad. What did she say? Why'd she want to meet with you?"

"She asked for my help. She wants me to call in a favor."

"What—" Nell started but Cap cut her off.

"She wants me to call in a favor with Em."

"How does she know Em?"

"She doesn't know Em. She figured that I had a favor coming to me, and she wants me to call it in so I can get the witness statements."

"Why doesn't she get them from the department?"

"You think Junior would give an inch here?"

He stopped at a red light, feeling an old wave of frustration and gripping the wheel.

"Asshole," said Nell, stewing. "Did you call Em?"

"No," said Cap. "No, I didn't call Em. I'm not calling Em. I'm not getting involved in this. And watch your language please."

"What?" said Nell, turning in her seat to face him. "Why not?"

"It's a police investigation. And I have my own cases to work."

As he said it, he heard the words differently. It was always like this with Nell: he'd already justified a thing in his head, but when he said it aloud, it got stripped down. There was the paltry sheath of it removed; all that was left was the truth.

"Because it's embarrassing? Because you're embarrassed?" said Nell.

My God, she would make a good cop, thought Cap. Or a journalist. Her questions just naturally sounded like someone who didn't want to demean you or pressure you—she just wanted to know all the facts. You couldn't teach a thing like that, he thought.

"Embarrassed, yes . . . and I couldn't put Em in that position."

"Dad, you covered for Em because he had little kids and a wife and a mother in a nursing home. You'd barely be asking for anything in return now."

"He could lose his job."

"So what?" said Nell.

"So what," Cap repeated. "That's a lot. That's everything to most people."

"You gave it up for him."

Cap felt a stab of guilt. Nell didn't have to say it; no one did, but still it was the theme that threaded through his family's life, that after he took the fall for Em, his marriage splintered and finally crashed, and even though he and Jules paid for it, and kept paying, no one felt it worse than Nell. He coughed and said, "And so the endgame is that both me and Em are out of a job? What's the positive spin on that?"

"You could help find the girls, Dad. Something you could do could help find them. The little one has asthma, for fuck's sake!"

Now her voice was raised so Cap raised his.

"Watch your mouth!"

They stopped at a light. Nell looked out her window and breathed strongly through her nose. That was another thing she'd done since she was a little kid, only when she got angry. Jules and Cap used to call her Baby Bull.

"There's another piece to this," said Cap, calm again. "I don't know who this woman is, the one from California. I read some articles about her, but she could have no idea what she's doing. Then I'd be taking a huge risk for something that has no legs to begin with."

"Don't we explore all avenues?" said Nell.

Cap laughed.

"I'm serious," she said. "Don't we look at every angle, every branch of the tree?"

"Yeah, we do," Cap conceded, feeling beaten down.

They pulled up in front of Carrie's house. Nell reached in the backseat for her bags. She faced straight ahead, thinking.

"Look," she finally said. "Remember when you quit your job and you explained it to me?"

Cap nodded. "Yeah."

"You said every day we make a million little choices, and we should try to make the right ones as much as we can. And you said rarely in life do the big choices present themselves, so when they do, we have to take advantage of the opportunity. We have to do the right thing."

Cap had no response to his daughter. He felt approximately six inches tall.

"Jesus, is there anything I say you don't memorize?" he said, his voice hoarse.

"Nope," she said cheerily.

She kissed him on the cheek and got out of the car.

"See you Wednesday," she said.

"Yep, Wednesday."

"I love you, Dad," she said, leaning through the window.

"Love you too," he said.

Then she was gone, up Carrie's steps. Cap watched her go inside and then took out his phone. He looked through his deleted items for Alice Vega's message. He sat in his car for a few long minutes.

Cap came back home. He parked in the driveway and rolled up the windows. It was still light outside, sun setting later and later these days, but it still felt like winter to him, especially in the evenings, the air cold and glassy with the sun sinking, everything in blues and grays. He saw the copy of *Othello* tucked behind the rear windshield and smiled.

As he walked up the path to his front door he didn't exactly hear something but sensed it, a movement close by. If he were a rabbit, his ear would have twitched. He turned around quickly. Alice Vega was standing across the street. She waved to him and crossed.

He couldn't help smiling and went toward her; they met in the middle of the street.

"Hey, hi, I just left you a message," he said.

"Oh yeah?" she said. "I haven't looked at my phone."

Then he began to notice things. Strands of hair frayed and out of place. Accelerated breathing. Light sweat on her forehead. She'd been in a rush recently. Adrenaline.

"Everything okay?" he said.

"Yes," she said, sounding so sure he felt stupid for asking. "Could you help me get something out of my car?"

"Yeah, sure," he said, but she'd already turned around and started walking away before he got the words out.

She walked fast, and Cap hurried to catch up. Something was off. Something was not fitting. He suddenly wished he had the Sig on him, which was not a wish he made often.

"Hey," he said, and he placed his hand on her shoulder.

The muscle pulsed there, a braided rope under his fingers. She shook him off, and they both stopped and faced each other. Cap held his hands up.

"Sorry," he said. "Are you sure everything's okay?"

This time she paused, appeared to think about it. ·

"I am. Could you come, please?"

She headed toward a generic beige sedan, and Cap thought how it wasn't that cold out. Why should his eyes be blurring? Why did it look like Vega's car was bouncing slightly up and down? But then he heard it, the squeak and scrape of the tires. The car was bouncing.

"What—" he said.

But Vega was already ahead of him, holding up her keys. *Beep beep.*

The lock clicked, and Cap caught up. She opened the trunk, and there was Brandon Haas, wrists and ankles tied with bungee cords, a collar of blue and bloody skin around his neck, urine stains on the crotch of his jeans, and a green apple wedged into his mouth. Frantic, angry raccoon eyes. He thrashed his body back and forth against the walls of the trunk and made long, muffled snorts. Cap lifted his hand to his mouth.

"This your skip?" said Vega.

"Yeah," said Cap.

Cap reached down and pulled the apple out. Haas gasped and started screaming.

"You crazy fuckin' bitch, I'm gonna kill you. I'm gonna fuck you up so bad—"

Haas then realized Cap was there as well and screamed at him, "She burned my cock. My cock is burning!"

"Did you do that?" asked Cap.

"I did," said Vega.

"I'm gonna sue the shit outta you, bitch. I'm gonna fuckin' rip your face off and beat the shit outta you and get your ass thrown in jail—"

She took the apple back from Cap and shoved it back into Haas's mouth.

"He'll just keep going like that," said Vega. "So how long do you need to take care of this? Couple of hours?"

Cap shrugged, a little stunned, said, "Probably."

"Help me get him out," she said.

Before Cap could agree, she threaded her arms underneath Haas's armpits and started to lift him. Haas wriggled and flapped his elbows around. Cap grabbed his ankles. Haas tried to kick him.

"Hey," said Vega to Haas, gripping his face in her hand like he was a dog she was trying to housebreak. "Stop it."

Haas paused briefly and then kept trying to buck. His T-shirt hiked up, exposing his stomach, white and sagging.

Vega dropped him from a few inches above the street and he landed on his shoulder blades with his head craning up. Cap dropped the legs, and Haas rolled back and forth.

"What does your voice mail say?" Vega asked Cap.

Cap was out of breath.

"Just that I wanted to have a conversation."

"I'll be back in a couple of hours," she said. "For a conversation."

She looked down at Haas like he was a traffic cone, then back to Cap. The very small trace of flirtation from earlier had gone. That had not been the real woman, Cap realized. This was her now, and she was working, and that's all there was.

She shut the trunk, walked around to the driver's side of the car, and got in. She did not look at Cap in her side mirror as she started the car, no thumbs-up or wave. Then he watched her leave again.

He was left with Haas, who'd worn himself out and was now just lying at Cap's feet, making halfhearted grunts.

"Mr. Haas," said Cap. "Someone who owes as much money as you do and has a bench warrant out on them shouldn't be threatening to sue anyone."

Haas made a sound that was like someone talking in his sleep. Cap squatted over him and pulled out his phone.

"So who's it gonna be first?" he said. "Your ex or the cops?"

Haas's eyes rolled toward him and blinked. Cap took the apple out of his mouth, and Haas took a breath like he'd been rescued from drowning.

4

CAP HAD FIFTEEN MINUTES TO CLEAN THE SHIT OUT OF HIS OFFICE before Vega would be back. This was after Hayley Haas's trashy lawyer had left with a signed IOU from Haas, and Cap had called a cab to take Haas to the hospital to have his dick iced.

He shoved every loose-leaf sheet of paper into a big black Hefty bag and tried to make the stacks on his desk look more like papers that were about to be filed instead of papers that were about to be shoved into a big black Hefty bag.

He thought only briefly about what exactly he was doing, why he was meeting with Vega again, what he would say to her when she arrived. He knew himself well enough and had had enough sessions with a shrink to know that the reasons that he did things were not immediately accessible to him until sometime later. Then, like seeing something on the street that he'd seen in a dream the night before, it would click. So that's why I did that.

He put his hands on his hips and surveyed the room. The motion sensor light in the driveway came on, and he could hear her coming, then the knock. He took a breath and held it.

He sat on the leather loveseat, Vega in a wooden chair, perched on the edge again. She leaned over her laptop on the low coffee table, started tapping various keys.

"Here's the feed from the parking lot, eleven forty-eight," she said, swiveling the laptop toward Cap.

Cap watched. The car containing the Brandt girls was not directly surrounded by any other cars. The lot was fairly empty. Spring Fest, thought Cap. One of the girls was in the front seat, passenger side, and he could see her shape but not her face. The feed was black-and-white, the camera probably thirty feet from the car and slightly to the left. The face flickered with movement, became lighter.

"She's turning her head," said Vega.

"Talking to her sister in the backseat," said Cap.

The face continued to flicker, back and forth, agitated.

"They're arguing," said Cap.

More angry flickering, then the girl in the front seat gets out. The girl in the backseat follows. Her dress shines: glitter, sequins, beads. Cap had put Nell in a hundred of them through age nine. The two girls go out of frame.

"Here," said Vega, typing.

Another square screen on the laptop opened, and new footage: an ice cream shop. The camera was a foot and a half or so above the counter. A woman, two kids, and a baby sit at a booth. The Brandt girls enter, led by the older one. The girl behind the counter gives them both miniature spoons with samples, and they eat. The older one licks her spoon, front and back, keeps asking for another. After five, the girl behind the counter tells them to pay or get lost. The older one says something smart-ass. (Cap could tell by the look on her face.) Squints her eyes and smirks, looks much older than ten. Then they walk out of the frame.

Vega closed the window, opened another. The parking lot entrance. The older one walks out, toward the street. The younger one stops, says something. The older one keeps going. The younger one runs to catch up. Out of frame. It is 12:02.

"So the older one sees someone, something, walks toward it. Younger one's reluctant but goes with her," said Cap.

"Maybe someone she knows," said Vega.

"So that makes your job easy, right?" said Cap.

Vega didn't turn to him, kept her eyes on the screen.

"Right."

"Relatives, family friends, teachers, dental hygienist, pizza delivery guy," he said. Then he pointed to the laptop. "How did you get this again?"

"I have a guy."

"Same guy who found Haas?"

She nodded.

"That's quite a guy. Hacker, right?"

She didn't exactly smile, but the muscles in her face relaxed. Affection, Cap thought. Familiarity.

"We call him that, but he'd say he's a contortionist."

"A guy who can squeeze into small spaces," said Cap.

"Yes."

"So," said Cap, "who do you like?"

"No one, until I get witness statements. You said you wanted to have a conversation."

She held out her hand. Here is our conversation.

"You want to help me."

It didn't sound like a question, and it didn't sound like she was attempting to brainwash him. It was softer; it was just the truth.

"How do you know that?" said Cap.

Vega sighed.

"Earlier when I left, you were sure you wanted nothing to do with this. Now something has changed. You thought about it, you had a revelation, a crisis of conscience. Maybe you thought about your daughter, or your ex-wife, or your mom. Maybe you talked to someone, and they changed your mind. Maybe you decided private practice isn't what you want. I listened to your voice mail. There's anticipation in it. Short breaths, your sentences end as questions; you sound hopeful."

Cap tried to keep a game face. He did it pretty well, had a lot of practice. But Vega seemed to see and hear everything, every wrinkle in the skin and catch in the throat.

"You made your decision already," she said. "Before I got here."

Cap glanced at the ghostly video feed on the laptop screen, the parking lot entrance, where he could almost see the smoke trail of the Brandt girls. Sometimes these things looked like fairy tales at first. But they never were. As soon as you got closer you saw the damage, the disease, not what monsters and wolves could do, but what regular men could do to a kid. Once he saw the body of a malnourished five-year-old boy left to decompose in a junkie's apartment. The ME who picked him up said he was as light as a doll.

"I did," he said.

"And either you agree with Haas that I'm crazy, or you don't, or maybe you do and you like it."

"But you don't care about that either, right? The why part," said Cap.

"Right."

Cap looked at the two open windows on the screen. Empty lot. The girls wandering out to the street like sleepwalkers. Dreaming.

Vega stayed in the car. They had driven together in Cap's but agreed she would not get out. Instead she moved into the driver's seat and watched from across the street. Cap stood in the lot where Vega had parked earlier. He leaned against a car and thumbed the screen on his phone. She watched a man come out of the building, down the steps, and around to the lot. He was overweight, pants a little too short.

He and Cap started with a handshake, then man-hugged, pat-pat-pat on the back. You haven't seen him for a while, thought Vega. They chitchatted. Small talk, easy back and forth, how's the wife, kids, house. Then it started to go on for too long. Four, five, six minutes. Come on, thought Vega. Too much time goes to this shit, she thought.

Should we play they could be . . . naked, raped, dying, dead? All of the above?

She sent a text to Cap and put her hands on the wheel. She watched him look at his phone.

STOP WASTING TIME. ASK HIM.

Cap paused.

"Y'okay?" said Em.

Cap smiled at him. Wiley Emerson. He was the same: always too loud and too fat, but earnest, honest, and surprisingly savvy when it came to police work. There had been a lot of talk when Cap left about how close they would stay, one very long night at Smith's Road House when Em had hugged him and cried, snorted into Cap's shirt and said, "Thank you, thank you."

Cap peered across the street at Vega in his car. She pointed at him, pressed her fingertip against the window. Ask him, said the finger.

"Yeah," Cap said at first. Then, "No, I need something, Em. I need a favor."

"Anything, man," said Em. He meant it.

"Nah, don't say that yet," said Cap. "I need *the* favor. The. Favor."

"Oh," said Em. Then as it sank in, again: "Oh."

"I need the witness statements, Em. From the Brandt case."

That took Em a second. Cap watched him deflate. Thanksgiving Day float style.

"What, what d'you mean?"

"I'm working the case. With someone the family hired."

"The woman from California?" said Em.

"Yeah, that's her. She went to see Junior. Obviously he doesn't want her help."

Em rubbed his chin, then his cheeks with his palms.

"Oh, man. Oh, Cap, I don't know, man," he said.

"Em, this woman, the one from California, she's good, and we can help. We can all work together. All you have to do is make me some copies."

Cap was not entirely sure when he had become so confident in the mission. But as he spoke he felt himself getting excited, felt popping and clicking in pockets of his brain where he hadn't noticed activity in a while. He used to feel it most days when he was a cop, but it came along with anxiety, tension, paranoia.

"Cap, I wanna help you, I mean, hell, we need you right now. You could cut through so much of this bullshit and get to the center of it, man. I know you could. But I don't, I don't know if I can do that."

"You're not going to get caught, Em. And Junior can't fire you anyway. He needs bodies."

Em looked over his shoulder cursorily.

"I thought they couldn't fire you either," he said, rubbing his eyes, red patches spreading underneath the lids. "And they did."

Cap nodded, said, "I resigned actually."

"I know, I know you did. For me. But I can't, I can't . . ."

Cap didn't make him finish.

"Can you at least tell me if you got anything solid?"

"Hell no. We got nothing." Then he leaned forward and whispered, "They say the older sister hugged the guy when she crossed the street, that's it." He shook his head. "I've slept like five hours in three days. Which is fine if we're getting somewhere, but we're going in circles. Junior said a Fed's coming in, but I don't see how that's gonna help because we got shit leads. It's like trying to hold on to sand."

Vega watched the fat guy get exasperated, wipe his face, his eyes. She watched Cap laugh, calm, steady. This is how he does it, she thought. He stays calm and steady while the other guy panics, until when, though. Pin him, she thought. Pin him like a goddamn moth on a board.

The fat guy shook his head, kept shaking it. Are you telling me no?

She took her hands off the wheel and opened the door. How many seconds would it take to cross the street and hit him in the temple.

Then she stopped. Junior Hollows at the top of the steps. She pulled her leg back in and shut the door.

Cap saw Junior, and Junior saw Cap, and Em turned around and looked guilty. Junior came into the parking lot, trotting, spry, to show how young and energetic he was feeling.

"Max Caplan," he said, sticking out his hand to shake Cap's at least a yard before he reached him.

"Hey, boss," said Cap.

They shook. It was not one of those hand-crushing contests between men, because, Cap knew, Junior didn't think there were any more contests between them. Junior was still a cop, and Cap wasn't. Junior had won.

"Got some more salt in your pepper there, Cap," said Junior, touching the sides of his head like he was primping in a mirror.

Cap said, "Forty-one in February, just learned how to send a Twitter."

"That's good," said Junior. Junior was big on approving of people and the funny things they said. "Em, I think Ralz and Royce have something for you."

"Oh, yeah," said Em with his shitty poker face. "See you, Cap. I'll get some dates from Hannah."

Good boy, thought Cap.

Em shuffled away, looking at Cap once before heading up the steps.

"You in the neighborhood?" said Junior.

"Something like that, yeah," said Cap.

"Busy time over here. Got everyone hustling."

"So I hear."

"How's business?"

"Good enough. Always someone cheating."

"There you go."

Junior took a serious breath through the nose now.

"It's not really a great time to be catching up, Cap, I gotta be honest. We've got our hands full right now."

"Yeah?" said Cap. "You get a promotion, now you're handling social calendars too?"

Chuckle, laugh, keep it light, thought Cap. Junior smiled too.

"No, I know you and Em go back, we just want to keep it on personal time."

He sounded like a middle school teacher at a parent conference. We don't want Em to get confused, do we? Cap tried not to feel the old spark of fury in his chest. He'd been to enough therapy, practiced enough breathing exercises. You are not mad at Junior anymore. You can't control other people.

"Because you're busy, right, I know. Then let me ask you this, Junior—why are you out here talking to me when you got your whole team inside busting their asses?"

"Just came to say hello."

Cap lifted his hand, waved at the knuckles. Hello.

Vega slid down in her seat, watched as the two men inched closer to each other while they spoke. A little shoot-out. She could see Cap smiling and nodding, too quick and eager.

Vega's phone buzzed. It was another email from the Bastard with a video attachment. The subject was "haystack." The text in the body read, "this would be the needle."

"Any reason you happen to be in the neighborhood now?" said Junior, smug. "Anything I need to know about?"

"Wait a second, now, let me think about that," said Cap. "Almost had something for you there but then I remembered . . . I don't work for you anymore."

He hadn't realized it, but he'd taken a step forward. Junior must have as well, because there suddenly wasn't a lot of space between them.

Junior laughed again.

"Seriously, you still crack me up, man. I mean it."

Then he backed off, turned around and started walking away. He pointed at Cap over his shoulder and said, "Good to see you, Cap. Stay in touch."

"Yeah. See you soon," said Cap.

He watched Junior go up the stairs to the station and thought about a word to mutter. "Fuckface," or "dickhead," or "asshole," or other words composed of "fuck," "dick," and "ass" that Junior's personality just naturally evoked. In the end he said nothing because it made him feel petty to mutter words alone in a parking lot after a conversation had ended.

He crossed the street to his car and saw Vega moving from the driver's seat to the passenger side, staring at her phone. It crossed his mind that the seat would be warm from her body.

"That was fun," he said, getting in.

"Is your friend amenable?"

"I don't know. We were sort of interrupted."

Cap stared at the building.

"What did he say? What was the head shaking?"

"They're disorganized, which I could have told you. They're overwhelmed, overworked. Junior won't admit they're overwhelmed and overworked because he's a cocky son-of-a-bitch who thinks he's in a James Patterson book."

"Did he say anything specific about the witness statements?"

"There's not a lot, but it's all varying reports—different colors, different makes of cars. Someone said Kylie hugged a man across the street from the mall."

Vega stared forward at the car parked in front of them. PHILADEL-PHIA EAGLES #1 FAN said the license plate rim.

"Watch this," she said, leaning over and holding out her phone.

It was another video. She pressed Play, and Cap watched.

It was two little boys eating ice cream.

"This is Dylan and Michael-John and we're all here stopping for ice cream on the way to Uncle Drex and Aunt Bert's," said a woman's voice, the woman holding the camera, Cap thought.

Either Dylan or Michael-John held up his spoon.

"I have cookie batter," he said. "With M&M's and Snickers."

The other boy was littler and just kept shoveling in the ice cream like it would be taken away from him soon. He had chocolate smeared across his mouth and cheek.

The first boy kept talking about ice cream and answered his mother's questions about how excited he was to see his aunt and uncle. Cap began to recognize the store, the parking lot.

"And we have Bitty-Love too," said the mother, turning the camera phone to a baby in a car seat next to her. "Just a little taste," she said, her arm extending from behind the camera to feed the baby white ice cream from a plastic spoon.

The baby smiled and kicked and made a sweet seal bark. Cap smiled.

There was ambient noise too, other voices off screen that Cap couldn't make out.

The mother kept feeding and tickling the baby and asking questions, and on the screen the baby started to sink to the lower right corner, because the mother was trying to talk to the boys opposite her and feed the baby with her other hand, Cap thought. The upper left portion of the screen grew, most of it capturing the parking lot outside.

And then there they were, Kylie and Bailey Brandt, on the screen, outside the store, facing each other, talking. Cap leaned in closer to Vega and her phone. He rubbed his hand over his mouth and chin.

Bailey pointed toward the lot. Let's go back to the car. Kylie still held a small tasting spoon from the store in her hand; she licked the back of it, which Cap thought seemed a strangely adult thing to do. Then Kylie stopped and took a few steps past Bailey, looking at something in the opposite direction, something across the street. Bailey's mouth still moved. Let's go back to the car. Mom will be angry.

Kylie waved to someone, cutting a big swath through the air with her raised hand, and then she smiled. It was really more of a grin, like there had been a joke. Bailey stood behind her, tentative.

Then the phone was placed down on the table and went dark.

"Where'd you get that?" said Cap.

"My guy found it. This lady put it on Facebook, called it 'Ice Cream in Denville.'"

"That was quite a smile," said Cap.

"Someone she knows," said Vega.

"Not just that," said Cap. "Someone she's glad to see."

Cap thought of it, Kylie's black smile, hovering in space like the Cheshire cat's. Jules read that one to Nell when she was little. Cap would stand at the door. *Please would you tell me why your cat grins like that?*

Vega handed Cap his keys and said, "You ready to meet Jamie Brandt?"

For as long as he had lived there, Cap always had many shitty things to say about Denville, but he actually thought it was a beautiful place at night. Beat-up streets with potholes became quaint in the dark, porch lights on to disguise the chipped paint and scratched siding on the houses. The expanding suburb developments looked better too; instead of cheap overgrown children's toys they had an almost English countryside look to them out of daylight. Not that Cap had ever been to the English countryside, but he'd seen plenty of movies.

Schultz's Bar was in Black Creek. The neighborhood was full of apartment complexes and single-level homes built in the '60s, brown and yellow exteriors with shag carpet and faux wrought-iron arches inside. When Cap and Jules had been shopping around for houses back in the beginning, they'd looked at one or two there, and driving away Jules had said, "If I have to live in a house like that, I will hang myself." Cap had said, "I will buy the rope." Then of course they'd laughed with the relief of their agreement on the subject. Ha. Suicide.

Cap had been to Schultz's once or twice. It looked like a hundred other bars, a black box from the outside with a single rectangular window, like an aquarium, but instead of fish there was a Yuengling sign. He and Vega parked on the street and went inside.

There were a few people scattered around, a group of men hooked around the corner of the bar, a couple making out at a table next to the bathroom, two women at the jukebox. And there was Jamie Brandt, Cap recognized her from TV, sitting at the far end of the bar with her head down. He and Vega made their way to her. Vega stopped when she was about a foot away, as if Jamie were a dog on the street.

"Jamie?" Vega said. She was quiet about it.

Jamie turned her head, languid, her lids heavy with exhaustion or drunkenness, or both.

"You," said Jamie, pointing at Vega.

"Alice Vega," said Vega.

"Right. Vega. Who's he?"

"Max Caplan," said Cap, friendly. He looked at Jamie's hands on the bar, lying there like leaves of a dead plant, and did not extend his.

Jamie licked her lips and said, "How'd you know I was here?"

"Your aunt said you might be."

Jamie laughed through her nose.

"What else she say?"

"Just that you went somewhere to be alone," said Vega.

Jamie paused to take a sip of what looked like a very light beer on ice from a mug.

"We have some more questions," said Vega.

"I'm sorta off the clock here," said Jamie. "I did three interviews today, and I talked to someone at CNN. Then I tried to find some pictures of the girls wearing different kinds of clothes other than dresses. The lawyer told us that they might be walking around in other kinds of clothes. So I been looking at pictures of them all day. Then we been hanging up flyers. So I come here to get drunk for two goddamn hours and then I'm going to go home and sleep for four more and then do it over again. Maggie's got an email into the *Today* show. She knows someone who knows someone."

"We need to make a list of people," said Vega.

"Cops made a list."

"We're going to make a better one. But we need you to come with us now so we can sit down somewhere and talk."

There was something a little hypnotic in Vega's voice, thought Cap, the evenness. Lost on Jamie Brandt, however.

"I need an hour. I need twenty minutes," said Jamie, grabbing at her mug.

She missed it, ran her fingers into the handle instead of latching on to it, and it spilled sideways toward Cap. Ice cubes slid down the bar and dropped into Jamie's lap, then hit the floor with little wooden taps.

"Shit," said Jamie.

The air around them seemed to freeze. Cap looked around, saw the bartender, not a small guy, coming toward them.

"Hey, Jamie, you okay over here?" he said, staring at Cap.

"I fuckin' spilled," she said, patting her lap with a wadded cocktail napkin.

The bartender wiped the bar with a rag and pushed a stack of napkins to Jamie. Then he folded his arms, which made them appear bigger. He had "Maya" and "Tori" tattooed on his knuckles.

"Maybe you two ought to take a walk around the block," he said to Cap and Vega.

"Jamie," said Vega, ignoring the bartender. "Come with us now, please."

"Hey," said the bartender. He nodded to Cap. "You wanna tell your girlfriend to chill the fuck out?"

Vega jerked her head in the bartender's direction.

"Or?" she said.

"You want me to come over there?" he said, leaning across the bar.

Vega's eyes went glassy like she'd just tasted something delicious.

"Wish you would," she said.

Cap inserted himself between Vega and the bar, touched Jamie's shoulder.

"Jamie," he said. "We don't have twenty minutes. We don't have one minute. Kylie knew who took her."

Cap watched as this information snaked its way into Jamie's brain. Her face contorted; her thin plucked eyebrows turned into little Spanish tildes.

"Cops didn't say that."

"They might not even know it yet. They're under a shitstorm of information, and they might not even have seen the footage we've seen yet."

"There's something else," said Vega.

Now they all turned to Vega: Jamie, Cap, Knuckles.

"They aren't telling you anything, right? They say it's part of an ongoing investigation?"

Jamie nodded.

"That's standard," said Vega. "But we're not cops. We'll tell you everything we know."

That seemed to wake her up. She looked from Vega to Cap, who nodded.

Cap said, "Kylie smiled at whoever took her. We need to make a new list."

Back in Cap's office, Jamie stared at the screen and covered her mouth with both her hands and made squeaking sounds into the hollow space. Vega closed her laptop. She and Cap looked at each other.

Jamie fumbled with her purse, a bright blue hobo bag with palm trees printed on it. She pulled out a pharmacy bottle of pills, flattened her palm against the lid, and tried to twist it. Her hands were shaking and the bottle fell into her lap.

"Here," said Cap, holding his hand out.

Jamie gave him the bottle. Cap unscrewed the top, glanced at the label: alprazolam. Generic Xanax. Jamie shook two into her hand and brought them to her mouth, chewed them up like SweeTarts. Cap looked at the symbol of a little martini glass with a line through it on the label, thought better of mentioning it.

Jamie still held a hand over her mouth, just grazing her lips.

"Son-of-a-bitch," she whispered.

Vega leaned over to her.

"Does anyone come to mind, someone she'd smile like that for?"

"No," said Jamie. "I mean, yeah, but she knows them for sure, that's all. That's what I'm thinking about."

"Most kids know their abductors," said Cap.

"Yeah, but how many make them smile?" said Jamie.

"She wouldn't know her father well enough that she would have that kind of reaction," said Vega, pulling her laptop onto her lap.

"Shit no," said Jamie. "They only seen a couple of pictures, and they're from a long time ago."

"So who's the first person, the very first, who you think of."

Jamie thought for a moment, rubbed the temples on her head roughly.

"My folks. That's stupid, huh."

"It's not," said Cap. "We want to rule people out, right? I was a cop for a long time, and that's how you do this. You just keep ruling people out until you get some good suspects. So put Jamie's parents on the list," he said to Vega.

Vega nodded at him, but he noticed there was some theatrics in it, exaggeration, so Jamie could see it. Her eyes were steady on him too. It was a familiar click; it was one partner to another.

"Okay, who's the next?"

Jamie shook out her shoulders like she had a chill.

"I don't know, my aunt?"

"Right," said Vega, typing.

Jamie went on, naming family members, a great-uncle, first and second cousins, a third cousin in the army who sent the girls emails from Afghanistan. All people Kylie might smile at. Then they were done with family.

Then her boyfriend, Darrell.

"What's he do for a living?" said Cap.

"He works at the Bagel Pub, over in Cherry Point."

"Would Kylie smile at him?" said Vega.

"Sure, I guess. I mean, they like him well enough."

"What about teachers?"

Mrs. Phillips for Kylie, Miss Ferno for Bailey. They had PE teachers too, but Jamie couldn't remember the names.

"What about, like, extracurricular types of things?" said Vega.

Bailey's soccer coach was a guy named Arnab, an Indian or something, Jamie told them. He seemed nice enough. Kylie's ballet teacher was Miss Savannah. Jamie thought she might be a lesbian.

"Are any of these folks angry at you for any reason? Do any of them hold a grudge that you know about?" said Cap.

Jamie tightened up her lips.

"No, everyone fucking asks me that. No. I mean, maybe I piss people off here and there because I say what I think, you know. I don't like to beat around the bush."

"Can you recall the last time you did that? Piss someone off?" Vega said.

Jamie coughed out a laugh.

"Take your pick, right?" she said. "Well, let's see, last week I flipped off a guy at an intersection and he yelled that he was gonna take my license number. I called him a pussy."

Cap smiled and said, "The other day I told a woman who cut me off to suck my dick, excuse me. I haven't said those words since maybe the seventh grade."

Jamie laughed.

"I know this might be a tough one—believe me I know, I have a sixteen-year-old—did Kylie have a crush on anyone? A teacher or an older boy she might have come in contact with?" Cap said.

"The girl's a natural-born flirt," said Jamie, and there was just a little pride in her voice. "I told her she should go into business school; she could sell space heaters to Egyptians. But I don't know about anyone in particular."

"What other men does she see on a regular basis?" said Vega. "Besides your family and your boyfriend, and teachers?"

"There's a kid lives in our complex named Sonny—he's probably fifteen, sixteen. He's always sweet to her," said Jamie. "But I seen him since Saturday walking around—his mom dropped off a crumb cake. He doesn't have the girls stashed in his closet."

Jamie shook her head, almost angry. Cap thought he should ask for the kid's phone number and address, not to put him on the list but to get Jamie's mind off the image of the girls safe and sound a hundred feet away.

"What about ex-boyfriends?" said Vega. "Men before Darrell."

"Before Darrell," Jamie said, spacey; then she seemed to focus again. "Before Darrell there was Chaney. Alex Chaney. I saw him about a month ago actually."

Vega glanced at Cap.

"Where'd you see him?" said Cap.

"I ran into him at Valley Diss. We kinda argued."

"What did you argue about?"

Jamie made a sound like *pssh* and said, "I told him he's a fucking druggie without a job. He said I'm an uptight bitch."

"What kind of drugs he do?" said Vega.

"He likes Vicodin and Perc, oxy when he can get it."

"He addicted, in your opinion?"

"Wasn't when I met him," said Jamie. "Then he got laid off and started hanging out with some other losers, and they started snorting that shit. He stopped wanting to hang out on the weekends. He'd show up at my place Sunday morning looking like a stray dog. And, you know, I like to smoke a joint sometimes but I don't want fucking junkies in my house."

"The girls like him?" said Vega.

Jamie thought about it.

"Yeah, they did. Before he got into the shit, he worked at Roma Pizza for a while and used to bring them stuff from there, like garlic bread and cannolis, stuff like that. I think Kylie had a little crush on him. She was upset when I cut him off."

"She comfortable with hugging him, you think?" said Cap.

"Sure," Jamie said. She looked at them. "You don't think he took them."

"I don't know. Do you?"

"No way, man. I mean, he's a loser, but a kidnapper? I don't think so."

"How'd he look when you saw him last month?" said Vega. "Physically."

Jamie shook her head in disgust. "Skinny, his hair was all long and greasy. I told him he looked like a homeless person."

She leaned her head against the back of the couch and yawned. The sedatives were hitting, Cap knew. Then her head popped back up suddenly.

"And his breathing was funny, like he'd just run up a flight of stairs."

Cap looked at Vega, and there it was again.

Click.

At one o'clock, Jamie fell asleep on Cap's couch. Cap covered her with one of Nell's comforters and gestured to the door leading from the office to the house. Vega went through, and Cap led her into the kitchen.

Cap's house was so impossibly cozy it could make a person depressed. The living room was filled with plush worn furniture, woven rugs on the creaking floors and framed photos on a brick mantel over the fireplace. The kitchen was cream-colored, retro speckled chairs at the table and a variety of magnets in the shapes of vegetables on the fridge. Vega peered toward the stairs and thought about what was up there, two or three little bedrooms, beds next to the windows so the sun could wake you up.

"Sorry about the mess," Cap said.

It was only then that Vega noticed the stacked dishes in the sink, the dust balls in the corners. She shook her head.

Cap took two bottles of water from the refrigerator and offered one to Vega. She took it.

"So you think Chaney's something?" said Cap.

"Could be," said Vega.

"Come on," said Cap. "Her gut is right—junkies don't become kidnappers overnight. They don't have the energy, for one thing."

"If they run out of money for drugs they'll find the energy. If he's out of breath after having a conversation, maybe he was in the starting stages of withdrawal. Doesn't get more desperate than that."

Cap squinted. "Then where's the ransom, the call. If he needs money so badly, why hasn't he asked for it yet?"

"Maybe he's panicking. Having second thoughts and stuck."

"Or," said Cap.

"Or," said Vega.

Cap pinched the bridge of his nose. "Or he doesn't want anything from Jamie."

"There's a lot of sick fucking people out there," Vega said, her voice flat. "He could want drugs or money from one of them."

"And wants to trade two little girls for it," said Cap.

"Worth a visit, right?"

"Of course," said Cap.

He placed a fist over his mouth and yawned.

"First thing tomorrow, then."

"What's wrong with now?"

"It's 1:30 in the morning," said Cap.

Vega stared at him.

"I'm guessing you don't sleep a lot," he said.

"No."

They did some more looking at each other; Vega could see the fatigue in his brow, his eyes.

"Okay," he said hoarsely, then cleared his throat. "Just have to stop for coffee first. You drink coffee?"

Vega shrugged. "I like a hot tea."

5

THEY WERE IN A NEIGHBORHOOD CALLED MAPLETON, ON A BLOCK where the houses were all narrow clapboards that appeared to be leaning slightly to the left or right. Cap parked across the street from Jamie's ex-boyfriend's last known address. The house was a sallow color with brown trim, and there was a window with a curtain drawn on the ground floor, a light on inside.

"Somebody's home," said Cap.

They got out of the car and crossed the street. Cap could hear music inside, classic rock, Allman Brothers or something, what Nell would call "old white guy music." Cap pressed his thumb on the scuffed doorbell button and heard no sound. He and Vega glanced at each other, and he knocked. There was movement inside, footsteps.

"You'll talk first, I assume?" said Cap. It had been a long time since he'd discussed tactics with a partner.

Vega nodded.

"And you won't necessarily throw boiling water on his crotch and stuff him in the trunk?"

"Sure," said Vega.

The peephole darkened.

Then, "Yeah?"

"We're looking for Alex Chaney," said Vega to the peephole.

"Who's looking?"

"Name's Alice Vega and Max Caplan."

"You cops?"

"No. Private investigators. This is about two missing girls. You've seen it on TV."

There was a pause. Vega wiggled the fingers on one hand. Then there were locks being unlocked, and Cap got ready. It was a familiar feeling, watching a closed door, waiting to see what was on the other side, but it was rarely good, especially in the middle of the night in a shit part of town.

The door opened an inch; there was a stripe of a man, not big, a white face with black stubble and a bloodshot eye.

"Mr. Chaney?" said Vega.

"Yeah," he said, looking at both of them up and down. "This about Jamie Brandt's kids, I don't know anything about it."

"I'm sure you don't. Look, we're not police. We're not here to interrogate you or search your property. We've been retained by Ms. Brandt's family. We're questioning everyone who knows Ms. Brandt and her daughters."

Chaney looked up at the sky and hesitated.

"A little late," he said.

"Honestly, Mr. Chaney, we don't have a lot of time. Every hour that goes by these girls get farther away from us," said Vega. "We only need about five minutes of your time."

Another pause. Chaney scratched at his scalp like a cat with a rash. Cap could see Vega's hand moving again, impatient.

"Yeah, okay," Chaney said finally. "Long as it doesn't take too long. I'm about to go to sleep."

Cap doubted that very much but smiled like a gentleman and followed Chaney in when he opened the door wide.

The room was spare, a futon and a ratty tan couch, a cardboard box between them like a coffee table. There was a huge flat-screen television on a small stand against one wall, and the lockup show about America's prisons on the screen.

Jamie was right about the homeless person thing. Chaney was like a stick figure in paper doll clothes, with long stringy hair to his shoulders. He picked up a lit cigarette from an ashtray on the cardboard box and brought it to his mouth, inhaled and made a face like it hurt his teeth.

"Do you wanna sit?" he said.

"We're good," said Vega. "When's the last time you saw Jamie Brandt?"

"Month ago maybe, couple of months. Ran into her."

"When's the last time you saw her daughters?"

Chaney thought about it. He looked at the floor and blew smoke out in an O.

"Shit, I don't know. A year ago? When me and Jamie broke up."

Vega let a few seconds pass before she said anything else, and Cap remembered this feeling. Getting the distinct impression they were being lied to.

"When was that exactly?" Vega said.

"A year ago February. Around Valentine's Day. Pretty rough."

He looked imploringly at Vega as if she would understand, being a woman and all.

"And you saw the girls around that time."

"Yeah."

"Anyone you remember, any friend or acquaintance of Jamie's stand out to you as someone who had an interest in the girls?"

"No, I don't know," he said, shaking his head.

"And when's the last time you saw the girls?"

Chaney paused, then said, "Uh, year ago."

Vega paused, and Cap turned to glare at her. Talk quickly right now, he thought. He'll crack but you have to press. You can't give him too much time to think. But she wasn't talking. She just stared at Chaney like he was a Rorschach blot. Cap began to doubt—she was a brawler but maybe interrogation wasn't her thing.

"So end of March, then?" said Cap.

Chaney and Vega looked at him. He avoided turning to see Vega's face.

"No, Valentine's Day, right?" said Chaney.

"You tell us. Did you see them the day you broke up with Ms. Brandt? Or before or after?"

"I don't really remember when, you know, it was around then."

"March," said Cap.

"Yeah," said Chaney, a light sheet of sweat forming on his forehead. Then he shut his eyes hard. "No, man, February."

"You were close to them, the girls?"

"No, I mean, sure, they're good kids, but I wasn't like a dad to them."

"Either one of them in particular, Kylie or Bailey?"

Chaney put his hand to his head like he had an ice headache. Okay, thought Cap. Brake.

"Which one were you closer to?"

"Kylie, I guess."

"You used to bring her cannolis."

"Yeah, Jamie tell you that?"

Cap nodded. "You had a friendship."

"Yeah, I brought her stuff like that. She was a good kid. Real funny. One of those kids with a grown-up sense of humor."

Cap believed him. They were all quiet. Chaney got nervous.

"I don't know anything about them missing," he said. He turned around and put out his cigarette in the ashtray. Stamp stamp stamp.

"No one said you did, Mr. Chaney," said Cap.

"I think those people are degenerates, all right? The ones who mess around with kids. Fucking degenerate motherfuckers."

He looked at Cap and Vega defiantly, waiting for them to challenge his position on child molesters.

"Can I use your restroom?" said Vega.

"Huh?" said Chaney.

"Restroom."

"Yeah, down the hall, your right."

Cap and Vega locked eyes for only a second. He could read nothing in her face, but was it because she was feeling nothing, or she wanted Chaney to see nothing, he could not say. Then she was gone.

"Was Kylie upset that you and Ms. Brandt broke up?" Cap asked.

"Yeah, I think so," Chaney said.

He had a wistful look. Now this is the truth, Cap thought.

"Yeah, she was sad about it," he continued.

"What made you think that?" said Cap.

"You know, she was just sad about it. The way kids get sad about things."

"So when exactly did you see her get sad about it? Was she there when Ms. Brandt broke it off with you?"

Chaney's eyes shrank in his face.

"No, no," he said, tripping over the words.

"Was it afterward then? Did you see her after?"

"Yeah, must have been."

"So then it was less than a year ago when you saw her last. Was it eight months ago, six? Four?"

Chaney shook his head and scratched at his neck.

"No, I don't know. I just know she was bummed out about me and Jamie."

"How would you know that, Mr. Chaney, if you hadn't seen her after you broke up with Ms. Brandt?"

Cap was calm. The situation didn't need much effort. Press a pen slowly into a water balloon and wait for it to burst.

Vega quickly, quietly, opened Chaney's medicine cabinet and examined the clusters of bottles on the shelves. NyQuil, Advil, Aleve. She took a ballpoint pen from the inside pocket of her jacket and used it to strip back the beige shower curtain. There was nothing in the bathtub except a brown ring and ashy spots on the floor.

She opened the door to the bathroom slowly and stepped into the hallway, heard Chaney chattering and Caplan's low tones.

Down the hall was a door with a light on inside. Vega squinted her eyes, saw shadows moving around in the crack under the door. Something was in the room. Here comes Little Bad, said Perry in her head. Vega slid her boots off and walked in her socks on the carpet down the hall. She pulled the doorknob toward her and tried to turn it. Locked. Vega leaned her head back and heard Chaney and Caplan still, Chaney's voice starting to rise.

She took from her wallet a Costco rewards card that never had belonged to her but that was long and flexible, with beveled laminated edges, and slid it directly in between the wall and the door, right above the doorknob.

She left it there, padded back to the bathroom, flushed the toilet and turned the water on in the sink. Then quickly back to the door with the light and the shadows, held the card tightly between her fingertips, wedged it next to the lock and jimmied it.

The door popped opened, and a black cat with white toes jumped off a table and ran out, sliding against Vega's shins on the way. Vega was about to lean down and grab the thing by the back of the neck but then she saw what was on the table in the room and thought, Let the girl run.

—

Cap saw the cat first. It lingered in the doorway for a moment and then curled around the frame into the room.

Chaney was saying: "I don't have a fucking BlackBerry, okay? I don't keep track of shit—"

Then he saw the cat and stared at it, froze and pointed to the hallway.

Cap held his hands out, didn't know what the big deal was with the cat except that it managed to look fed in a druggie's house.

"Where—" Chaney started to say.

Then Vega came in, taking big strides, and threw something at Chaney's head. It hit him and bounced to the floor, sounding like a maraca. Cap finally got a good look at it—a sizable prescription pill bottle.

"What the fuck?!" Chaney said, crouching in shock.

Cap looked at Vega expectantly but said nothing. Vega picked the bottle up and showed it to Cap, then shoved it in Chaney's face and pulled him down to the futon by the shoulder.

"He's not just a junkie," she said. "He's a dealer. He's got a room back there with six boxes of pills."

"That's trespassing!" said Chaney to Cap.

"You let us in, Mr. Chaney," said Cap.

"The fuck you care I got oxy—you said you weren't cops."

"We're not," said Cap. "But we can call them right now and draw them a little map to your back room."

"When's the last time you saw either Kylie or Bailey Brandt?" Vega said, standing over him, very close.

Chaney panted and wiped his mouth.

"Okay," said Chaney. He ran his fingers through his hair. "I saw Kylie about a month ago. She took a bus here after school. When Jamie and I ran into each other she was in the car and saw me."

"Why did she come to see you?" said Cap.

Chaney sighed.

"She's a kid. She said she missed me and wanted me and Jamie to get back together. It's just 'cause they don't have a father, you know?"

He looked up at Vega, then at Cap.

"Look, when I heard about it, that someone took them, it broke my heart, okay? They were real cute kids."

"You got a little scared too, right?" said Cap. "Thought people might come around and ask you questions."

"I don't want any trouble."

"What did you do when Kylie showed up at your door?" said Cap.

"I took her to her grandparents' place. Drove her myself."

"And you didn't think to call Jamie Brandt and let her know her child was here?" said Vega.

Chaney shook out his shoulders.

"Kylie begged me not to tell. And no one knew she was gone. The old man watches her in the afternoon. She made up some story to tell him. And I . . ."

Chaney paused.

"I had clients here. People get freaked out they see a kid."

"Makes them less likely to buy illegally obtained opiates," said Cap.

He shook his head again.

"I didn't have anything to do with those girls disappearing. Not a fucking thing."

Cap kept the stern look on his face for Chaney's sake, glanced at Vega, whose wide, steady eyes confirmed what he already thought, that this asshole was telling them the truth.

Then Cap said, more softly, "Do you remember what you talked about in the car? Did she tell you anything that stands out?"

Chaney leaned back on the couch and stared at the ceiling for a moment.

"You know, we already had all the drama back here, so I wasn't going to give her any more shit about running away. She told me she finally decided she wanted to be an actress. Like she's been thinking about this a long time, right? She's finally decided on a career."

He thought about it and laughed. Cap smiled too. How serious they could get.

"I asked her if she told her mom that, and she said no, that it was a secret and she was only telling certain people."

Chaney paused. He put his hands behind his head as he thought of something.

"She was telling me she and a girlfriend, they had this little club—what she call it? 'Secrets Club' or something. They wrote down their secrets together in diaries."

"You remember the friend's name?" said Cap.

"Nah, man, it was a month ago. It was like a boy's name though, I remember that. I asked if it was a boy. She said no and looked at me like I'm crazy."

He nodded at Cap.

"You know the way a girl looks at you like you're crazy?"

Cap nodded. Because he knew.

In the car Vega was silent, glanced at Cap's face in profile. She could tell he was trying not to yawn, his lips pinched closed, eyes watering. As soon as they got to the stoplight on the corner of Chaney's block, and Vega was sure there was no way Chaney could see them through his busted curtains, she spoke.

"We said I was going to talk," she said quietly.

"What?" said Cap.

She didn't say it again because she knew he had heard her the first time. It was a bossman thing. They made you say it twice so then you sounded like you were complaining. Even if they weren't doing it consciously.

He sighed.

"I thought I would jump in. With guys like that you have to keep the pressure on and not give them time to think up a lie."

Vega didn't answer. At the next stoplight, she watched him yawn into his fist toward the window, knew she had about one full second.

She reached over, pushed the shift to Park and turned the engine off, let the key dangle.

"What the fuck are you doing?" Cap said, looking in his mirrors, disoriented.

"I know guys like that too," she said, raising her voice just a little. "This is my case, and you're the special guest star. So when we say I talk first, I fucking talk first."

"Hey, you know what," said Cap, starting the car. "You're used to working alone, I get it. But you have to trust me a little bit. I saw an opening, and I took it. And we still got him to talk. Both of us fishing, you on recon and . . . gentle assault."

"Trust doesn't matter," she said. "We just have to agree."

"Fine, then let's agree on who talks first, but if an opportunity presents itself, the other one should take it."

"Sure," said Vega.

"Great," said Cap.

They drove in silence until Cap pulled up at the inn.

"He would've talked eventually. Chaney," he said, "I had him. You didn't have to come in like that."

He sounded a little hurt about it. Jesus, thought Vega, now we have the ego.

"You know what the problem with that is?" said Vega.

He shook his head.

"Eventually."

Cap looked surprised, almost in a pleasant way.

"Have a good night, Vega," he said.

She didn't answer him, got out of the car, went inside.

After three hours of sleep she woke up with boys' names that could be girls' names playing on repeat in her head. Dylan, Sam, Shane, Aidan, Peyton, Morgan.

Standing on her hands, she took slow breaths in and out through the nose. Her head started to get quiet, the only noise the heating unit humming in the corner. Cloudy paint splotches swam on her lids.

And there they were. The Brandt girls in white dresses with black velvet bands around their waists. Kylie to the left, Bailey to right, facing Vega. Vega didn't believe in psychic visions or premonitions, but her mind wandered during the handstand, projected hazy filmstrips. It was pleasant in an autopilot sort of way, as long as it wasn't a memory. So stay, thought Vega. Stay right where you are.

The girls inspected her like she was a painting in a museum. Then Kylie said, unexpectedly loud: "Better check your email."

Vega's eyes opened with a jolt, and she brought her legs down. She sat on the floor and raised her head too quickly, felt the heat leave her head and rush to her chest. After a few seconds she stood and went to her laptop, flipped it open and clicked her email. There was a new message, a Gmail address she didn't recognize. No subject. It was a single line:

FIND NOLAN MARSH AND YOU WILL FIND THE
BRANDT SISTERS

6

CAP WAS SHOCKED OUT OF SLEEP BY THE SOUND OF BOSCH NEXT door yelling, then his own doorbell. He jumped up from the couch, still in his clothes, disoriented, his head running through the slideshow of the night before. He smelled the coffee brewing from the programmed machine in the kitchen, glanced at the blue numbers on the cable box (7:01 a.m.) as he hustled to the door, didn't look through the glass panel before opening it. And there was Vega, looking exactly the same as she had hours earlier, except her hair was wet from the shower.

Bosch stood on the edge of his driveway and was waving his arms like he was trying to flag down a tow truck. He wore a bathrobe over his clothes.

"Cap, Cap, I tried-a teller she can't park there," he said.

Then Cap saw. Vega had parked in Bosch's spot in front of the lawn where he liked to walk his dog and his mother's cat.

"I'm not blocking the driveway," Vega said, quiet, not defensive. She searched Cap's eyes for an explanation.

"Cece won't do business on a car, she don't like the wheels," Bosch shouted.

Cap smiled apologetically.

"We don't park there," he said. "You can park behind my car."

Vega turned and stared for a moment at Bosch, who continued to talk.

"Cece gets upset, then Monty gets upset, then they don't eat, Cap . . ." he said.

She walked down Cap's front steps and headed toward her car.

". . . then Ma don't eat . . ."

For a moment Cap's head flooded with concern while he watched them, Vega approaching Bosch slowly as he chattered. Then she unlocked her car with the beep from her keys and got inside, started the engine, and pulled into Cap's driveway.

". . . she's gotter iron supplement, she can't take it with any dairy else it don't work," Bosch was saying, though he was beginning to slow down.

Vega got out of the car and nodded to Bosch.

"Thank you, thank you, ma'am," he said.

"Welcome," said Vega.

"Thank you, thank you," said Bosch again. "Cap, is Nell home there? Gotta book for her. She might like it."

"Wednesday. Best to Iris," called Cap, as he held the door open for Vega.

She passed underneath his arm, barely producing a draft. If he'd had his eyes closed he might not know she was there.

Cap let the door close and followed Vega in. Only now did he feel tired, the exhaustion of the night before pressing on him.

"Is Jamie awake?"

"I don't think so. You want coffee?"

"No thanks," said Vega. "I got this email a couple of hours ago."

She handed him her phone. Cap peered at the screen.

"Who's Nolan Marsh?"

"Twenty-five-year-old white male, disappeared three years ago. Took a walk after dinner from the home he shared with his mother and never came back. Listed as a 'vulnerable adult.' "

Cap leaned on the back of the couch and rubbed his eyes.

"Mentally challenged or ill," said Cap.

"Yes. Detective Ralz is listed as the police contact."

Cap thought.

"What's the connection to the Brandt girls?"

"Nothing obvious. I have Marsh's mother's home address and a land-line," said Vega, examining her phone.

"Your guy get that?"

"He did."

"We should call her."

"Yes, we should. Let's talk to her first," said Vega, nodding toward Cap's office.

"Yeah," said Cap. "Wait. Let me get coffee."

He went to the kitchen and pulled out two mugs, filled them.

"You sure you don't want?" he said, tipping one toward Vega.

She shook her head, impatient.

"Okay," he said. "Let's go."

He ran his hands through his hair in a weak effort to appear more presentable, and went to his office door, Vega right behind him. He opened the door to his office slowly. The room was dark and stuffy, the blinds still drawn. He heard Jamie Brandt snoring softly as they got closer to the loveseat. She was curled up like a prawn, her face pressed against the back cushions, mouth open.

Cap walked around and sat on the table. He looked up at Vega. Who's going to do this?

No one had to. Jamie convulsed awake, blinking at Cap and Vega hard and fast, struggling to see them.

"What is it? Where are they?" she said, hoarse, her hand on her forehead.

"It's okay, Jamie," said Cap. "You're in my house. Max Caplan," he said, tapping his chest.

"Yeah," she said, sitting up, breathing. "Yeah, right. I remember. What time is it?"

"A little after seven."

"I have to go," she said, alarm setting in.

"We have to ask you a couple more questions," said Vega.

"I don't have time," she said, reaching for her purse. "I have to go."

"We have information. We have to ask you some questions," said Vega, firmer.

"What do you mean? What information?"

"Here," said Cap, handing her the coffee.

She sat back and took a small sip.

"Do you know someone named Nolan Marsh?" Vega asked.

Jamie thought about it for a second and shook her head.

"No, doesn't ring anything."

Vega and Cap looked at each other. Then Vega handed her the phone.

"I got this email this morning."

Jamie looked at the screen. Cap watched her eyes go wide.

"What is this? Who is this from?"

"We're trying to find out," said Vega. "Nolan Marsh is a missing adult, disappeared three years ago."

"Does he have them? Do you think he has the girls?" Jamie said to Vega.

"We don't know if there's a connection, but we're going to speak to his mother soon and ask her about it."

"It's very possibly a false lead, Jamie. The police told you about these?" said Cap.

"Yeah," she said. "Sickos who just want attention, stuff like that."

"Exactly. On the surface this doesn't sound too promising, but we'll still check it out. We just wanted to ask you first."

"Okay."

She took an aggressive sip of her coffee, set the mug on the table with a clink.

"Thanks," she said. "That it for now?"

"Something else," said Vega. "Does Kylie have a girlfriend with a boy's name? I have her class list, but it doesn't show gender."

"Yeah, it's Cole. Cole Linsom. Parents are a couple of snobs, but Cole's a sweet thing. Real polite. The police already talked to her though. All of Kylie's friends."

"Linsom," said Vega, writing it down on a small chit. "We need to speak with her."

"Why? You think she knows something?" said Jamie, fresh paranoia in her voice.

Before Vega could say a word, Cap said, "We're not sure, but we need to clarify a couple of things, make sure Kylie didn't mention anything to her about someone she was going to meet at the mall."

"Okay, yeah," said Jamie. "I can . . . uh, call her mom. She sent me an email, I think. Said if there's anything she can do."

"That would be great," said Cap. "Should we take you back to your folks' place?"

"Yeah. Could I use your bathroom first?"

"Out the door on your right."

Jamie picked up her purse and left, closing the office door behind her.

"Why didn't you let me tell her about Chaney?" said Vega, writing another note.

"We tell her about Chaney, she gets upset about Chaney. She calls him, shows up at his house—Why didn't you tell me you saw Kylie? and so on. Then we have her off the rails, which we don't need, right? We need her focused."

Vega looked at him and didn't speak for a moment. Cap felt slightly disarmed.

"I tell my clients everything," she said. "No one can help us more than the client."

"And usually I would agree with you. But you have to go case by case."

"I told her last night we'd tell her everything we knew. Now I'm lying."

"You never lie, Ms. Vega?" Cap said, mostly out of curiosity.

"Not to clients."

The toilet flushed; there wasn't much time. Cap leaned in.

"This is your investigation so you run it however you want. But my opinion: we hold back on Chaney now, tell her later when we need to. Now we drop her off at home, let her get her day in order," he said quietly. "We don't need to push her further down, right? The more time that passes, she's going to get there on her own."

Vega's face didn't move, her eyes still on him. Jamie came back in, on the phone.

"I'm coming. They're driving me. . . . Jesus, Mom, I'm coming, shut up, okay?" She hung up and put her phone in her purse, then looked up at them. She was awake now, scared and sick all over again. "Can we go?"

Cap glanced at Vega and tried to read her, but she was a stone.

"Yes," she said, nodding up at Cap as if they'd already discussed it: "Your car, right?"

"Right."

Cap took another quick sip of coffee and grabbed the jacket off the back of his desk chair. Brand-new day, and here we go.

Every fucking one looked the same, thought Vega, as Cap parked on a wet dirt road. All the houses here looked like they'd suffered a few winters without maintenance; they all had water stains on the siding near the ground, the gutters on the roofs over the garages twisted dripping glum puddles into the driveways. The homes varied by style, either row house or ranch style or A-frame, but they were all old, all depressing in their disrepair. Her house in the Sacramento Valley was nothing special, two small bedrooms and a narrow kitchen, arched doorways and bright blue tiles in the bathroom. Spanish eclectic, the realtor had called it. It didn't evoke any emotion in her in particular; she didn't miss it when she was gone, had no feelings either way about sleeping in her own bed or taking a bath in her tub the way other people seemed to, but this place, Denville, made her miss the heat in the air when she left the screens open on the windows in her kitchen, and the squat peeling palm tree in the backyard.

She watched Cap pocket his keys, listened to him ask her something and thought, Except his place. Something about it she liked; something made her want to sit in his living room in the summertime and feel a warm breeze blow through.

"So? What do you think?" Cap said again, squinting through the windshield at the house.

"About what?" said Vega.

Cap glanced sideways at her, a smile creeping onto his mouth. He knew she hadn't been listening and was amused.

"We go straight to Cole Linsom's house after. Unless we get a break."

"Sure."

"And you talk first," said Cap.

They got out of the car and walked the short distance up the road. The house had a little land around it, overgrown grass and shrubs and a few trees framing the property. It was raining lightly, speckling the grass, tapping the roof of the porch as Vega and Cap stepped up. Cap knocked on the wooden pane of the screen door; it rattled under his fist.

They waited a couple of minutes, and then a woman opened the door behind the screen. She was thin, with curly red hair and no eyebrows. She also had a plastic tube running across her face with a prong in each nostril, the tube running to a nylon bag she wore on her shoulder, and which contained, Vega suspected, a portable canister of oxygen. Vega felt just for a moment like she'd been punched in the nose, all the bones in her face radiating heat. And it came to her: cannula. That's what the tube was called, a nasal cannula. Just one word in the lexicon of the sick and dying, one stone in an endless riverbed.

"Hello, Ms. Marsh?" said Vega. "I'm Alice Vega; this is Max Caplan—we spoke on the phone?"

Maryann Marsh opened the screen and smiled, a weak, crooked line.

"Hello, come in," she said.

She seemed to struggle with holding both doors open until Cap stepped in and pushed them to the wall. Vega followed him inside, wiped her shoes on the gray mat by the door like he did.

The house was dark inside and smelled old, like water had been spilled on the carpet a long time ago. There were tables and sideboards against every wall with no space in between, and on top of them, knick-knacks and pictures and ashtrays with hardly a spot of bare surface showing.

Maryann walked slowly ahead of them and sat on a pink brocade couch, the upholstery faded and shredded in spots on the arms. Cats, thought Vega. But she saw none.

Maryann touched the cannula, pressed the prongs up her nose with two swollen fingertips.

"Sorry to keep you out there," she said. "Don't move too fast."

Vega nodded.

"Ma'am, I received this email this morning."

Vega unfolded the sheet of paper and handed it to Maryann. She squinted at it and looked disappointed.

"Who sent this?" she said to them.

"We don't know. The email address is just a Gmail; we're trying to trace the actual machine it was written from. Do you have any idea why someone would link your son's disappearance to the Brandt girls?"

Maryann paused to consider, then shook her head. The red hair, which was now very clearly a wig, moved stiffly on her shoulders.

"He's been gone three years November. Other than the fact that there's all three of them missing now, I'm not sure. . . ." She took a deep breath through her nose then and coughed.

Vega felt everything that was bothering her just then—the toe she had stubbed that morning, a cut below her knee from a razor two days before, most of all the smell of the house, some kind of lotion and mold, like a cellar stuffed with old clothes. It seemed to be getting worse.

"Could you tell us what happened to your son, to Nolan?" said Vega.

Maryann nodded.

"Yeah, I can," she said, resigned to the task. "He was what you call a disorganized schizophrenic, which is just like what it sounds like. Everything about him was disorganized, his head and the way he talked, and his emotions. I first knew something was wrong when we were at my mom's funeral when Nolan was, oh gosh, about twenty-one, and he was laughing during the service. But I could tell he didn't think he was doing nothing wrong—he just didn't know how to be. Before that, he was a normal boy. Played all kinds of sports, had a couple nice girlfriends. Here," she said, waving her hand toward a small white table. "Get those pictures, will you, hon?"

Vega stood and went to the table, saw two pictures in dusty frames and brought them over.

"That one, that's him in his soccer gear," Maryann said, pointing to Vega's left hand.

Cap and Vega looked. A boy, big and brawny, with red cheeks, on one knee in a soccer uniform. He had the look, Vega thought, the one reserved for teenaged boys, the one that says there's nothing but girls and beer and sports in the world and I am goddamn okay with that.

"Looks like a forward," said Cap.

"You got it," said Maryann, proud. "Went to State that year. Lost in the end but made all the papers."

"When was this taken?" Vega said, nodding at the other photo.

It was the same boy but obviously transformed, wearing a white shirt buttoned up to his chin and his hair combed neatly. He smiled but was shy about it.

"Then that's him right before he disappeared. He was in the community college when he was diagnosed, and then he just lived with me and my youngest. Their dad's way far out of the picture."

She paused to take a breath through the tubes in her nose and pressed them again to her nostrils, as if to get every last bit.

"That must have been challenging," said Vega.

Maryann laughed. "You know, you'd think so, right? But by the time he left, we were doing okay, the three of us. Nolan knew he had to take his meds, and he smoked a pack and a half of Camels every day, but it was no bother. He always smoked them on the porch or in his room."

"There's something I have to ask you," Vega said, leaning forward in her chair. "Did Nolan ever show any interest in underage children?"

Maryann breathed strongly through her nose, coughed and laughed. "No, my dear, he did not."

"And he never had any violent tendencies? I hear that can happen with schizophrenics."

Now Maryann seemed to try to steady herself, placed one hand on the arm of the couch. Vega could see the white in the knuckles. Maryann held up one finger.

"One time he pushed me. Once. When we were still trying out different meds, before we got him on the Zyprexa. But he was like a starving dog that ain't been fed yet. Just wild and sick."

"And that was it," said Vega.

"That was it."

"What happened when he disappeared?" said Vega.

Maryann shut her eyes.

Please do not cry, thought Vega.

"He and I got in some silly argument over emptying the dishwasher—he was usually really good about chores—and I told him I was too tired. And then I told him, 'Nolan, I'm going to bed early and tomorrow morning that dishwasher better be empty.' I was working a fifty-hour week back then, before I got sick. And I woke up next morning, and he was gone. All his clothes still in his closet. No note. Just took his wallet and his cigarettes."

She looked at Cap and Vega then, and wiped tears from the corners of her eyes with her clubby fingers.

Cap leaned forward and handed her a square brown napkin from his pocket. She nodded and took it, wiped her eyes.

"Youse have kids?" she said.

Vega had heard that a few times since she'd gotten to Denville—the "youse." It made her think of old movies, newsboys waving papers on the street corner.

"One," said Cap.

"No," said Vega.

Maryann focused on Cap.

"I've been to every morgue in eastern Pennsylvania. I've seen a baker's dozen of John Does, anyone who's male between the ages of twenty and forty. All's I want is a body. All's I want is some dust or some nails or something to bury and say the Lord's Prayer over. Can you imagine that, wanting something like that?"

Cap shook his head.

"I can't, ma'am."

"You shouldn't have to. Nobody should."

Her nose crinkled up, lips tightened and released. Vega knew she was trying not to cry, and that this was not an unfamiliar effort.

"You went to the police," Vega said, trying to move things along.

Don't let them get emotional unless you're looking for a confession. Otherwise you get stuck in tears and reminiscing.

"Well yeah. That's what I'm supposed to do, right?" she said. "They put him up on the NamUs website; they questioned the neighbors. Did a lot of paperwork for about a week. Turns out no one cares too much about a grown man who goes missing, especially one they think's retarded."

She somehow, thought Vega, did not sound bitter saying this. It was like she was observing it all.

"I guess you can't blame them," she said, and then her tone went flat. "He wasn't as cute as those two girls."

"Were there ever any solid leads?" asked Vega.

"No. Not that they told me about. I put up flyers and kept updating the profile on NamUs. Once we got close—they had a body down in Philly that matched him, but the face was all decomposed. Then they did the teeth and no go. Ain't him. I got sick about a year later, so I don't do much anymore. My youngest keeps up with it more nowadays."

She shrugged.

"Is it your lungs?" asked Vega.

Cap turned to her, startled.

Maryann nodded.

"I'm stage 3B. Which means I'm only seventy-five percent screwed as opposed to a hundred percent screwed. Funny thing, I only smoked here and there when I was younger. Doctors don't know if it was Nolan's smoking or my folks' or the asbestos around Beth Coal where I worked for twenty years."

She crossed her hands in her lap and smiled at them.

"And really, who cares? *Machs nix,* as my dad would have said."

"Is it in all of your lymph nodes?" said Vega.

"Oh yes, hon. It's everywhere. Survival rate is shit, excuse me."

"I'm sorry to hear that," said Cap.

Maryann shook her head as if to tell them not to worry. Vega's mouth was unbelievably dry just then; she bit the tip of her tongue to create some liquid.

"Could we speak with your other son at some point, Ms. Marsh?" Cap said.

"I don't see why not. I'll give you his number," she said. Then she reached into the pocket of her sweater and pulled out her cell phone. "You know," she said, pausing, "the detective called me yesterday. The one who I filed the report with originally."

"Detective Ralz?" said Cap.

"Yes, Ralz. He said he was going over old files and wanted to know if I'd ever heard anything. I told him no. We talked for only a couple of minutes."

Cap glanced at Vega. Maryann put on a pair of reading glasses and held her phone in her lap, tapping the face of it.

"You know what they say about coincidences," she said, still eyeballing the phone.

"That there are none?" said Cap.

Maryann looked up at a point above their heads. "Is that what they say?" Then she shrugged. "I thought they said something else."

The Linsoms lived on a cul-de-sac in the Sherwood Forest subdivision, part of the Sprawl, as Cap called it—rural edges on the north side of town transforming into Monopoly-house planned communities. He'd seen a billboard on the highway on the way in: LIVE LIKE A KING IN SHERWOOD FOREST. Then the list of amenities, if the name was not enough to grab you: 2-, 3-, 4-BEDROOM NEW LUXURY HOMES, JACUZZIS, WINE CELLARS, OUTDOOR GRILL ISLANDS. There was the happy family right in the picture, standing in their front yard. See them waving? See how cheery they are? You'd be that happy too if you had your own outdoor grill island. Instead you have a boring indoor oven, and your kids think you're a failure.

"You talk to the kid, okay?" said Vega as they walked up the driveway.

They had not really spoken after leaving Maryann Marsh's house. Cap couldn't tell if Vega was working something out in her head or if it was something else—the vaguest sense of grief seemed to rinse over her face, but there was no way he was going to ask her about it. Maybe in the future, over beer or tea or motor oil—whatever she consumed in her leisure time.

Lindsay Linsom answered the door and let them in. Her face was an arrangement of delicate bones, her hair pulled into a neat bun. Everything inside was white—white walls, white carpet, white furniture, the only standout a mahogany upright piano against one wall with a nickel-plated table clock on top, ticking audibly. Mrs. Linsom led them into the sunken living room and offered them drinks and seats on the couch.

"We met with the police at the school yesterday," she said. "They asked Cole some questions already."

"We understand, Mrs. Linsom. Like I said, we have some new information that we have questions about. Cole might be able to help us with it. It will take only a few minutes."

Mrs. Linsom looked at both of them and touched her hair gently.

"Of course we want to do everything we can to help. I can't imagine what Jamie must be going through. We just had Kylie over last weekend," she said, shaking her head. "I'll get Cole. She said her stomach hurt, so I kept her home today. I think she's just worried about Kylie. You never know how kids will process these things."

She left, up a carpeted staircase. Cap looked around, at the straight stack of hardback books on the glass coffee table, the throw pillows angled in the same way in the corners of the couch, not a thread out of place on anything.

"Cozy," said Cap.

Vega nodded, examining a glass deer centerpiece on a table behind her.

Mrs. Linsom came down the stairs with Cole, a slight girl with white-blond hair and pink lips. She stood in front of them, wide-eyed, uneasy.

"Cole, this is Mr. Caplan and Miss Vega."

Cole stared at them and took a step closer to her mother.

"Hi Cole," said Cap, as gentle as he could.

He'd actually forgotten how small ten-year-olds were. He had come to see Nell as an unstoppable force of development, since she had gotten out of the baby stage and started outgrowing clothes and shoes every other month. Cap's reaction to her was still, I can't believe how big she is. He would look at her on the soccer field and be awed, watching her slide tackle the ball with her long legs, her arms coming out like pea shoots from the sleeves of her uniform.

But this girl wasn't like that; she seemed younger than ten, smelling faintly of baby powder. Kylie is this age too, he thought, but she seemed older somehow. He couldn't put his finger on it, so he stopped, focused on this pale girl in front of him.

"How old are you now?" he said, like he was any family friend.

"Ten," said Cole, soft and airy.

"Ten's big. When will you be eleven?"

"August sixteenth."

"It'll be here before you know it. When my daughter was ten, she had about twenty of those Webkinz—you have any of those?"

"Yeah," said Cole, her face splitting into a smile. "I have the cocker spaniel because we can't have a real one."

Cap laughed.

"Well, that's the next best thing. A lot easier to take care of," he said.

He looked up to Mrs. Linsom, who laughed with some relief.

"Can I ask you a question about Kylie?" he said then. "You're friends with her, is that right?"

Cole nodded.

"You know her mom's working really hard to find her and her sister, right? And that we're helping her?"

Nod.

"You can do a lot to help us, Cole. All you have to do is tell the truth, okay?"

Nod.

"Good. Okay, did you guys have any games you liked to play together?"

Cole scrunched up her face.

"Like video games?"

"Sure. Or other kinds of games, like pretending to be in a club."

Cole looked up at the ceiling.

"A club," she said.

Mrs. Linsom leaned forward in her chair.

"I'm sorry, Mr. Caplan, what do you mean?"

"I think Cole knows what I mean," said Cap. "Cole, did you have a club with Kylie? Just the two of you?"

"Um," said Cole, now looking at the floor.

"Cole?" said Mrs. Linsom, facing her. "Answer Mr. Caplan. This is very important."

"It's a secret, though," said Cole.

"Cole, this is to help Kylie. I promise she won't be mad if you tell," said Cap.

Cole let out a small breath.

"We had a Secret Journal Club. We wrote down our secrets in journals and put them in a hiding place." Then she turned to her mother and said urgently, "We didn't even tell each other what was in them. We were supposed to keep it secret till we died or got married."

"Cole, where are they? The journals. We need to see Kylie's," said Cap.

Cole turned to him with heavy eyes and pointed out the picture window.

They all followed her through the kitchen gleaming with appliances and clean countertops, through the back door, across a small paved patio, and into a backyard with short green grass and a cluster of four trees at the rear of the property, overlooking a thin creek.

Cole started running then, toward the trees, her mother behind her. Cap and Vega stayed on the patio, next to the grill island made of stucco and stainless steel.

"It's in the tree," said Vega.

"Huh," said Cap.

They watched as Cole kneeled, reached into a hollow in the second tree from the left, and pulled two spiral notebooks out. Mrs. Linsom said something to her that Cap couldn't make out. Cole's face dropped, and Mrs. Linsom pulled her back to where Cap and Vega stood.

"Go ahead," said Mrs. Linsom.

"This is Kylie's," she said, and she handed Cap the notebook with the baby-blue cover. It had three heart-shaped stickers at the top and frayed edges.

"And what else?" said Mrs. Linsom.

"I'm sorry I didn't tell sooner," she said, and her lips started to turn down.

Cap squatted a bit so he could look her in the eye.

"Don't be sorry. You just helped Kylie a lot. Thank you."

"Do you need mine too?" Cole said, holding out the other notebook, with a pink cover.

"You can keep that one secret, what do you say?"

Cole smiled, held the notebook to her chest, and left, walked toward the house.

"I'm so sorry," said Mrs. Linsom, looking at both of them. "I had no idea. The police just asked general things—if Kylie had said anything to her about running away, things like that."

"She didn't do anything wrong, Mrs. Linsom. She didn't know we would want to know. And there might not be anything in here, but we have to take a look."

Mrs. Linsom nodded and then something caught her attention from the front of the house, and her smile dissipated.

"Daddy's home for lunch!" Cole yelled from inside, more alarmed than happy.

"Oh," said Mrs. Linsom. "My husband. Excuse me."

She hurried inside. Cap turned to look at Vega, raised his eyebrows. She gave a small shrug, nodded toward the house. They went.

Cap saw Mrs. Linsom talking in a hushed voice to a tall man in a white shirt and tie, suit jacket over his arm, laptop bag in the other. His face was tense, turning red under blond eyebrows and thinning straw-colored hair.

Mr. Linsom turned and saw Cap, put on a businessman smile, and went to meet him, hand extended.

"Press Linsom," he said, confident.

"Max Caplan," said Cap. "This is my partner, Alice Vega."

They all shook hands, and Press Linsom stood back and put his hands on his hips. Mrs. Linsom stood behind him, shrinking before Cap's eyes.

"You want to tell me what this is about?" he said.

"We, Ms. Vega and I, we've been hired by the Brandt family to find Jamie's daughters. Cole and Mrs. Linsom just helped us a great deal by helping us find this."

"Uh-huh," said Press, skeptical.

I know this guy, Cap thought. Met him a hundred times. These little pissing contests are the highlight of his day.

"So you're not with the police?"

"No, sir. We're private investigators."

"And what makes you think I'll just let you take an item from my property?" he said, stepping forward.

"Press, Jamie Brandt called me herself. She sent them here," said Mrs. Linsom quietly.

Linsom turned his head to the side and held his hand up to her. She stepped back. Cap had a feeling she was familiar with that side of his hand.

Cap smiled, scratched his chin, and turned around to Vega. She kept a straight face.

"I'd think you'd want to assist in finding these two girls, being a father yourself and all," said Cap.

Small parts of Linsom's face reacted—the corner of the mouth, the tip of the nose twitching as if he were smelling something.

"Max Caplan," he said. "Why is that name familiar to me?"

Cap glanced away, felt caught and couldn't help it.

"Have we met before?"

"I don't believe so," Cap said. "I used to be with the police."

Now Linsom smiled, victorious.

"I know who you are. I've done business with Kit Samuels. You're the one who let his boy die."

Cap shut his eyes for only a second, forced himself to open them, and wished a lot of things: for a beer, to be at his kitchen table with Nell, to go back in time and go to law school, to have supervised Em that goddamn night to make sure he was doing his job, to have checked that junkie kid's pulse himself.

"Why'd you let them in?" Linsom said, turning to his wife. "The police fired this guy for incompetence."

"He resigned, actually," said Vega.

Everyone looked at her.

"Splitting hairs, sweetie," said Linsom. "I want you both out of my house now, and I want that book. I'm sure the police would be interested in its contents. Qualified professionals."

"You heard your wife, sir," said Cap. "Jamie Brandt asked us to come here and talk to Cole. We're bringing this book to her."

Linsom tossed his suit jacket on a counter and held his hands out.

"You're not bringing it anywhere, Caplan. Caplan, right? What kind of name is that anyway, Jewish?"

And a Jew-hater too, thought Cap. This guy is a winner across the board.

"Yes, it is," said Cap.

Linsom took another step. He had a good six inches on Cap. He could smell the coffee on Linsom's breath.

"True what they say, about sex through the sheet and everything?" Linsom said, smirking.

"All true," said Cap. "It's surprisingly effective."

They were locked there for a moment, and then Cap could sense, not really hear, but feel Vega stirring behind him. Then she was next to him, both of them facing up to Linsom.

"Look, we don't want any trouble," she said.

Her voice was high suddenly, youthful.

"Oh yeah?" said Linsom. "Then you shouldn't have come here."

"We're working with the police. Captain Hollows knows all about it," she said. Then she looked back and forth to Mrs. Linsom and Cap nervously. "Do you really think Jamie Brandt would trust us otherwise? If we bring this to them . . ."

She stepped closer to Linsom, gazed up at him. Cap tried not to smile.

"Well, it'll look really good for us." She shook her head, humble. "You can, uh, check out my credentials, I have a business card somewhere."

She patted herself down, fingers going in and out of pockets. She turned around to Cap.

"You don't have them, do you?"

She looked so earnest Cap almost believed maybe this had been the real Vega all along and the whole tough girl thing was the act. He put his hands in his pockets.

"Why would *I* have them?" he said, annoyed.

"Press," said Lindsay, pulling gently at his arm.

Linsom kept his eyes on Cap and Vega and let his wife tug him away for just a second. She spoke quietly and rapidly, and Cap could only imagine how many times she'd had to do this before—talk her husband off the angry bridge. Linsom spread his feet apart, seemed to relax a bit. There you go, Tiger, thought Cap.

"So if I let you walk out of here, and I call the police captain in a couple of hours, he'll know exactly who you two are and he'll have that notebook as evidence?" said Linsom.

He sounded like a high school principal, and Cap could tell he enjoyed it; the smirk had reappeared.

"Absolutely," Vega gasped. "You have my word."

Linsom thought about it for another full minute, making the fake Vega squirm.

"Get out of here before I change my mind," he said.

"Thank you, thank you so much. I'm so sorry, we're so sorry to have bothered you."

She pumped his hand and rushed out.

"Mrs. Linsom, I'm so sorry," she said.

Cap followed her. He smiled sheepishly at Linsom, and said, "Yeah . . . sorry."

Out they went, through the front door. Cap ran to catch up with her as she crossed the street.

"Give me your phone and yell at me in a second," she said, eyes straight ahead.

Cap handed over his phone. Vega bounced it on her fingertips like a volleyball and dropped it to the pavement.

"Goddammit, Alice!" Cap shouted.

Vega bent down to grab it, and they got to the car without looking behind them, but Cap didn't have to. He knew the Linsoms were still at the door, watching. He and Vega got into the car, and Cap bit the insides of his lips to stop himself from bursting into laughter from relief and awe that Linsom was just another safe that Vega had cracked.

"Park when we get out of here, yeah?" said Vega, looking down.

"Yeah," said Cap, tucking the notebook between his seat and the cup holder.

He pulled out and down the block, glanced in the rearview and watched the Linsoms and their absurdly spotless house get smaller and smaller. He drove out of the Sprawl and parked next to a brown field, which he felt certain was soon to be Extended Sprawl.

He and Vega sat in silence for a moment. Then she placed a small black hook on the dashboard. It made a little clink.

"Where'd you get that?" said Cap.

"From the grill on the patio. It's a magnet. I think you hang tongs on it."

"So that was plan B, huh?" said Cap. "To hook him like a bass?"

"Something like that."

Cap thought about it, rubbed his chin. "I wouldn't have minded, tell you the truth. He was a special guy."

Vega reached her hand out the window and adjusted the side mirror. "I had a feeling we could get out of there clean so I went with it."

Cap nodded and picked up the notebook.

"Let's do this now?" he said.

"Yeah, hold on," said Vega.

She pulled out her phone and scooted toward Cap.

"Lean over," she said to him.

He leaned into her, and she held the phone and aimed the camera. He pressed his shoulder into hers gently and could smell her hair and skin. Something herbal but not flowery—sharp and aromatic. He tried to ignore it the best he could, the desire to just turn and take a deep breath through his nose. He opened the notebook to the first page.

"Good?" he said.

Vega looked at the frame on her phone.

"Yeah," she said, tapping the screen. Snap.

Then they huddled together and peered down at the first page, a list of boys' names. "5A" was at the top of the page and the middle of the way down, "5B." Next to each name were letters, a code: FH, BF, FF, G. Thankfully Kylie had added a key: FH: Future Husband; BF: Boyfriend; FF: Friend Friend; G: Gross.

Cap smiled at the honesty of it. At least you knew where you stood.

"Boys in her class," he said.

"I have the class list—we can match the names, make sure there're no discrepancies," said Vega.

They flipped through the next few pages, more lists of boys' names, more codes, some scratched out and changed from FF to BF and back. Ballpoint garlands of flowers and vines around the borders.

They came to a page with "MY MOM IS A BITCH" written at the top, angry black spirals beneath it, covering up a sentence or two.

"She felt bad about whatever she wrote," said Vega, running her finger over the scribbles. "Crossed it out."

There were only about ten pages in all with writing; the rest was blank. The last page was covered with wobbly edged hearts, the initials "KB + WT" inside every one.

"Who's WT?" said Cap.

"Go back to the lists," said Vega.

"Wesley. We can get his last name. And he's a FF, so it's probably not him."

"Wait," said Vega.

She ran her thumb through the rest of the pages like a flip book and stopped on one with a crease at the corner. She opened it. Tiny letters at the bottom: "See you soon he said!"

They both stared at the words.

"So what do we do in two hours when Linsom calls this in?"

"How about we beat him to it?"

"You want to call it in?" said Cap.

"We could use it. Trade it for whatever they have that we need."

"You want to go back to Junior," said Cap, staring straight ahead. The prospect made his teeth hurt.

"You want me to call, I'll call," said Vega.

"No, I'll call. I'll call," he said again, talking himself into it.

Vega's phone buzzed, and she scanned the screen and said, "My guy got the location of the email source—it's a Kinko's on North Haven Street. He's working on security footage."

"At least he's close, but it's a public device," said Cap. Then he thought about it. "Shit, was it too much to ask for it to be a single-occupant residence?"

Vega didn't answer him. She gazed out the window.

"Why don't you bring that to Hollows too?"

"What—the Kinko's?"

"Yeah. He doesn't want our help," she said. "Doesn't mean he can't help us."

"Let them do the legwork there, talk to the staff," Cap said.

"Why not. Keep everyone busy, going in the same direction. Here," she said, handing him his phone.

Cap rubbed the top where it was nicked from the fall.

"Why'd you have to drop my phone and not yours?" he said.

Vega turned to face him and said, "I like my phone, Caplan."

7

EVAN MARSH MOVED LIKE HE HAD A PAIN IN HIS SHOULDERS OR his neck. Vega stood just outside the loading dock of a supermarket called Giant, light rain landing in her hair, the temperature dropping. Marsh met her eyes and sped up, jumped off the dock and around the fork of a manual pallet jack with boxes stacked on top.

"Hey, Alice?" he said.

"Vega, yeah. Evan Marsh?"

"Yeah, that's me."

"Do you have a minute to speak?"

They shook hands, and Marsh said, "Yeah, my shift hasn't started yet. So you talked to my mom?"

"Yes, earlier today."

"You have any idea who sent that email?" he said.

Vega watched his eyes. Big and brown, she couldn't even separate the pupil in the low light. His hair was brown too, his skin smooth. Unlike his brother, who looked to be too big for his body in the pictures, Evan Marsh was in his midtwenties but looked about seventeen, young and lean like a greyhound.

"Not yet," said Vega. "Do you?"

He laughed through his nose. "No. Nobody's talked about my brother for three years except me and my mom. The police got the same message?"

"We think so."

"And they didn't do anything about it," he said. "Not a surprise."

Vega saw the tension in his lips, pushing his chin forward in frustration. She knew if there was something he wasn't telling her, she could find it out, just by passing the tip of the blade over the wound that was already wide open.

"You don't have to tell me," she said. "I been in some small towns with some goddamn incompetent police departments, but this one is up there. They couldn't find their assholes with a mirror and flashlight."

Marsh smiled with half his mouth and nodded to the parking lot.

"You wanna walk?"

"Sure."

As they walked out, Marsh took out a cigarette and lit it with a Zippo, silver with a cast metal skull on the face. He offered the pack to Vega, and she took one, let him light it for her.

"I don't smoke around my mom," he said. "Only started when Nolan disappeared."

"I'm sure it was a stressful time," said Vega.

"You do this for a living, right? Find people who are missing?"

Vega nodded.

"So you've seen all of this before—parents who can't find their kids?"

"I've seen it. Every one's different though."

Marsh brushed the rain off his hair.

"What do you think the email means?" said Vega.

"I don't have any idea. Doesn't make a whole lot of sense."

"You're right about that. But let's say you had to guess. Let's say your brother and the Brandt girls are connected in some way. What way do you think that might be?"

Marsh frowned, shrugged.

"I don't know. I was kinda hoping you would. You're the professional, right?"

"Yeah. But you'd be surprised how much you might already know, just instinctually. I mean, you can't be any more off base than the cops, right?"

Marsh smiled again.

"So you just want my gut?"

"Yeah. Your gut."

"Maybe the same guy who took those girls took my brother, and someone, like a third party, knows about it and sent the email," Marsh said, looking down, almost embarrassed.

"Hey, it's possible," said Vega, encouraging him. "So are they all in the same place—Nolan and the Brandt girls?"

"No, no way," said Marsh. He stopped walking. "My brother's dead. I know that. My mother knows that." He took a long drag from his cigarette, shook his head and shut his eyes hard for a second. "She tell you that she's sick?"

"Yeah, she did."

"She seem upset about it to you?"

Vega watched him. Finger flicking the cigarette at his side.

"Actually no, she didn't."

"You think some people are just at peace with a death sentence, right?"

Vega thought about the cannula again, the way it scraped the insides of the nostrils.

"I don't know."

Marsh shook his head more slowly for dramatic effect, like that would make Vega listen closely.

"She doesn't like the pain," he said. "She's got a lot of aches, says her bones hurt, hurts to cough and breathe. Her mind's pretty sharp though, but she forgets to take the pills that will shrink the cancer cells. Get it?"

Vega got it but wanted him to explain it to her. She shrugged dumbly.

"She doesn't mind the cancer because it's the last thing he gave her."

Vega was glad it was raining, and that it was cold, that the water was getting into her socks and wetting the back of her neck and starting to chill her skin. Then it was easier to play the trick on herself. She'd started it a long time ago, on a humid day in South Carolina doing side lunges, the nail on her pinkie toe peeling off. Count the grass blades, smell the cigar smoke. This is not your body, she thought. This is not your pain. When a two-hundred-pound beast of a Mexican with a tattoo on his bald head that read BEBE AMO MAMA threw her across a table in a bar she thought it as she hit the floor: Focus on the sticky-sweet smell of tequila on the boards against your cheek. This is not your body. You don't feel a thing. Right before she reached for the Springfield.

And she did it again, right now, looking into Evan Marsh's angry young face, feeling cool drops slide into her bra, let herself shudder.

Marsh's hair was dark and soft, glued to his forehead in wet curls. His eyes were big and round and liquid. This is not you.

"I'm sorry," said Vega.

"I know," he said. "So what do you think, Alice? It's Alice, right?"

His eyes went over her, down to the waist and back up to the face.

"Right."

"What do *you* think, you know, in-stinct-ually?"

He drew the word out and managed to make it sound inappropriate.

Some part of Vega wondered what he was getting at. Are we flirting now? she thought. Well, okay, then, Evan Marsh, I will be whoever you goddamn well want me to be.

"I think it's probably random, someone with an odd sense of humor. That doesn't mean I won't look into it."

"I appreciate it. You know, for my mom."

He wiped the water off his face and his hand lingered there, over his cheek. Vega looked at his hand and saw a series of fresh scratches, vertical on his forearm. He dropped his hand to his side, and she grabbed him by the wrist. He didn't pull it back. His skin was warm.

"You have a cat?" she said, turning his hand up, showing him the scratches.

"Roommate's got two," he said.

He let his knuckles rest on her wrist, held her eyes. She let go and smiled, tried to picture herself younger and lighter.

"How are you not freezing out here?" she said.

He looked back over his shoulder at the loading dock.

"Hard labor, Alice," he said. "It's a bitch."

"I thought you said your shift hadn't started yet."

Evan flinched only a little bit, smiled and started backing up, toward the loading dock. He held his arms out and called, "Guess I'm just warm-blooded."

Cap leaned against his car and watched two kids, a boy and girl, probably four years old or so, turn dizzy spirals on a small steel merry-go-round. One of their mothers sat on a bench texting on her phone and smoking. She seemed young, and it momentarily concerned Cap, made him think, Why aren't her eyes on the kids?

A blue midsize sedan pulled up across the street, and Junior Hollows stepped out, nodded to Cap and jogged over.

"Twice in twenty-four hours," he said. "That's twice as many times as I've seen you in the past three years."

Cap shrugged.

"Unusual twenty-four hours."

"What's this about, Cap? You want to explain to me what you have to do with my case?"

"I'm working it."

"You're working it? From your rec room?" Junior said, amused.

"Alice Vega hired me. I'm working with her."

Junior's smile dissipated, and for a rare moment Cap could see the age lines around his mouth, ironed creases in a napkin.

"You really think that's a good idea?" said Junior.

"Yeah, I do. The more hands the better."

Junior laughed and shook his head, weary.

"Would you ever say that as a cop? Would you ever have wanted PIs up in your shit? Come on, Cap."

"If they could help my investigation, yes, yeah I would."

"And how can you and Alice Vega help me exactly?"

"I have Kylie Brandt's diary."

Junior's eyes got a little bigger; then he tried to look cool about it.

"Kylie Brandt didn't have a diary."

"Says who."

"Her mother."

"In what universe are you operating where girls don't keep secrets from their mothers?"

"We've been through Jamie Brandt's apartment," said Junior. "It's the size of a shoebox. We didn't find a diary."

"Kylie didn't keep it at the apartment. It was at a friend's house."

"The friend gave it to you?"

"Yes."

Junior shrugged with cynicism.

"What makes you think the friend didn't make it up, for the attention?"

"Jamie Brandt's ex-boyfriend says Kylie told him about it. That's how we found it."

Cap watched Junior process it.

"You have it here," Junior said, nodding to Cap's car.

"Yeah. Also you got an email recently about Nolan Marsh?"

Junior shook his head no, a reflex.

"I know," said Cap, fatigued by the exchange. "You don't know what I'm talking about. Okay. Let's say the DPD received an email about a guy named Nolan Marsh. Alice Vega got the same email."

Junior stopped shaking his head, just listened.

"She had it traced to the Kinko's on North Haven. I don't want to tell you how to do your job, but maybe you want to send someone over there."

They both stood there; Cap let his eyes drift to the kids on the merry-go-round, the boy dragging his foot along the ground, slowing it down.

"All right, Cap," said Junior. "What do you want for all this? For the diary."

"Just the open exchange of information. You don't want to work with us, fine. But at least we can all have the same facts. Like witness statements, for example."

"I have to check with Traynor," said Junior. Then came a big sigh. "You know he likes it clean."

Cap nodded. He knew Junior wasn't necessarily lying. The chief of police liked detail and transparency. He kept a twenty-year medallion from Alcoholics Anonymous in a frame next to the picture of his kids. The files in his file cabinet were alphabetized and color-coded, the Post-its stacked in towers from large to small on his desk. Cap knew for a fact there was a canister of Lysol wipes in his bottom right drawer. The only thing worse than telling Nell and Jules about his resignation was facing Chief Traynor, who was under the impression it really had been Cap who had let the junkie kid die.

"Caplan, I didn't think you had these kinds of fuckups in your blood," he'd said.

It hurt Cap like a sunburn.

Light rain had started to fall. Junior wiped drops from the hair that hung over his forehead.

"Fine," said Cap.

He went into his car and grabbed the book from the seat, shielded it under his jacket from the rain. Junior eyed it and his lips twitched, like he was hungry and just a little too far from the dessert cart. Cap enjoyed the moment of cruelty, let his hand linger on the book before handing it over. Junior slid it under his coat.

"Thanks," he said, blinking from the rain. He ran his hand over his face and shook it out. "I'm glad you called. It was the right thing."

Cap stared at Junior, thought maybe it was not at all the right thing.

Then they heard screaming. It was the little boy from inside the playground. He'd fallen off the merry-go-round and hit the rubber playground mat headfirst.

"Goddammit," Cap said.

He ran into the playground as the mother got up from the bench and went to the boy, not in a rush.

"Hey!" he shouted to the mother. He could feel his ears getting hot.

She turned to Cap as she leaned over the boy and helped him stand up. Cap put her age at twenty-one or twenty-two; she had the face of a girl.

"Listen, ma'am, there are three entrances to this playground. One of them leads to a street where people frequently run the stop sign, and either of these kids could have run out there at any time. And I've been standing here a full fifteen minutes, a strange man just watching your children play, and you haven't looked up from Candy Crush. Just watch the goddamn kids. That is your only priority."

Cap's hands started to shake so he stuffed them into his pants pockets.

The mother sneered and said, "Hey, mind your own fucking business, aright? He's fine."

Cap and the boy stared at each other for a minute, the boy with a couple of tears on his pink cheeks, both of them breathing heavy.

"Is he lying?" Vega asked as Cap drove them down a four-lane state highway.

"He could be," said Cap. "He's a liar, generally."

"No one lies all the time unless there's a compulsion."

"I don't think that's the case. He just lies to cover his ass like the rest of us," said Cap.

Vega's eyes wandered to the signs of small businesses flashing past: AKA COPIER SERVICE, PERSONAL APPEARANCES HAIR SALON, ROUTE 61 BAR AND GRILL.

"You don't," she said. "I don't."

"Well, Vega, I can't really imagine the situation where you'd need to cover your ass for any reason."

"Then you have a limited imagination, Caplan," she said, turning to him. "So what's the takeaway?"

"He might help us, and he might not. Traynor, the chief, might help us, might not. . . ."

"So we keep going our own way," said Vega.

"Yeah. What was Marsh's brother like?"

"Strange. He's hiding something, but I don't know what. I asked him to imagine why he thought someone would send that email, and he had a theory."

"What was it?"

"That his brother and the Brandt girls were taken by the same person."

"So who's the sender of the email?"

"Next-door neighbor, guilty accomplice, doesn't matter. Point of it is, he'd thought about it, while his mother was completely hard-pressed for an idea."

"So . . ." said Cap, taking the exit for Raven Run. "You think that's suspicious."

"He also was a little out of it, running his words together," she said, remembering. Without thinking she touched her lips and said, "Warm."

"Huh?" said Cap.

"He was really warm. We were outside in the rain a good ten minutes, temperature's probably forty degrees. He had short sleeves and was warm."

"Drugs?"

"Seems most likely," she said.

She thought for a moment and turned her body to face Cap.

"How much trouble you think it would be to find out what happened to Nolan Marsh?" she said.

Cap blew air through his lips in an O.

"Three-year-old cold case, missing vulnerable adult with no viable leads?"

"We don't know we have no viable leads."

"Look, Ralz may be Junior's errand boy, but he knows what he's doing. If he couldn't find Nolan three years ago, chances are it's a lost cause."

Vega reared back like she'd been pushed.

"Tell that to his mother."

"Hey," said Cap. "I don't like it, but I know that's how it is. You do too," he said quietly.

"So what if it is related to the girls? Then it's not just an exercise."

"No evidence either way," said Cap.

Then, suddenly, he looked discouraged.

"But we have to explore every branch of the tree," he muttered.

"Explore every branch of the tree?" said Vega. "Did you see that on a motivational poster?"

Cap glanced back and forth between her and the road.

"I'm sorry, Vega, are you making a joke at my expense? Do you actually have a sense of humor?"

She ignored him, tapped her knuckles against the window, said, "I think we have to put both cases side by side and see what the connection is. Nobody writes an email like that without a motive."

"Fine," said Cap. "When we're in bed with Junior and Traynor and Ralz we can ask for the file on Nolan. Until then can we focus on WT?"

"Sure. Can you think about more than one thing at once?"

She was honestly not trying to be difficult.

Cap seemed to know that and said, "Why, sure."

The very corner of his mouth turned up, and Vega thought if that corner ate all its vegetables, one day it could grow into a real smile.

They found Jamie Brandt in front of a Kmart talking to a blond woman in a windbreaker with a Fox 29 logo on the back. There was a man loading equipment into the back of a van, and a small group of people handing out flyers. The sun was just about down.

A tall, older woman who Cap thought had a slight hunchback came up to them.

"So," she said to Vega, indignant. "Any news?"

"Not yet," said Vega, who seemed to know her. "We need to talk to Jamie."

"Who's the we?" the woman said, nodding to Cap.

"Max Caplan," said Cap.

"This is Jamie's mother, Gail White," said Vega to Cap. Then she turned to Gail and added, "I've hired him as a consultant. He's a former police officer."

"Good thing you're a former," said Gail. "Talk about a bunch of ignorants. Your IQ probably went up fifty points when you walked out the door."

Cap couldn't help smiling. He liked Gail White.

"I'll get her for you. She just did an interview with Hallie Summers from Fox in Philly. She's just trying to make her cry again, asking her the same dumbass questions."

Gail seemed to be one of those people who said things without expecting or needing a response. She left then and went to Jamie, who saw Vega and Cap and started to run, saying something in haste to the woman from the news.

"What is it, anything?" she said.

She was puffy eyed and her skin was dry, flaking around her temples and her mouth. Her hair was wet from the rain—she didn't have an umbrella and didn't seem to notice. Cap knew the hours were stacking up on her, and soon she would take the slow turn from despair to mourning.

"No," said Cap. "But we have to check something with you. Will you step over to my car?"

"Yeah, Maggie made these," she said, handing them soggy flyers.

On each were the most recent school photos of Kylie and Bailey, their stats and the word "MISSING" at the bottom of the page.

"Kylie did have a diary. She kept it at Cole's house," said Cap.

"What, really? Where . . . where is it?" she said, panicky, stretching her neck so she could look into Cap's car.

"We gave it to the police, but we have pictures."

Cap held his umbrella over the women as Vega showed Jamie her phone, the image of the last page of the diary. Jamie squinted. Her breath sped up.

"That's her writing. That's how she does letters."

"Good," said Cap. "Do you know who WT is?"

"No," she said. "Maybe a boy in her class?"

"We checked the class list," said Vega. "Only one 'W'—Wesley McPherson. No WT."

"Anyone come to mind? William, Walker, Wayne?"

Jamie pressed her hand to her forehead, as if she were applying a compress.

"No, I can't think of anyone," she said. "Fuck, why can't I think of anyone?"

"It might not be an obvious person. We'll check everyone in the school, every class, teachers."

"The police are following their leads too."

"You think this WT had something to do with it?" said Jamie.

"It's an idea. She wrote some notes about him in the diary too."

Vega scrolled so Jamie could see the initials.

"Shit," she said. "Who the fuck is he?"

Cap's phone buzzed, and he handed the umbrella to Vega and stepped away. He saw Em's name come up, and he picked up.

"Em."

"Hey, Cap, can you meet?" said Em under his breath.

"Yeah, when?"

"Fifteen minutes, the luncheonette?"

"Yeah. Everything okay?"

"Yeah. Got something for you."

Cap heard something different in his voice. When Em had first started at the department, he'd been all cocky frat boy, maybe a little too enthusiastic when pinning and cuffing a suspect, calling the rest of the guys bitches when they went home early from drinking after a second shift. If they needed someone to sit on an amped-up PCP freak, they'd send Em, who didn't care if he got black eyes and chipped teeth before holidays. Then he got his girlfriend pregnant. Then she was his wife and she got pregnant again, the second time with twins. Then Em was tamed because it was simple, Cap knew, because he had the fear, because he had three kids and a wife and a whole life he could fuck up.

But just now he heard it—the old Em, the one who made a prank call to Junior and pretended to be a hooker.

"Oh yeah?" said Cap, smiling into the phone. "Can I have a hint?"

"It's bigger than a breadbox."

"Great. See you soon."

Cap hung up and looked back to the women. Jamie stared at the image of her daughter's phantom handwriting on the phone; Vega met Cap's eyes and saw something there. She sniffed, a fox sniffing out a jackrabbit.

Vega ran a napkin over a smear of ketchup left on the table by the previous customer. She sat next to Cap in a booth, and Wiley Emerson was opposite them, breathing heavily and perspiring. Rain streaked up the window next to them.

"Here you go," said Em, sliding a white envelope across the table toward Cap.

Vega placed her palm gently on top of it, intercepting it, and picked it up, opened the flap. Cap raised his hands in surrender. All you.

"I didn't include the ones that didn't see anything, or from the Kmart or anything. These are just the people from the parking lot."

"Three," said Vega.

"That's it. It was a slow day over there, I guess."

"Are they consistent?" asked Cap.

"More or less. One of the witnesses is an eighty-something man; some of his stuff doesn't make sense, but there's a type there. You'll see it—Caucasian male teenager, baseball hat and sweatshirt."

"Car?" said Vega.

"Tan, white, beige compact."

"Three witnesses, three colors," she said.

"Yeah, no one saw plates."

"No one ever sees plates," said Cap.

"So they couldn't see his face," said Vega. "Because of the hat."

"None of them got a good look, no."

"Who took the statements?" said Cap.

"Ralz and Harrison."

"The word's getting out?"

"Every cop in Pennsylvania has the description, but they can't pull over every tan, white, or beige vehicle on the street."

Cap nodded.

Em tapped all his fingers on the table and bounced back and forth on the seat a little bit.

"I better get back. I told Junior I needed some coffee that didn't taste like cat shit."

"Thanks for doing this," Cap said. "What changed your mind?"

Em exhaled loudly and said, "I'm just thinking about it. Went home to my kids, you know. Jake's the same age as the little Brandt girl, and I was like, what the fuck am I doing? Why not, why fuckin' not? Let's get this thing by the fuckin' nuts, right?" he said, looking at Cap. Then, to Vega, "Excuse me."

"Talk about nuts all you want," she said. "Did Traynor bring in a Fed?"

"Yeah, his name's Cartwright. He just came in this morning and been locked up with the chief."

Cap nodded, said, "Look, I shared some information with Junior earlier. We might all be working together real soon."

"Good. That's good, right?"

"Right. Thanks, Em."

Em grinned, looking a little dopey. He turned to Vega, waiting on something, like he'd asked her a question that she hadn't answered yet.

She stared back, unsure of what he wanted. She glanced at Cap, who made some eye rolls in Em's direction.

"Oh, thanks," she said.

"My pleasure," said Em. "I'm gonna go. Nice to meet you, Miss Vega," he said, standing up from the booth. "Talk soon, Cap."

Then he headed for the door. He grabbed a toothpick from a dispenser on the counter on the way out and stuck it in his mouth like a cowboy.

Vega watched him out the window for a second longer as he walked through the parking lot, while she handed the envelope to Cap. Please thank you, please thank you, please thank you, she thought, because it helped to practice.

A half hour later they were at Cap's house, their notes and the statements spread out on the kitchen table. Cap put on a pot of coffee and then winced and shook a finger at Vega.

"I don't have tea," he said.

"I'm fine," said Vega, looking over the pages.

"So three people," said Cap. "Rachel Simmons, twenty-three, getting into her car after returning a Blu-ray player at Best Buy, notices the girls crossing the street, sees one of them hug a boy, presumably the driver, wearing a white baseball hat and light-colored sweatshirt. Girls get into the car, which she thinks is tan. Doesn't think anything's strange about it, thinks the girl and boy must be boyfriend and girlfriend."

"Carl Crain," said Vega. "Forty-five, loading baseball equipment into the back of his truck with his son. He sees the girls cross the highway and thinks, Where're their parents? Then sees the bigger one hug a Caucasian male dressed in a gray sweatshirt and white baseball hat. They get into the car and drive away. Son doesn't see anything."

"And Roy Eldridge, eighty-seven, as he's being driven by his niece out of the mall parking lot onto the highway, sees a boy hug a girl. Then he says two girls get in the car with Harry. Ralz asks who Harry is. The niece says Harry is Eldridge's son; Eldridge is old and confused. Thinks the boy in the baseball hat is his son."

"Or looks like his son. And the niece didn't see the boy or the girls."

"Right."

"It doesn't say anything about what Harry looks like," said Vega, staring straight ahead.

"No, but the niece wouldn't necessarily know that. May not be relevant either. Eldridge is almost ninety and prone to bouts of"—Cap looked back at the statement and read—"'disorientation and aphasia.'"

"We could still check. All of them, see if their memory's been jogged at all since they talked to Ralz." She took a deep breath and tapped her fingers on the table. "Maybe he didn't write everything down either."

"It's a possibility," said Cap, his phone buzzing in his pocket. "They were probably rushing trying to talk to everyone at the mall who might have seen something. That's a lot of statements to take and only two police."

Cap looked at his phone. A text from Nell: "Have you seen the news??? Break in your case. Turn on 6."

"What is it?" said Vega.

"Nell. My daughter. Says there's a break in the case."

Cap went to the living room and dug the remote out from the couch, turned on the TV, and stood there with his arms folded. There was footage of a boy, a teenager, long-limbed and lanky, being led out of a cruiser, a sweatshirt pulled up over his face, and up the steps of the station. Cap recognized most of the cops standing on the steps, waving off the press like mosquitoes. Ralz guided the boy through the front doors.

"—brought in for questioning this evening," said the anchorwoman. "The police are releasing no information about the underage suspect except to say they have reason to believe he may know the whereabouts of Kylie and Bailey Brandt."

The image cut back to the anchorpeople with their moderately concerned expressions and moderately detached commentary.

The woman said, "Kylie and Bailey Brandt were last seen at the Ridgewood Mall on Sterling Road East and Highway 61 last Saturday morning. If you have any information regarding their whereabouts, please call your local authorities. Scott?"

Scott had a downcast sort of look and said thoughtfully, "Terrible." Then, a pause. "A Reading man pleaded guilty to two counts of homicide this morning—"

Cap muted it. He turned to Vega, who had the phone pressed to her ear.

"Who are you calling?"

"Jamie Brandt." Vega's eyes focused as she listened to a voice on the other end. "Why?" she said into the phone. Then she pulled it from her head and tapped it, held it out in front of her.

"That's Sonny Thomas," said Jamie's voice, sharp and strained on the speaker.

"The boy who lives in your apartment complex," said Vega.

"Jamie, it's Max Caplan. Why would the police want him? Did you tell them anything about Sonny you maybe forgot to tell us?" Cap said, feeling his heart rate speed up.

Something about it wasn't right, he knew, but it was useless to try to pin it down now.

"What's 'Sonny' short for?" said Vega, staring at Cap.

"What?" said Jamie, distracted, her mother's voice in the background.

"Sonny," said Cap. "The name, is it short for something?"

"Son-of-a-bitch," said Jamie, realizing. "It's Wilson. Wilson Thomas."

Jamie said she had to go and hung up on them.

"Why did we cross him off our list again?" said Cap, agitated.

"Jamie didn't think he was a viable candidate."

He shook his head to some internal rhythm.

"You have a lot of experience letting your clients call the shots?" he said with an edge.

"Only when their arguments make sense," said Vega. "How would a fifteen-year-old who lived a few doors down from the Brandts coordinate the abduction, stash the girls somewhere, and then keep showing up at home, business as usual?"

"It's possible," said Cap.

"Not probable," said Vega.

"The kidnapper is someone who's not probable," said Cap. "Otherwise it would be obvious who he is."

"Did Em call you back yet?"

Cap glanced at his phone.

"No."

"Then we can't do anything. Junior's going to want Sonny alone in a room before his mother can get a lawyer to him—he's not going to call in the witnesses until tomorrow midday at the earliest. Let's talk to them first."

Vega watched Cap as he chewed on his lips. He looked at his watch.

"We can't knock on their doors now," he said.

"Probably not," said Vega. "But we can call, set it up for first thing before they go to work."

Cap bit his lip and nodded mechanically, all his pissiness replaced by fatigue.

"I'll call them," said Vega, closing her laptop, tucking it under her arm. "I'll be here at seven. I'll park across the street, so your neighbor can walk his cat."

She saw the first curl of a smile on him before she left, before he had a chance to say anything, probably either "Thanks" or "Okay," muttered into the empty space of his living room.

She held her breath, all of her abdominal muscles hugging the organs, stretching her legs up to the ceiling. Fingers out—they're duck feet, they're oven mitts. The idea was that it should be all parts working equally, but that was for Indian gurus and vegan socialites. Vega's was circus yoga, a magic trick, and it always felt like there was one thing pushing harder than anything else. Today it was her forearms. Vega knew it was her body making the selection (her core was weak from riding around in a car for so many hours, shoulders stiff from pulling Brandon Haas across the parking lot), but a skittering bug in her brain told her it was for a reason. The forearms are active because you will need them more today.

Then her phone began to hum on the table, moved toward the edge like it was drawn by a magnet. Vega felt a strange predatory affection for it: Come here, little thing. Come closer.

8

RACHEL SIMMONS LIVED IN HER PARENTS' GARAGE IN BLACK
Creek; it was a large room with one small window near the ceiling facing
out onto a balding lawn. She sat in between Cap and Vega and squinted
at Vega's phone, at the picture of Sonny Thomas that Jamie had sent.

In the picture Sonny was wearing a floppy beanie with a ball on top
and an oversized T-shirt. He was leaning to the side hugging Kylie.

"Um, I don't know," said Rachel. "I mean, I was in the parking lot,
you know? This all happened across the highway."

Vega tapped on Sonny's face to zoom. Cap thought he looked like a
TV show's idea of a teenager: unthreateningly handsome, check; mild
acne, check; nearly imperceptible smirk, check.

"Yeah, I really didn't see his face," said Rachel.

"But it's possible this was him," said Vega.

"I guess so," she said.

"Is there anything else you can remember," said Vega, "Anything that
stands out at all?"

Rachel picked a piece of lint off her jeans with her long fingernail,
painted blue.

"I was far away," she said, turning her head from Vega to Cap. "I'm
real sorry, I just got one little look."

She frowned, her face framed by frizzy blond hair, her eyes big and
shaky, and Cap could do nothing but believe her.

Carl Crain kept them on the porch.

He was a big man with a belly and a buzz cut. He closed the screen
door behind him and was panting, like he'd been rushing.

"Kids are getting ready for school," he said by way of explanation.

"That's fine," said Vega. "We only need a minute of your time."

He smiled at her awkwardly and then looked past her to Cap and said, "I saw on the news they got him. They got the guy who took those girls."

Women get hellos, Vega thought. Men get business.

"Not quite," said Cap. "They've only brought someone in for questioning."

"Do you recognize this boy?" said Vega, and she held up her phone to Carl Crain's face.

He peered over the phone and said to Cap, "Is this him? Is this the kid?"

Vega turned around to look at Cap too,

"Yes, he's the one the police have brought in," said Cap reluctantly.

"I know I was across the street," said Carl, "but this is him."

"Your statement says he was wearing a hat that covered his face," said Vega.

Carl looked at her sideways, confused, either by her asking questions about the case or by her speaking words at all.

He responded to Cap, as if Cap had asked him the question. "Yeah, but he was tall and skinny like that. You know, long armed. You think they're going to bring me in to do a lineup?"

He put his hands on his hips and cleared his throat, as if he were preparing to identify someone in a lineup at that moment. He rocked back and forth on his feet.

"Possibly," Cap answered him, over Vega's head. "They have all your contact information, correct?"

"Yes, sir," said Carl, as if his contact information were a great source of pride.

"I'm sure they'll be in touch," said Cap.

Vega said nothing, stood between them like a dumb little ghost.

As soon as they got in the car, Cap started the engine and said, "Look, some guys around here only want to talk to other guys about anything substantive. I don't like it, but that's the way it is."

"Sure," said Vega. "You do a decent impression of one of those guys."

Now she had offended him. He took his hands off the wheel and turned to her.

"No, hey, give me a small break, Vega. I was trying to get information and move to the next thing."

"Then let's move to the next thing. My lead."

"All yours."

"You don't have to be so fucking supportive," said Vega. "You can just let me work."

Cap shrugged. "Fine."

They didn't speak until they got to the last witness on the list. A woman named Alyssa Moser let them in but was anxious about it. She wore a chunky wool sweater with a large spiral pattern on it. Her face was covered with freckles like a girl, though Cap put her age at about fifty.

"I keep going back in time in my head, wishing I'd turned around and seen something that could help you," she said. "You have to understand, my uncle isn't well. We told the police. I don't know what you could get by interviewing him again."

"He seemed to remember a few things when he gave his statement," said Vega, not combatively.

"Good days, bad days," she said, looking sad. "He used to be so funny is all," she added, as if to explain her sadness.

"He said the suspect looked like Harry?" said Vega.

Alyssa gave them a wounded smile.

"Harry was my cousin. Uncle Roy's son. He died in Vietnam in 1970."

"I'm sorry," Cap and Vega said at the same time.

"He gets confused. He keeps thinking he sees people who've died—his parents, my aunt who passed four years ago," said Alyssa.

"What about Harry?" said Vega. "Does he think he sees Harry?"

"Sure, sometimes."

"Do you have any pictures of him?" asked Vega.

"Who?" said Alyssa, confused.

"Your cousin, Harry."

"Yes, sure, just one moment."

She left the room, and Cap looked to Vega. His look said, So what's the point of this now?

Alyssa Moser came back with a photo in a chipped gold frame.

"This is him and me," she said, smiling. "He was five years older than me, and I just loved him to pieces."

Cap and Vega came to her side and examined the picture.

It had that muted color of photos from the '60s, like the film was developed in murky water. There was a little girl, twelve or thirteen, wearing a headband and a denim dress, smiling with a mouthful of braces at the camera. She leaned against a boy who looked like a man, tall and burly with a healthy head of hair and a respectable mustache.

"This is Harry?" said Vega.

"Yeah, that's him," Alyssa said. "'Course when he went to Vietnam they cut his hair and everything."

"He was a big guy?" said Cap.

"Oh, yeah. Over six foot."

She paused, eyes dulled in thought.

"He was six-two when he shipped out, and he was six-three when they shipped him back," she said. "Weird to think he grew an inch over there."

"He looks husky too," said Cap.

"Made it to State for wrestling. All he would eat was bananas and peanut butter so he could bulk up."

They looked back down at the picture, at Harry Eldridge's honest smile.

"Roy Eldridge is the definition of an unreliable witness," said Cap in the car, determined to shred the morning's work to dust.

"I understand, but stack it up. Two witnesses claim Kylie hugged a skinny teenage boy, slight in build."

"The current suspect fits that profile," said Cap, sounding bored.

"Sure. But one witness describes a totally different body type."

"The witness has dementia."

"Stack it up. Let's just not forget it; that's all I'm saying," said Vega.

Cap looked at her sideways. She could see the doubt in his face.

"What do you want to do?" she said, tapping her hands on the dash, conciliatory.

"We should've talked to the kid first. He should've been on the fucking list," said Cap through his teeth.

"He wasn't on the fucking list. Get over it. What do you want to do?"

Cap rolled his head to the right. Vega heard a snap.

"I don't think Jamie's good for us right now," he said. "Her kids have been gone for eighty hours. She's cracking. She's going to rip apart the first person who takes her off the leash."

"She wants to think the kid did it."

"Maybe the kid did do it," said Cap, raising his voice. "Maybe he killed them and dumped the bodies in the Beth Hill mine, and we've been chasing bullshit for the past two days."

"We have to go back to Jamie."

"Are you listening to anything I'm saying?" said Cap. "Jamie is useless."

"We can get more detail about Sonny Thomas; we can tell her about the three witness descriptions and Nolan Marsh and see if anything pops. She might be the only person other than the kidnapper who knows where the girls are, and all we have to do is sift through the mud in her head a little bit."

Vega paused and watched Cap rock side to side, settling in his seat, think it over. He had a little conversation with himself, sighing theatrically and moving his lips, and when he started to shake his head at nothing in particular she knew she had him beat.

They climbed the exterior stairs of Jamie's complex to the second floor, brown boxes of apartments stacked up like kids' building blocks. Cap saw spiderwebs stringing from the corners of the stucco ceilings to the doorways, graffiti tags here and there. Vega was silent and stoic, and it pissed him off, made him think maybe there was less going on behind the mask as opposed to more. That maybe she wasn't a natural after all, just some delinquent who'd gotten lucky.

They heard a muted series of thumps coming from inside; it reminded him of when he and Jules couldn't afford a drum set; Nell would practice on couch cushions and pillows. Then there was the shimmery crack of glass breaking. Cap bounded for the door.

"Jamie?" he said loudly. "Jamie, it's Max Caplan."

"It's open!" she shouted.

Cap opened it, and they came into the living room—a small space with a mismatched couch and chairs, a large tube TV balanced precariously on an oblong table. To the right, the room opened up into a galley kitchen—a counter covered with stacks of glasses and plates, and some cabinets, all open. Jamie was on her hands and knees, holding two semicircles of glass, a thin ribbon of blood spreading on her hand. She stood and went to the sink, dropped the glass pieces with a crash, looking disgusted. She crossed in front of Cap and Vega and nodded at them.

"I'm glad you're here," she said, weird and calm. "You can help me look."

Her hand fluttered to her hair, pushing strands out of her face, smearing red on her forehead.

"Jamie," Cap said evenly. "You're bleeding."

She looked at her hand, distracted, then shook her head.

"Look for what?" said Vega.

Jamie ripped a paper towel off a roll on the kitchen counter and wrapped it around her palm.

"Anything," she said. "You found her diary in a goddamn tree. Who knows what else she has here. There's got to be something somewhere, something about Sonny, something . . ."

Cap looked at her face, could tell she was thinking, calculating, but there was chaos in it. Like she'd just gotten a concussion and was trying to do trigonometry.

"The police have been through here already, Jamie," said Cap.

"So what, you think they don't need help now? Isn't that what the fuck you two are for?" she said, chewing her thumbnail. "I already kicked Darrell outta here because he's totally frigging useless. I already been through their room. You can start in the bathroom if you want."

She stopped talking then, just went to the couch and started lifting up cushions, brushing coins to the carpet.

Vega nodded at Cap, nudging him to the other room. Cap was thankful. Maybe Vega could get through to her, do a woman-to-woman thing. Because she was so naturally sensitive. Cap shrugged it off and went into the next room, glad to have a break.

Kylie and Bailey's room was sacked, the twin beds pulled apart, blankets and sheets in twisted piles on the floor, a white dresser with chipped edges, drawers open and vines of brightly colored little girls' clothes spilling over the sides. Cap saw a pair of pink leggings. He remembered Nell wearing a lot of leggings when she was eight, nine years old. He wanted to smell them but felt like it would be disrespectful somehow, so he only touched them, lightly between his thumb and forefinger. They were unbelievably soft. The knees on them were worn, thready. They must be Bailey's, he thought, still running, skinning knees.

"Fuck," he heard Jamie say from the other room. "Oh fuck. Fuck, motherfucker, oh fuck, fuck, fuck!"

The fucks started low and throaty, then they rose to alarm quickly until they were screams.

Cap ran into the living room. Jamie was on the floor in front of the TV, DVDs scattered around her. Vega was closer and leaned down to her, grabbed her shoulders.

"What is it? What's wrong?"

Jamie looked up at them, her face all black lines, electric, furious. She held up a DVD. *Pirates of the Caribbean.*

"This fucking movie." She spat out the words like they were tobacco she'd been chewing. "Guy in it named Will Turner, she's seen it a million times. *That's* WT. It's not Sonny Thomas. It's not anyone."

Cap's forehead tingled and burned. He put a hand up to it, felt the breath kicked out of his chest. Then his instinct came back and he saw Jamie for what she was: an unstable element, a cut wire spraying sparks.

She slapped her hands over her eyes. She must have liked the way that felt because she did it again. Then she started hitting her face like her hands were flyswatters, first in a pitter-patter way, then harder until she knocked the heel of her hand into her nose and blood leaked from it.

Cap jumped from where he stood to stop it, but Vega was closer and quicker. She clamped her arms around Jamie from behind and pulled her to a standing position.

"Let me go!" Jamie yelled.

She thrashed and twisted against Vega, who'd pinned Jamie's arms to her body. They were about the same height, Jamie and Vega, but Jamie's fury was nothing next to Vega's discipline.

"Call her mother," said Vega to Cap.

"Lemme go, bitch," Jamie screamed.

Cap could see into the cave of her mouth, black and bottomless, as her eyes grew to globes, and he reached for his phone.

She was in the bathroom vomiting when her mother arrived. Vega pressed a wet towel to the back of Jamie's neck and heard Gail White yelling at Cap. Jamie was weak, had gone for too many hours straight on pills and beer and coffee, and now her insides were kicking up like mud off tires.

Gail burst into the bathroom, Cap behind her.

"All right, get the hell outta here," she said to Vega.

Vega stood back. Gail pushed her out of the way and knelt behind Jamie, whose head was lolling around on the toilet seat.

"A lot of fuckin' good you're doing, all of you," snapped Gail. "Just get out now, go!"

Cap and Vega backed up and left. They walked through the scraps in the living room, and then Vega saw something.

"I'm calling Em," Cap announced, heading for the open door.

Vega stepped around DVDs like they were bombs and picked one up, examined the back of it. She stared at it and followed Cap without looking up. She heard him speak.

"Where is he . . . ? Okay, WT is a dead end. Jamie Brandt thinks it's from a movie. . . ."

Vega walked behind Cap, out the door, down the complex stairs and to his car. She ran her thumb over the front of the DVD and opened the case.

"Just have him call me if he wants to talk. Or he can talk to Jamie, but she's sick right now . . . like sick, vomiting. . . ."

They got into Cap's car. Vega reached to the backseat and brought out her laptop, set it on her thighs.

"I'm saying you have no more leads; he's a character from a god-damn movie. . . ."

Cap's voice rose; he massaged the bridge of his nose. Vega slid the DVD into the laptop and turned down the sound.

"Sure. Fifteen minutes," he said, and hung up.

He bounced his fist on the top of the wheel. "Em wants to meet at the diner. We have no reason to hide anything from him at this point. We all have shit."

Vega pressed Fast-Forward on the movie, watched the picture jump and split.

"Yeah. Okay."

Cap hung up and put his hands through his hair. He started the car. "The hell are you doing?"

Vega didn't answer him. She had stopped the fast-forward and was now watching the movie in real time. She pressed Pause.

"Is this him?" she said, pointing to an actor on the screen. "Is this Will Turner?"

"I think so," said Cap, leaning over. "Yeah, it's not Johnny Depp; it's the kid."

Cap put his seat belt on and began to pull the car out onto the road.

"What are you doing?" he said, more slowly.

She stared at the kid's face, the movie star, at his dark eyes generously spaced apart, delicate features, smooth skin. It had been hard to tell from the DVD case, but now, watching him move and speak, it was clear. She tapped her fingernail on the screen.

"This kid looks exactly like Evan Marsh."

———————

EM WAS WAITING FOR THEM IN THE SAME BOOTH. HE TAPPED A quarter on the table and hopped in his seat when he saw them. Vega slid in first, her laptop under her arm, Cap next to her.

"What's going on, Em?"

Em showed them what he was holding—not a quarter. A flash drive.

"That for us?" Vega said, opening the laptop.

"Junior released Sonny Thomas an hour ago because they got nothing on him," said Em.

"Yeah, no shit," said Cap, nodding to the laptop screen where the movie was frozen on the young actor's face. "Because that is Kylie's dream date. A fictional character in a goddamn movie."

Em handed the flash drive to Vega, and she plugged it in. He stared at the screen.

"I don't think I get it," he said.

"The character's name is Will Turner. We all thought Kylie was writing about Wilson Thomas, but instead it's a guy who doesn't exist."

"Shit," said Em. "It's this guy? What's his name, Rodrigo something?"

Another video screen opened, the blurry chevrons of a security camera. Retail floor, a row of computers on a counter with one user, seated, back toward the camera.

"You got the Kinko's footage," said Vega.

Em pulled a finger gun on her and winked.

"Give the lady a stuffed banana."

Cap leaned in for a closer look. The figure in the video stood up. Tall, thin, wearing a sweatshirt with the hood pulled down over the top half of his face. Bottom half a mess of static fuzz. He walked out of the frame.

Vega pressed Pause.

"Could be Evan Marsh," she said.

"Related to Nolan?" said Em.

Vega nodded. "His brother."

"The guy working the register doesn't remember him," Em added. "We're trying to lift prints."

"You want to lift prints at a Kinko's?" Cap said, incredulous. "You're going to get sludge from those keyboards."

"Not impossible," said Vega.

Cap stared at her, at her hair swept back into a neat ponytail at the base, two or three wisps draped across her cheek, as if she'd planned it that way. It enraged Cap suddenly, her arbitrariness. Some things neat and some things messy. Maybe there was no method here. He suddenly felt duped.

Vega looked away from Cap and across to Em now, suddenly on the same side.

"Can we think about this critically for a second?" Cap said to both of them. "Where would Evan Marsh and Kylie Brandt meet? Where would they be in the same place at the same time?"

"I don't know," said Em, shrugging. "Maybe the supermarket."

"That Giant's clear across town. Jamie Brandt would shop at the Walmart in Black Creek."

"We can figure it out later," said Vega.

"No, let's figure it out now," said Cap. "I'm not chasing the invisible fucking man, here."

"Maybe . . ." said Em. "Maybe that's not the right question."

Cap and Vega turned to him.

"Oh yeah?" said Cap, laughing a little bit. "All right, Stephen Hawking. You tell me. What's the right question?"

Em scratched his chin and shifted his gaze to Vega. She raised her eyebrows. Go for it, kid. Knock yourself out. Em coughed, nervous.

"So maybe there's a room," he said. "Evan Marsh and Kylie Brandt are in it together. I can't tell you where it is, and I can't tell you how they got there." He pointed to the laptop screen. "Kylie loves this movie, loves this movie star, and meets a guy who looks just like him. Right?"

Vega grabbed the line.

"She's a flirt, romantic, a boundary tester," she said. "She's pissed at her mom, she's pretending she's a princess, she's pretending she's in a movie. Evan Marsh is nice to her. Maybe he flirts with her, makes her feel special. Maybe he's teasing her. Maybe he's stoned. He lights a cigarette and she sees a skull on his Zippo, just like the one the hero wears on a necklace in her favorite movie. She believes in signs, fate, love at first sight. All that shit a happy little girl believes in.

"Maybe he gets something from her—an email, a phone number, a way to communicate, tells her he'll see her soon but doesn't know where or when exactly. Then he trails her from home, picks up her and her sister from a mall when Mom's shopping."

"Why?" said Cap. "Is he a pedophile? Any history of that?"

"Not that we are aware of," said Vega.

"So what would be the motive here? What would make a twenty-one-, twenty-two-year-old kid who's not a pedophile kidnap two girls? Risk jail time. With a mother who's dying."

Cap had flashes of Maryann Marsh, her filmy eyes and drawn lips as she looked at the picture of her missing son.

"His mother," said Vega.

"What's the story with the mother?" said Em.

"She's dying," said Vega. "Evan told me his mother didn't mind having cancer because it's the last thing Nolan gave her. He was a smoker."

"Oh, shit," said Em, covering his mouth. "That is some rough shit."

"Yes," said Vega.

"I bet he was pissed the police didn't do more," Em suggested.

"How'd you know?" said Vega.

Em threw his hands up.

"Missing adult? Ralz probably just checked the box. File the report. Move on. We have some staffing issues," Em explained. "In that we are understaffed."

Cap asked, "How pissed?"

"Hard to say," said Vega.

"Desperate?"

She nodded.

"Maybe."

"His brother goes missing, Mom gets sick, kid's life falls apart," narrated Cap.

"He stops going to school, gets into some drugs," added Vega.

Em picked up: "Somewhere, he meets Kylie Brandt."

Cap continued, "And he has an idea. Take the girl—"

"Or girls," said Vega. "Write an email to the police as ransom. Only instead of money, he wants them to find his brother."

"Then he sends us the email," said Cap, "because the police aren't doing anything. Probably on a healthy dose of oxy to get rid of the anxiety."

"But he's not a criminal, right?" asked Em. "He's just some druggie who made a shit-ton of bad decisions."

Vega nodded at him. "I would think so."

"If he has the girls, all we have to do is pull a thread," said Cap.

Vega's phone buzzed. She looked.

"That your guy?" said Cap.

"I got a home address. You know Sisilia Street?"

"Yeah," said Cap.

He studied Em across the table. He hadn't aged much since that night the kid had died, since he had run to get Cap in the break room looking like a chunky pre-teen nerd who'd just got spooked from playing the Bloody Mary game in the mirror. No gray hair, no wrinkles, still with the sweat rings under the arms, but there was something different now. Cap couldn't put his finger on it, but if he had to guess it might have been the maturity of experience, knowing what was instinct and what was optimism.

"I'll go back to work," Em offered. "Try to get the original report on Nolan Marsh, see if we have anything on Evan."

"Good," said Cap.

"Thanks, Emerson," said Vega.

Em grinned and gave them two thumbs-up.

9

IT WAS CALLED BETHLEHEM HILL, THIS AREA, BUT IT FELT PRETTY flat to Vega. Cap told her this was the Bethlehem Coal Mine before it closed in the '70s. When it was operational, the runoff would flow into the creek and powder the water black, and there you had it, Black Creek. Cap said some towns turned their old mines into museums, gave tours and sold chips of anthracite on key chains, but Beth Coal had been abandoned and trashed after an underground fire was set by an arsonist around 1980. The surrounding roads caved and looked like they'd been suctioned with a giant vacuum from below. Every once in a while there'd be an item on the ballot to clean it all up, but there was always somewhere else to put the money.

The streets within a couple miles' radius consisted of mostly commercial properties, mini-malls and offices spread out about a hundred feet from one another. The building they were looking for was only two floors, a dusty block of brick sticking up like a rotten tooth.

Cap parked on the street. There was one other parked car, a beige compact under a carport behind the brick building. The sun was almost down.

"Apartment two," said Vega, reading from her phone.

"Gotta be up there," said Cap, pointing to the second floor.

Evan Marsh's apartment was above an eye doctor's office, a monument-style sign in front that read BETHLEHEM EYE ASSOCIATES, along with the logo of an eye, wide open with lashes. The office was closed.

Vega followed Cap to the stairs, metal and rattling under their feet. On the landing, Cap knocked hard on the door, and they waited. Vega put her ear to the door and heard nothing. She leaned over the railing to look through a small window and could see a part of a living room—a recliner and beanbag chair. She looked at Cap and shook her head.

She eyed the gold-finish doorknob and stretched the bottom of her shirt over the fingers on one hand. It was locked but cheap, clicking back and forth. Cap glared at her, vaguely disapproving.

"Okay, now, we can wait in my car," he said.

"That's got to be his car over there," she said, reaching above each ear and pulling out two thick bobby pins.

"You're probably right," said Cap, peering over the railing. "And it's beige."

"We're friends with the cops now, right?" she said.

She turned her head around to see his face—tired and put-upon. It made her imagine him waiting for her outside a dressing room. In another kind of life wherein she didn't order her clothes online and would drag a man shopping. And in which Cap was the man. The whole fantasy was so weird it made her smile, and that made him smile, contagious like a yawn. The lines around his eyes softened up.

"Right," he said.

She extended one of the pins, bent the other, and stuck them both in the lock. She felt around for the driver pins inside, turned the plug, and the door snapped open.

"We're doing this now," Cap said.

Vega went first into the living room, saw the recliner and the beanbag she'd seen from the window. Also a television, shaggy carpet, an outdated light fixture hanging from the ceiling on a garland chain. The space was not big, and there was a musty smell in the air—body odor, dust.

She sensed a familiar element shifting—something chemical, like a change in altitude. Early decay: she knew what it was even before she saw the body.

There was Evan Marsh, the boy from this morning, now smaller and whiter and lying on the ground faceup, legs buckled, with his forehead blown open. Vega stepped back without thinking about it, almost into Cap, but stopped right before she hit him. It was a few seconds before she spoke.

"I'll check the other rooms," she said.

"You want company?"

She shook her head and drew the Springfield, kept it pointed at the floor, stepped lightly toward a partly open door. It was a bedroom, sparsely decorated: a mattress without a box spring, an uneven set of gray blinds over the window. She pushed open the sliding door of the closet with her foot and there were three shirts on hangers.

She went into the bathroom, flipped the light switch with the nose of her gun. It was dim and dirty. There were two fat prescription bottles without labels on the sink. Frosted shower door slid open. The Zippo with the skull and an ashtray full of butts on the edge of the tub. Vega hovered over it, leaned down and picked up the lighter with two fingertips, careful not to touch the tile. She held it up for a second, then slid it into her back pocket.

She came back out and saw Cap squatting over the body, stretching his neck around, examining the head.

"All clear?" he said, without looking up.

She nodded and let her eyes follow the blood sprays and clumps of pulp. The biggest spatter was on the cabinets above the kitchen counter; it was streaked and had dripped onto the counter below, into coffee cups, over the edge and down to the floor in thin lines. Bullet hole in the cabinet door.

She stayed there for only a second and then went to the body, kneeled opposite Cap.

Evan Marsh's eyes were open, the lids either gone completely or mashed into the scramble that had been his skull, brain and hair a clotted mess. A halo of blood had spread underneath his head, dried into the threads of the carpet.

Vega thought of another body in another cheap room. It was in some Inland Empire meth den with plastic tablecloths tacked over the windows, mice darting across the countertops, the stench of meat and milk left in ninety-degree heat. She'd shoved the butt of her Browning into some punk's chest and shot another one in the foot, left them both scuttling around on the floor moaning and yelling. Into a back room where she found her skip, a nineteen-year-old black kid named Zion, lying on a bed with his limbs stretched out so far they looked gummy, fingers extended like they were webbed, eyes and mouth open in shock. Dead.

It was the first time she had felt bad for a skip, on account of him being so young and so freshly dead. Could have been because he wasn't alive to call her a cracker dyke, which would have eroded her sympathy a bit. But it was easier to pistol-whip and cuff them that way. She had kneeled and stared at him for a few minutes first, and then placed her head on his chest, ostensibly to listen for a heartbeat but really, truthfully, to narrow the gap between him and her, or was it the gap between life and death? Whatever it was it hadn't worked, because Zion was dead and gone, and now so was Evan Marsh.

"Fuck," she said, quiet and pissed.

"Yeah," said Cap. "Happened a few hours ago. Blood's separating."

Vega looked where Cap was pointing, the blood on the cheeks was dried, yellow and thin at the edges of the splotches. She was confident she knew the details but wanted to be sure.

She slid a hand under Evan Marsh's shoulder, felt the still weight of it, and then Cap's hand clamped down on her wrist.

"Don't," he said.

It sounded like a warning. His eyes searched her face.

"Let go now," said Vega, which also sounded like a warning.

Neither moved. She had her right hand free and knew Cap favored his right side, so she would need only a second, or less than that, to shove her palm into his nose. His fingers were hot on her skin.

He let her go.

"We have to wait for the ME," he said.

Vega clenched her teeth and felt a pressure in her ears. She held her hands up to them.

"Fuck that, Caplan."

"You'd like to know what happened here, right?" said Cap. "Then we call Junior and Em. We wait for the ME and we find out."

"How long does that take? You really think your boys and the coroner are going to get to the bottom of this one quick? With all their spare time and powers of deductive reasoning?" she said.

"If you fuck with this crime scene, you contaminate a hair or a print that could lead us to the killer, and—"

Vega sat back on her haunches and shook her head.

"—and it could, it *could* bring us the girls. If Evan Marsh has some connection to the girls, which we have yet to figure out."

"If we wait we're losing more time."

"Wait for what? What are you going to find out by moving this body around right now?"

"The entry wound."

Cap smirked.

"So you got a forensics lab back at the bed-and-breakfast, you're gonna analyze some residue and bullet-casing striation?"

"Stop it," said Vega calmly, and she stood up.

"Stop what?"

"Stop being a dick."

"This is me," he said, and he stood up too. "I have some experience here too. Maybe you think it can't stack up to all your street guerrilla bullshit, but I've seen a lot of bodies and a lot of evidence get trashed because of sloppy police work."

"Good thing we're not police," said Vega.

That almost made him laugh but he stopped himself.

"What do you need to know exactly that you can't guess?" he said, holding his hand over the body like he was in a séance. He walked to the door. "Okay, so the shooter is either invited in or the door is unlocked—no forced entry. Victim's standing at the counter when shot from behind, six to twelve inches, I'd say. Vic flops forward, bounces back to the ground. Bullet's probably in the wall behind the cabinet. You got anything else?"

"Shooter was invited in. Victim knew him," said Vega quietly.

"How do we know that?"

Vega pointed to the counter.

"Two coffee cups. Can of Folgers."

Cap sighed. "Yeah, looks like he was going to make the guy coffee."

Cap put his hands on hips and stared down at the body. Vega watched his face change as he thought of something disappointing, swept his open hand over his mouth.

"Oh shit, Vega. Maryann Marsh. Fucking Maryann Marsh," he said.

This seemed to exhaust him; he slumped where he stood.

"Yeah, I know," said Vega.

"Okay, okay," Cap muttered, like he was talking to himself. "Okay,

Vega, look. You want to put your hands all over the stiff first, go for it. You want to drag your feet through this place, muddy up the fibers, do it. Can we please just give the ME a shot here after, see what he can pull?"

Vega wondered if this was how he got women to sleep with him, disarming them by giving in to them on one thing and asking for something else at the same time.

So she made him wait for a few fat seconds before she said yes.

An hour later there were six cops on the scene, two paramedics and the ME, a guy named Baker who had been smoking for forty years and looked like it, his skin a mess of pale folds. Baker and the cops seemed glad to see Cap, their faces expectant, surprised. They looked at Vega like she was a spiky tropical fruit, some exotic unknown thing. They had started to comb the room, splitting it into a grid of squares, Baker kneeling over the body making a disappointed hound dog face.

Cap and Vega waited on the landing outside, watched as the cops dusted and bagged. One of them, Torres, a young guy in a wrinkled uniform, took pictures with a digital camera.

"Any idea why they're not questioning us?" said Vega, leaning against the railing.

Cap's gaze went to the road, to a tan sedan pulling in next to the ambulance and the cruisers. Cap nodded to it.

"I have an idea."

The car door opened. It was Ralz.

"Hey, Ralz," said Cap. "We going for a ride?"

Then they were in the goddamn cruiser. In the backseat behind the filmy polycarbonate partition like a couple of drug dealers.

Ralz drove them and didn't speak, kept glancing at Vega in the rearview.

"Junior does this. This is his thing," Cap said to her.

"Wasting time during an investigation?"

"He gets angry, asserts himself, calms down. Happens very quickly."

Cap looked out the side window into traffic. He patted his knee with his hand; Vega watched the fingers curl. She glared at Ralz's face through the partition. Maybe 180 pounds but mostly muscle. Dead-eyed and stoic, which seemed to be his signature look. He would win in a fight between the two of them with his eyes closed, one hand tied behind his back, without breaking a sweat, and all the rest. Unless she had one or two seconds on him.

Perry would have said that if someone crosses you on the wrong day, you grab the nearest pint glass and shove it in their teeth. Don't stew in your juices, don't let anything sink in. Don't wait, don't bide your time, don't save your breath, don't sleep on it. You don't have the weight, kid, but you got the fire, so burn the motherfuckers to the bone.

The wind had picked up, blowing leaves and trash in spirals in the street outside of the station. As they pulled up, Cap saw Junior standing on the front steps like an angry dad. Hands on his hips and everything. Em and some other cops filtered out behind him.

Ralz opened the doors for Vega, then Cap.

"What the fuck!" Junior yelled to him.

"Hey, Junior," said Cap, checking the impulse to grin.

He came down the stairs and stood in front of Cap and Vega, pink in the face and sweating through the blond fuzz on his upper lip. He pointed a thin finger at Cap's chest.

"You got some bad fucking luck, Cap, you know that?"

"I'm pretty keenly aware of it, yes."

"This is cute, asshole?" said Junior, hushed. "You think turning up at a murder scene with your girlfriend after I told her to stay out of my town is funny?"

Cap felt a prickly numbness on the back of his head, something sour in his throat. His mild amusement at Junior's pissy little face started to shift.

"You want to give us shit or you want our statements?" said Cap, dry mouthed.

"Wow, Cap, how about both?" said Junior, snotty. "The two of you can sit in the box until you scrape some lawyer off the bottom of your shoe, and then I'll have you arrested for obstruction anyway. Then you can add gross misdemeanor to your list of fuckups. . . ."

He kept talking. Cap watched a drop of foam form in the corner of Junior's mouth, and couldn't hear him anymore. Cap looked down at his hands, front and back. Shaking.

He remembered times like this before. A lot when he was younger, so skinny and scared he couldn't do anything about it, in high school in Sheepshead Bay when those goddamn gangster Russian kids jumped him and beat him with an umbrella. Then later, when he was a cop, when he wasn't skinny or scared anymore, some punk they had in for armed robbery kept calling him a Jesus killer and talked about how Hitler was A-OK in his book. And then he saw the picture of Jules on Cap's desk and said, "Your wife looks like she likes gettin' raped." Cap had to go in the bathroom so he wouldn't slam the kid's face into the desk edge. Then fights with Jules, the time she said so incredibly fucking coldly, "The worst part about you, Max, is that you don't even know why you're angry at me anymore—you're just too lazy to figure it out." So he threw the beer bottle at the door and it cracked into a few unsatisfying pieces and dented the old damp wood.

Stop, Junior, please stop.

Cap made himself step back.

"What's the problem, Cap?" said Junior, a smirk spilling across his face. "You think you might hit me?"

Then came Vega. Before Cap could answer or think or move, she put herself between him and Junior, chin angled up. Junior almost looked charmed.

"You got a thing to say, sweetie?"

Cap could sense her body filling up with some kind of current, the warmth from her back on his chest. For a second he thought he could feel her heart beat.

"I know guys like you," she said with an air of discovery. "You're the kind of guy has to beg girls to let you screw them."

Junior coughed out a laugh now.

"Sure, sure," he said. "You missed your calling, California. Should have been a shrink."

"You beg your wife to marry you too?"

Junior talked over her, said, "That's enough, now."

Vega did not think that was enough; she kept talking fast and low in his face.

"She's so *active,* Hollows," said Vega. "So much time at the gym."

Junior was caught off guard and speechless for a second, and Cap saw just the smallest hint of painful recognition in his eyes.

"Miss Vega, every word you say digs you a deeper hole. It's a little pathetic," said Junior, still calm.

"I saw her Facebook page—not the one with your kids and your dog and all that shit. I'm talking about the good one, GymBabe80?"

"Watch your mouth," Junior snapped.

Cap realized, finally, where she was going. Ralz pawed at the ground a little next to Cap, and the air in their little circle turned to glass that was about to break.

"She really likes spin class, right? A lot of nice pictures of her, but not one of you or the family. That's a little funny, huh?" said Vega, whispering now. Then she grew thoughtful and almost humble: "Now, I don't know a lot about social media. What does it mean when you have a ton of 'likes' from guys?"

"Watch your fucking mouth, I said," said Junior, pointing a finger in her face.

Vega leaned into the finger and said, "They seem to know her really well."

Cap kept his eyes on Ralz, who looked unsure as to how to proceed. He could almost see the hamster wheel in Ralz's brain rattling around as he ran through the options.

"Detective Ralz, please place Miss Vega under arrest right now," said Junior, his voice a little hoarse.

"What for?" Cap said. "Talking trash about your wife? You'd have to arrest half of Denville."

Cap was just gambling now; he'd never heard anything about Junior's wife, but saw that Junior was sure as shit uncomfortable talking about her, and that made Cap very happy. Junior glared at him.

Vega shrugged, her shoulders rising and dropping casually.

"You're right, doesn't matter," she said to Junior, cheery and concilia-tory. "Probably doesn't mean a thing."

Junior's shoulders came down a fraction of an inch at the prospect of her backing off. He even looked like he might turn around and go back to being his regular shithead self.

But then Vega snapped in a loud, clear voice, "My guess is they clicked 'like' because there's no 'I fucked her' button."

And that was it. Junior lunged, grabbing for the collar of Vega's jacket, and suddenly Cap felt all his limbs loosen and an old blind confidence fill him up, and he stretched his arm out to bat Junior away, but couldn't get there before Ralz landed a punch on his jaw, smashing Cap's lower lip between his teeth.

He hadn't been hit in a few years and was unprepared for it, lost his balance and stumbled sideways onto the ground.

Cap sat up, saw Em standing with Ralz in a headlock, Ralz's face red, both of them tumbling backward with the momentum, and Cap was so dazed he started laughing. When he stopped there was a buzzing in his ear, like a bug was deep in there. He shut his eyes and heard his name over and over through the static. Caplan, Caplan, Caplan.

He opened his eyes. The noise cleared. Traynor, the chief of police, stood above him.

"Caplan, you need a medic?"

Cap shook his head, tasted the blood on his tongue, and stood up carefully. All at once he felt the various points of pain on his body—shoulders, coccyx, jaw. He pressed his palm against his chin, trying to adjust it. He knew in an hour it would swell, in four it would bruise.

Then he looked around. They were all staring at him, frozen. The chief, right in front of him, fit and attentive. Here were Ralz and Em behind him, both sweaty and no longer attached to each other. Here was a slightly hefty guy in a blue suit and a burgundy tie, alert, clear eyes—must be the Fed. Here was Junior, panting and dazed. Here were a few cops, some in shirtsleeves and some in uniform, some Cap knew, a couple young ones he didn't, on the steps and on the ground.

And there was Vega, standing next to the chief, loose strands of hair waving like spiderweb filaments, her fair skin punctuated by red blots on her cheeks and forehead, chest rising and falling in measured surges.

They were all watching Cap. Cap looked back at Traynor.

"What's going on here, Caplan?" he said.

Cap knew there was rage in there, contained and primed. Cap

thought that back when Traynor was a drinker he must have been a bastard; he'd heard stories about him showing up for work with black eyes and bloody knuckles, blowing .12 on the Breathalyzer at eight in the morning before coffee. But now he was wide-awake, chewing the end of his mustache, waiting for an answer.

Cap didn't plan, just started talking.

"I'm working for the Brandt family, Chief, with Alice Vega, over there. We think there's a connection between the kidnapping and the dead kid we just found, and we'd like to tell you about it."

Traynor glanced at Vega, then back to Cap.

"Get inside."

"He can't enter the premises," said Junior, pointing at Cap. "It's in the terms of his agreement."

"What terms?" said Traynor.

"My resignation," said Cap.

Traynor thought about it for only a second.

"Was the condition negotiated on behalf of the family or the department?"

"Department," said Cap.

"Good," said Traynor. "Consider the condition suspended for the length of this investigation."

"Chief, legally speaking it might not—" Junior began.

"You get yourself a JD, Hollows, in your spare fucking time?"

Junior stepped back and appeared to shrink in volume.

"Then we worry about it later. Let's go," the chief said, loud enough for everyone to hear.

He turned and headed toward the steps, striding, and everyone else was quick to follow, jumping to attention like they were already late. Vega held her hand down to Cap. He took it, feeling her soft cold skin, and she pulled him up. She let go, said nothing, straightened her jacket out and clapped her hands together once softly like they were chalkboard erasers she'd just finished cleaning.

10

SHE SAT AT A LONG OVAL TABLE IN A DIM BLUE ROOM WITH A bunch of cops.

Cap was next to her, and the chief of police and the FBI agent were at the front of the room, projecting images from a laptop onto a ratty screen. Cap and Vega were near the head of the table. The presentation was for them.

There was a school photo of a girl on the screen, round faced, with straight blond hair to her chin. She smiled out at the camera, but it was one of those trained-kid smiles. Smile, smile, smile, Vega could hear the photographers in her head. Always laid it on thick for the girls— Come on, princess, you're gonna be Miss America, smile for me. All the boys got was a Hey buddy, say cheese.

"This is Sydney McKenna," said the chief. "Disappeared on her way home from school two years ago near Harrisburg. She was eight years old at the time. You remember?" he said to Cap.

Cap nodded. "I think so, yeah."

"Splashed around the news for a couple of months. Never found her."

Traynor nodded at the kid with the mouse, who clicked.

Another photo, another little girl, wearing a sailor top and a navy bow in her hair. She was younger than the last, her hair a darker blond, but still there was a resemblance.

"Ashley Cahill, age six, was seen getting into a car in the parking lot of a public swimming pool in Lebanon four years ago," said Traynor.

He let it all sit for a moment.

"Gone. Never seen again. Either of them. We think," he said, nodding to the Fed, "what we have is an MO, which is not much, but it's similar, and there's a physical resemblance between all the girls. That and they all took ballet classes. These two and Kylie Brandt."

Traynor nodded at a cop by the door, who flipped on the lights. The photo of Ashley Cahill stayed on the wall behind him, overexposed, the top half of her face whited out.

"We've talked to every registered sex offender who fits the profile between here, Harrisburg, and Reading. Everyone ruled out aside from five we can't locate. Agent Cartwright has people working on that.

"As you know, we have three witnesses of varying reliability, two of whom have a similar description of the suspect, which matches the image of the sender of the email we got from Kinko's. You say you have something similar?"

Vega nodded.

"We'll want to have a look at that afterward to line it up. You tell us—Caplan, Miss Vega—what brought you to Evan Marsh?"

Caplan looked at her and held his hand out, opening a door.

"After we received the email about Nolan Marsh we talked to his mother," said Vega. "She didn't have anything new as far as we could tell. I talked to Evan Marsh just to cover the base. He seemed under the influence of something—your team will find the pills in his bathroom. And your ME should look at his right wrist—I saw scratch marks there.

"We, Caplan and I, we think Evan Marsh had some opportunity to meet Kylie, even though we're not sure where." She paused. "We think he was the kidnapper, initially at least. His plan was to take the girls and use them to get his brother's case revisited. Then, we think, he would've returned them. He wasn't a pedophile, didn't want to raise them as his own, just wanted his brother's body so his mother could put on a funeral. But he obviously didn't do this alone, and whoever helped him or worked for him got angry.

"But now, this guy, Marsh's killer, has the girls and an unknown motive. Maybe he's one of your five."

The Fed, Cartwright, leaned forward.

"You talk to Marsh's acquaintances? Co-workers? Girlfriend?" he said, no blame in his voice, just a slight southern accent.

"We didn't get that far," said Cap. "This is our theory as of"—he looked at his watch—"two and a half hours ago. And we've been tied up."

"What about your team?" said Cartwright to Traynor. "They get anything from Marsh before he was killed?"

"Hollows?" said Traynor.

Junior sat at the opposite end of the table. He looked at something on the palm of his hand.

"Lieutenant Ralz spoke with the mother. She indicated she had no involvement."

"Which is probably the case," said Traynor. "What did Evan Marsh say to you?"

Hollows paused and glanced at Ralz.

"We didn't speak with him."

Traynor combed his mustache with his bottom lip. He turned his head halfway, in Cartwright's direction.

"Let's get two people to the mother's house now to break the news and get the information while it's fresh." He turned back to the group at the table. "We'll keep the team we have now at Marsh's apartment and have them look for anything, specifically financial records and statements, get his phone and computer so we can get the tech in here. Miss Vega, Cap, you two," he said, pointing to Junior and Ralz. "Stay two seconds with me, please. Everyone else, let's move."

The rest of the cops scattered and filed out the door. Vega watched Traynor and the Fed. Traynor gripped the edge of a chair and leaned down slightly. Nervous energy, she thought, but holding it together. The Fed's face was round and red. He tapped a pen on his knee and watched the cops leave, moved his jaw like he was cleaning something out of a molar with his tongue.

The door closed, and Junior held his hands up, indignant.

"This is what we're going on now?" he said. "This is the working lead?"

Cap laughed lightly. He's used to it, Vega thought, this little fucker's attitude and sycophantic bullshit that passes for work. Doesn't make a move unless it makes things easier for him, less paper on the desk. Or, worse, he just can't have anyone else be right first. Even cleaning five bloody, shit-stained toilets with her own T-shirt in Basic was better than working in a goddamn office with goddamn office people trying to climb a ladder, crushing knuckles along the way. Vega squeezed her hand open and shut around her pen.

Traynor shoved the chair into the table.

"Yes, Captain, it is one very viable lead seeing we've had an abduction and a homicide within four days' time that appear to be related. Just so you can get a nice sleep tonight, we'll still chase the five SOs and the father. That okay with you?"

Junior shifted in his seat.

"Yeah, Chief."

"You sure? You sound a little depressed about it."

Junior stopped moving, and Traynor stepped back toward the wall, crossed his arms. Vega watched him, noticed how he got relaxed as soon as Junior appeared to be getting nervous. She could see the cop in him then, could imagine him in an interrogation room firing questions out one after another before the suspect had a chance to think up a lie.

"It's clear to me you and Miss Vega have met before, correct?"

"Yes, Chief," said Junior.

"When was that?"

"Monday, Chief."

"Did you discuss this case?"

"Yes, sir. She wanted to pool resources."

"And what was your response to that proposal?"

Junior's face contorted for a second. Sniffing bad milk.

"I told her we don't work with civilians, Chief."

"You said no thanks," said Traynor.

"Yes, sir."

"You turned down help from an experienced private investigator hired by the family."

Junior rolled his shoulders back.

"Yes, sir."

"Why would you do that?"

"Policy, sir. We don't work with civilians, never have."

"And you didn't think this case might warrant a different approach, when we're maxed out on manpower and officers are working triple shifts?"

Junior didn't answer. Vega wove the pen through her fingers and stared at him, thinking he looked like a mouse that had just hit the glue.

"I take your silence to mean, No Chief, I did not think that because I thought I could handle this myself, and I'm too self-satisfied to admit I need help. Here is a fact, Captain: your pride was a useless thing to me before, but now that it has gotten in the way of this investigation it is a fucking abomination. After we find these girls we're going to sit down and brainstorm about some methods you could utilize to improve your performance. Until then we, and by we I mean you, don't sleep, take your meals and piss in a cup either in your car on the way to interview witnesses or at your desk with the paperwork so we don't waste any more time. Got it?"

Junior slumped in his chair and cocked his head to the side, cracking his neck with no sound.

"Yessir."

Traynor put both hands behind his head, ran them down to his shoulders.

"Now," he said. "You and Detective Ralz can have the honor of telling Marsh's mother her only remaining son is dead, and I want you there for however long it takes to get the name of every known associate she can spit out through her grief. Meantime, you can hope Miss Vega and Cap won't be pressing assault charges." He waved the two of them off with a stroke in the air, sharp as a salute. "Go."

Junior and Ralz stood and walked out. Junior nodded at Cap and Vega as he left. Vega didn't do a thing, didn't even stare, just let her eyes rest on him like he was scenery.

"Okay, Miss Vega," Traynor said when they'd left. "You have my attention and cooperation. What do you want to do next?"

Cap and Vega stood in the freezer section of the Giant waiting for the manager. They'd talked with Traynor and Cartwright for thirty minutes about next steps, about their preferences and what they'd done so far, agreed to frequent communication. Cap felt high on it, the energy and the planning, and yes, the vindication and approval from the chief, which came only in the form of Traynor looking Cap in the eyes and asking what he thought of this or that. He remembered the feeling from a long time ago, and it made him feel younger. Awake.

The supermarket manager came through two gray swinging doors. He was a kid in short sleeves and a tie, beady eyes and a cluster of pimples on his forehead.

"Hi, Mr. Caplan," he said, shaking his hand. "Drew Bennett."

"Mr. Bennett," said Cap. "This is Alice Vega."

"Hi, ma'am," said Bennett, holding his hand up in a motionless wave.

Would have tipped his hat if he had one, thought Cap, but no handshake for a girl. "Come back to my office, please."

They followed him through the double doors, through the back room filled with boxes, the rear of which opened up into a loading dock, and past that, the parking lot. Bennett led them to a small cluttered room on the side with a yellow-tinted window that looked out onto the boxes. He closed the door and stood in front of the desk.

"So is this about Evan Marsh?" he said to Cap.

"What makes you say that?" Cap answered.

"Ran out an hour before his shift ended and didn't say anything about it. Not returning my calls either."

"He do that before?"

"He's been calling in sick more and more, leaving early, but he always lets me know. Except today. He in some kind of trouble?" Bennett said, crossing his arms. Cap thought he must have seen a lot of actors on TV say that.

"Yeah, he's dead," said Vega.

Now Bennett acknowledged Vega. He stared right at her, leaned on the desk.

"No way," he said.

"Yes, actually," she said. "He's dead."

"How? Was it an overdose?"

"Cause is yet to be determined. Would you not be surprised if it was an overdose?" Vega asked.

Bennett stared at the space between them, eyes glassy, and now Vega stepped directly in front of him so he couldn't look away from her if he tried. She stacked the questions quick, one right after another, so he didn't have time to be stunned.

"No, I guess not."

"Were you aware of him using drugs?" she said.

"Yeah, I mean, not directly."

"What does that mean—'not directly'?"

"I didn't *see* him use drugs but just figured he was."

"Why is that?"

Bennett blew air between his lips.

"He lost some weight, started acting spacey, like groggy, you know?"

"How long would you say that behavior had been going on?"

"I don't know, really. . . ."

"Three months, six months?"

"More like six."

"Can you remember anything specifically about when the behavior started? Anything he told you or did that might have tipped you off that something was going on in his personal life?"

Bennett thought about it, and his gaze snapped back to Vega.

"I had to fire this guy, maybe eight months ago. He was a first-class loser, and Marsh was buddy-buddy with him."

Then Bennett paused and regarded them both, unsure now.

"You said you were detectives?" he said, suddenly paranoid.

"Private investigators," said Vega. "Not police, but we're working with them and the Brandt family."

"Can I see some ID?" he said, his voice lower, trying to act tough.

Fucking TV, thought Cap.

Vega pulled her wallet from her jacket pocket and pressed it against his chest.

"Here," she said. "What's his name?"

"Who?" said Bennett, genuinely disoriented.

Just then Cap pictured a kid passing the ball down the line to Nell in a soccer game, how it sailed right to her cleat like she had a magnet on it. His turn.

"The first-class loser?" said Cap.

"Charlie. Charlie Bright."

Vega took a step back from Bennett, made room for Cap.

"Did you have a good reason to fire him?"

Bennett laughed. "He was never here. And when he was here he was too stoned to work half the time. Dropping boxes everywhere. One time a carton of Cokes in the glass bottles? In the summer? Ants and bees all over the dock for a month," he said, exasperated.

"That's terrible," said Cap. "He and Marsh were friends?"

"Yeah, they might have known each other before. I remember one time, they came in late, two hours late, and I laid into them a little."

Bennett pointed to himself. "I'm a pretty reasonable boss, you understand, but I can't be missing two loaders for two hours—we got all kind of stock backed up. And I was telling them they had to shape up, and they were just laughing. I said, 'Keep laughing, assholes, next time you're late you're gone.'"

"So what happened?"

"So Bright was late a couple of days, a week later, and I fired him."

"But not Marsh?"

"No, he was on time mostly, but then, like I told you, he started coming in late more and more the last couple months."

"Why didn't you fire him?"

Bennett sighed.

"Because he always called, said he had to take care of his mother. I know she's sick, and I'm the type of guy who's sensitive to that. I'm not some heartless boss."

Cap nodded. He generally didn't like the type of guys who went out of their way to tell you what type of guys they were.

"But you didn't believe it, that he was late because of his mother. You thought he was into drugs."

"A little of each, I guess. When he was here, he'd work, but if there was a minute of downtime, he'd literally nod off for that minute. Just sitting on the dock, leaning on a box." Bennett paused. "I can't believe he's really dead. He was a nice kid," he said, wistful.

"We're going to need a list from you, Mr. Bennett," said Cap. "Every employee who came in contact with Evan Marsh, addresses, phone numbers."

"And Charlie Bright," said Vega.

Bennett nodded.

"Of course, Mr. Caplan, Miss Vega," he said, standing straighter. "Anything I can do to help."

He handed Vega her wallet back and looked very sorry about everything.

"Thanks, Mr. Bennett," said Vega. "Mr. Caplan and I appreciate it."

Here was the message from the Bastard:

Hey, AV, can't find residence for Charles Bright in Denville, PA/

surrounding areas, just PO Box from old payroll. IRS is wrecking my shit, can't get in.

Vega played with a pair of nylon restraint cuffs in her hands, shine from the streetlights passing over her like little camera flashes. Cap had pouches under his eyes; he stretched his lips out, trying not to yawn.

"My guy doesn't have anything. He's looking," said Vega.

Cap nodded, stopped at a light.

"We can call it in to Traynor and Junior. I doubt they can get something your guy can't. Where did you get those?" he said, examining the restraints in her lap.

"I got them off Junior's belt when he grabbed me."

"Of course you did," he said. "Hey, so, how did you know all that stuff about his wife?"

"I didn't," she said. "I saw the Facebook page—it's all about fitness, but all the likes are from guys. I just figured Hollows was insecure enough about it that it must bother him. Just a guess."

Cap's phone buzzed and he glanced at it. He smiled so faintly Vega couldn't tell if it was from something he was reading right now or something he was remembering that was vaguely pleasant.

"My daughter," he said, shaking the phone. "Telling me to eat something."

Vega made herself smile politely.

"Hey, are you hungry?" Cap said.

"What?"

"Hungry, you know, food?"

"Not really."

"Yeah, I could've seen that coming," he said. "I'm pretty starving, and my daughter made some dinner. So look, why don't we go to my place—we're a few blocks away, have some food. We can look over the files from Traynor and wait for your guy. Go from there?"

Something about the way he asked made her embarrassed. She couldn't remember the last time she was embarrassed. Junior high school, maybe. She'd refused to wear a bra. Boys stared at her breasts. She looked out her window.

"Unless you're one of these gluten-free, dairy-free people? Or a pescatarian?" he said. "You are from California. Don't you all eat locally farmed kelp and stuff like that? Mashed yeast?"

"Mashed yeast?" she said, turning to him, confused. "No, I eat anything. I don't eat much but I eat anything." Then she looked out the window again and repeated, quietly, "Anything."

"Then we're good," he said.

He smiled a little, like he had a secret, and took the corners quick.

It felt like a first date. Vega had never been on a first date. She could not remember sleeping with someone she hadn't been in a fistfight with first.

This wasn't a date, she said to herself. This was a pause.

Cap's house looked like one of those houses in a miniature Christmas village, lit from the inside with yellow light; Vega almost expected to see artificial snow sprayed on the windows, smoke puffing from the metal flue on the roof.

Cap pulled into the driveway, and Vega stepped out into the air. It was dark and cold, and she breathed in fast and held it.

"Come on, you can't back out now," said Cap from the front steps, teasing.

Vega shook her head and followed him inside. The house was warm and full of food smells. Garlic and onions and oil.

"I'm home," called Cap. "And I have a special guest star."

Vega looked at her hands and felt like a freeloader suddenly, someone Cap just picked up off the street out of charity. Then a girl appeared from the kitchen, tall and athletic looking with a thoughtful expression. Here was Nell, Vega thought, the owner of the sneakers by the door and the copy of *Othello*. When the girl's eyes landed on Vega she looked nicely surprised.

"Hello," she said.

"Nell, Alice Vega," said Cap.

"Nice to meet you," said Nell, coming forward to shake her hand.

"Hi," said Vega.

It was a firm handshake for a young girl. Self-assured. When she let go, she backed up and examined Cap's face.

"Are you swollen?"

"Yeah," Cap said, touching his chin. "I got in a tussle."

"What kind of tussle? Who hit you?" she said, calm.

"Brad Ralz."

"Brad Ralz hit you? Why would he do that?"

"There's a story," said Cap. "Let's eat and we'll tell you all about it."

"Well, okay then," she said. Then, confessional: "I made too much food."

"Great," said Cap. "You ate, didn't you?"

"Not yet."

Cap shrugged at her, incredulous.

"It's after nine," he said.

"I had an apple after practice and I've been studying." Then she looked at Vega. "My dad has a tendency to worry. Have you noticed this, Miss Vega?"

"I have."

"He forgets I'm not seven," she said.

"There needs to be at least one person in the household who maintains healthy eating and sleeping habits," said Cap, removing his jacket and dropping it on the couch. "It was specified on the census."

Nell sighed and said, "Whatever." Then she went back to the kitchen.

"What?" said Cap, holding his hands out. He looked at Vega like, Can you believe this kid?

She knew right then he was a dorky dad, like one on TV. Here in this cartoonishly inviting house with a smart, witty teenage daughter. And she, Vega, was here with them.

She smiled, and it was real.

Nell was impossibly good with people, Cap thought, as he watched her pile whole wheat spaghetti onto Vega's plate with tongs. It was like she was the perfect mix of him and Jules: She had Jules's intensity and sincerity that came from the education background; the look on her face said I am listening to everything you're saying and taking it very seriously. This combined with Cap's easy smile and ability to make a stranger comfortable and therefore likely to tell him secrets.

But there was no calculation in Nell's demeanor; she asked Vega polite questions and passed her bread and butter, refilled her club soda, apologized for the lack of lemons. Vega said more words in ten minutes than she'd done in two days. And there was something so surprising and soothing about it, listening to them talk, watching Vega actually smile, one tooth overlapping the other like the one in front was trying to hug the one in back.

Somehow Nell made it all sound natural and noninvasive: What's the origin of the name Vega? Are you married? Have you always lived in California? Do you have family there? What's it like living there? And Vega's answers, similarly, were direct, but she seemed not at all uncomfortable responding between small bites of pasta: It's Mexican—you can call me Alice; No; Yes; My father and my brother and his family live about ninety minutes away; it's warm most of the time.

Vega pulled out her phone and looked for something on it, then handed it to Nell.

"This is my backyard. That's my palm tree."

Nell's eyes got huge.

"Oh my God. Dad, did you see this? She has a palm tree in her backyard."

Nell stretched across the table to give Cap the phone. Cap saw the picture, a thick, short palm tree that reminded him of an ear of eaten corn. The sky was a ridiculous Windex blue behind it. No clouds, just power lines. It looked like a set from a science fiction movie.

"Wow," said Cap. "You should not look in our backyard."

"Yeah, it's a little overgrown. We don't do a lot of landscaping," said Nell.

"The palm tree was there when I moved in," said Vega. "I don't have to water it or anything."

Cap smiled and couldn't look at her for a second, something about how she was trying to not make Nell feel bad, fusing a connection through shitty backyards. It made him feel shy.

"So," said Nell, looking at the clock on the coffeemaker. "I have to go up in ten minutes to finish Civ. You want to update me on the case and tell me about your jaw?"

Cap glanced at Vega, who nodded. Be my guest.

"I'll give it to you in five."

Cap gave her the highlights, as he'd been doing since she'd been about ten or eleven. Back then he left out the worst details: the ones that involved abuse of children, or anything particularly bloody, but now she could take it. She listened intently and crinkled up her face at certain points, covered her mouth in shock when Cap told her about Evan Marsh.

"That's awful—he was shot in the head?"

"Looked like it."

"This all happened today?"

Cap nodded. Nell thought for a moment.

"So why did Ralz punch you in the face?"

"Getting to it."

Cap described the fight; Nell looked back and forth between him and Vega, dark eyebrows arched.

"So you basically taunted him into attacking you?" she said to Vega.

"Basically, yeah," said Vega.

"This is, like, a lot of drama, you guys."

"Serious drama," said Cap.

"So that kid they had in custody had nothing to do with it?" she said.

Cap shook his head.

"And you think Marsh was involved?"

"Would be a heck of a coincidence if he wasn't," said Cap.

"So what's the link?"

Cap leaned back in his chair and stretched his arms up, swallowed a yawn.

"That's why me and Vega are here, Bug."

"Can I see the paperwork?" she said, getting her determined look.

"Finish your Civ and then I'll show you what we have."

"Oh, fine," she said, standing, sweeping up her plate and glass. She leaned against the sink. "I can't believe you saw a dead person today."

"I know," said Cap, quiet.

"Let me know before you leave, okay?" said Nell. "Excuse me for eating and running, Alice."

Vega nodded and said, "Thank you for dinner. It's really good."

"The next time you come, maybe my dad will make shrimp tacos. It's his thing."

Vega looked at Cap.

"It's my thing," he admitted.

"I'm sure it is," said Vega.

Nell didn't linger. She bounded up the stairs like a deer and shut the door of her room. Cap looked up, heard the floor creak, and traced her steps. Bed, earbuds in, over to the desk where she sat in her wheeled chair and rolled gently back and forth while she read.

Cap and Vega were quiet, pushing food around on their plates. Cap sipped his beer and became instantly self-conscious that he was drinking it instead of club soda.

"You tell her about your cases," Vega finally said.

"Yeah, I do."

"She's the reason, right, why you changed your mind about me? Working with me?"

Cap smiled. "Yeah. Usually I don't know what I think about something until I tell my daughter about it."

His phone buzzed on the table and he looked.

A text from Nell: "She's not a guy, Dad. Call her Alice."

"If I hadn't met her, I might not believe that," said Vega.

Cap thought hard about the acronym for Mind Your Own Business, tried to type "MYOB."

"But if I had a kid like her, I'd probably do the same," Vega continued.

He hit Send, then realized he had hit the "V" instead of the "B," and his phone had autocorrected to "Myocardial."

The text came back from Nell in a second: "Are you trying to say myob? Lol Dad."

"She's a piece of work," said Cap, placing the phone on the table. Then he chuckled, almost just to himself. "That's something my father says. Let's put it this way: I think she's pretty extraordinary for a person, not even just for a kid. But as a parent you can't go around saying stuff like that. I mean, you can, but you'd be one of those parents you meet at Back-to-School Night who can't stop talking about how little Timmy doesn't play any video games and just loves practicing the violin all the time."

Then Vega laughed. Actually laughed. Cap saw the teeth again and felt out of breath. He realized he had forgotten what it felt like to make a woman laugh. It was almost better than making them come. With Jules, even when their marriage was in the mud, he could still make her laugh unexpectedly, and boy would she punch the brakes as soon as she realized it. The look on her face could sear you like a steak—No way you are making me laugh, motherfucker.

Stranger still, laughing made most women, including Jules, look younger, the spontaneity of it trimming the years off, letting you see the little girl on a merry-go-round, the sixth grader at the roller rink. But with Vega, she looked older in some appealing way, the skin around her eyes and lips falling into easy creases. It made Cap think, This is what she will look like at forty, fifty, sixty with spotty skin and filmy pupils, spine curved over like a fishing pole. But then you will make her laugh and all the light will pour right out of her just like it did that first time at your kitchen table.

"You ever think about it?" he said, feeling like he could ask her anything just then.

"What?"

"Kids?"

Out loud the word was toxic. Vega looked at her plate and didn't respond right away.

"I'm sorry," said Cap. "Way too personal, right?"

"No," she said plainly. "Not too personal. Kids are . . ." She paused but only for a moment. "Not for me."

Vega washed her hands in Cap's bathroom. She looked at herself in the mirror and thought about death. Which was what she usually did when she looked in strange mirrors in strange bathrooms. It made her think of hospitals and morgues, how a body could look peaceful but only in the way a piece of luggage looked peaceful—it was simply an item that didn't move.

However, as Vega had seen with her mother's body, the opposite could be true. A body could be animated in one last shock, neck twisted, limbs shriveled. Why did you have to look at her face? thought Vega now, in Cap's bathroom. Why did you have to see the teeth comically large for her head like those vampire choppers you got from quarter machines?

Is this you?

Cap loaded the dishwasher, cleaned out the soft spaghetti bits from the drain in the sink, opened another beer. He could still think clearly after three beers. Some nights he'd get to the end of the six-pack without thinking about it and wouldn't feel any different, would still possess his powers of critical reasoning, was just able to sleep easier and more immediately. But he could still work. If the call came in with Charlie Bright's address, he'd drink a pot of coffee with a lot of milk and sugar and be on the way.

He squeezed the dishwashing goo into the dispenser, and the bottle made a retching sound. He glanced toward the hallway, the bathroom door, to see if Vega was emerging. He did not want her to think that *he* had made the retching sound, or worse, that the sound had been him passing gas.

Not after he'd seen the picture of the palm tree in her backyard, after she'd allowed herself to be charmed by Nell and the three of them had sat around a table in a family-like formation. There was something, wasn't there, some delicate strand between them, hovering like a jelly-fish arm. Couldn't there be more, when this was all over, when they found those girls, however they were going to find them? Couldn't he take her to dinner and couldn't she possibly have some wine and fix her focus on him, walk around the table and lean down to tell him some-thing, press her face against his and breathe in his ear so he could smell the salt in her hair?

His dick woke up a little, and he knocked his fist against his fore-head and sat at the table.

"Pull it together," he said aloud. Let's not have an erection like a twelve-year-old boy during his first slow dance.

He opened the file on Ashley Cahill and his eyes fell on scattered words: blond, blue, 44 inches, 45 lbs., Holling Pool, mother bartender, father worked at a sporting goods store, missing, missing, missing.

Then Vega came back. She nodded at him and sat back down at the table.

"Everything's clean," she said.

"Yeah . . . dishwasher," he said. "You want anything else to drink?"

She shook her head and opened the file on Sydney McKenna. Cap looked back down at the Cahill police report. No one saw anything. She'd been at the pool with a group of kids, and one of their moms said one minute she was playing Marco Polo with the rest of them, and the next minute she wasn't. Cap picked up the 5x8 matte school portrait. Nell didn't have them done anymore, but Cap remembered them from grade school, her image in varying sizes—big, medium, a sheet of wal-lets. Rows and rows of Nells.

The girl, Ashley, was cute in the way all six-year-olds were cute. Large eyes, unblemished skin. There was, in fact, nothing extraordi-nary about her. Except, Cap thought, to her parents.

Vega closed the folder on Sydney McKenna and placed her hands on top of it. She looked intently at Cap, and he saw something strange about her eyes; they were clear and wet but not like she'd been crying. It was like she'd dunked only her face in a pool.

"I have to tell you something," she said.

"Okay."

She took a quick breath in and looked at the folder under her hands.

"My mother died when I was twenty. She had lymphoma," she said. They both waited. "Then my friend Perry, the guy who was kind of my mentor in fugitive recovery, a skip stabbed him in the kidney and he died walking out to his car. On the lawn."

"I'm sorry," said Cap. He was unsure about a lot of things.

She continued: "Then I started working freelance. I got lucky right away with Ethan Moreno." She paused, then said, "The biggest mistake people make is that they think they're special. They're not."

She nodded, more to herself than to Cap, and seemed not to know what to do with her hands. She tapped her fingertips together like there were castanets on them. Cap didn't like it, didn't like her sad and some-what confused. Could I hug her? he thought. Will she slam her forearm into my face if I hug her and kiss the crease between her eyebrows?

He didn't have a chance. She put her hands flat on the folder again and said, "Is there a gun shop open this late?"

Quiet again in Cap's car. Vega felt strange, unused to a stomach full of food. Especially pasta, all that wheat swelling up like a pile of wet shoe-laces. For a few years now Vega had a neutral attitude about eating, bor-dering on animosity, frustration at the braking of her body's systems when she was hungry. Watching people eat in restaurants, she thought it seemed like such a waste—Do you think you have this kind of time? she wanted to say to them. Hours and hours sitting over bread and butter and Big Macs. Perry had Diet Cokes and grilled cheese sandwiches with bacon three times a day every day she knew him, so he wouldn't spend any seconds considering the options. So Vega did that too—bananas, power bars, milk, juice. Some vitamins, some fat, some protein. Every day.

"You're gonna like this," said Cap.

He parked on a dark street, and they got out, walked to a two-floor brick house, picture window on the ground floor with a paper sign, a certificate—SMOKEY'S GUN SHOP. Below that, in big black letters: GLOCK.

Then a woman came through a door to the right of the window with a ring of keys. She was round and short, with a boy's haircut, the skin on her nose and cheeks red and speckled. When she saw Cap her face opened up, the keyhole mouth grew into a smile.

"Mister Caplan, ain't seen you much anymore," she said.

"Hey, Jean," said Cap.

They hugged. Vega stood back.

"This is my colleague, Alice Vega. She'd like to look at some firearms. This is Jean Radnor. This is her shop."

"Hiya, Alice."

Vega shook hands with her, watched her unlock a series of locks on the glass door.

"Come on in, then."

They followed her in as she flipped the light switches, fluorescents flickering on in succession. Handguns with orange tags in glass cases like jewelry. Shotguns and rifles on the wall racks.

"What you been doing, Cap? How's your daughter?" said Jean, pressing a code into an alarm box.

"She's well. Sixteen years old."

"You gotta be kidding me," said Jean, genuine surprise in her voice, almost to the point of being offended. "That makes us what, a hundred goddamn years old or what."

"Something like that. How're your sons?"

They kept talking about kids and houses and births and deaths. Vega looked at the semiauto rifles on the wall, arranged by popularity as far as she could tell: Bushmasters, S&Ws, Sporticals, a Colt at the end of the row.

"Jason and his wife had twins, I tell you that?" said Jean. "Sweet kids, but ugly. Don't know how they got that way either. Jason and Melanie are attractive; it's some kind of mystery."

"Could I see your Colt?" said Vega.

Jean and Cap turned to her, both seeming surprised to hear her speak.

"You got it, hon," said Jean, going behind the counter. "You know I can't sell it to you, right? Have to wait for regular store hours."

"That's fine," said Vega. "I just want to try it out."

Jean found a key on her ring and unlocked the case, lifted the rifle and handed it to Vega over the counter, continuing her conversation with Cap.

"Names are Boyd and Blaine. I said, 'Isn't Blaine a girl's name?' Didn't go over so well."

One hand on the grip and the other on the underside of the barrel, Vega held the rifle up, pressed her cheek against the stock. She could smell the alloy in the back of her throat, the tinny burn of it. The stock pushed against her shoulder; something wasn't right. A Goldilocks feeling.

"How long is it?" Vega said to Jean.

Jean thought.

"Thirty-two I think, with the stock retracted. Something wrong?"

"Seems long to me."

Jean pulled out a lip balm stick and unscrewed the top, rubbed it across her lips, the color of rare meat.

"Well, what're you comparing it to, hon?"

Vega glanced at Cap and could see him putting something together; she knew the look now, his eyes got a little dreamy, and his head bobbed slightly from side to side, like he was weighing two things. Like they were hanging on his ears.

"An M4," said Cap. Then he looked at Vega. "Right?"

She relaxed the grip, held it to her side. Cap was grinning like he had won a poker hand.

"Right," she said.

"Oh, you're military?" said Jean. "My nephew's in the marines."

"I only went through basic," said Vega.

At the mention of the word she felt the heat, dirt from the ground in her mouth, triceps and deltoids humming, mashed like lemon pulp.

And the hunger that started in her bones instead of her stomach, for any kind of calories—meatloaf between bread dipped in whole milk to get it down quicker and as much coffee as she could swallow, throat already burned from breakfast.

"Army," said Cap, pointing at her.

"Right."

He smiled, pleased with himself. Almost made Vega smile too.

"Mind if I strip her?" said Vega.

Jean shrugged one shoulder.

"Help yourself. It's brand-new, though; you're not gonna find any deposits."

"Sure. I just want to field-strip it," Vega said.

Jean's eyebrows arched up and she smiled peacefully, knowingly, reminding Vega of yoga teachers, the way at the end they would say, "The light in me bows to the light in you," or some kind of bullshit.

"It relaxes you, right? Me too," Jean said. "I'll get you an Allen wrench."

"That's okay," said Vega, pulling back the charging handle.

She took one of the pins from her hair.

"Ha!" shouted Jean. "She's prepared. You got a good one here, Cap."

Vega slid the front pivot pin to the side. The snap of the receivers coming apart had a soporific effect on her; finally she could rest a second.

At the inn, Vega went through the motions of someone getting ready for bed: took a shower, brushed her teeth, rubbed some of the complimentary gardenia-smelling lotion into her hands and on her legs. She lay down on the bed, closed her eyes, and did not sleep, ping-ponging questions back and forth in her head. Soon it was five or six, blue light out the window as the sun rose somewhere close. Vega got off the bed and onto the floor on all fours. Then into down dog, where she didn't linger, walking her feet up to her hands until they met. She held her breath, tensed her abs, and brought her legs up above, then stretched them out. Widened the fingers. Breathed.

Then her mother in the hospital, the last time, Vega leaned down to kiss her forehead, and her mother grabbed her head suddenly and tried to pull her down, but she was not strong at that point. Vega was startled and a little terrified because she'd thought her mother was asleep. Her mother pushed her lips out like Vega was a drink she was trying to reach, and kissed the ridge between Vega's nose and cheek. Then she went back to dying.

Vega came down from the handstand and sat on the floor with her knees bent and her head between them. She had been at her father's house when she heard the news. She'd always thought she would just know, that there was a cosmic alarm clock built in her chest linking her to her mother, but no. Her mother had died, and Vega had no idea.

And the Brandt girls were not even blood. These things weren't real, these connections between family members, husband to wife, parent to child. This psychic trash of people saying, "I knew when so-and-so died because I felt it in my soul or my heart or my pockets." You didn't, thought Vega, you had no idea. Those girls could have been in the ground two hours after they disappeared, and all of us have been running like hell in our mouse maze since then, tapping our bells and flags, desperate for pellets.

11

THE NEXT MORNING THEY ARRIVED AT CHARLIE BRIGHT'S MOTH-
er's house early. A garbage truck rambled down the street. Cap pressed
the doorbell, a grimy little button set in a rusty diamond.

"Do you want to talk about goals?" he said.

Vega's right shoulder jerked, the suggestion of a shrug.

"No change," she said. "Right?"

"You're asking me?" said Cap.

"Yes," said Vega.

Cap almost believed her.

Then a dog started barking. Low bark, big dog, he thought. He could
hear it sniffing at the door.

He pulled the screen door open and knocked, and the dog continued to alternately bark and sniff. He turned back to Vega.

"Your guy sure she's here?"

"Yes."

Cap kept knocking, driving a stick in an anthill and shaking it
around. Up and out, everyone.

Then footsteps, and a voice shouted either at Cap or the dog or both,
"That's enough! That's enough!"

The door opened, and there was a slice of a woman, fat, loose gray
curls on top of her head like Easter basket grass, and the dog, medium-
sized, pushed his black-olive nose on either side of the woman's legs.

"Yeah?" she said.

"Mrs. Lanawicz?" said Cap.

"Who's askin'?"

Great start, lady, thought Cap.

"My name is Max Caplan; this is Alice Vega. We're private investigators working with the Denville Police."

Mrs. Lanawicz remained unmoved. She eyed them both.

"I'm all paid up on tickets," she said.

"Ma'am, we're hoping you might help us locate your son, Charles Bright."

A little flare in the dull eyes at the name.

"He ain't here," she said quickly.

"Do you have any idea where he might be?"

"He lives up Camden. I don't know; I ain't talked to him in six months."

It was like she had rehearsed a few different things but forgot she was supposed to pick only one story.

"It's very important we find him," said Cap. "It's about the Brandt girls."

Mrs. Lanawicz puckered up her mouth.

"He's got nothing to do with anything like that," she said.

"I'm sure he doesn't," said Cap. "We're looking for someone he used to work with at the Giant, hoping he can give us a lead."

Mrs. Lanawicz stepped back, a little disarmed.

"Like I said," she said, quieter now, secretly sheepish. "He ain't here."

"Do you have a phone number where we might reach him?" said Cap.

From the side Cap saw Vega step back, off the walkway, toward the street. Now where are you going, girl?

"Nah, he uses those disposable cell phones because he can't afford a plan, a monthly plan."

"Address?"

She placed her hand, thick and arthritic, on the doorframe.

"He's living with my niece, I think. It's, uh, 2040 Filbert in Camden."

Cap watched her eyes wander to where Vega was. He didn't turn around.

"2040 Filbert in Camden," he repeated. "That a house or an apartment?"

"It's a house," she said, still watching Vega.

"Your niece have a phone number?"

"Yeah, I have it, I think some—" she said, and then she stopped, mid-thought and mid-word, and she made her mouth into a little O and her eyes shot open wide.

"What?" she said, pointing past Cap.

Vega charged by him and shoved the door open, Mrs. Lanawicz falling backward but managing to steady herself against a table an eighth her size. The dog looked like a large hamster, a shaved square patch on its side, and continued to bark.

"What the hell are you doing?! You can't do this," Mrs. Lanawicz shouted, bringing her claw hands to her head.

"He's upstairs," Vega said to Cap, heading for the stairs.

"Vega, wait, goddammit," Cap said to her.

Vega stopped at the bottom and shot him a glare.

"This ain't right! This ain't right!" said Mrs. Lanawicz, waving her arms. "You people think you can do whatever you want."

Cap looked around, faded floral-patterned couches facing each other, green carpet flipping up at the corners, narrow staircase to the right.

Mrs. Lanawicz struggled to walk, her legs bowed, back bent at the base. She made her way toward Vega, shouting various threats: "You can't come into my property. I have a lawyer. This is a home invasion situation. . . ."

"Mrs. Lanawicz," Cap said loudly. "Shut up for a second."

She shut up and blinked, and sort of a whirring sound came from her throat, reminded Cap of an eggbeater.

"We're not going to hurt you or your son. We're not going to arrest either of you. But if we leave and find out you were holding back information or harboring your son here, then there will be a good deal of trouble landing in your lap."

Then she started to cry and let out a plaintive moan. Sometimes it really didn't take too much.

"He's sick; he hurt his back. Please don't hurt him," she said to Cap.

Vega looked at Cap once more and then took the stairs, two at a time.

Cap turned to follow, and Mrs. Lanawicz grabbed his sleeve.

"He hurt his back working construction two years ago," she whispered, spitting on him a little bit.

"I understand that," said Cap, unlatching her.

He followed and Mrs. Lanawicz started to climb slowly behind him. The dog ran in a little circle at the bottom, barking and wiggling.

On the second floor, Vega glanced at the closed doors and approached the one with Eagles and Flyers stickers lining the border.

"Can you wait a minute?" said Cap in a hushed voice.

"He's right in here," she said, finger touching the door.

"How do you know?"

"Cigarette butts all on the right side of the lawn, tamp marks on the sill. This sill."

Mrs. Lanawicz kept coming, bellowing.

"He's sleeping right now! He needs his sleep!"

Cap whispered, "You don't have to break every fucking door down, Vega."

This seemed to surprise her.

"Not every door, Caplan," she said, almost sweetly. "Just this one."

She pushed open the door, slammed it against the back wall.

The room was dark and humid, dirty curtains drawn over the single window. Posters of wrestlers, male and female, covered the walls. Cap doubted the décor had changed since Charlie Bright had been in junior high. There was a figure in a twin bed stirring under a blanket, without urgency.

"Charlie!" yelled Mrs. Lanawicz, almost at the top of the stairs. "They're police, Charlie!"

This got his attention. Charlie Bright sat up on his elbows, long hair and a raggedy beard and small eyes lolling around.

Cap held his hand out to Vega. Stand back for one second, he said to her in his head. To his relief, she did.

"Charles Bright?" said Cap.

"Yeah?"

"We need to ask you some questions about a former co-worker of yours, Evan Marsh."

Bright coughed and spit into a mug on the floor next to his bed.

"Don't know him," he said.

Cap sighed.

"Charlie, they wanna ask you questions!" yelled Charlie's mother from the hallway.

"I worked at the Giant six months ago," said Bright. "I'm out on disability."

"What's the injury?" said Cap.

"Back. Got a pinched nerve between L4 and L5."

"I would imagine you're medicated for that," said Cap.

Bright sucked on his two front teeth.

"Got legal prescriptions from doctors."

"He's got a pinched nerve," said Mrs. Lanawicz, breathing heavy in the doorway. "Between L5 and L6."

"I told them!" yelled Bright. "They don't want to listen."

"So just to clarify," said Cap. "You were employed by the Giant during roughly the same time frame as Evan Marsh, but you never met him or associated with him in either a personal or professional context?"

"Uh," said Bright. "Yeah, that's right."

Then he yawned.

You dumb motherfucker, Cap thought. He looked at Vega and said, "I'll get Mama."

Vega's eyes lit up, Roman candle style, and then she charged the bed. Bright was so surprised he pulled the blanket up to his face, trying to hide. Vega gripped the sheet beneath him and yanked. Bright shouted and rolled out of the bed, landing hard on the floor.

"No! My boy!" screamed Mrs. Lanawicz, lurching forward.

Cap held his arm in front of her, not forcefully.

Meanwhile Bright moaned, and Vega stood above him and shoved her boot into his neck. Bright coughed and grabbed her ankle. He tried to build some rocking momentum with his legs, lifting them up and down, but he was overweight and doped and didn't have the sharpest reflexes, it turned out.

"What are you—cops?" cried Mrs. Lanawicz.

"Evan Marsh," said Vega, crouching down. "We know you knew him."

"I don't know where he is," said Bright.

"He's nowhere," said Vega. "He was shot in the fucking face."

Bright stopped squirming.

"Marsh is dead?" he said.

"You ain't cops!" announced Mrs. Lanawicz, departing from the doorway. "I'm calling the cops!"

"That's right, Charlie," said Cap. "He knew something about the Brandt girls and someone didn't want him to talk. So if you know something about the Brandt girls, someone might not want you to talk either. You following this?"

Bright's face was red, veins squiggling down his temples.

"He came to me."

"Who did?" said Cap.

"Marsh."

Cap nodded at Vega, and she removed her foot from Bright's neck. Bright sat up and coughed, rubbed his Adam's apple.

"He offered me money. Fifty K to move two girls."

He stopped talking and looked up at them, embarrassed.

"I didn't do it," he said, scissoring his arms in front of him like an umpire. Safe. "I didn't take it. I didn't want to get involved in all that. Come on."

"He flat out asked you?" said Cap.

"We were smoking after work one day, and he said it all off the cuff, that he's got a way for me to make fifty K, and all I gotta do is drive the car."

"And you weren't interested in that at all?"

"No, man. You can clean this place out; you're not gonna find fifty K."

"Where did Marsh get that kind of money?"

"I don't know," said Bright. "I swear, I don't know who was laying it out."

"Do you have any idea who might be interested in a deal like that?"

Bright struggled to sit up, hunched over his knees.

"Shit, man, this is fuckin' D-Ville," he said, laughing, sad in a way. "Take your fuckin' pick."

Traynor had a list.

They'd put Bright in a small room with the cop named Harrison, and out had come a list. Now Vega was in Traynor's office with Cap, Harrison, and the Fed. She stood in the corner while the men talked.

"Revs Cleary, John McKie, Harland DeMarco, Jason Boromir, goes by Bent. You remember these guys?" Traynor said to Cap.

"Little bit," said Cap.

"They've all been in and out two, three times for possession, but nothing sticks. If they're dealing, they clean out before we get to it."

"We're just going on Mr. Bright's opinion at this point?" said the Fed.

"That's correct," said Traynor, looking up from his notes. "You're saying this might not be the best use of our time?"

The Fed didn't move. "I'm saying that, yes."

It was maybe the most civilized exchange Vega had ever heard. It was like they were discussing what color to paint the living room.

Then she said: "It's Bright's opinion, but these are Evan Marsh's known associates, right?"

The men turned to her.

"Right," said Traynor.

"And they're dealers or fences or whatever?"

"Right. Users at the least."

"So you'd agree that's a demographic likely to traffic in large sums of money illegally obtained?"

"Ma'am," said the Fed. "I have no doubt these gentlemen are likely candidates—what we're looking at is men and the time it will take to chase all of them down. We're looking at the most likely, and how do we discern that in the quickest amount of time possible."

She stretched her fingers at her sides, thought, Well, we stop sitting around fucking chitchatting about it for one motherfucking thing. Then she glanced at Cap. He was staring at her intently, and then he tilted his chin downward, nodding. She was confused by the gesture at first, couldn't identify his expression.

It was conviction, that thing underneath. I am calm because I believe in you. I am right here.

"So ten minutes, okay?" she said, her mouth dry. "You have something on them, right—pictures, priors?"

"Yeah," said Traynor.

"Let me and Caplan look at them for ten minutes, that's it, match up the names to Maryann Marsh's list. See if anything jumps?"

She said it like a question out of respect. I am not pissing on your investigation, Chief. I will not make trouble, Special Agent. I will stay out of your way and keep being right, and you all can come around any time you want.

—

In the blue room Ralz laid out photos and files. The faces were all familiar to Cap—he wasn't sure if that was because he knew them personally or if they just looked like a hundred other drug dealers he'd shoved into the back of his car when he was a cop. Same dim stares, same dumbass tribal tattoos, same line of bullshit too—I wasn't there, been outta town since Tuesday. Where's your warrant, asshole? And then the ones who wanted to get to him, threats spit through their hillbilly teeth: You got kids, officer, I'll find 'em. Sure hope you have a daughter.

"So," said Junior, impatient. "What's the course here, Cap?"

Cap looked at the three of them—Hollows, Ralz, and Vega—and realized they were all waiting for him, and also that it might be a nice thing to stop and take a little dip in the moment, but there was no time.

"We're taking ten minutes, seeing if anything jumps for anyone. We're looking for a type desperate enough to get past dealing or fencing or possession into kidnapping."

"Okay," said Junior, picking up a mugshot. Shaggy red-eyed stoner. "Revs Cleary, last time in was last year for speeding; we found marijuana in the car but just under thirty grams. He was in County for a month and released."

Cap flipped through the file and handed it to Vega.

"Jason 'Bent' Boromir. Busted for possession of oxy, but the cognitively impaired prosecution couldn't manage to prove that he had intent to sell. Apparently he had a couple thousand pills and ten boxes of commercial food service sandwich bags for his own personal use. Did just one year at Allenwood."

Cap and Vega stared down at the photo—shaved head, teardrop tattoos. Cap handed her the paperwork.

"Harland DeMarco," said Junior.

"I know this guy," said Cap, remembering.

He held the picture in his hand. DeMarco was older than the rest, with white hair and tinted glasses, looked like he should have been at the other end of a craps table.

"I thought Forman got him," said Cap.

"Forman did get him," said Junior. "On back taxes. DeMarco lived in a new development, kept his stash in the damn wine cellar. The warrant said we could search the immediate premises, and his lawyer, some ringer from New York, got the jury to agree that the wine cellar didn't count as immediate. We could have him on a felony. Instead we get back taxes."

"Fuck me," said Cap.

"Classic Denville clusterfuck," said Junior.

Cap passed the file to Vega, said, "I can't see him getting into kidnapping kids."

"Why the hell not?" said Junior. "He's got his hands in everything else from here to Harrisburg, why not kidnapping?"

"Junior," said Cap. "Likelihood. Odds."

Junior pawed at the ground with his foot.

"All right," he said. "Then I say Bent could do it—he smokes a little meth himself; he's pretty shithouse crazy. Revs, no—if we're placing odds, no."

"Why not?" said Cap.

"He's a stoner, he has family money, and the only reason he deals is because he got kicked out of private school. I don't like him for this."

"John McKie," said Vega, sliding a folder toward Cap.

She held on to the picture.

"Sure, McKie could do it," said Junior. "Did a little time for assault and possession. And sexual assault, I think."

"But not of a minor," Cap said, reading.

"So what? We're just looking for kidnapping, not abuse, right?"

"Right."

"Caplan," said Vega.

They all turned to her. She stared at John McKie's photo, her eyes covering the page quickly, manically.

"Yeah?" said Cap.

"Look familiar?" she said, flipping the photo around.

He saw and thought, Goddamn yes it did, it really truly did.

It made Alyssa Moser smile, the mugshot.

"Yeah, I see it, sure," she said. "And he's having a good day, but still, you shouldn't, you know, get your hopes up."

"We understand," said Cap. "We just want to see if this photo sparks anything at all in your uncle's memory. We're comfortable with long shots, Miss Moser."

Alyssa shook out her shoulders and said, "Okay, then, let me go make sure he's awake."

She left them, went down a hall, into another hall; then Vega heard her speaking softly. She looked at a glass case full of plates and thin-stemmed glasses.

"You realize—" Cap started.

Vega held up her hand to him, said, "I realize."

"You're not even going to let me finish?"

"I'm not," said Vega. "I realize."

"Well, okay," said Cap. "Miss Vega realizes."

She started to smile, and Alyssa Moser returned.

"You can come in," she said.

They followed her down the hall, into a room where an old man lay, propped up by pillows, his head thin and spotted.

"Uncle Roy, these are the folks I told you about. They're trying to find those girls," said Alyssa, her voice amplified.

Roy Eldridge stretched his neck, his head reaching toward them.

"Hello," he said with some effort.

"Hi, Mr. Eldridge," said Cap. "We'd like to show you some pictures, and if anyone looks familiar to you from last Saturday at Ridgewood Mall, or if you remember anything at all from that day, we're hoping you could let us know. Does that sound all right?"

Eldridge wet his lips with his tongue, and Alyssa held a glass of water underneath him. His mouth found the straw, and he drank.

"Sure," he said. "Shame . . . shame about those girls."

"Yes, sir," said Cap. "Now first, could you tell me, are these the girls you saw when you were leaving the mall last Saturday?"

Cap brought the school photos of Kylie and Bailey to Eldridge.

"Wait!" said Alyssa. "Wait, wait, wait," she muttered.

She went to the small table next to the bed, opened a drawer and pulled out a glasses case and a pair of large-rimmed black bifocals.

"Here," she said, placing them on Eldridge's head. They made him look like he was wearing a costume—a librarian for Halloween.

"Were those the girls you saw in the car?" said Cap.

Eldridge inspected the picture, like he was looking at a germ under a microscope.

"I'll tell you, sir, I think so, but you understand my eyes aren't what they used to be."

"That's fine," said Cap, reassuring. "That's not a problem. Now I'm going to show you another picture and if you could, please tell us if this person looks familiar to you."

Cap pulled the mugshot of John McKie from his folder and held it up to Eldridge.

"Yeah," said Eldridge, happy. "Now, that looks like Harry. Doesn't it look like Harry?"

"Sure does, Uncle Roy," said Alyssa.

"Except Harry's never in a bad mood," said Eldridge. "He's a glass half full."

"Mr. Eldridge," said Cap, gentle, quiet. "Did you see this man with those girls in the car when you left the mall last Saturday?"

"Well, sure I did," said Eldridge. "He was driving. I tried a get his attention, but Harry's a good driver; he's looking straight ahead."

Vega glanced at Alyssa, who looked back at her, her face a mixed grill of sad and worried.

Then Eldridge placed a giant hand on the expanse of his forehead, his fingers crooked at the knuckles.

"Aw, hell, Lyssie," he said. "Harry's dead, isn't he?"

"Yeah, Uncle Roy," said Alyssa, crying a little bit. "Over in Vietnam."

"This fellow, he only wears his hair the same way," Eldridge said to Cap.

"I think so, Mr. Eldridge."

Eldridge's lips curled in and milky tears rolled down his face.

"'Cause Harry's dead. Long dead."

"Yes, sir," said Cap, so soft and sweet it made Vega want to lie down and go to sleep. "Do you remember anything else about this man who looked like Harry, or the little girls, or the car?"

Eldridge pinched his nose with his thumbs.

"I don't think so," he said. "Car was tannish, I think. Had a bumper sticker," said Eldridge. "Giants, New York Giants." Eldridge laughed. "Harry never woulda had that, would he, Lyssie? He was a true blue Eagles fan."

It made Cap smile, the way Eldridge said "Eagles" like "iggles."

"You bet, Uncle Roy," Alyssa said, laughing too.

"That's incredibly helpful, sir," said Cap. "I can't tell you how much we appreciate it."

"Thank you," Vega said, louder than she had planned, so even Cap turned and appeared surprised.

"We're glad to help," said Alyssa. "Isn't it so, Uncle Roy? If we could help find those missing girls?"

Eldridge did not seem glad to help. He lowered his brow, looked wistful, could have been trying to remember what he had for breakfast or how he was a paper boy in the Depression. Could be anything, Vega thought.

"Aw hell, Lyssie, looks like I peed," he said, shifting around.

"It's okay, Uncle Roy, I'll get the stuff," said Alyssa. She turned to Cap and Vega. "You folks need anything else?"

"No, thank you, this has been very valuable to us. Thank you both," said Cap.

He continued to talk to her as they left the room. Vega looked back once more at Eldridge, gazing up like he was trying to make out words on the ceiling. For a second Vega looked up there too, just in case.

Cap hung up with Traynor, stared at some boys in long T-shirts, hair falling in their eyes. They sat at a table in the food court, drinking juice from giant cups, straws squeaking in the plastic lids.

He saw Vega behind the counter at the Peking Express, showing photos to a large woman wearing a polo shirt, the manager. The woman also had papers for Vega and flapped her hands while she talked like she was swatting flies. Vega stared at the hands, and it made Cap smile because she looked like just another cop, listening to all the details a witness wanted to tell you along with their opinions and psychological diagnoses.

"Mr. Caplan?"

Cap turned around, saw a lovely tired woman with a toddler asleep in a stroller in front of her. The last time he had seen her, a couple of days ago, she had been just as lovely, only angrier.

"Hey. Hi, Mrs. Svetich," he said. "Who's this?"

"That's Cammy," she said. "He's my youngest. This is when he's the cutest."

Cap laughed and started to say the thing about little kids, little problems, but she cut him off.

"I'm glad I ran into you," she said. She was not shaking, but it looked like she was about to start. "I wanted to tell you I'm sorry for how I behaved the other day. In your office. I shouldn't have taken out my anger about my shitty marriage on you."

She said it quickly, as if she'd said it before. Cap pictured her rehearsing in the mirror. Mr. Caplan, I'm glad I ran into you.

"Please," said Cap. "You have nothing to apologize about."

"I do," she said firmly. "I tell my kids all the time: just because you're in a bad mood doesn't give you the right to take it out on the world."

"What do they say to that?"

"They don't listen to a thing I say," she said. "But you know, I figure I keep telling them this shit, and then one day they'll be twenty-five and they'll remember it."

"And where will you be then?" said Cap, not even thinking about what he was asking or why he was asking it, but if he thought about it he would know it was her, Mrs. Svetich, at exactly this point, with no filters, clogs removed from the drains, speaking plainly, and it made him want to do the same.

"When they're twenty-five?" she said, charmed by the idea. "On a beach somewhere, I don't know."

Then she laughed, embarrassed, and Cap laughed and thought how this would be a part of her divorce story years from now, how she ran into the detective a few days after he had caught her ex, and he made her laugh.

"There you go," said Cap. "I'll expect a postcard."

She laughed in a burst, and then tears filled her eyes.

"Mrs. Svetich—" Cap began.

She leaned forward and kissed him on the cheek and hugged him then, clung to him, pushed her face into his neck. Cap could feel her breasts against his chest, the moisture from her eyes and nose, her lips. Very slowly he put his arms around her and closed his eyes, did the hair-smelling thing (some kind of berries, but that could have been coming from Jamba Juice). Her arms were thin but strong like belts, stretching around his neck and pulling him close.

So much of it was unfamiliar, he had a hard time parsing it out—the smell, the skin, the closeness, the need. But all of it was good, glorious, exquisite.

Finally she stepped away. Cap let her go instantly, did not want her to think he might have enjoyed what was probably a peak moment of loneliness for her. She patted her damp cheeks and looked at him, not shy in the least.

She said, "Everything happens at the wrong time, doesn't it?"

Cap felt spun and skinned by that one.

"Yes," he said. "It does."

She turned around and looked at her kid. "He'll be awake any minute. It was nice to see you, Mr. Caplan. I hope I see you again."

Her eyes were huge and dark, and there was nothing hidden away behind them. Cap was so caught off-guard by her honesty all he could say was "Yes."

Then she left, wheeled the stroller around, shopping bags dangling from the handles. Cap watched her go, the shape of her moving under a flimsy drape of a dress that looked insubstantial for the beginning of spring. He watched her get smaller and smaller, turn a corner at the Old Navy and then disappear.

He looked at his hands, front and back, could still feel the warmth from Mrs. Svetich's body, and leaned against the table so he could breathe, stoned from the intimacy.

Vega held the mugshot of John McKie in her hands and waited for the manager to come back with his original job application, which was the only information on him that was available. She examined the people standing around, sitting, eating, shopping bags at their feet. She studied their shoes and their earrings and the way they held their spoons. Noticed the irregularities of their faces: unevenly spaced eyes, discolored skin, moles, beards.

She realized Cap had been gone for some time, and turned to find him, and there he was, across the food court, hugging a woman. "Hugging" didn't seem an accurate word to describe how they were touching each other. The woman was clinging to Cap like she was drowning, and he was the life raft, which made Vega the one on some distant shore with broke-ass binoculars.

The woman left Cap and wandered off, slowly pushing a stroller. Cap watched her and didn't move. He was a little too far away for Vega to see his face, but she took in his posture—most of it was as she had observed before: minor slump in the shoulders, feet rooted slightly farther apart than the hips, neck curved and head tilted, quizzical. But one difference now: his hands were out in front of him a few inches, like he was waiting for the woman to come right back.

Vega's phone buzzed with a text from the Bastard.

"Still looking for K. Brandt the person but found someone else looking for him too. Seems like you guys have a lot in common. Email coming with details."

Vega put the phone in her pocket and looked back at Cap. Still facing the direction of the woman but on his phone, texting the way he did with an index finger tapping out one letter at a time. Then he turned around, eyes scanning the crowd for her. She didn't wave or come forward, just waited for him to find her, and when he did he waved broadly, relieved or resigned, she couldn't tell.

12

CAP TAPPED THE NUMBER AT THE TOP OF HIS RECENTS AND SET the phone in the cup holder. There was a gulp in the air and then the ring, then a pickup: "Kendrick."

"Officer Kendrick, this is Max Caplan. Sorry I missed you."

"That's fine," said Kendrick on the phone, his voice wavering loud and quiet. "You want to know about John McKie?"

"Yes. You met with him the last time—" Cap paused.

Vega held up one finger and mouthed, "Year."

"A year ago, is that correct?" said Cap.

"Yeah, that's right. He completed his parole."

"You have any idea where he is now?"

Kendrick laughed.

"We didn't talk too much, socially. So no, I don't know where he is. Can I ask why you're looking?"

"We'd like to question him in an ongoing investigation. The Brandt girls. Can you tell us anything that might be helpful in that regard?"

"In finding him? The guy lived with some friends but not for long. Had a job at the mall, right?"

"Yeah, we just came from there."

"He had a girlfriend too—she'd been down in Riverside in Philly. Charming girl."

Cap smiled and looked over at Vega, who did not smile.

"He stayed with her for a long time. Her family was up in Wilkes-Barre. I'd try her. Even if he's not with her, she might know."

"Great, can you get us her name?"

"Yeah, give me a few minutes to go through the notes. I'll send you a text."

Cap said thanks, and Kendrick said he was happy to help and then hung up. Cap tapped the wheel with his thumbs.

"So we get the name, maybe we send it to your guy? Vega?"

He looked over. Her eyes were closed, her head leaning into the sling of the seat belt, asleep. Her hands were in her lap, fingers twitching. Cap smiled, glad she was getting rest. Also realized he worried about her getting rest. Realized he was worried about her at all. Some loose strands of her hair fell across her cheek, into her eyes, and Cap thought what was the harm in it, really, just to sweep it off her face and bring it behind her ear. I'll barely touch her, he thought.

Vega was not asleep, just shut down for a while. She pictured John McKie, and she pictured Evan Marsh, head shots and camera flashes behind her eyes. They were dots on a map with roads sprouting out from each like veins, and only one road was the one, only one lit up from underneath with runway lights, but she couldn't see where it led.

Cap's phone dinged, and Vega opened her eyes and sat up. Cap grabbed at his phone but somehow knocked it onto the floor, near Vega's feet.

"Fuck," he said, disoriented. Like he had been asleep.

Vega picked it up and read from Kendrick's text aloud.

"The girl's name is Dena Macht. In Riverside for eighteen months for assault and possession of drugs and stolen property. Corresponded with John McKie while on the inside and then reunited when they were both out. Kendrick said before they were arrested their hobbies included smoking meth, snorting Vicodin, picking pockets, and stealing from family. He would not be surprised if they were involved in one or more of those activities currently."

Vega scrolled, read more.

"That's how Dena Macht got busted in the first place. Her parents called it in."

"Her parents," said Cap.

Vega typed in a message to the Bastard on her phone, and then Cap's phone buzzed again and she read the text on the screen.

"Who's that?" he asked.

"Traynor. He wants us to come in."

"Why?"

"They have Kevin Brandt."

Then she had to put both phones in her lap because of the sweat budding on her hands. Also on the bottom of her feet, muddying the insides of her shoes, and a single drop slipping down her arm. She opened the window and stuck her head out. It was getting dark, and there was a little rain in the air.

Cap was asking her questions but she didn't answer; she breathed and tried to count five on the inhale and five on the exhale. Push, pull, said a yoga teacher in her head. In breath to the out breath.

Fuck you, said Vega to the yoga teacher. I want the shallow breath, and I want the sweat, and I want the headache. It means I'm close.

Cap huddled in a hallway with Traynor, Junior, and the Fed. Vega stood with her back flush against the wall, not leaning. She had her jacket draped over her forearm and her skin was wet and white. Cap tried to get her eye, but she wouldn't look at him.

"Brandt's in A," said Junior.

"Who's with him?" asked Cap.

"No one right now," said Junior. "Says he has a lawyer coming."

Traynor added, "He claims he doesn't know where the girls are, hasn't seen them in eight years. Same story Jamie told us."

"Where'd you find him?"

"Town in southern Ohio," said the Fed. "Living under the name Miss Vega's contact provided. We had people search his home, where a number of illegal recreational substances were recovered."

"But not two girls," said Cap.

"No. His alibi checks out as well."

"Which is what?"

The Fed paused, looked at him sideways.

"That he was in southern Ohio at the time of the abduction. He's got half a dozen people who can vouch for him."

"Yeah, but he lived here once," said Cap. "He could still have connections here."

"He didn't know Evan Marsh," said Traynor. "Says he didn't."

"Who's talking to him?"

"Harrison could," said Traynor.

"Let Vega do it," said Cap.

She looked up, pushed gently off the wall.

Junior stiffened up, ready to talk. Traynor cut him off.

"She's not a police officer," said Traynor, but he wasn't digging in.

"Brandt's not a suspect," said Cap. "They're perfect for each other. He also owes eight years of child support—he doesn't have a lot of cards here."

Traynor and the Fed glanced at each other. Cap felt them tipping. Come on, he wanted to say, she's having an anxiety attack; this will be just the thing to snap her back. Some girls need a spa treatment to unwind; this one likes an interrogation. Vega looked at him, brows heavy over her eyes, tired and a little grateful.

It was a little room, had the coppery smell of office machinery. Kevin Brandt sat at a square table, texting on his phone when Vega came in.

"Who are you?" he said.

"Vega."

"Yeah, who are you? Cop, lawyer, FBI?"

His voice was nasal, congested, and he had a flat face like an inbred dog.

"No," said Vega.

She sat opposite him, and he sniffed loudly.

"Then why are you here? You know my ex-wife? Huh?"

Vega folded her arms.

Brandt dropped his phone on the table and pressed a fingertip hard on top of it.

"You can't keep me here without charging me, you know that, right?"

Vega was quiet.

"I got a lawyer," Brandt said. "He's coming."

Vega leaned forward and laced her fingers together on the table like an altar boy.

"Where are the girls?" she said.

"How should I fuckin' know?" said Brandt.

"When's the last time you saw them?"

"Eight years ago," he said, not having to think about it.

"You know a guy named Evan Marsh?"

"Nope."

"You sure?" she said. "Be sure."

"Hey, fuck you, bitch. Nothing wrong with my faculties. I heard you and I answered you, and unless you or a real actual cop is gonna charge me with something, I have somewhere to be."

Brandt crossed his arms and waited for the insults to sink in. Vega just leaned back in her chair. She stretched her arms up, kept the fingers laced, palms up. Just like a yoga instructor would tell her. And then she yawned.

Cap and Junior stood on the other side of the glass. Junior was moving around, nervous, not sold.

"So she's tired? That's the plan?"

Cap watched Vega yawn, having never seen it happen before. There was no way she was tired. She didn't get tired. Or she was just young enough to fight it off.

"Just wait," he said to Junior.

But to Vega in his head he said, You got a plan, right, girl?

She let her hands drop to her sides, rolled her head from side to side, hearing little cracks from the cartilage in her neck.

"So you're *sure* you don't know where the girls are?" she said again, almost friendly, almost cute.

Brandt stared at her, shoving his confusion into a corner to make room for the agitation.

"Yeah, that's what I've been fucking saying for fucking two hours since I got picked up. Now charge me, or I leave through that door, right there, right now," he said, pointing to the door in question.

Vega turned around to look at the door like she'd forgotten where it was.

"Right," she said. She exhaled in a whistle. "Okay, then, I guess you're free to go."

—

"I'm going in," said Junior, at the end of whatever frail cord he'd been hanging by.

"Wait," said Cap gently. "Just give her a minute."

He watched her expression, totally foreign to him, this one a little flaky, flirty. Another brand-new Vega in front of him, unwrapped from her box, new clothes, new face, new pose.

Brandt didn't move.

"And you all are just gonna let me walk outta here, unmolested?"

"Well, sure. You're not under arrest, right?" said Vega.

"Right," said Brandt.

They watched each other for another minute, Brandt still confused and angry about it, Vega weirdly cheery. Finally she took out her phone and started thumbing the screen. Brandt stood up slowly and grabbed his own phone from the table.

"Sorry we wasted your time, Kevin," said Vega, smiling distractedly.

"Yeah, whatever, fuck off," Brandt said as an afterthought.

He grunted an unintelligible thing and headed for the door, behind Vega.

"Oh, hold on," she said, tapping her screen, not turning to look at him. "Quick question. You know a guy named Antoine Sutton?"

Brandt paused, his hand on the door handle.

"No," he said, shaking his head, flustered.

"You sure?" she said, turning her head just a little bit over her shoulder.

"Yes, I'm fucking sure. Don't know anyone named Antoine St-st—" He struggled to remember the last name.

"Sutton."

"Sutton, yeah, don't know him. Is that it, goddammit?"

"Yeah, that's it," Vega said. Then she tapped the screen once and lifted her phone to her ear, making a call. "I guess he has a nickname though—some people call him Rascal?"

Brandt turned back to face her, dropped his phone to the floor, looked like he'd been rabbit-punched.

"Oh, you know him?" she said, genuinely curious to know. "I'm calling him right now. You want to talk to him?"

Brandt jumped for her, but she stood and hiked her jacket up to show him the gun.

"You owe him some money, right? Like ten K or something? All for what, poker and blackjack and horses."

"Give me the phone, you bitch. Give me the fucking phone."

Vega moved to the other side of the table, pushed her jacket back, rested her hand on the grip of the Springfield.

"It's ringing," she said, excited.

Brandt had begun wheezing, gripping handfuls of dirty wheat-colored hair.

"Please," he whispered.

"Is this Rascal?" said Vega, suddenly calm and unamused. "You're looking for a guy named Kevin Brandt, right? That cocksucker is standing right in front of me."

"Please!"

"Hold on a second." Vega lifted the phone away from her ear and tapped the screen with her thumb. "He's on mute. Do you know where the girls are?"

"No, I swear," said Brandt. "I haven't seen them in eight years."

"Do you know someone named Evan Marsh?"

"No," he said, shaking his head to show her how serious he was about it.

"No one has contacted you within the last week about their whereabouts and you've observed nothing out of the ordinary that you can recall."

"No, I swear. I promise."

"Don't promise," said Vega, disgusted. "What are you, a fucking cub scout?"

Brandt gripped the end of the table and rubbed his nose, eyes, trying not to cry.

Vega touched her phone screen and began to speak.

"Sorry about that. Wrong guy. If I find him, I'll call you."

She hung up, put away her phone and gun. Brandt began to take choppy breaths through his mouth, still gripping the table's edge.

"Okay, so listen," said Vega. "You don't need a lawyer. Tell the detectives everything they want to know and stay close for a few days. You step on a crack, I call Rascal."

Brandt continued to gasp.

"Say you understand me," said Vega, now annoyed.

"I understand you."

"Great," she said. "Have a seat."

She turned to face the mirror, knowing it was Hollows and Caplan back there. She hoped she was looking at Caplan when she nodded, not at Hollows or into the space between them, but it was hard to tell. From this side, all she could see was her own face, unrecognizable in the room's yellow light.

Kevin Brandt looked like a different guy when he came out of the room with Vega. Suddenly his clothes seemed ill-fitting, his skin pallid.

"You need anything else from Brandt?" said Vega, as if he weren't next to her.

"We'll get his contact information. We can arrange for you to stay at a motel the next few nights, Mr. Brandt. That all right?" said Junior.

Brandt nodded, said nothing.

"Detective Ralz can take care of that for you."

Ralz led Brandt away quietly, and Cap couldn't help smiling.

"Rascal?"

"That's the man's name," Vega said, not smiling exactly, but her eyes suggesting that she might start soon.

Then she looked at her phone, and everything in her face hardened up.

"What?" said Cap.

"It's Gail White," said Vega. "She called me three, four times."

Vega pressed the phone to her ear while she kept her eyes on Cap. He thought about how you never knew you were going to get good news before you heard it, but bad news you could always sense coming; you didn't even have to guess.

Cap and Vega drove to Jamie Brandt's parents' house, where there were four news vans parked but none of their lights on and no correspondents or producers outside. Vega glanced at the numbers on the vans, everyone local, no cable. That meant word hadn't got out yet, or there was just bigger news at the moment, which was possible.

Cap parked across the street, and they walked across quickly. Vega heard a van door slide open as she and Cap hit the driveway, past the line the reporters could cross.

"Miss Vega, any break in the case?" a man called to her.

Vega thought of bones and glass, and the front door opened, Maggie behind it.

"She's been up there an hour," she said.

"That them?" Gail called from the other room.

"Yeah, that's them," said Maggie, annoyed. "Who else you expecting?"

Vega and Cap came into the kitchen, where Gail stood wearing a down coat, the back door open.

"You're the one she asked for, missy," she said to Vega sourly. "Arlen put a ladder out, but she don't want anyone up there."

Arlen White appeared, coming in through the back door, out of breath. He cast his thumb over his shoulder behind him, pointing outside.

"Did she talk about hurting herself?" said Cap.

Gail shook her head at him.

"No, sir, she just took a bottle of Smirnoff with her."

Cap caught Vega's eye, and she nodded at him. Got it.

Everyone stood around for a second, not moving.

"Well, go on, then, if you're gonna go," said Gail to Vega.

Vega went out the kitchen door, through the garage to the outside, along the back of the house. The house next to the Whites' was only a few yards away, a chain fence dividing the property. There was hardly any light at all, no moon that she could see, only a dim sconced bulb above the back door.

An extension ladder was propped up against the house, next to one of the living room windows. Vega climbed it.

"Better be you, Alice," Jamie said before Vega reached the top.

"It's me."

Vega stepped off the top rung and onto the roof, where it tilted at a small angle around the perimeter. Jamie sat in the middle, where it was flat, with her knees to her chest, holding the vodka to her side.

Vega approached her but didn't get too close, stood next to her facing what she was facing, which was the street, a patch of woods, a satellite from one of the vans.

"We have a new lead," said Vega. "A guy named John McKie—do you know that name?"

Jamie tried to shake her head, but it was like there was a delay between her head and her neck.

"What about Dena Macht?"

"Nah," Jamie said. "I never heard of 'em. Who are they?"

Vega told her and couldn't tell if Jamie was listening. She was drunk, and her head kept tipping forward and snapping back up as she almost fell asleep and caught herself.

"Also I met your ex-husband," said Vega.

Jamie registered this, turned to look at Vega and laughed.

"Yeah? He didn't know anything, right?"

"Right," said Vega. "You should talk to your lawyer—the government will garnish his wages for child support, but he might go to jail before that."

Jamie nodded mechanically.

"I don't even care," she said. "Money, no money, jail, no jail." She closed her eyes and breathed deeply, like she was at the beach. "This guy I read about killed himself by cutting his wrists and *then* jumping off a building."

"You can't kill yourself, Jamie," said Vega. "Your girls are going to need you."

"Oh, come the fuck on," said Jamie, turning on Vega, lips dark with lipstick or just chapped from being bit. "This is what I wanted-a ask you. What are the odds of them being alive, now, really? You do this for a living. I've read a bunch of shit online."

She did not finish her thought, just peered straight ahead, into the woods.

"What I do," said Vega, "has nothing to do with odds."

Jamie rolled her eyes and took a swig from the bottle.

"That's some *Fast and Furious* shit right there," she said, pointing at Vega. Then she mimicked her: "What I do has nothing to do with odds, baby."

Jamie started hiccupping, a wet indigestive sound. She pressed her fingers to her lips.

"You going to be sick?" said Vega.

Jamie didn't respond, just put her head down and shuddered her shoulders.

"Jamie?"

Vega moved a little closer, tried to see her face, but the streetlight wasn't bright enough.

Jamie still didn't look up, and now the bottle dropped from her hands and hit the roof dully, rolled toward the edge. Vega ran to her just as Jamie went limp, and Vega caught her before she tipped fully over.

"Jamie, Jamie, Jamie."

Vega said her name over and over, but Jamie couldn't hear her; she was in another place now, foam bubbling out of her mouth and lying in Vega's arms, still warm.

At the hospital, Cap paced in the waiting room while Jamie had her stomach pumped. Cap had seen the process a few times as a cop, and every time he thought about the accuracy of the term because it was like something you would do to a septic tank to flush it out—stick in a tube and apply suction until everything comes up and out.

Jamie's parents had been taken into the Resus area with her; Cap and Vega were left in the waiting room, while Maggie filled out forms with the triage nurse. Vega stood typing on her phone with her thumb, leaning against the wall. She had a streak of Jamie's vomit across her shirt. She hadn't looked Cap in the eye since right before she'd gone to the roof. He had an urge to tell her it wasn't her fault, none of it was, but he couldn't figure out a way to do it that wasn't patronizing.

His phone buzzed with a text. Nell.

"U OK? It's late even for u."

Cap typed, "I'm OK. Jamie swallowed a bunch of pills with half a bottle vodka. At ER."

He watched the three dots flash at the bottom of the screen and pictured Nell's face.

"Terrible!" she wrote back. "Will she be OK?"

"Hopefully," texted Cap. "Usually 4-hour window good."

He paused, then added, "Go to bed!"

She sent back a rolling eye face, and Cap smiled. He tried to find a face that implied fatherly worry without being pushy, but there was really nothing in that department. Just heart eyes.

Then Arlen White emerged from the back, looking stunned. He turned a flat wool hat around in his hands like a wheel. Maggie, Cap, and Vega gathered around him.

"Arlen, what is it?" said Maggie, a plea in her voice.

Arlen coughed into his elbow, then said, "She's gonna be all right. They took everything out of her. They're gonna keep her overnight at least."

"Oh, thank God," Maggie said, and she pressed her clasped hands to her chest, as if she were going to start praying right then.

"That's good news," Cap said to him.

Arlen smiled very faintly, then turned to Vega and said, "Ma'am?"

"Yes," answered Vega.

He stopped turning the hat and said, "Been gone a week now."

Vega exhaled a small breath and said, "Yes."

Arlen nodded. Then he addressed all of them: "You can go. Gail wants to stay, 'course."

Maggie asked if he was sure, and he said, yes, he was, and that was all. He turned and went back through the swinging double doors to where his wife sat next to a cot that held his daughter, knocked out from the trauma to her insides.

The three of them left the ER in silence and made their way to the parking lot where Maggie said good night but didn't make a move to leave.

"You okay, Miss Shambley?" said Cap.

Maggie nodded, distracted. Then she said quietly, her eyes cast down, "How many of the eighteen people took more than a week to find, Miss Vega?"

Vega's nose crinkled up as she paused. Cap knew she didn't have to think about it, that she knew how long it had taken her to find every one of the eighteen, because she thought about them all the time when she wasn't working a new case, because she kept living and reliving the old cases over and over; that she probably dreamed about them the way a starving man dreamed about food.

"Three," said Vega.

Maggie put her hand to her cheek like she was checking herself for a temperature.

"And out of those three, one of them was dead, and one was alive but," she said, tapping her head, "dead."

Vega nodded.

"Right," said Maggie solemnly. Then again, "Right. You'll let me know how your lead goes?"

"Yes, of course," said Vega.

"I'll send you a text in the morning," Maggie said. "Tell you how Jamie's doing."

"That would be great," said Cap, wanting to make everything easier for everyone.

Then they all said good night and got into their cars. Cap headed for the inn and drove a few blocks before saying anything.

"Alive but dead," he said. "What did she mean?"

Vega rolled her shoulders one at a time, stretching. Then she spoke.

"It was a girl in the Valley, near L.A. Christy Poloñez. Twelve years old. Her uncle kidnapped her, put her in a basement, filmed her with three men at a time, four men at a time. Knocked her teeth out so she could give them a smoother ride. She'd been down there two weeks when I found her, real out of it, but I thought it was the drugs they'd given her. Her parents were so happy she was alive that they didn't care at first that she wasn't talking in sentences.

"Then they did a press conference. They wanted to thank the city, the police . . . me."

Vega paused, rubbed her hands on her pants legs as if she were wiping something off.

"So the press is asking, 'Christy, how does it feel to be back home?' and Christy's just smiling. Smiling, smiling, smiling like a drunk. And everyone's happy and laughing and being encouraging, you know, because this is a good story for everyone. Everyone likes to see the kids come home. And Christy's looking at the cameras and starts taking her clothes off, because in her brain, now, and forever, when she sees a camera, that's what she's supposed to do."

Vega stopped, and Cap could tell there was more, but that she was deciding whether or not to tell him.

"What happened to her?" he asked.

Vega sighed.

"Her mother covered her up and took her away. Last I heard they were homeschooling her because she couldn't function in a regular school. That's what happens, Caplan, when they're gone more than a week, two weeks." She pointed to her head. "Train goes off the tracks."

"Not unequivocally," said Cap. "Every case is different."

She stared out the passenger window now, removing herself from the conversation.

"Vega, everyone's had a shitty night. They're all just hitting an emotional wall. We've both seen this before," he said.

"You don't have to do that," she said.

"Do what?"

"Attempt the pep talk."

"I am not attempting pep talk," he said. "I am sharing my experience."

"Okay, that's enough," said Vega.

She wasn't laughing or even smiling, but she seemed suddenly to have more energy, inspired in some odd way by his sappiness.

As they pulled up to the inn, she checked her phone and said, "So Wilkes-Barre is what, fifty miles?"

"Sounds about right," said Cap. "What's in Wilkes-Barre?"

"Dena Macht's parents," she said, getting out of the car. "You'll tell Traynor we're heading there in the morning?"

"I guess I will," said Cap, taking a sip of a four-hour-old coffee from a wax paper cup. "Pickup at seven?"

He looked at the time on the dash. 3:06. Vega shrugged.

"Seven-thirty," she said, and turned and went up the path to the inn, lit on either side by gas lamps for charm purposes.

Cap laughed once and loudly before starting the car.

She may or may not have slept. But when it came down to it, did she need to? As long as she was lying down with closed eyes, pretending to be asleep, could a body really tell the difference?

She thought about this while standing on her hands. There was congestion in her nose; she felt the block as she tried to breathe deeply. She gave up and breathed through her mouth. A no-no in yoga. So turn me in, she thought. Call the yoga police.

She heard a bird, but it wasn't a song, more like an effort at communication: persistent, repetitive, rhythmic. No birds answered him; it was just that one. And the more Vega heard his weird calls the more she swore he was actually speaking English, one word over and over: Here. Here. Here.

She opened her eyes, and there were the girls again, in their white dresses with the black sashes. Vega knew this was not really Kylie and Bailey speaking to her. She knew her mind was feeding her the images, pulling them from horror movies—the *Shining* twins, the little girl with the braids who kills her classmates, the gang of blond kids with their glowing eyes.

But they sure looked like Kylie and Bailey, even if they were fakes. They looked at each other, at Vega.

"What?" Vega said to them, sweat trickling up her chin, onto her lips.

That's when Kylie got on one knee and came up close to her face. Vega could feel the warm air of her breath as she spoke:

"You're probably gonna die today."

13

DENA MACHT'S PARENTS LIVED OUT IN WILKES-BARRE. CAP DROVE on a county road, and out the window were woods and farmhouse conversions. How could anyone sleep listening to crickets and cats and a car down the street once a day? Out here you would watch it come and go from your window, anxious, then relieved.

They found the house down a road that was paved but just barely. They parked and could not find a path of any kind, so they walked in the grass toward the house, which had two boxy stories with an A-frame roof. Cap expected to see some chickens or a pig running around in the front yard, but instead of animals there were about fifteen dishwashers, tented under a blue tarp.

Cap rubbed his eyes reflexively, as if the gesture would make him more awake. But he wasn't. He was on the ropes of consciousness, even after he'd drunk a cup of coffee while he shaved and finished a thermos in the car on the way to Vega's. He still knew if he closed his eyes for more than a few seconds he would collapse. He felt like a senior citizen even though he knew that forty-one wasn't old anymore, that lots of men became first-time fathers in their forties, or dated women half their age, went back to school. Allowed themselves to be in love. But not him, and not now.

Vega was showing signs too. She had seemed aggressively youthful back in the old days earlier in the week, energy buzzing off her even while she sat silent in the passenger seat. Now she was moving slowly, head tilted down, weighted.

A woman came through the screen door and stood on the porch, looking at them. Pockmarks lined her cheeks, her eyes clear and blue. She didn't speak.

Cap stood up straight and said, "Mrs. Macht?"

"Yes. You Mr. Cappan?"

"Caplan, yes. This is Alice Vega."

Mrs. Macht nodded at them, a little suspicious.

"May we come in for a minute?" Cap said.

She nodded again and went inside, holding the door open.

They followed her. The living room seemed too small for all the furniture, tables and couches and chairs, lining the walls, a rug with woven concentric circles in the middle of the floor that made Cap dizzy.

"Let me get my husband," Mrs. Macht said.

She stood in a doorway leading to other rooms and yelled.

"Mitch, these folks are here!"

Mrs. Macht did not sit and did not tell them to sit. She crossed her arms and pulled her thick sweater tight across her chest. Then Mitchell Macht came in. He was fat and had a mottled blond goatee on his chin.

He shook hands with Cap, nodded at Vega, and seemed to be out of breath.

"You're looking for Dena?" he said.

"That's right," said Cap.

"She's staying at my dad's cabin down Woodgrove."

"Where's that exactly?"

"About ten, fifteen miles east of Frackville, back toward you in Denville, I'm afraid—you got to go a bit off the interstate."

"Is your father with her there?"

"Nah, he's dead," said Macht, no emotion in any direction. "She's been staying there while she looks for work."

Mrs. Macht emitted a sigh that sounded like a honk. Her husband glanced at her, and she left the room.

"You looking for her ex, for John?" said Macht.

"Yes."

"He's trouble. I always knew it. Dena was doing okay before she met him. She was going to junior college and had a job, everything."

Cap nodded, pictured Nell.

"You said ex—they're not together romantically as far as you know?"

"Yeah, she got rid of him," said Macht proudly. "She knew he was bad news."

"Do you have a number where we could reach her? We'd like to ask her if she has heard from McKie at all in the past month."

"She just changed her cell phone. She couldn't get reception up there with AT&T."

Cap thought for a quick second, remembered Charlie Bright's mother making excuses for him.

"Is there a landline?" he said.

"Yeah . . ." Macht paused. Cap watched him struggle, eyes batting around, lips tightening over the teeth—all marks of a witness who was not a great liar, trying to decide whether or not to admit something.

"It's been outta order for a while," he added quickly.

"So what would be the best way to get in touch with her?"

"You could, uh, leave her a message on the cell, and when she gets it she'll call you back."

"We don't really have too much time to wait for that, Mr. Macht," said Cap. "You understand, we're looking for the Brandt girls. Every minute we lose we get further away from finding them alive and safe. I'm sure you can appreciate that."

"Yeah, 'course," said Macht, pained. "I could drive you up there myself—I usually go see her every other Friday. I don't want to take her by surprise."

Cap's jaw throbbed where Ralz had hit him, made him feel foggy, like he had to unpack things more than usual.

"I'm sorry," he said. "Can I ask you what you mean by that? You don't want to take her by surprise?"

Macht took a few seconds to compose a response. Then Cap heard Vega's voice.

"You know what he means by that?" Vega said.

Cap turned, saw that Vega was talking to Mrs. Macht, who had reappeared in the doorway, smoking a cigarette.

"Yeah, I know," said Mrs. Macht.

"Ro, we talked," Macht said to her.

"I know we talked about it, you damn old fool," said Mrs. Macht, not at all affectionately.

"My wife, she doesn't have a lot of patience for Dena," said Macht.

"Just shut up, Mitch," snapped Mrs. Macht. "Shut your mouth and quit telling lies."

Macht looked like he was about to protest but then didn't, sank back into the couch like a sandbag.

Mrs. Macht came into the room and addressed Cap and Vega, didn't look at her husband.

"That girl didn't need John McKie or anyone else to turn her into a deadbeat," she said, spite drawing down the corners of her mouth. "She did that all by herself. Started sniffing glue and paint thinner when she was twelve years old. First abortion at fifteen, second at seventeen."

Mrs. Macht tapped the side of her head forcefully. "Something missing up here. Always was."

"Ro," Macht said sadly.

"No, Mitch," she said. "I tried to sit here and listen to you lie to these people to make yourself feel better. I ain't doing it."

She shook her head, laughed to herself.

"She faked my signature on a check; that's when I called the cops. We work our whole lives and then we're gonna lose our damn house 'cause she wants to smoke drugs? No way. No way, José."

She looked at her husband over her shoulder, dismissive.

"He didn't want me to do it either. If it was up to him, we'd be on welfare 'cause of her. 'Cause he's a fool."

Macht said nothing, stared at the globe of his stomach.

"Ma'am," said Cap. "Do you think your daughter is still involved with John McKie or do you agree with Mr. Macht?"

"I don't agree with Mr. Macht about anything," she said. "So, yeah— I'm sure they're still together, and I'm sure he's with her right now at that cabin. And what Mr. Macht didn't wanna tell you is there was a landline, but she's never paid a bill in her life so there's no electricity and no running water up there. They just smoke drugs by candlelight; it's a real romantic scene. Only way you're gonna find them is if you drive there yourselves."

"We can do that," said Cap.

"I gotta give you directions," said Mrs. Macht. "Address won't come up on Internet maps."

She went to a small table where there was a phone and scratched out notes on a slip of paper.

"If you talk to her, if she isn't passed out or what have you," she said, handing Cap the note, "can you give her a message for me?"

"Of course."

Mrs. Macht blew out a cloud of smoke, aimed above Cap's head to be polite, and she looked a little shaky just then. Maybe the screws and bolts that locked up her daily rage were loosening, Cap thought.

Then she said, "Tell that dumb bitch she still owes me sixty-eight hundred dollars."

They followed a series of splintered roads according to Mrs. Macht's directions until they were officially lost. There was a house every quarter mile or so, each one more rustic than the last, smaller and smaller windows and doors, lawns shrinking and turning into woods, until they didn't see any houses or cars for ten minutes. The landscape reminded Vega of a program she'd seen on TV once, something like "When the Humans Die"—vegetation growing wild, vines covering houses and cars, doing the quiet work of decomposition.

She watched her phone, which still retained a flicker of reception, but the message kept coming back that the Internet could not find her location. The tics of the circle in the upper left corner spun. Searching, searching.

Cap decided they better turn around, but then Vega saw something up ahead, a flash of white, headlights and tires jutting out from the trees. A truck.

Cap rolled into the gutter of the road and turned off the car. Vega got out, smelled the salty smoke of a fire somewhere close. She heard a dissonant birdsong, three mismatched notes on a loop. She examined the pickup, the paint faded to beige, dirt coating the tires and fender. Her eyes followed the scrap of a driveway back to a cabin the size of a gas station bathroom, surrounded by trees, and on the porch, a man kneeling, working at something.

Cap went first, stepping quietly around the truck.

"Excuse me," he called, his voice amplified.

Vega nodded, approving his volume. Best not to surprise anyone out here.

Closer to the house now, she saw the man crouching, cleaning a stool with a spray bottle and a rag. There was also a folding chair and an old tube television.

The man glanced up as they came to the clearing, and said, "Folks lost?"

He was in his seventies, with hair that looked recently shaved, just sprouting white spikes in a semicircle on his head and also his face.

Cap came forward and said yes, introduced himself and Vega. The man didn't offer his name.

"We're looking for a woman named Dena Macht. Do you know that name?" said Cap.

"Macht, sure," said the man. "You're all turned around, realize?"

He stood now, wiping his hands with the rag.

"Yeah, we thought as much," said Cap.

The man gave them some directions. Turn around, a left where they had taken a right, follow the unmarked road with the broken roadblock sign to the Macht cabin.

"I've seen the girl and her boyfriend in town," said the man with the air of a conspirator. "They got problems."

"What makes you say that?"

"That girl, Dena?" said the man. "I used to see her with her grand-dad when he built the place. She used to be cute; now she's got holes in her face from the drugs."

He seemed genuinely saddened by it.

"Have you seen them lately? In the last few days?"

"Nah, I ain't seen them," he said. "Couple weeks probably. You friends of theirs?"

"We know Dena's parents," said Cap.

The man nodded. That was enough for him.

"Well, she owes money to everyone in town. Surprised they haven't torched the place yet," he said. Then, as an afterthought: "I don't trust people from New York, personally. Think they got an attitude."

At first Vega thought somehow he'd picked up Cap's trace Brooklyn accent, even though Vega heard it only in a few of his words, when he said "coll" for "call." Cap met her eyes, registering the anomaly.

"Who's from New York, now?" said Cap.

The man dropped the rag on the folding chair and pulled a tissue from his pocket, rubbed it on the back of his neck.

"Her boyfriend, right? The tall guy. He's got a damn Giants sticker on his car," he said, impatient suddenly, like Cap and Vega were dense not to get it before.

Vega's head burned in the middle, the realization blistering outward, fire eating up the fuses. She turned around and left first, heard Cap thank the man and not wait for him to say anything back before Cap followed her, both of them walking, then running through the white trees which were peeling, flaps of bark hanging off with the red wood underneath. Vega knew it was probably natural for whatever kind of tree it was, but it still looked like a disease, a hemorrhage, something to be cured or killed.

They found the roadblock, faded orange stripes on two planks with a handwritten detour sign. Vega got out and moved the sign to the side of the road while Cap tried dialing Traynor, then Junior, then Em, but there was no answer, no click and no ring—just the low hum of not connecting.

Cap leaned his head out the window and said, "I have no bars. No dots. Do you have service?"

Vega got back in and ran her thumb over the face of her phone.

"No," she said.

Cap pulled ahead slowly, hearing the wheels crush gravel, the car rocking unevenly over the dips. He kept one hand on the wheel and the other on the phone, hitting Traynor again. Traynor . . . calling work. Nothing.

"Caplan, brake," said Vega.

Cap glanced up a little too late, and the car slid into a ditch. He yanked the wheel right and pulled out, the fender cracking the edge.

"Shit."

"Caplan," said Vega. "Maybe we should walk awhile."

"Yeah," he said, pulling over.

He turned off the engine, and they both stepped out. The morning was turning warm, the air clear, clouds moving fast. Spring for real, thought Cap. Vega straightened her jacket at the bottom and shrugged one shoulder, adjusting the holster and the pistol underneath.

Cap typed out a text to Traynor, Junior, and Em as he walked to the trunk: "We are 15 miles east of Frackville. Bumper sticker on McKie's car matching descript of ridgewood mall car." He hit Send and watched the bar at the top hang in the middle.

He opened the trunk and reached for the MicroVault, tapped in his code (1107—Nell's birthday), and pressed his right index finger over the fingerprint scanner. The lock clicked and he opened the case. There was his Sig, right where he had left it the day he lost his job. When he was a cop he'd carried it every day and kept it clean, but never had been one to fetishize it like some other cops, never gave it a woman's name or obsessively polished the steel, never had a collection at home or subscribed to publications for gun enthusiasts. It had just been a tool of the job, a stethoscope for a doctor. And when he lost his job he had put it in the vault in his bedroom closet and forgot about it. Until this morning.

He loaded the clip and peered down the barrel.

"When's the last time you had that in your hand?" said Vega.

"Day I lost my job."

"That's all kind of pathetic," she said.

Cap smiled and slid the gun down the small of his back, undid and fastened his belt to the next hole to tighten it up.

They walked the road, which grew narrower still, the width of a compact car and not an inch more. Cap looked at his phone again, cupping his hand over the top to shade the screen from the glare. The texts read as delivered, but his phone was so old he never knew. He wrote one more: "Copy back." Hit Send. Then redialed Junior. Not even a ring, the screen black.

"Can you get anything?" he asked Vega.

She shook her head.

Cap stopped walking. He remembered plenty of times when young cops were too hot to see some action, started making poor decisions. Jules had told him some boys' frontal lobes, the part of the brain that processes consequences, didn't develop until they were in their mid-twenties, and Cap could believe it. Taking a bad shot, searching and seizing without a warrant, walking into an unknown situation without backup.

He could just see the outline of the cabin about a hundred feet away, the shape of a one-story A-frame, shimmering through the trees.

Vega continued to walk ahead of him and soon realized he wasn't right behind her, that he had stopped. She turned and held her hands out, impatient.

"Coming?"

Cap didn't speak, gestured come here with one hand. Vega looked at him sideways and came back, small clouds of dust kicking up from her feet.

Then she was right in front of him, breathing fast and heavy.

"What is it?"

There was no way to say it except to say it, no bubble wrap he could duct-tape to the thing to make it more attractive to her.

"We have to go back," he said, calmly resigned.

"What's that?" Vega said back as if she had a bad ear.

"To the old man's house, see if he has a landline we can use."

Vega stared at him, her mouth a little slack, in shock.

"We're right here," she said. "The girls are in there right now."

She spoke slowly so he wouldn't miss anything.

"They could be," said Cap. "And McKie and Dena could be armed. So let's say we have a little gunfight, and they shoot us, and we die. Then the girls are still in there, and no one knows where they are."

Cap watched her face for a reaction but there was none. She gazed at him, forehead wrinkled.

"And we're dead," he added.

"They're junkies, not gangsters. They got in over their heads," she said. "We can handle them."

"All circumstantial. We're talking about thirty minutes here. That's the trade—thirty minutes for odds of a significantly better outcome."

Vega stepped closer, up to his face, close enough so he could smell the herbiness of her breath and see her nostrils puff with air.

"This could be the thirty minutes, Caplan," she said, her eyes shining, reflecting the severely clear sky. She continued: "When they rape them or kill them or cut off their thumbs and their ears because they're panicking."

She was earnest and not angry, and Cap knew the real bitch of it was that they were both right.

"This is the thirty minutes," she said, firm. "This is it. Right now."

Cap thought of this: When Nell was twelve she learned about 9/11 in school. They had covered the basics before then, but when she was twelve, in the sixth grade, they really gave them the details, watched videos and read newspaper articles, wrote reports and glued clippings to posterboards. Not long after Nell wrote a short story about a freak snowstorm in the middle of September, all the planes grounded, all airports shut down. Cap and Jules were stunned: even though it was a child's rewrite of history, isn't that what we all did in our heads, tapped the clock icon and scrolled the hours back, played endless versions of if this, then that.

He wanted to tell Vega what he never told Nell, that the terrorists just would have done it on September 12.

"We can't control that," said Cap. "We can control what we do."

"Yes," she said, lips curling up on her teeth. "We can."

She turned and headed purposefully toward the cabin.

"Vega!" Cap called.

She whipped around and walked a few steps back to him.

"I'm going in there right now. You can come or not come. If the girls are in there, I'm going to get them and bring them out here. You can come or not come."

He looked at her and really saw the color of her eyes, a mix of green and blue, thin yellow rays spiking out from the pupils—two watercolor suns.

She turned to go again, and this time Cap put his hand on her shoulder with the intention of pulling her back. In a second she grabbed his wrist and flipped it and kept twisting it like a pipe cleaner; the pain shot through the tendons, and he grabbed the collar of her jacket with his free hand and grunted. She shoved her other hand hard against his sternum, the heel sharp right over his heart. Cap knew it was some martial-arts move, something where you use the muscles of your back and midsection to push forward. He wondered if they fought, really fought, who would win. Vega's reflexes were faster, but he was probably ultimately stronger, just the cruel benefit of being bigger and a man. That said, if he had to put a dollar down on who would get up more quickly after being hit, that would be Vega.

They both froze, barely breathing.

"Here's the thing, Vega," he said, barely louder than the chattering birds around them. "I think you made a mistake too, just not the same one as most people."

She wasn't moving. Her fingers stayed cold and clamped around his wrist.

Cap kept going: "Except instead of thinking you're too special to lose someone, you think you're special because you already have."

Vega stared at him, eyelashes coming down halfway, not even a full blink.

"I'm very sorry about your mom and your friend—Perry, right? But losing them doesn't make you special. My grandfather died from Alzheimer's, and he killed a fucking Nazi with a knife."

His voice choked high when he mentioned Art. His mother's father, a small bowlegged man, the human equivalent of a Jack Russell terrier, always busy, building Cap cars and trucks out of thick wooden blocks. When Cap was ten, Art had told him to lose the "Grandpa." "You're practically a man, Max, you can call me Art like my friends." And then the shitty, undignified end—a bed in the vets' hospital in Bay Ridge, playing with a child's tower of rainbow rings.

His nose stung, and he swallowed salt. Vega still didn't move, kept her hand against him, the other on his wrist. Cap let go of her jacket.

"If they're dead, they're already dead," he said. "If they're alive, they'll probably be alive in thirty minutes."

Vega cocked her head a little and started to open her mouth.

"We play the favorites," said Cap. "Not the long shot."

She bent her elbow, and the palm on Cap's chest relaxed. Slowly she let go of his wrist with her other hand. Then she leaned forward and kissed him forcefully on the mouth.

It happened so fast he didn't have too much time to react. He felt the pressure from her lips (soft, dry) as if she were trying to pass something through them to him, a message or a germ. Their arms were still tangled together, her one hand still resting lightly on his chest, and then she pulled away. Her eyes moved up and down his face, the neck of her black T-shirt shaking. There was no wind; it was from her heartbeat.

He instantly regretted not holding tight to her shoulders and kissing her back, kissing her cheeks and her forehead and her eyelids. He realized he couldn't think of a thing to say that made sense, so he thought of what Nell would say.

"WTF, Vega?"

The corner of her mouth turned up in a smile she wouldn't allow to fully occupy her face, so he focused on that tiny movement, a miracle really.

Then the deafening crack of a gunshot split the air around them, and it was over.

14

THEY BROKE APART INSTANTLY AND RAN TO THE RIGHT SIDE OF the road, each behind a tree. Vega pulled the Springfield from the holster and flipped the safety. She watched Cap do the same with his ancient Sig. They waited for another shot, which didn't come. But then they heard voices, loud but unintelligible. Fighting. Vega peered through the branches to the cabin but could see no detail, all the windows dark.

"One of them didn't want the other to take the shot," she said.

"Are we certain they're shooting at us and not each other?" said Cap.

Vega strained to hear specific words but couldn't get anything, just a "goddammit" here or there from McKie and high-pitched screeching from Dena.

"Doesn't matter. They're getting itchy in there, and they're armed," said Vega. Then she said, as if it were a full sentence, "So."

Cap squatted, looked over his shoulder and around the tree at the cabin, then back up to Vega. There was a bluish tint to his face, from either the early light or exhaustion.

"So this is the thirty minutes," he said.

Vega said again, "And they're armed."

Cap exhaled through his nose audibly and then barely shook his head, ending a conversation between himself and himself.

Finally he said, "Why don't you go around back, see if you can get in. I'll get in the front door."

Vega huffed out a laugh. "And then what the hell are you gonna do?"

"If the girls aren't in plain sight, then I'll talk, distract them while you look around."

"What if they are in plain sight?"

"Then I'll talk, distract them, wait for you, then we shoot to wound.

Below the knees, no torso. Stay away from arteries. We need to know what they know."

Vega nodded.

"Let's get a little closer first," he said, standing.

He took a few steps to another tree, and then another. Vega followed him, hiding behind the same trees. Soon they reached the clearing around the cabin, which was wider than the house of the old man with the truck, more square footage but still shabby, the exterior a chipped red wood with metal-paned windows and an open porch running along the whole front of the house.

"You good?" said Cap.

Vega nodded, and then started to make her way around, moving through the trees, kept the Springfield pointed down, both hands on it. Through a side window, she saw shapes, people moving. She glanced at Cap, who was staying low and thin against the tree, and she pointed to the window and then to her eyes. I see them right here. Cap gave her a quick up nod.

She continued, slowly, tree to tree, passed a pair of sloped cellar doors and an old beige Honda with a peeling New York Giants sticker on the fender. The car the girls were taken in. When did Kylie realize Evan Marsh was not her friend, and neither was John McKie? When did the fear close in? Vega shook it out. Not her concern, and as usual, the wrong questions.

Vega left Cap's line of vision, went behind the house. McKie and Dena were still fighting, the volume sounding the same, which meant, Vega hoped, that they had not moved too much, that they were still where Vega had just seen them, toward the center of the house and not right up front. Cap knew he had to get the twenty feet to the porch unseen, then under the window.

Why don't I keep my goddamn vest in the trunk anymore? he thought. It was in the attic at home, in a cardboard box with untaped flaps, covered in dust. The short answer was that he had not foreseen this particular situation. He had not predicted a week ago that he would be working on a police and federal investigation and would be participating in an armed hostage rescue. He momentarily grabbed hold of the idea, allowed himself to feel the fear of it, closed his eyes and thought to Nell over the father-daughter telepathic hotline—I love you, Bug.

That was it for the fear. He opened his eyes, gripped the Sig tighter, and ran for the house.

There was no porch at the back of the house, just three narrow steps leading to a rusted screen door, wires frayed at the bottom. The inner door, red with a square window, was closed behind it.

Vega stayed in the trees. She could still hear the fighting but faintly. She tried to see through the window in the door, but the shadow from the screen was too dark. So she crouched and hustled to the door, up the three steps.

She looked in.

A small room, full-size bed in the corner, with a sheet and a thick blanket in a pile, a dresser with a lamp on top. Bottles, papers, candy wrappers on the floor.

Vega opened the screen door slowly; a squeak came and went. She grabbed the handle, pressed her thumb down on the thumbpiece, and the door was not locked. The country, she thought, with an element of disdain. She pushed the door open with a little bit of pressure; it opened with the soft pop from the rubber door sweep. Then she was in.

She took a couple of light steps. The door to the rest of the house was wide open, but Vega couldn't see anything except a hallway wall. Where are you, Little Bad?

And then her answer: a girl's scream.

Cap heard it as he squatted underneath a window on the porch, facing the woods, the hoarse cry followed by sobbing and garbled words in the same high child's voice. The hair on his arms straightened out, the skin on his neck iced from the sound. He heard Vega in his head: thirty minutes.

Now he could hear McKie clearly: "Shut her up, Dena, shut her up!"

"Fuck you!" Dena shouted, then murmuring to the girls, Cap assumed. Babysitter of the fucking year.

He felt footsteps shake his ribs as they grew closer, stopping right behind him. He made himself as flat as he could against the wall, guessed that McKie was looking out the window above his head.

"They're fucking gone," said McKie. "They're gonna bring the fucking National Guard on this place."

Cap could hear the slur—drugs or booze or both. Suspect not thinking clearly, volatile, armed.

"Get her out," yelled McKie, his voice cracking.

Her. A child—Kylie or Bailey—made a mournful sound like a wounded animal. Cap's eyes fell on the cellar doors in front of the porch, and then there was movement, two or three sets of feet coming forward, to the front door, right next to him.

He ran on his haunches, keeping the Sig tight in one hand, pushing off the porch with the other like a chimp, and turned the corner just as the door opened. He sat against the side of the house now and peeked around the edge, tried to breathe and slow his heart rate as he saw who came out.

Vega still couldn't see. She heard the front door open and people run out, so she left the small bedroom and stepped into the hallway, pressing her back flush against the wall. Now she saw more of what she guessed was the living room, a yellow wingback chair, another open door leading to a bathroom. Dead mice and boiled meat filled her nose; she pictured hot dogs in a pan of oil-topped water.

She heard no sound in the living room except a small rustle, and she imagined Bailey Brandt gagged and tied and nearly passed out on a pile of newspapers where they made her sleep.

Wrong! Perry would have said, knocking his fist against his head like it was a door. The hell, Vega, your number-two fuckup (number one was not bringing enough firepower): Never assume you're gonna find who you're looking for. Assume you're gonna find the other thing. Which will generally be someone who wants to kill you. Sometimes they're the same.

He was telling her, over and over, just like Little Bad and Big Bad, to get out of her head, stop projecting and imagining and hypothesizing, because even if you're thinking of the worst thing, it was still a kind of optimism, being cocky enough to think you could see the future and get a handle on it. You have no handle—you got your gun and you got the fire; sometimes it's enough, and sometimes it isn't.

She got closer to the end of the hallway, and she saw more of the living room—a couch with a sheet over it, a pile of clothes. And just as she realized the hallway was more of a partition, a thin wall between the back room and the front of the house, she heard a creak and a catch of breath, and she turned the corner with her Springfield out. But McKie was right there, waiting for her, swinging a plank of wood at her, and he cracked it over her forehead and right eye. Then it was shock, blood, bright white, then black.

Dena Macht wore cutoffs and a pink tank top, dressed for summer in not-yet-fifty-degree weather. She had the same eyes as her mother— blue and set close together; except hers were bright and agonized whereas Mrs. Macht was past all that, long since resigned to bland disappointment. Dena had a gun in one hand but held it awkwardly, no finger on the trigger. Her other arm was wrapped around Bailey Brandt.

Cap curved his body around like a ribbon and pressed his face against the side of the house so he could get a better look: Bailey's face was buried in Dena's ribs; her blond hair was stringy and snaky down her back, and she wore the pink dress she'd been kidnapped in, the tulle wrinkled and ripped in the skirt. Cap shook his head to an invisible audience and bit the inside of his cheeks—those fuckers hadn't given her a bath or changed her clothes for six days.

Dena did not have the gun pointed at Bailey, but it could be there quickly. These things could unravel in a second, Cap knew. There was no fight and then there were fists, no accident and then a pileup, no gunshots and then, suddenly, blood and brains.

Dena was steering Bailey slowly toward the car when McKie called from the house: "I got one, Dena, I got one!"

He sounded giddy, like a kid catching frogs. Cap cringed. Dammit, Vega, how'd you get caught?

Dena's eyes went wild as she held the gun up, pointing it at the sky.

"Get her in the car!" shouted McKie.

Dena shuffled toward the car, pulling Bailey, who moved like she was sleepwalking, her bare feet turned in slightly, head still pressed against Dena's midsection. Cap brought his head back from the edge and just sat for a second against the side of the house, tapping his head on the wall.

He knew a few things: he knew McKie and Dena were planning to take off soon, and he knew he was a man down. Once they were in the car it was over; there would be no way for him to get to his car fast enough, especially if he had to make sure Vega was still breathing. He knew people were easier to talk to when they were apart; together they got mobby, gave each other ideas. He knew he had a matter of minutes to convince Dena.

He knew it was time to talk.

Vega tried to open her eyes, and then the pain landed. She put her hand over her right eye, which was wet, muddy. She looked at the blood on her fingers and touched again right above her eyebrow, and it was like a fucking ocean of pain there, blood rushing from an actual hole in her head. She gasped before she could realize she should keep quiet, looked around and saw she was right in the hallway where she'd been hit, and then he was above her again.

She struggled to prop herself up on her elbows, but McKie grabbed her by the shirt and pulled her off the ground.

"Who are you? Who the fuck are you?" he said, spraying spit in her face.

Vega moved her tongue around in her mouth but it felt gigantic. She tried to say what Perry told her to say to every dumbass skip who asked the same thing, but all she could do was grunt. His breath was rotten, and his teeth were uneven like the broken piano keys in a cartoon.

He asked her one more time and then dropped her, the back of her head smacking the floor. Then it was all snowy static as her eyes rolled up behind the lids.

Cap led with the Sig held in both hands and turned the corner.

"Dena!" he called.

Dena and Bailey both jumped. Dena raised her gun with a shaky arm, aimed it in Cap's general direction as her eyes scoured the woods, looking for him. Bailey flipped around so Cap could see her face (scared, thin). Dena's arm slid around Bailey's clavicle and clutched her tight.

Cap took a step on the porch, made sure she could see him.

"Dena, it's okay," he said, as levelheaded as he could sound. Ready to get the cat out of the tree.

Dena tightened her grip on the pistol and pointed it at him.

"Don't tell me that when you got a gun on me, mister," she called, her voice high like a much younger girl's.

"Fair enough," said Cap. "I'm going to stay right here, okay? I'm not coming any closer. And I have no plan to use this gun—I only have it for Kylie and Bailey's protection right now."

He watched the words coil in Dena's head. She allowed herself to take a breath and readjusted her arm around Bailey, which was a good sign. It meant that Dena was thinking and not yet locked into anything she saw as inevitable. Bailey stared at Cap with giant exhausted eyes; he couldn't tell how much she was registering.

"My name's Max Caplan. Your folks told me where I could find you."

"I know," Dena said. "My dad called."

The old softie, Cap thought with a mix of bitterness and sympathy. Probably paid the phone bill for his little girl and didn't tell the missus. And totally screwed the ambush factor, but Cap didn't let the anger in because this was the opening. This was the door.

"I talked to your dad for a long time," he said. "He's a real good guy."

Dena bit her lip.

"He loves you a lot, Dena. I think he'll do just about anything for you," said Cap. "I know how he feels—I have a daughter too. She's sixteen. And she's everything to me. She's the reason that I don't give the hell up and drink beer all day. She's why I'm alive."

Cap listened to his words as they trailed out of his mouth, echoing back and forth. He took the smallest step forward.

"I think your dad feels the same way about you."

Dena scrunched up her nose, trying not to cry. This was good. If he could get her crying, he had this, and no one had to get shot. Cap knew this was the time. Make the jump.

"You have to know, Kylie and Bailey's mother feels the same way about them. You know that, right?"

He waited. Nobody moved.

Slowly, Dena nodded.

Vega woke up in the hallway again. She was on her side now, the blood a steady stream across her forehead. The front of her skull throbbed, and every muscle ached, like she'd just run ten miles without stretching. She opened her eyes just a little and did not see McKie but could hear him in the small bedroom, muttering and moving things around.

She lifted her head, and the pain increased, pounding now, but she pushed, and looked around, didn't see her Springfield.

Goddammit, Vega, said Perry in her head. You let that redneck grab your dick? Make that shit right quick or you're dead. Then he would whistle the sound of Pac-Man getting sacked by a ghost, punctuated at the end by a cheerful "Wup Wup."

She heard thumps from the small bedroom, McKie opening and slamming drawers shut. Vega flipped onto her stomach, the gash above her eyebrow beating like a heart, and she watched blood drip from her head to the floor. She pushed up with her arms and her feet at the same time, her body a plank, and she started to move like that, crawling without her knees touching the ground, close to the wall, until she could just see into the bedroom.

McKie was leaning over the bed, shoving clothes into a cardboard box. He was breathing fast and heavy. Her Springfield stuck out of the back of his jeans. The strip of wood he'd used on Vega was on the floor, a foot from the doorway, two black screws sticking out of the end, dipped in Vega's blood.

Vega walked her legs to her hands and squatted, the springs of her hamstrings ready. McKie stopped packing and ran his hands through his hair. Vega pinched two fingers into her pocket and pulled out Evan Marsh's Zippo. You got spare change, Perry would say. Throw it. Buys you three or four seconds, and that's all you need.

Time was funny that way when the shit got thick—slow then fast.

Vega threw the lighter so it sailed past McKie's head before hitting the wall and landing on the bed.

He turned his head to the side as he twisted around and reached for the Springfield in his pants, but Vega was already up on her feet. She grabbed the board with one hand, digging her fingernails into it, the pain in her head revving like a chain saw, and she swung at McKie's hand just as he touched the gun, putting everything from her upper body into it. The Springfield flew to the floor, where it skidded and spun to the corner, and Vega shut the door with the back of her foot, careful not to slam it. McKie screamed, his mouth the end of a black tunnel, and Vega thought, *Ugly, ugly, ugly,* as she hit him again across the side of the head. Now he fell and quieted down, stunned, and she brought the board down on his back where it broke, snapped in two, the jagged half twirling up in the air.

"What was the question?" Vega said, sounding genuine.

She stomped his ribs with her heel and kept kicking.

"What was the question?" Vega said, louder. "What was the question?"

McKie screamed again and tried to turn onto his back and cover his abdomen with his bloody hand.

"Who am I, right? Right? Right?"

She held her foot right over his face, let it hover. And then she said what Perry had taught her—someone asks who you are, you tell them the only thing they need to know:

"I'm the motherfucker who gets. Shit. Done."

Then she kicked him once more in the face, and he was out.

The birds got louder, overlapping chirps and squawks that sounded like arguing, but Cap knew that was just him tracing human emotion over it. He thought he heard a thump or two from inside the cabin but couldn't be sure; it might have been the pounding in his ears.

He had gotten closer, off the porch now, on the ground, level with Dena but still a few yards away. Dena still wasn't crying yet but was close, her arm loose around Bailey, the hand with the gun wiggly, like the weight would bring it down soon.

"Dena," Cap said, tried to put on his best Dad voice—firm and kind. "I know this all probably got out of hand very quickly, right?"

She nodded.

"I know, and your dad knows, that you really didn't have anything to do with this—that John talked you into it, and you did whatever you did because you love him."

She kept nodding so he kept talking.

"You don't want anything bad to happen to these little girls. You're just trying to find a way to fix all this."

Now the tears came, just some thin trickles, her cheeks pinched.

"So let's fix it," Cap said softly. "I can help you. I can talk to the police for you. They'll listen to me."

Dena's jaw jutted out in belligerence.

"How'm I supposed to know that?" she said, her voice tense and muted from her stuffed nose. "Why should I believe you anyway?"

Cap tried to sift out where she'd go next. She was damaged enough to have come this far, but how much further could she go, and which way would she break? Was she so desperate she was about to give up, or would she instead take a nosedive into a dry quarry and take whoever she could grab with her? He had to place a bet and pray on that ticket like anyone else.

"Because I'm going to put my gun down. Right here, okay?" he said, gesturing to the ground at his feet. "That is how sure I am that you'll know what to do next."

Dena sniffed and her mouth went slack. Cap continued.

"That is how sure I am that your dad was right about you."

Dena shut her eyes for a short second and wiped them with the top side of her wrist.

Cap started to kneel.

"I'm putting my gun down now," he announced. "No fast moves."

He placed the Sig on the patch of wild grass in front of him. Came back up to standing with his hands in the air. Dena watched him, her breath staggered and short. Bailey watched him too and started to move her mouth, trying to talk, but no sound came out. She gripped Dena's arm like it was a pull-up bar.

"Okay, Dena," Cap said. "Now it's really up to you."

The moments that followed stretched long, each one packed full. Acid swirled in Cap's stomach, coffee surging in his throat. Dena kept her gun pointed at Cap, her hand still shaking. Cap reminded himself to breathe slowly, drops of sweat running from his underarm down to his ribs.

Then Dena began to unlock her arm from Bailey, slowly at first, Bailey still hanging on. Dena moved quicker then, shaking Bailey off and putting her free hand on the gun. Bailey stood motionless, arms at her sides but fingers extended, tense. She was looking at the ground, but her eyes moved all around, to her feet, Cap's feet, the porch. Cap thought she looked possessed.

His mouth was dry but he swallowed anyway. He had to keep talking but not patronize her. She still had the gun.

So all he said, all that was in his head, was the simplest thing he could think of.

"Thanks, Dena. Thank you."

Then he shifted his gaze down, to Bailey.

"Bailey?" he said.

Bailey made little fists. Her arms were impossibly thin. Pretzel sticks. The pink dress hung off her, too big. She didn't look up, but blinked. Cap knew it was good to get any kind of reaction because it meant that even if she was out of it she was not in shock.

"I know your mom," he said.

Bailey looked at him like he was speaking a language she understood only a few words of.

Dena breathed hard through her nose and pointed the gun at Bailey for a second, only to nudge her.

"Go," Dena said. "Go with the man."

Something about Dena's delivery wasn't convincing, a singsong bounce in her voice, her eyes skimming from Bailey to Cap and back. Cap glanced at his gun, thought about how long it would take to grab it, just in case she was having second thoughts about where this was going.

Bailey took a couple of steps and then stopped, arms still pinned to her sides. Cap kept his hands raised slightly above his head but watched Dena move from side to side, like a catcher settling in his spot.

"Come on," Cap said to Bailey, just above a whisper.

Bailey started moving forward again and was almost to him. Sweat streamed down his temples. He could hear nothing—no birds, no breeze, just the sound of Bailey's small feet shuffling through the dirt.

And then the front door slammed open and there was Vega, half her face covered in blood, aiming her pistol at Dena.

Dena fired at Vega, missing, hitting the door and shattering the frame, splinters falling on the porch in a cloud.

Bailey froze and screamed, a foot away from Cap, and Cap yelled, "Vega, don't!"

But Vega wasn't hearing him.

Cap threw his body over Bailey, nesting-doll style, as Vega started to shoot. Shot one was at Dena's hands before she could fire again; the gun flew to the ground and Dena let out a piercing scream that sounded like a birdcall, blood spraying. She fell back against the car, hands curled into her chest, and howled, started to slide down but didn't get far.

Vega came down the stairs of the porch, loose-limbed and wobbling like Dorothy's Scarecrow, and shot again, hitting Dena's right shoulder. Then one knee, then the other. Four shots. Dena was on the ground now, convulsing, vomit bubbling from her mouth.

Cap pushed Bailey's face into his shoulder so she wouldn't see. Vega staggered toward Dena.

"Vega!" Cap called, trying to wake her up.

She turned to him and lowered the gun. He got a better look at her face now, the blood coming from someplace on her forehead that was distended and starting to swell. She regarded him with her non-bloodied eye, but Cap knew she couldn't see him—the eye was rolling and squinting, her head starting to droop and then snap back up, like someone falling asleep on a plane.

"Where's Kylie?" she said.

She fell to her knees, then forward, and passed out, dirt swirling around the outline of her body.

Cap wanted to go to her but didn't want to let go of Bailey, who was gripping his sleeves. She pulled her head away from him gently and looked up at him, whispered with her puppy breath, "Kylie's not here. Evan took her."

15

VEGA WAS FULLY CLOTHED ON THE BEACH, AND IT WAS HOT AND bright. She tried standing, but it was a lot of work, first to get to her knees, then upright. Was it the Pacific, that little beach near Monterey, darker as it got deeper, whirlpools spinning in the distance? But the sand was different here than she remembered, muddy, her feet in her boots sinking and sticking every time she took a step.

That's because you're dreaming, asshole. She tried to take off her dream clothes, but they were heavy, draped around her like towels, each second that passed making her hotter and hotter, blood roiling and bones rattling in her torso as she made her way to the water.

Then she was in, her head under, but still she was breathing, taking water into her nose and mouth and throat and lungs, and then she heard the voice of the boy in the tank.

"Can you hear me?"

That brought her back to Hyacinth Avenue, in the neighborhood where all the streets were named for flowers. It was a cute little town, except for all the meth. Trees and fences and pinwheels in the breeze.

Was it that day again? This is death, then, she thought. Reliving all the big days.

It had been three months since Perry had died, and Vega was working freelance for a couple of different bail bondsmen, guys you wouldn't necessarily cross the street to avoid but not people she would call friends or even business partners.

She'd stopped drinking for the most part, had started and quit yoga, ran five miles every morning and did pull-ups on a bar in her closet. She'd mostly stopped talking. Ordered what she could online so she wouldn't have to speak to people: protein bars, toilet paper, mags for her firearms. She'd started carrying a Springfield in a shoulder holster instead of the Browning rifle on jobs, kept the out-the-front knife strapped to her calf.

The neighborhood was quiet, people at school or work or locked inside watching talk shows, lifting shaking spoons of cereal to their mouths. She found the block, then the house. Not the nicest of either. She opened the gate, went up the path, and not up the porch steps but around the side. Looked in the windows but couldn't see anything— blinds shut, frames locked.

Then a back door. She opened the screen door, doorknob jammed. Push-button lock. Took a minute or two with a paper clip. Click, then open. She drew the Springfield, held it with both hands.

She stepped into a moderately messy kitchen and smelled cigarette smoke, bacon, sweat. She could hear the television coming from another room and stepped around the table, got close to the doorway and took a little look.

There was her skip, Quincy-Ray Day, lying on the couch smoking a pipe with a girl asleep on his lap. She did not have to look at her phone to make sure it was him. Tiny brass-snap eyes, cheeks red with acne and scars, oily ginger hair. She didn't see a gun anywhere near him, which meant a little. Could be one between the couch cushions, under the girl, stuck in the back of his pants. But if it was not immediately visible, then it was also not immediately accessible. Add that to both his hands being occupied, one with the pipe, one with the lighter, and that gave Vega a nice fat set of seconds.

She moved quickly into the living room toward Quincy-Ray, pointing the Springfield right at him. She watched his fuzzy eyes focus on her, making sure she wasn't a hallucination, and then when he realized it, he dropped the pipe and jumped off the couch, the girl falling hard to the floor, screaming. And Quincy-Ray scrambled to his feet and raced for the door.

Oh, Jesus, thought Vega. You dumbass saltine motherfucker.

"What the fuck, what the fuck?!" yelled the girl.

Vega glanced at her, saw no features except brown teeth and a white tongue lolling around like a piece of fish.

Vega took one more step and pressed the Springfield into the back of Quincy-Ray's neck.

"Stop," she said. "Stay on your knees."

He stopped and stayed. The girl kept chattering but Vega ignored her.

"Reggie Guff's looking for you, Quincy-Ray," she said. "Put your hands behind your back."

Vega took one hand off the gun and reached for her belt where her cuffs were hanging. She knew a second before it happened—he was taking too long to bring his left arm back.

Vega turned around just in time. The girl was lifting a bowl, about ten inches in diameter, and had started to bring it down on Vega's head.

Vega blocked it with one arm and dropped the cuffs but not the gun. She hit the girl in the mouth with it, while Quincy-Ray tackled her. They both fell to the ground then. He was on top of Vega for only a second. His weight was soft and heavy in a somnambulant way, and he tried to grab her gun but ignored her left hand, so she hit him in the nose with the heel of her hand, and he rolled off her. She grabbed his hair and yanked his head off the ground, blood starting to run from his nostrils, and turned him over. He flailed and she sat on top of him, gun to the back of the neck again.

"Put your hands behind your back. Again," she said.

The girl moaned and cried in a pile next to them.

"He's got a boy in there, bitch," she said to Vega.

Vega cuffed Quincy-Ray.

"The fuck you talking about, Choppers?" Vega said, standing.

"He's got a boy in the bathroom," she said, holding a newspaper to her lips, the split in the middle gushing blood.

"Fuck you," said Quincy-Ray. "He ain't mine. He belongs to the guy who owns the house."

"They're all into some sick shit," said the girl.

"I didn't do nothing to that boy," said Quincy-Ray, arching his back, trying to flip over.

Vega went to the front door and unlocked the locks, opened it up. She heard some birds and smelled the air.

"You," she said to the girl. "Get the fuck out of here."

"I'm telling you the truth, bitch," she said, her lips and cheek starting to blow up.

"Get the fuck out of here or I will break your fucking fingers in this fucking door!" Vega shouted, gripping the doorknob.

The girl jumped, grabbed a backpack, stepped over Quincy-Ray like he was a puddle, and left, dripping blood on the carpet as she went.

Vega slammed the door.

"I'm serious, girl," said Quincy-Ray. "I had nothing to do with that boy in there. I's just staying here a couple weeks."

Vega left him and drew the Springfield again. She walked softly the way she'd come, moved through the kitchen except took a left, passed a room she guessed was a bedroom though there wasn't a bed in it, only stuffed black garbage bags.

Then a narrow door that she opened slowly into a dark room that smelled rotten, the only light in the room coming from a small gray window on the other side of a filmy shower curtain.

She kept the gun in front of her and let her eyes adjust, held her breath. It was then that she realized there was someone else in the room, breathing shallowly, much lower to the ground than she was.

She kept both hands tight on the Springfield, felt around with her elbow for the light switch and flipped it.

There was a lot to see, all at once. A bathroom that wasn't unusual. Toilet, bathtub, sink. Except under the sink, across the floor, was a tank, like a big iguana tank, open on the top. Later she would learn it was thirty by thirty by eighteen and made of acrylic.

There was not an iguana inside. There was a boy.

He was younger than a teenager but not little; he was naked, in a fetal position, covered in shit and blood. His head had been shaved, and his eyes were closed, but he was breathing, shivering. Hands cuffed with cheap restraints around the pipe under the sink, his arms stretched unnaturally above him, fingers blue.

Vega felt dizzy and remembered to breathe. She squatted and put her gun in her holster, rubbed her hands over her mouth. She looked at his face and recognized the crinkle of his bottom lip, the attached earlobes. She had seen him on TV, missing from Modesto, thirty miles south. She sifted through the trash in her mind for his name.

"Ethan?" she said. "Ethan Moreno."

He stirred but didn't wake up.

"Ethan, can you hear me?"

His lids fluttered, just a small beating of wings, his eyes not staying on her.

Later she couldn't remember exactly what had happened or how she felt. She told the cops; she told CNN. It was like she'd climbed into the backseat and let someone else drive, but she was still giving directions. First the kitchen, under the sink, looking for a wrench or a hammer but found a small fire extinguisher instead. Then back to the bathroom, where she slammed it against the pipe, over and over, for ten, twenty minutes until it busted and water sprayed them both, and she untangled his hands and reached inside the tank and put her arms under and around him, feeling his cold, wet skin, the bones of his hips and back, and she lifted him out, his eyes still fluttering.

Then she ran out the back door the way she had come, to her car, curling his head toward her chest.

"Ethan, can you hear me?"

He spoke into her shirt, his breath a hot burst.

"Can you hear me?" he repeated.

She smiled without meaning to, said, "Yes, I can."

Then: "Can you tell me your name?"

Then he was gone, and so was that street and that day, and so was Vega for that matter; she couldn't see a thing except the flashlight in her eyes, and all she kept hearing was that doctor asking if she could hear him and if she could tell him her name. She started to speak, but the words turned to salt in her mouth, and her eyes sealed shut as she tried to get back to the boy in the tank.

Cap had never seen media like this.

Twenty or thirty vans and trucks with every three-letter and double-digit combination on their doors were parked outside the emergency room entrance. Men with cameras, correspondents in sportswear, antenna masts spinning. Cap watched them through the spotted beige blinds of a hospital administrator's office in Frackville, a town that made Denville look downright cosmopolitan, where the sole local ambulance and one sheriff's car had brought Dena, McKie, Bailey, and Vega to be treated.

"You can't contain these things anymore," said the Fed, standing a foot or so behind Cap. "When I started, twenty-five years ago? It was easy to stay five steps ahead of them. You could get someone in and out of the hospital or the courthouse. Jail. You could go through a back door and throw a coat over their head. Now one person takes a picture with a phone and you get this shit."

Cap scrolled through the flipbook of potential responses in his head: "You got that right, what a bunch of dicks," or "Hey, they're just trying to make a living like everyone else," or "This could help us—the more attention, the better," or "This could hurt us—the more distractions, the harder it will be to find Kylie."

He said none of them, instead whispered, "Watch the language, okay?"

The Fed nodded, remembering.

Then they both glanced to the corner of the room where Bailey sat on a chair, drinking Pedialyte from a straw. She didn't seem to hear them, staring at the ground, still in the dirty dress, legs kicking the air like a lazy swim stroke.

Vega sat straight up in bed, hips and torso shuddering with a single jolt. She looked around quickly for clues. Green plaid curtains, green plaid chair, television mounted to the wall. It could have passed for the world's most uncomfortable motel room until she looked down at the stiff white sheets, flimsy gray blanket, adjustable side rails, remote with worn arrow buttons. Another goddamn hospital.

She saw the IV needle stuck in the top of her left hand. With her right she touched her chest, looked down the gown in the front. Bra and underwear still on. She pressed her lips against her teeth, then rubbed them together, realized she was taking too long to do these things and enjoying things too much—they must have given her painkillers. She touched her lips, smelled her fingers, saw the residue sprinkle on the tips and the imprint from the handle of the Springfield like little tire tracks on her palms.

Then she remembered Dena Macht on the ground, Bailey Brandt with her arms hooked around Caplan's waist, the snapping of a wooden plank over McKie's back, and then she lifted her hand and touched the bandage above her eye. The pain was dulled by the drugs but pulsed from the pressure, a drop rippling through a puddle.

Vega heard noise outside the window—voices, vehicles. The first thing she thought of was a stock car race, the time her mother took her and Tommy to see NASCAR racing at the Sonoma tracks, the swell and grind of the engines, the hiss and howl of the crowd. But this was not a sprint.

Vega pushed the twisted sheet off of her and swung her legs to the floor. Slowly she stood, one hand on the rail, the other on the IV stand. The bottoms of her feet felt spongy, the muscles in her legs weak, but she knew it was just the drugs; she hadn't been in a coma, for Christ's sake. She walked to the window, tugging the IV stand behind her, and pulled back the curtain.

She saw Jamie Brandt, Gail and Arlen White on either side of her, holding her arms, and Maggie behind them, in the middle of a herd of vans. A pack of newspeople waving mikes and cameras. Gail shoved one of their arms away as they ran toward the emergency room doors, leaving Maggie Shambley's lawyer in her unwrinkled suit behind to talk to the press.

Vega went back to the bed to sit, pushing the IV stand in front of her. She examined the needle in her hand and thought. She'd seen enough nurses do this with her mother. Only one or two of them were good, the rest were always stabbing and re-stabbing her hands, muttering, "Small veins," with disdain like it was her mother's fault. But by the end she was so high most of the time it didn't matter. She didn't notice the blood drops on the mattress or the bruised skin below her knuckles.

Those were actually sweet memories for Vega, when her mother was stoned on morphine, because she seemed to enjoy things and she wasn't debilitated by anxiety as she'd been before the cancer. Her mother had stopped driving a couple of years previously because she was afraid she'd crash, so she'd made Vega and Tommy and her second husband, TJ, drive her everywhere. Then she stopped riding in cars altogether because she said they felt too small.

But on the morphine, she laughed and swore, leaned back on the pillow and gazed at Vega as if she were a gently waving daffodil. Vega thought her mother looked pretty then, with her little scraps of hair and thinned eyebrows, clear white skin and deep-end eyes, like an old elf queen.

Vega stared at the bag and the slow drip of liquid into the tubing. She reached up and rolled her thumb on the little wheel to pinch off the tube inside, shutting down the flow. Then she looked around, grabbed a tissue from the tray table next to the bed and folded it into a tiny square. She unpeeled the tape from the needle, pressed the tissue square over the entry point into her skin, and pulled the needle out, slow and careful, then strapped the tape over the tissue.

I could have done that for her, she thought briefly, sadly. She slapped her palms against her thighs, rubbed them through the gown. For a moment she felt very old and very scared. Then she stood and walked on her rubbery legs to the door and pushed it closed. Her shirt and jacket hung on a hook on the back, pants folded neatly over a hanger, black boots against the wall. She gave them a tight little smile and pulled the gown off over her head.

Bailey didn't seem to hear the noise coming from outside. She had finished the Pedialyte, and had asked for more, which Cap didn't have access to in the administrator's office, so he'd given her a small cup of water. He knew he couldn't give her too much, that she was at least mildly dehydrated and would need more electrolytes, salt, and sugar. Cap squatted in front of her while the Fed looked at his phone.

"She's here," he said to Cap.

Cap smiled at Bailey, examined the slender curvature of her cheeks and chin. She really did look like the Shrinky Dinks version of Jamie, not just younger, but everything in miniature, down to the expressive almond eyes.

The child was calm and seemed to trust him. He didn't flatter himself that he had a way with kids; he knew to her right now he was merely the agent of change, taking her from somewhere terrifying to another place, and considering the instability of Dena's and McKie's state of mind, another place was better no matter where it was. Because there were a ton of worse things you could do to an eight-year-old girl besides kill her.

But she had held on to him after Vega passed out, listened to him when he asked her to wait in the car while he went inside the house of the old man with the truck to use the phone, stood next to him and pressed her head into his side and under his arm when the sheriff and the ambulance showed up.

"Your mom's here," said Cap to her.

"Is she sick?" asked Bailey.

Cap breathed out an airy laugh and tried not to burst into tears like a maniac. Having had what would probably prove to be the singular most traumatic experience of her life, here was Bailey Brandt worried about her mother.

Before he could say yes, there was the ding of the elevator and then a rush of noise in the hallway, chatter and footsteps and Jamie Brandt's burnt voice above them all, yelling, "Bailey!"

Bailey jumped in her chair and stood. She looked once more at Cap, and he smiled at her and nodded. She appeared unsure of everything, but not afraid. She peered toward the doorway.

Then Jamie was there, nearly hyperventilating, her jean jacket and purse falling off her, like she had climbed a rope ladder to get there. She was thin and pale and weak but still she ran and stumbled to Bailey, hitting the floor on all fours and crawling the last step to her. Bailey said, "Mama," and slung her arms around Jamie's neck, and Jamie grabbed her and moaned, her mouth open, cupping Bailey's head and sweeping her hands over Bailey's hair.

Then everyone was in the administrator's small office: Traynor, Junior, Gail and Arlen, Maggie, two doctors and two nurses. Gail went to Jamie and Bailey and started hugging them too and thanking God, and Cap started to back out and make his way to the door.

Then Arlen was in front of him, pumping his hand, saying thank you and asking how can we thank you and remarking on what a blessed day this was. And Cap thought the day was blessed until it turned on you, and if they couldn't find Kylie it would turn quick, sweet cream into bad milk.

A blessed day. Well, whatever you say.

Then a dark blot clouded the corner of his eye, and he turned and saw that it was Vega, standing against the wall at the end of the hallway. Dressed in her black uniform, the pants and sleeves coated with dust and dirt from the Macht cabin. Her face was scabbed and scraped on one side, a bandage over her eye where McKie had hit her with something hard and sharp.

Gail White called for her husband, her voice strongly reminiscent of a bow saw on plywood, and Arlen immediately stopped thanking Cap and God and hustled into the office.

Cap turned back to Vega and took some steps, and then she took some steps until they were close, and he could really see the scratches on her cheek like an animal skin pattern and the gloss of the bacitracin, the gray-blue bruise rising around the puncture wound, swelling her eyebrow.

"I didn't think they'd let you out so soon," said Cap. "They said you were dehydrated."

"I'm okay," she said, pressing her lips together. "They got me on some kinda painkiller."

She squinted one eye at him and looked a little tipsy.

"You're not supposed to be up, are you?" he said.

She shrugged, nodded to the office.

"They all in there?"

Cap nodded.

"Bailey tell you anything?" Vega said.

"Not really. We were holding questioning until Jamie could get here."

"Where's Dena?"

"In ICU. Which in this hospital is a room with a sign on the door that says ICU. She's conscious but not at all lucid."

"What about McKie?"

"He's in a bed. Local sheriff's watching him."

"Awake though?"

"Yeah. Concussed," Cap said, then smiled at her. "What'd you do to him anyway?"

"Hit him with a plank-a-wood," she said, words running together. Then she pointed to the bandage. "Same one he got me with."

Cap looked at the bandage, imagined a plank of wood hitting him in the forehead, a jagged edge or a nail punching a hole in his skull.

He took in the parts of Vega's face, including the puffy eyebrow and scrapes, and did not think he would look as good in such a situation. The kiss in the woods came back to him fast, his embarrassment and desire taking the form of a stomach cramp. He pulled at his belt.

"You okay?" Vega said. "What's wrong with your pants?"

"Stomach thing," he said.

She ignored him, because she was either high or disinterested, and he was grateful. Then he wondered if she remembered it at all, the kiss, if it had been wiped away by the trauma or if she'd slipped it into the inside pocket where she kept all things vulnerable and emotive.

Then a crowd came out of the office: Traynor and Junior and the Fed, the doctors and the nurse, the hospital administrator, and Maggie Shambley. The administrator shut the door.

"Family needs a few minutes," said Traynor in Cap's direction.

"Miss Vega," said Maggie, rushing up, then to Cap, "Thank you both. I knew you could do it," she said to Vega, taking one hand in both of hers. "I read about how you found that boy in Modesto, and I just knew it."

She whispered the last few words, overcome. Vega gave a mandatory smile, and her eyes were lazy from the drugs, also sad because she was Vega—it was Friday and they were still one girl down.

After everyone had thanked everyone two or three times, and Traynor and the Fed had laid out the schedule, they'd all decided that it made sense to do the interviews right there in the hospital to (a) get the freshest statements; (b) play keep-away from the media; (c) get McKie and possibly Dena to talk before they figured out they wanted lawyers.

They were gathered in the hospital staff room, just marginally larger than the administrator's office. The Brandt-White family lawyer was named Sam, tall and horsey with blond highlighted hair and a blouse with a silky ascot attached. Gail White had whispered to Vega in the hallway, "She's from Philly," to explain the sophistication, foreign and apparent. As Sam spoke she held out one hand and cut across it with the other, like she was chopping onions.

"Jamie's ready, and Bailey's ready," she said. "You've got to wait for the social worker from CPS or you're going to get heat from your DA."

"We're fine with that," said Traynor. "We know most of them. Do we know if Dena Macht's awake?"

"In and out," said Cap, rocking slightly on the balls of his feet. "McKie's awake."

"Anyone coming for either of them?" said Traynor.

"Hospital notified Dena's parents," said Junior. "They're on their way. Still looking for next of kin for McKie."

"I'll take McKie," said the Fed, fairly definitive. Then, "My supervisor's meeting us in Denville."

"I'd like someone in the room," said Traynor. "Junior?"

Junior nodded. Cap cracked his neck to one side quickly, without sound. Vega recognized it as a signal that he was getting ready to be pissed off.

"Hey, we brought him in," he said, looking at Vega. "We should be in there too. At least one of us."

Traynor shrugged very gently and said to the Fed, "I have no problem with that."

The Fed thought about it for a minute and then said, "I lead."

"Of course," said Cap.

And Junior will be there as window dressing, thought Vega.

"You can't interview McKie right now," said Sam the lawyer to Cap.

He shook his head, incredulous, preparing again to be pissed off.

"Why the hell not?"

"Because the Brandt-White family wants you to interview Bailey. With the social worker," she said.

Cap was confused now. All the men were, actually, but Vega knew exactly what was coming. She'd seen it when she'd come down the stairs from the Macht cabin, the blurry vision of Bailey's arms linked around Cap's waist, the little girl's face turned up to him, making a study of his chin.

"Jamie Brandt asked for me?" he said.

That made Sam the lawyer smile, tickled that he didn't understand.

"Jamie agreed, but it was Bailey who asked for you," she said.

They all took a second to absorb that. Vega watched as Cap's brow softened.

"Fair enough," he said, his voice hoarse. "Then Vega can be the third with McKie."

Junior bristled and said, "Maybe not the best idea seeing she so recently beat the crap out of him?"

"I'll stand somewhere where he can't see me," she offered.

The Fed perked up and pointed at her.

"You keep yourself controlled, ma'am. We can discuss ahead of time what you want covered, but you don't make a sound, and you don't make yourself known. Yes?"

He reminded Vega of someone, but it was surprisingly not the high school vice principal. There was nothing condescending about the tone, only firm and informative. Like a stern museum docent: Stand right behind this piece of tape, please. And do not touch a thing.

For the first time that day, Cap noticed there was a ripe smell coming off Bailey, like something fermenting, not entirely unpleasant. She had not been bathed and was in a frayed gown with sleeping tigers printed on it, sitting on her mother's lap on the edge of a bed. Even though she was slight, she was still about fifty pounds and four feet tall, and Jamie struggled to hold her but showed no sign of letting go, one hand around Bailey's thigh, pulling her legs into place, the other on Bailey's head and hair. Bailey leaned her head on Jamie's shoulder, the tips of her toes grazing the floor.

The CPS rep was young and named Krista. Cap remembered her a little from when he was a cop; there were only so many social workers in the county dispatched to do the uncompromising work of child abuse investigation. She blended in, though, with all the human services professionals he knew—mostly women, smart and overworked, usually with clothes that didn't fit quite right, slacks and cardigans bought on sale.

The pediatrician, a stocky woman in jeans with a string of tiny hoop earrings on one earlobe, had just completed a basic head-to-toe exam on Bailey, confirmed the EMT's diagnosis of mild dehydration, found no broken bones, but there were two small bruises and irritation around her right wrist where she'd possibly been tied up.

Cap watched as Krista tried to broach the topic of a rape kit, but since getting Bailey back Jamie had run the bases of Gratitude and Fragility and was now tagging Adamant and Pissy, or doing the best she could in her state.

"We're at risk of losing any possible evidence of that type of activity," Krista said, speaking as formally as she could, Cap sensed, so the adults would understand but the meaning might go over Bailey's head.

"She don't need it," Jamie whispered, her voice thrashed from the tubes. "She told me they didn't touch her like that." She said gently into Bailey's hair, "They touch you like that?"

Bailey shook her head sleepily.

"She may not remember for some time everything exactly as it happened," Krista said, more quietly. "Wouldn't you want to know?"

That caught a thread for Jamie. She considered it. Then she turned to Cap, her eyes heavy.

"What do you think?" she whispered, pointing at him with her chin.

Krista and the pediatrician looked at him, and he thought he could see a glint of Bailey's visible eye peeking out from Jamie's neck too.

"Well," he said, "how recent does the activity have to have been in order to show up in the kit?"

Krista shrugged, said, "Depends. Certain physical elements degrade obviously. But bruising . . . scratches."

"I looked at her," said Jamie, more helpful now. "When she used the bathroom, she looked fine. Everything looked normal."

"Sure," he said. "I think what Krista's saying is there are some things we can't see, right?"

Krista nodded.

"But," Cap said with a small cough. "I think the odds are that there has not been this type of activity, committed by these particular suspects."

Krista opened her mouth to speak, and Cap held his hands up in humility and kept talking.

"I'm not saying it's not possible. Just saying from our investigation, me and my partner's, these suspects—"

He paused, stopped himself from saying "didn't want her for that" because it sounded crude in his head.

"Had other goals," he finally said.

Krista almost spoke again, then closed her mouth and gave a tight little smile.

"But if we're ready for some questions," Cap said, looking to Jamie, "we can, I hope, get some more information. Right?"

Jamie pressed her nose against Bailey's head.

"Mr. Caplan's gonna ask you questions now, okay?"

Bailey brought her face out of Jamie's neck and leaned back on her.

"Yeah," she said. "I'm okay with it."

Then she smiled at him.

Cap smiled too. The more he looked at her, the more he thought she was a gorgeous kid, the more he wanted to do things that would make her happy.

"Okay," said Cap, tapping the Record button on the DVR. "So can you tell me what happened last Saturday morning at Ridgewood? After your mom went to Kmart?"

"Like, right after?" she said.

"Yeah, right after," said Cap. "Your mom gets out of the car. What do you and Kylie do?"

He watched Jamie's eyelids twitch and nearly shut, like hairs were being removed from her head one by one.

Bailey, however, had the advantage of youth and did not yet view her ordeal as a tragic story. For her it was merely one thing after another, which, if her recollection of events didn't fuse together, would be very helpful for Cap.

She told him everything, and her voice was high and thin, no real dip or modulation through the story of their leaving the mall and getting into the car, stopping for Blizzards at Dairy Queen on the way to the Macht cabin, even when she admitted to getting scared and missing Jamie, even when McKie pushed her into the kitchenette roughly because she was in his way. It was only when she got to the part detailing the realization that her sister was leaving with Evan Marsh, how she had grabbed and scratched his hand and wrist trying to hold on to him to make them stay; it was just when she was left with Dena and McKie, when she realized it was getting dark outside, that she started to cry in front of Cap just like she had in front of the strangers who had kidnapped her.

Vega swayed forward and back on her feet like rocking chair legs, the painkillers still suppressing whatever receptors they were meant to suppress in her central nervous system. She could sense the medication ebbing, though, as she pricked her cuticles with her thumbnails and felt startled when the spike of skin separated. She stood on one side of a grimy curtain between a vacant bed and an old heart rate monitor, the Fed and Junior on the other side of the curtain with McKie, who was cuffed to the bedrail and not in the greatest mood. Vega swore she could smell him too, the same scent that hung in the cabin—something gamey and just beginning the process of decay.

They had started nicely enough, the Fed lobbing plain questions, McKie saying yes and no like a good dog, but then it turned quickly into McKie playing pin the tail on the bad guy, who was Evan Marsh of course, McKie and Dena having been victims of unfortunate circumstances.

"So how exactly did Mr. Marsh talk you into kidnapping an eight-year-old girl?" said the Fed, all clean lawyerly manners. "I'm curious to know how he phrased it so you could think you weren't doing anything wrong."

"All he said was he needed me to hold on to a kid for a couple of days. We were never gonna keep her," McKie said.

"That's supposed to make me feel better, sir?" said the Fed. "Kidnapping a child for a week is as bad as a month is as bad as a year."

McKie's breathing accelerated, turned into a wheeze.

"Look, if you find Marsh, he'll tell you everything—he took the older one."

"Mr. Marsh is dead, Mr. McKie," said the Fed. "We think someone shot him."

"Fuckin' Marsh," McKie muttered. "Dumb motherfuckin' Marsh."

"Yeah," said the Fed, quiet, calm. "Where would someone like Marsh get fifty thousand dollars, Mr. McKie?"

McKie didn't respond right away. Vega heard nails on skin, scratching an itch. She wondered what kind of medication they had him on, how long it would take him to go into withdrawal.

"A guy," he said. "I don't know who. Some guy paid him to take the girls."

"Then why would he give one of them to you?"

Vega knocked her head lightly against the wall behind her. She pictured Kylie's face in the video at the ice cream store, the smile. *The girl's a natural-born flirt.* She knew what McKie was about to say.

"Because the guy wanted the older girl. *Just* the older girl. I guess ten-year-olds gave him a stiff but not eight-year-olds, the fuck do I know," McKie said.

Then he laughed a little at his joke.

"I'm glad you find the potential rape and murder of Kylie Brandt funny, Mr. McKie," said the Fed. "I'm sure Captain Hollows here will remember that when he speaks with his district attorney."

"Hey—" started McKie.

"Don't speak unless you're spoken to, please. You're a moron, and it grates on me," said the Fed, getting angrier. "What do you know about the man who paid Mr. Marsh to bring him Kylie Brandt?"

"Nothing," said McKie, drawing the word out. "Nada."

His tone was careless, and it made Vega want to pop his front teeth out with a flat-head screwdriver. But if he were lying he would be more committed, somber even. He was not smart enough to lie casually.

"Captain Hollows," announced the Fed, "if you have any questions, I encourage you to ask them. Mr. McKie's made me so tired with his cerebral impairment that I can't trust myself not to slap his mouth if I continue to conduct the interview."

Vega extended her neck like a weed trying to reach the light, listening.

"Yes, I have some questions," said Hollows. "Where did you say you met Evan Marsh for the first time?"

Vega heard the creak of the mattress as McKie moved around.

"Stag's Bar on Seventh."

"When was that?"

"I don't know. Year ago."

"And how did you get to know each other?"

"What do you mean?" said McKie, confused.

"In my experience," said Hollows, "drug addicts get to know each other because they buy drugs together, sell them together, do them together. It's like a burrow of rats sharing the same pile of garbage. And Denville's not a big place. So did you and Evan Marsh share that type of relationship?"

Vega smiled. Hollows could sound sanctimonious and bitchy reading a grocery list, and she recognized that it probably made him good at his job.

"Yeah, sure, we bought from the same guys," said McKie.

"You traveled in the same circles?" said Hollows.

"Yeah," said McKie, sounding exhausted from the repetition. "Yes."

"So how exactly would Evan Marsh meet Kylie Brandt, if these were the types of people he was associating with?"

McKie was quiet.

"I'll rephrase that," said Hollows, ever more condescending. "Where would a little girl meet two dumb junkies like you and Evan Marsh?"

"I don't know, man," said McKie, angry and annoyed. "At a party or some shit. I wasn't there."

Vega pictured a room. Beige walls and beige floors. No furniture, no windows. There was Kylie in her party dress on one side; there was Evan Marsh in jeans and a T-shirt on the other. No one else.

"Come on, John," said Hollows. "Where would that party be? You think Marsh went to her middle school dance?"

Vega filled in the room. Flat-screen TV. Cardboard box for a coffee table. One black cat with white paws. She touched the bandage above her eye, and the ache rushed across her brow.

"One of Marsh's hookups," said McKie. "He was buying, and she was there."

In her head a blue needle moved across the spiking red sound waves on an audio memo, a scratchy voice saying, "I had clients here. People get freaked out they see a kid."

"That's what he told you?" Hollows said, skeptical.

"Yeah, that's what he told me, the fuck I know!" McKie shouted, banging his fist into the bottom of his food tray.

Back in Vega's room: Evan Marsh, Charlie Bright, guys who looked like one or either of them—doubled and tripled, smoking weed, drinking beer, counting money.

And then Evan and Kylie in the corner of the room, talking, getting to know each other in the few minutes it took for Evan Marsh to get hold of a bad idea, and for Alex Chaney to get his keys so he could drive Kylie back home.

They were in Traynor's SUV, Junior driving with Traynor sitting shotgun, twisting his body so he could talk to the passengers in the backseat: Cap and the Fed, with Vega between them like the little sister on a road trip. Vega's thigh was lined up against Cap's, the warmth blocked by the fabric of their pants, but it crossed his mind his palm could likely span the width of her leg, that she was actually far more delicate than either of them wanted to think. She reminded him of birds he would see hanging on the feeder Nell had strung in the backyard a few winters back, puffing out feathers to protect brittle bodies.

On the way out of the hospital, the administrator and a gray-faced doctor stopped them and made Vega sign a form, saying they weren't responsible for the consequences of her removing her own IV and releasing herself. The doctor gave her a Band-Aid for the spot on her hand where the IV needle had been, and told her there might be irritation where they'd administered the tetanus booster in her arm. He told her to keep the wound on her forehead clean and change the dressing once a day. Vega seemed bored by the instructions, took the pen impatiently from the administrator and scrawled "AV" on the black line. To Cap, she looked smaller, her head bowed, taking careful tightrope steps to the car.

Cap realized it was his turn to talk, after the Fed had debriefed them on the interview with McKie, and Junior had instructed Ralz to bring in Alex Chaney for questioning. He tapped his fingertip on the Fast-Forward button on the recorder and gave them the highlights.

"After Kylie leaves with Marsh, McKie and Dena give Bailey some food and water and tell her she's going home soon, so she does what they tell her for two days; she notices they nod off on the couch around the same time every night. I'm guessing that's when they shot up or took their Vikes or whatever. So on the third night she waits until they're asleep and then tries getting out the back door. McKie comes to and catches her, ties her by the wrist to the bed with an extension cord.

"She said he and Dena started fighting, fed her less, kept her tied up and made her pee in a cup. That was the last two days. Then we showed up."

"Did she hear Marsh say anything about the man with the money?" said Traynor.

Cap held his fingertip to the Fast-Forward button.

"Just one thing," he said.

He let go, clicked up the sound.

"*I know this is hard,*" said Cap on the recorder. "*Was Kylie upset to leave you . . . when she and Evan left?*"

"*Yeah*," said Bailey, sounding even younger and squeakier than eight years old. "*We were, like, hugging and crying.*" Bailey's voice shook and rattled. "*Evan said it would be okay; he'd bring Kylie back soon and we could see our mom soon. . . .*"

"*What did Kylie say?*"

"*She told him she didn't want to leave me there, in the cabin, with John and Dena. And he was like, we'll be right back after we visit your friend.*"

Cap tapped the Stop button.

Traynor looked at the Fed, then Vega, then Cap. He shrugged and shook his head at the same time.

"*Your* friend," said Vega.

"Yes," Cap said. "Bailey, quoting Marsh, who says *your* friend to Kylie."

"I heard that," said Traynor. "You're thinking that means Kylie knows the moneyman?"

"Maybe," said Cap.

Traynor turned to the Fed and nodded.

"Easily a slip of the tongue or memory," said the Fed. "It's a stretch."

"Sure," said Cap. "Stack it up is all I'm saying."

Traynor waved his hand in the air directly above his head. Reminded Cap of the white-wigged politicians in British Parliament he'd seen on TV.

"So noted," said Traynor, a red light flashing over his face. "Captain," he said to Junior, aggravated, "pull over and let all this pass."

Junior pulled over, and they all watched the caravan: the Whites' car containing Jamie and her parents and aunt and Bailey, the lawyer's car close behind, two state police, three local, and then the news vans—ten that had become twenty while the authorities had been conducting the interviews in the hospital.

A helicopter cut the air above them, hanging low like a mosquito. Cap lowered his window, leaned his head out and peered up, shutting one eye to the rough wind from the rotors. The sound amplified and became less choppy, turned into a booming rumble. There was something strangely peaceful about it; Cap had the feeling that if he closed his eyes and opened his arms the gust might lift him up, he might rise and float—until a voice or a car horn shocked him awake, brought him back down fast.

16

VEGA WATCHED THE TV IN THE BREAK ROOM BACK AT THE POLICE station, saw Jamie hobbling out of the hospital clutching Bailey to her side, Sam the lawyer stepping between them and the cameras, then Hollows, Cap, herself. Her eye twitched when she saw her face on the screen, the gravel scratches and the bandage, the bruise around her eyebrow. It all looked worse than it felt, although now that the last of the drugs had worn off, the pain was manifesting as weariness, joints and muscles cracked and stretched. She swallowed the rest of the room-temp Lipton tea from the cup in her hand.

"Vega."

It was Hollows in the doorway. He nodded at her, and she nodded at him, and the nods meant that she should follow him. They went to Traynor's office, where Vega felt like she had missed something. It was Traynor behind his desk and Cap leaning on the wall, the Fed and the Fed's boss, who was silver haired and looked like a businessman instead of an agent—tie clip, cuff links, clean lines on the pants. He was tired in the face though, thin but swollen skin under the eyes and jawline. He spoke quietly.

"This is Miss Vega?"

"Yes, sir," said the Fed. "Miss Vega, this is my supervisor, Special Agent Gatlin."

Gatlin stood and shook her hand, glanced and read the screen on the tablet in his other hand.

"Miss Vega, I understand you shot and wounded a key witness in this investigation, and now she is unresponsive?"

He did that question-mark ending, reserved for lawyers and teenage girls. It was difficult to know if he actually wanted an answer. He closed the cover on his tablet.

"That's not the ideal outcome," he said to her, as if they were the only two in the room. "I imagine you'll have to appear before a grand jury at some point."

"Is this really your jurisdiction, sir?" said Cap, agitated.

"Caplan—" said Traynor.

The Fed rubbed his eyes.

"No, let's just hold on," said Cap, coming off the wall. "You're coming in here and threatening my partner with indictment after she acted in self-defense and defense of a minor. We don't need that kind of help. She doesn't give a shit if she goes before a grand jury. She doesn't give a shit if she goes to jail."

Gatlin smiled thoughtfully, like he was doing math in his head, and said, "What a relief that must be."

"Yes, it is," said Cap. He patted his hand over the middle of his chest, flattening an invisible tie. "It's fucking heavenly. So, sir, do you have anything you can bring to this case, or did you just come here to slap us on the wrist? Because if that's the case, however much the Bureau paid for your plane ticket, it seems like too much."

Vega knew he was tired, could hear the cords straining in his throat, could see his eyes watering as he got more and more pissed off.

For just a second, the room was quiet and airless, and in that peculiar space Vega thought of him unclasping her bra and wondered if he could do it with one hand.

Traynor coughed as an intro and said, "Sir, we've all been working round the clock here, and I think what Mr. Caplan is getting at is we've made it a point not to get caught up in digressions. Do you have anything new for us?"

"Just one thing," Gatlin said, not angry, no longer bemused.

Vega got the impression nothing moved him much in any direction.

He opened his tablet again and tapped the screen. He showed it to Traynor but spoke to the room.

"We've been re-examining the Ashley Cahill and Sydney McKenna cases," he began.

"*Re*-examining?" said Cap. "Aren't they still open?"

Gatlin turned to him and poked his tongue around his cheek.

Traynor touched one finger to his temple like he was about to tell the future. Vega felt a laugh shudder through her chest and throat; she kept her mouth shut tight.

"Yes, Mr. Caplan, they are open, just a bit chilly. We found one more connection—both Ashley and Sydney took ballet classes at small studios."

"So did Kylie," said Vega.

Everyone thought about it.

"Yes," said Gatlin. "And all three of those studios used the same distributor—Moreland Athletics."

"So are we talking to them?" said Traynor.

"We are," said Gatlin. "We have a man there going through employee lists, looking at who has made deliveries or sales to all three locations."

"Wouldn't it be better to isolate Kylie Brandt's first?" said Junior. "In the interest of time?"

"Can't be too many guys who've worked there over four years, in deliveries and sales in those three areas," said Vega.

"That's exactly right. By looking at all three scenarios, Captain, we'll actually narrow our suspect list," Gatlin said.

"Moreland Athletics didn't come up in the ballet teacher's statement, far as I know," said Traynor, standing. "While we're waiting for lists, let's cover it again, everyone who works there. The suspect profile is someone with substantial disposable income, probably male, probably Caucasian. Special Agent Gatlin, you and Special Agent Cartwright can accompany Captain Hollows to the location if you'd like to see it."

"That's fine," said Gatlin, eyes on his tablet.

"Vega, Cap—Alex Chaney's waiting for you."

Chaney was pacing and gnawing his fingertips when they came in. He wheeled around and shut his eyes in relief when he saw them.

"Hey, you guys . . . could you guys tell them I didn't have anything to do with this—you know I didn't have anything to do with this, we talked about it, we had a—"

"Sit down, Alex," said Cap.

He was past exhausted and anxious and was now feeling like he had felt when Nell was a newborn and he was working certain cases—

awake but not awake, when coffee didn't work anymore and it was just sugar he wanted, candy and soda.

Chaney dropped into the chair and put his thumbs and forefingers on his temples, making an awning out of his forehead.

Cap sat across from him, and Vega stood behind Cap.

"You sell drugs to a guy named Evan Marsh?" Cap said.

Chaney shivered and shrugged.

"Yeah, sure. Works at the Giant, right?"

"That's right," said Cap. "Now you need to think—the day Kylie came to see you, was Marsh there too?"

Chaney looked back and forth between them, cornered.

"He got something to do with Kylie?"

Cap cut the air with his hand.

"Just listen to what I'm asking," he said. "The day Kylie came to see you, was Evan Marsh there?"

Chaney bit his lips so they disappeared.

"Yeah, I think so. I think that's right. I mean, it makes sense. Timing's right. Marsh comes by once a month, toward the beginning."

"But you don't remember them talking to each other specifically, or anything like that."

"No, man, I wanted to get her out of there. I said to her stay here, in the corner with the cat—she was playing with my cat—and I went to get my keys and my jacket."

"So when you came back to the living room, was she still playing with the cat?"

"No," said Chaney. "She was talking to some of them, the dopeheads, and I remember thinking she looked so much older than when I last seen her."

"Was one of them Marsh?" said Vega.

Chaney gazed up to her, his eyes wandering around her face, registering her injuries.

"I don't know. Maybe." He looked back to Cap. "I just wanted to get her out of there."

Cap tried to picture Chaney's house in daylight, tried to see Kylie there with the cat, talking to Marsh and whoever else.

"Does Marsh usually come to your place by himself?" Cap said. "Does he come with people?"

Chaney perked up, eager to answer.

"Yeah, he does," he said. "Lately a guy named Bruce."

Cap scrolled through the list of Evan Marsh's known associates in his head, thought he remembered a Bruce.

"Bartender, right?" said Vega.

Chaney rapped his knuckles on the table.

"That's right. At Stag's."

"You got a number for him?" said Cap.

Chaney pulled out his phone and tapped some buttons. Vega put the number in her phone, and then Chaney looked up at both of them and sniffed dramatically.

"We'll walk you out," said Cap.

"That's it?" said Chaney, looking like a kid who just found out he didn't have to get the flu shot.

"That's it," Cap said. "We don't have any questions or concerns regarding your small business aspirations. If you could keep track of your clientele, maybe work up a list for us of people who come to see you at the beginning of the month, that would be helpful."

"You got it, man," said Chaney. He stood and made fists, unsure of how to process the energy. He made a sound like "Hoo," part sigh and part whoop.

The three of them left the room, entered the second-floor hallway, which was narrow and crowded with circles of cops. They headed for the stairs, and then Vega stopped short in front of Cap, and Cap put his hand up in reflex, felt the lats in her back turn to clay, and then Cap saw why: Junior holding Jamie Brandt's arm, coming up the stairs.

Jamie started to smile when she saw Vega, but then her face hardened up when she caught sight of Chaney lurking behind Cap.

"The fuck is he doing here?" she whispered.

"He's helping us," said Vega.

"Helping you," said Jamie, incredulous. "He never helped anyone but himself. "What do *you* know about anything?" she said to him.

Chaney held his hands up.

"I swear, I'm here to help find her."

"The fuck are you talking about? The fuck is he talking about?" she said to Vega, her voice cracking into a shriek.

"We need to bring you up to speed, Jamie," said Cap.

"Yes, you goddamn do, Mr. Caplan. I don't know anything that's going on right now; that's what I'm doing here. What are we doing to find Kylie? What's this asshole got to do with it?"

"Jamie," said Vega. "One thing and then the other."

Jamie blinked twice like Morse code, and Vega said it again more quietly:

"One thing and then the other."

The words had a pacifying effect on Jamie while she considered the situation. She studied Vega's face, and the hallway took on the feel of a junior high basketball court before the free throw, all the parents holding their breath, hoping to hell the kid would make the shot.

At a stoplight, Vega opened a small foil envelope and shook two Advils into her mouth, tasted the sugary coating in the back of her throat and waited. The sun was starting to sink again, the temperature dropping fast after a deceptively warm day. Her window was open, and a burst of cold air shot through the car and hit the open cuts on her cheek.

She thought of when her mother used to take her and Tommy to the Russian River, and they'd wade into the water, walking on a million pebbles and then smooth, round rocks that seemed made to fit the arches of her feet. The water was cold, but she'd get used to it quickly, her body heat sinking to match it.

But then the riverbed would drop off, and the plunge wouldn't startle Vega as much as the temperature of the water, which would turn to freezing cold, the real cold, enveloping her, and she'd realize, this is what the river actually is—it is this cold, the kind that makes you blue.

That's what she felt in the air now, and that's the problem with this whole coast, she thought. They tell you it's spring, they say out like a lamb, but it's still winter underneath, barbs of ice packed deep in the dirt and gusts of Arctic air turning whipped cream wheels in the sky.

The light went green, and Vega followed the GPS to Stag's Bar, a red-brick building on a small street with houses on either side. There were two small windows and a Coca-Cola light-box sign above the door, an American flag dancing around in the wind.

Inside, the counter was U-shaped and white and looked cheap and beat-up under the fluorescents in the corkboard ceiling. There were three customers, two young guys together on one side talking to the bartender, one old man on the other. The bartender had illegible script tattooed up and down both forearms and drowsy eyes. He was not particularly tall or husky.

They all gawked at her when she came in, none of them the least bit shy, the old man sipping his beer and staring at her face like he was watching a football game. The bartender walked away from the two young men, and they immediately erupted in laughter. The bartender glanced back at them and laughed too, in on the joke. He came toward Vega, smirking.

"What can I get you?" he said, shuffling his skater sneakers on the checkerboard floor.

"You Bruce Pastor?" said Vega.

He nodded up once. It was the who-wants-to-know nod.

"I'm Alice Vega," she said. "I left three messages on your phone."

Pastor snapped his head to the side.

"Battery's dead," he said, both hands on the bar. "Who are you again?"

"My name's Vega. I find missing persons. I'd like to ask you some questions about Evan Marsh, about a time you and he bought drugs from Alex Chaney a month ago."

She could see Pastor hedging in the dimly lit hallways of his head. She could almost hear the idiot chorus: lie to her.

"I don't know either of those guys," he said. "So I don't know what you're talking about."

"I'm not a cop," she said. "I don't care if you buy drugs or use drugs or if you're on drugs right now. I need to know if you remember seeing a little girl at Alex Chaney's house the last time you were there with Evan Marsh."

Pastor was quiet; he was looking everywhere but at her eyes.

Vega leaned over the bar.

"The little girl was Kylie Brandt," she said, close enough to his face to smell cinnamon gum. "We found her sister this morning, but Kylie's still missing. I need to know what she and Evan Marsh talked about at Alex Chaney's house a month ago."

The two guys in the back chattered away. Pastor looked over his shoulder at them, then turned back to Vega, pursing his lips, gathering spit to speak.

"If you're not buying a drink, you're gonna have to leave."

Vega sighed. She could tell he felt kind of bad about it but not bad enough to talk. He started to walk away, and Vega grabbed his wrist.

"Don't do this," she said. "Please just tell me if you remember."

He yanked his arm away and shrugged, and even that was lazy, his bony shoulders barely making the arch.

"Sorry, girl. Wasn't me."

Now he no longer felt bad about anything. Now he was just a kid who wanted to cover his ass, like a million kids before him wanting to cover their asses. He walked away from her, and she watched him go with his skinny-boy slouch. He went back to talking with his friends, and they sputtered and laughed some more.

Vega honestly couldn't determine if she was more angry or tired. Her face was tingling, but she was fairly sure it was the injuries and not roofless rage. She stared at her hands, palms and tops, the dirt and blood packed under the nails, and thought of the day she had had. Then she saw the three boys at the end of the bar and tried to think of the day they had had—probably woke up at noon and smoked weed and played Grand Theft Auto and jerked off.

She looked at the old man on the other side of the bar, sipping his beer, and felt like him, or felt like she imagined he was feeling—creaky and sore.

Then she thought of Caplan and his daughter. For some reason she imagined him helping Nell with homework at the kitchen table. Vega actually doubted that Nell needed much help with anything, but still she pictured Cap standing over her while she worked on math or chemistry, something with definitely right and wrong answers, nothing wishy-washy. She thought of Nell getting it, drawing a neat box around a string of numbers and letters. Cap would say, "You see, Bug [that's what he called her, wasn't it?], you don't even need me." And Nell would smile and say something smart. Maybe they would high-five. They would both be proud.

Maybe Cap and Nell had not done that today, but whatever it was, no matter the detail, Cap and Nell were unequivocal in the decency of their lives; it ran through them like thread and colored everything they did. And these guys, well, how was she to know, really; maybe they helped an old lady with her grocery bags and had run a tutoring session for at-risk kids today before they came here to get hammered at five p.m., but likely not. Vega stared at them, put a box around the answer.

She moved slowly at first toward them, her right hand running along the bar, when she came to the taps—Yuengling, Yuengling Light, Bud, Bud Light. She made a fist and hit one after another, and down came the tired streams, one by one onto the rubber mat on the floor. It was only during a pause in their conversation that Pastor noticed the sound.

"What the fuck, girl—" he said, managing to sound offended and hostile at the same time, and then he started to run.

Vega picked up a highball glass in each hand and lobbed one at him. He caught it like she knew he would, so she fired the other one at his head. It hit him, and he screamed, probably more from the shock of it than the pain, though he went down anyway.

The other two were coming at her fast, one taller than the other, both scrawny, and Vega thought she could fight one but not two, especially if they did that thing that boys were so fond of, where one held your arms back and the other took shots.

And then there was the interest of time. So she pulled the Springfield from her holster and waved it at them casually.

"Go away," she said.

They both stopped where they stood. The tall one's jaw fell open like a puppet without a hand, but the short one was galvanized, high off the possibility of violence.

"I'm-a call the cops on you and your busted-ass face, bitch!" he said.

They lingered for a second, the short one rattling off imaginative threats punctuated with "cunt" and "bitch," and didn't seem to be wrapping it up.

"Go away!" she shouted, this time aiming the Springfield at the short one's chest, and he finally shut up.

They both ran out, the front door flying open, letting in the cold and the light for a second.

Vega put her gun away. She jumped the bar, swung her legs around, and knocked over a few mugs. Pastor was trying to stand, still stunned, a thin line of blood trickling from his eyebrow. He was mostly moaning.

The old man on the other side of the bar had not moved, still drank his beer.

"You got something to say, Papi?" she said.

He put his mug down, pinched his upper lip to wipe the foam, and pointed at her.

"You remind me of my late wife," he said thoughtfully.

Vega was too distracted to laugh, so she nodded. Then she looked back down at Pastor, who was sitting up with his knees bent and his head down. He asked her to turn off the taps, so she did. One by one the streams stopped, reminded her of ceiling leaks getting plugged. Then she sat on her heels next to Pastor, who thanked her before he told her everything he knew.

17

CAP SAT WITH JAMIE IN JUNIOR'S OFFICE. AS SHE LISTENED TO HIM, ruddy splotches appeared on her cheeks and forehead, tears spilling loosely from her sealed eyes. She rubbed them with her fingertips.

"Jamie, we're getting all the security video we can and canvassing the strip mall near the ballet studio," Cap said. "Do you remember anyone who stood out? A delivery person or a salesman maybe?"

"No, it was just a strip mall, and it was just her ballet class. I don't remember a delivery guy," whispered Jamie, coughing. She smacked her forehead with her palm gently. "Part of me feels like I got Bailey; there's no way I'm gonna get Kylie too, right?—that's just too much luck."

Cap knew he should speak, but he couldn't think of anything that didn't sound patronizing.

"I just," Jamie started, "I just think I could handle anything. . . . I think I could live with just Bailey if I had to, I just, I just . . ." She kept braking on the "just." No new tears were coming; her eyes were small and dry, her face wet like a stone. "I just couldn't handle it if they cut her up. You know, her body parts. I've thought about this a lot. Then I'd do the overdose right. Bailey could live with my folks."

She touched her hair dreamily, still gazing past Cap as she thought about it. Cap stood up and saw confetti in the corners of his eyes, held the edge of the table with one hand, queasy.

"Wait here. I'll be right back," he said.

Jamie nodded, still spacey.

Cap jogged out of the office, down one floor to the break room, fed dollars into the vending machine. Two packs of peanut M&M's dropped to the tray, and Cap grabbed them and ran back upstairs to

Jamie. She was still staring blankly ahead, resting her head on her fists, stacked on top of each other.

"Here," said Cap, setting the candy on the desk in front of her.

She raised her head and looked at the yellow bag like it was a rock from the moon.

"Have you eaten any solid food yet?" Cap said, ripping open his own bag.

"Yeah, I had some toast and soup."

"Try a couple," he said. "They'll give you a little energy."

He tilted his head back and poured some of the candy into his mouth and started crunching. Then the syrupy sweetness of mass-produced chocolate hit him, and he accidentally made a little grunting noise.

"You *really* like M&M's," said Jamie, opening her bag with two hands.

"The cheap sugar's the only thing that keeps me going when I'm this tired," he said. "Might help you too."

"Kylie doesn't love anything like she loves sugar," she said. "I tell people that and they're all, duh, she's a kid, but it's different. I have two kids, and Bailey loves ice cream and cake and Twizzlers as much as the next, but Kylie . . ."

She paused, shook her head, stared at the bag of candy in her hand.

"Go on," said Cap.

"I still have to stop her from sucking on ketchup packets when we get hot dogs. She puts them in her pocket. It's like a drug problem."

She set the bag down on Junior's desk.

"Do you think . . . they actually lured her with candy, like the stuff they used to tell us when we were kids?"

Cap swallowed and the candy went down rough—a collection of unchewed peanuts.

"This sounds a little more organized than that," he said. "Which is good for us actually. Random's usually harder to figure out."

Jamie nodded. She picked out one M&M, bright unreal blue, and ate it. She closed her eyes and held it in her mouth for a good long time.

In the big blue conference room, Vega connected her laptop to a projector, and the image, split into four, appeared on the beige screen: the parking lot of the strip mall on Church Street; the western entrance where the ballet studio was visible, in between a shoe store and a juice bar; the eastern entrance; and the rear parking lot for trucks making deliveries.

The Fed and Traynor stood and stared, watching footage in black-and-white, people coming and going.

"How'd your guy get this so quickly?" said the Fed.

"He has a talent," said Vega.

"Maybe he should come work for us," said the Fed, glancing back at his boss, who sat and drew delicate slashes with his fingertip on his tablet.

"He's an independent contractor," said Vega. "How far you want to go back—six months?"

"Six months?" said Cap. "Come on."

"Let's start with one," said Traynor. "Emerson?"

Em sat near the head of the table chugging an energy drink, sur-rounded by three officers still in their blues from their previous shifts.

"Yes, sir, we'll each take a screen. Looking for a white male who shows up more than once, probably near or around the ballet studio."

"Anything that stands out, anyone who looks familiar," said Cap.

"The ballet instructor remember anything?" said Traynor, nodding to the Fed.

"We talked to her for about an hour," said the Fed. "There's a guy who works for Moreland—came in to measure mirrors a while back. She said she didn't like the way he looked at her and some of the older girls."

"Was Kylie one of the older girls?" said Cap.

"No. Oldest was twelve. But that may not make a material difference to a pedophile," said the Fed. "Our man at Moreland is going through his records, trying to find the guy he sent to measure their mirrors—he'll send it as soon as he has it."

"Does he need someone to help him along?" said Junior, annoyed.

"I'm sure he's capable, Captain," said Traynor.

"There's only nominal information in the McKenna and Cahill files about the ballet classes, so we should get the parents in here."

"The McKennas are on their way now. Anything from neighboring businesses?" asked Traynor.

The Fed shook his head.

"Everyone's got a story. You ask people enough questions, they start to think the UPS guy looks suspicious."

"Vega?" said Traynor.

"Pastor was with Marsh at Alex Chaney's the day Kylie was there. He didn't realize it was Kylie—in his memory she only stood out because she was a little girl in a roomful of dopers. He thought she was Chaney's kid sister or something," she said, glancing at the video feed. "He remembers she told Marsh she wanted to be a movie star. And he asked her how old she was and where she went to school."

"So he gives her his number?" said Cap. "That doesn't seem plausible."

Vega shrugged.

"Who cares," she said softly, as if it were just the two of them in the room. "He knew enough about her to find her. Name, school. Denville."

"We've got people canvassing the strip mall on Church," said Traynor, charting maps in his head. "Detectives and lieutenants calling the parents of the kids in the ballet class. Let's get prepared for the mirror man."

"We can do the interview," said Vega.

"No," said Traynor definitively.

Vega stared at him, surprised, and Cap stiffened up, ready to fight. Really, Chief? she thought. Now we're taking our dicks out?

Traynor swabbed at the air with his hands like they were windshield wipers, erasing it.

"It'll take some time to get him IDed and in the house. Let's put it to use. Sydney McKenna's parents should be here soon. Cap, Vega—why don't one of you talk to them?" he said.

"What about Ashley Cahill's parents?" said Cap.

"They're divorced. Father lives in Philly, but the mother still lives in Lebanon, right outside, so we'll talk to her first and then if we need to, go to the father. I want all of this face-to-face."

Vega got it. People thought more when you were in the room with them. They had better memories, consciences. And you could see their eyes.

Traynor continued: "Apparently Mom can't leave the house, says she's ill. Didn't sound so stable when I spoke with her."

Vega remembered lying in her bed in junior high and high school, falling asleep listening to Eminem or Black Flag on headphones, and then waking up long after the CD ended. How she'd hear her mother making her rounds around the house, checking doors and windows, murmuring the mantra of her neuroses: "Safe, safe, safe."

"I'll go, I'll see Ashley Cahill's mother," she said then, so firm, so assured, you'd think she'd made the decision years ago.

Cap's phone hummed and jumped with texts on the desk in front of him. He was in Traynor's office alone. Messages were stacking up, flashing at the top of the screen from people he knew and sort of knew, friends he hadn't talked to in a few years, and also his parents in Florida, his cousins, of course Nell, and even one from Jules, who usually only contacted him about logistics.

The texts said things like this:

"Buddy you are on CNN!!!"

"I just saw you on the news you look old"

"Please call me dad is so proud he says xoxo mom"

"U and Alice are on every network! Any closer to finding kylie? . . ."

"Cap, be careful."

That last one was from Jules, and Cap smiled at her use of punctuation, even in a text. Formal and academic, except with his name. When they'd been married she called him Max, but after the split, on the rare days she actually used his name to address him, he was Cap. It sounded casual enough coming from anyone else, and from her it meant exactly that. She was anyone else now. Still, he stared at her text and felt something resembling joy.

He wrote back a restrained "Trying. Thx for checking in."

Then he wrote to Nell, "Don't stay up too lateral," the autocorrect button popping up.

"I wolfs :)" came back.

Then the door opened, and it was Junior, with a couple behind him.

"Max Caplan, Toby and Erica McKenna."

Cap shook their hands. They were both young and attractive, tan and brunette. The man, Toby, was tall with a full head of thick hair and glasses, his wife petite with a perfectly oval face. They all sat in a small circle of chairs Cap had arranged because he hadn't felt comfortable sitting behind the chief's desk.

"Thank you for coming," said Cap. "Especially so late."

"Happy to do it," said Toby McKenna, his voice deep.

With the small circle frames on his glasses, Cap thought he was a twin for Clark Kent.

"I realize this can't be easy."

Neither responded to that. Both smiled politely, looked at their hands and each other. Even unnerved, their faces retained their clean beauty.

There were plenty of young parents in and around Denville—Cap found it to be a function of the suburbs. People had bigger houses, more rooms than they did in cities, so they filled them up with kids. This was not what he had experienced growing up in Sheepshead Bay. When Cap was four or five and begged his mother for a little brother, she'd said, "Where we gonna put him, Maxie? The bathtub?" He grew up with pots and pans stacked on top of one another in cupboards that could never quite close, the fan of handles jutting from the doors. Later he found out his mother'd had her tubes tied when he was a year old. We don't have the money, and he's just about perfect, his mother had said to his father. Why tempt fate?

But around here, you had kids and you had them young and you had a few. Even knowing that, though, Cap thought the McKennas looked awfully young to have an oldest child who was twelve years old. He put their age at about thirty, so of course it was possible that they'd had kids in high school or right after, but there was something off-center about them; he couldn't quite pin it down.

He remembered from the file that Toby McKenna had been driving for a livery car service in Harrisburg at the time of the abduction. But Cap didn't read that now. Not from the brown leather shoes with a black rubber outsole, tan blazer, Clark Kent build, and glasses with designer frames.

"Mr. McKenna, can I ask, are you still working for the black car service—what was the name again?" he said.

"No, not Elite Fleet, not anymore," said McKenna, adjusting his glasses shyly, humbly dapper, Cap couldn't help but think. "We opened, me and Erica were able to open our own service a year ago in Middle-town—a few cars, a few drivers. Catering to high-end clients."

He said it quickly, made Cap think it was something he didn't want to dwell on.

"I see," Cap said, smiling, friendly. "Going well I hope? Always tricky with a small business. Believe me, I know."

"Yes, it's going okay," said McKenna, quick again.

"We've been very lucky," added Erica McKenna. "Right place at the right time."

She smiled then, and Cap saw a twinge cross her face. For a moment it looked as if she might cry.

"I'm pleased to hear it," Cap said. "If anyone deserves it, it's you folks."

They both nodded, looked down and away. Shutting the door on pain or hiding something. Or both.

"So," Cap said. "I'll get right to it here so you can go back to your lives and your family."

He leaned forward and rested his forearms on his knees, clasping his hands to show them: this is a conversation, not an interrogation.

"We have reason to believe that Kylie Brandt's kidnapper had some kind of connection to her through her ballet class initially. Ashley Cahill in Lebanon also took ballet, and I understand Sydney did as well, that right?"

"Yes," said Erica. Her husband nodded.

"I guess what we just need to know here is if you remember anything strange surrounding the ballet class in particular. Did you take her to ballet generally, Mrs. McKenna?"

"Yes," said Erica again.

"Great. Let's start with the teacher—her name was in the file." Cap reached behind them and grabbed the folder, opened it. "Nancy Topper?"

"Miss Nancy, they called her, all the girls."

"Miss Nancy," repeated Cap. "Anything seem off with her? Anything stand out?"

"No, I don't think so," said Erica, glancing at McKenna. "Syd liked her well enough."

"Okay," said Cap. "Now can you recall anyone, anything that didn't seem right at the class, or maybe where the class took place? At the"—he flipped through the pages of the file, searching for the name—"Junior Tiptoes Dance Studio?"

Erica shook her head, appeared confused.

"I'm sorry, like what?"

"Anything," said Cap. Still they both looked at him with blank faces. "I apologize, I'll be a little more specific. Do you remember anyone else, besides Miss Nancy, who was in and out of the studio and may have seen Sydney? A deliveryman, a salesman, someone who worked in a nearby business?"

Erica gripped the small purple handbag in her lap.

"No," she said, sounding genuinely sad. "I'm sorry, I just don't remember anyone like that."

"The police asked us all these kinds of questions when she first disappeared," added McKenna. "We made lists of all the people—all the parents of the other kids, names and numbers."

"I understand," said Cap, holding his hands up. "And again, I'm sorry to have to rehash this. It's just that we can't take anything as a coincidence right now, and three little girls who all took ballet—and the same equipment distributor serviced all three ballet studios—it's something we noticed."

Cap flipped through the pages in the folder and didn't speak for a minute. He wanted to see if the McKennas might offer up anything else without his prompting. The thing about it was, he believed what they were saying, both of them, but he could not shake the feeling of a bad tooth decaying in the gums.

That's when he saw the picture. It was a Christmas card showing the whole family—a glossy green strip with all of their smiling faces, the girls in green dresses, the boy made to wear a sweater vest, and McKenna and Erica, both at least twenty or thirty pounds heavier. Their tragedy explained the weight loss easily, but their faces were different too, Erica's nose now smaller and turned up at the end while in the picture it was longer and thicker. McKenna's eyes now wide without a wrinkle, while for that Christmas, tired and furrowed after undoubtedly driving a third-shift hack. In Cap's experience it was seldom that parents looked better and healthier after losing a child, yet here the McKennas were, right in front of him, two years after their eight-year-old had vanished, looking like superheroes on their off day.

It was close to ten when Vega pulled into Laurel Acres Mobile Home Park Estates, which sounded to her like the result of a word jumble game. The GPS continued to announce she had reached her destination because the roads of the park were not registered on any map except its own internal directory. Now she was going from the notes on her phone, given to her by Hollows, who'd gotten them from Ashley Cahill's mother.

The roads were paved, set out in a grid, two or three lots per block, all the homes raised on concrete foundations, built long and narrow. Most were in decent shape with fresh vinyl siding, flower boxes under perfectly square windows.

Vega found the street and then the number. There was no curb or driveway so she turned in and parked perpendicular to the house, next to an old hatchback. She got out, saw that the place looked the same as the others more or less, blue gray in color, dim lights on inside, a blue bulb over a screened porch.

She went up the steps, pulled back the screen door, and stood on the porch, a blank wiry mat under her feet. She pressed the doorbell and waited. Cool air blew through the screen and went right into her ears, a sharp little sting.

The woman who opened the door had milk-white hair pulled back in a ponytail, wore a sleeveless jersey dress with bare legs and feet underneath. Her eyes were such a dark brown they were almost black. She puckered her lips, chewing gum, Vega assumed.

She said, "You're someone else."

Vega paused, then said, "Alice Vega."

"The guy I talked to said he'd send someone else, meaning not him."

"Yes, Hollows, right?"

"Yeah, that's it."

"And you're Stacy Gibbons?" said Vega.

"Yeah. Used to be Cahill. I'm her," said Stacy, moving the gum to her molars, jaw clicking and clamping. "You can come in."

Vega stepped inside, and Stacy moved behind her to shut and lock the door. Like the whole park, everything was laid out in neat squares here, the living room first with an L-shaped couch fit perfectly to one corner and its walls, leading into the square of the dining room with a square glass table. There was nothing on the table except an empty bowl in the middle. Vega glanced around and saw every table and surface was the same—no knickknacks, cups, magazines. Her eyes jumped to paintings on the wall—nondescript flowers in vases, a sailboat on a calm sea. They reminded her of pictures hanging in a hotel room.

"It came like this," said Stacy, reading Vega's mind. "Furniture and everything. My ex gave me the down payment so I'd stay away from him and his new wife." She glanced around the room, then, and added, "It worked."

She studied Vega quickly, head to feet and back up again. "The guy, Hollows, said there wasn't anything new about Ashley. That this is about those other girls up in Denville."

"That's right," said Vega.

Stacy did some short nods, continued to work the gum in her mouth, pursing and relaxing her lips.

"Okay, then. You can have a seat."

Vega sat on one side of the L, Stacy on the other. The jersey dress hiked up a bit, revealing bald, bruised knees. Stacy didn't make a move to cover herself, didn't seem to notice. She tried to keep her hands in her lap but was having some trouble doing so, rubbing her thumbs between fingers like she was kneading a knot of dough in each hand.

"You think it's the same guys, whoever took Ashley?" she said.

"Maybe," said Vega. "I want to ask you a couple of questions about her ballet class. Kylie Brandt also took ballet. We're thinking the kidnapper might have seen or gotten to know the girls that way."

Stacy pressed her front teeth against her bottom lip; Vega could see her temples pulse.

"Like a stalker?" said Stacy. "Someone stalking ballet classes for kids?"

"Yes, maybe. Does anything come to mind?"

"No," she said, right away. Shook her head and kept shaking it.

She had voluntarily removed herself from remembering, Vega knew. Nothing on the walls, nothing on the shelves.

"Do you have any pictures of her taking ballet, or a video of a performance maybe? Anything I could look at that might help me?" said Vega.

Stacy stopped shaking her head suddenly. "You mean something that might help me, don't you?" she said, popping her jaw down.

"Maybe," said Vega.

"You probably think I got rid of all of Ashley's things, just because I don't have pictures of her everywhere."

Vega didn't respond.

"You're wrong," Stacy said. "I have everything. Everything. I have her hair. I have her underwear. I just don't have it out here. Because of this."

She pointed to her jaw, clamping and unclamping, still. She opened her mouth, white teeth, a salmon-colored tongue. There was no gum. There had never been gum.

"I tried putting pictures of her up. I'd look at them and get muscle spasms or pass out. Gnawed my teeth down to stubs. Then I got a shit-ton of meds so I can operate in the world, but I still do this twenty-four seven, three sixty-five," she said, tapping her jaw again.

They were quiet, the only sound the clicking of Stacy's teeth. She had an aggressive spark just then; Vega thought she might jump up and bite her. She thought of what Cap would do and started talking. She thought of her mother.

"People pay me a ridiculous amount of money to find their kids," she said. "They come to me and they're out of their minds. So I find them, most of them. And the parents either live their own lives and hope that works out for their kids, or they live their lives *for* their kids, and the kids still grow up and fuck up, and the parents still worry about them until all their hair falls out. . . ."

Stacy watched her, listening, moving her chin around in tiny circles fluidly, like she was hearing soft music.

"Or I don't find the kids at all," said Vega, quieter. "And you know what that's like. And either way, anyway, you've got scraps. My mother never got more than four hours of sleep at a time because she was so amped up with worry that something would happen to me and my brother. It was like her religion. And then she died when she was forty-one."

Vega's injuries started a little marching band, throbs and beats, forehead, cheek, knees. Everything hurt, all her skin hot like it had been grazed by an oil fire.

"Was it suicide?" said Stacy.

"No. Cancer."

Stacy nodded, but it wasn't pity or sympathy—Vega had seen many of those nods, the glistening eyes and Halloween mask frowns. This nod was her seeing all the layers at once. Copy that.

Vega looked down at her hands through blurry eyes, and they appeared to be vibrating in her lap, shaking.

Stacy stood up from the couch.

"When Ashley was three or four she used to say, 'I hate you, Mommy.' Back then I'd get all out of shape about it—I'd yell at her and send her to her room and get all rankled—but now when I think of it, when I think of her face . . ."

Stacy cupped her hand in the air in front of her.

"I know she didn't mean it. She was doing it just to see what I would do. I was like her lab rat. She was trying to figure us out. What makes us sad, what makes us happy. She figured it out too. Always the same answer."

She lowered her hands to her sides, rubbing the fabric of her dress between her fingers.

"I'll get the pictures," she said.

She started to leave the room and then paused in the doorway, craned her head over her shoulder to speak.

"I don't think your mother worrying about you gave her cancer."

Then she left.

Vega wiped tears from her cheeks, forgetting about the raw skin, and twitched at the pain. Her breath was choppy, a washboard in her throat. She fumbled for her phone in her inside pocket and skimmed over about twenty texts. She tapped her brother's name. His read, "Saw you on TV. Kick all kinds of Ass ;)"

Vega smiled, and that hurt her face too, and she wrote back, "Shut up."

There was also one from her father, but she skipped it, went straight to Cap's: "Can your guy get financials on Toby and Erica McKenna quick?"

"Probably. Why?" she typed back.

While she waited for his response, she sent an email to the Bastard, and then Cap's text came back: "I think they have too much money and look too good."

She was about to write him back when Stacy returned holding an orange shoebox. She sat on the couch and placed the box on the low table between them. She didn't open it right away.

"This has pictures from ballet class, I think," she said. "You can take them with you if you want."

"Are you sure?" said Vega. "I can look at them here."

"I can't," said Stacy. "Please take them. You can bring them back."

She ground and snapped her teeth in the front now, incisors on incisors. Vega stared at them, glowing white.

"You have really nice teeth," she said.

"I should," Stacy said, a laugh crowding her throat. "They're all crowns, every one of them. My ex paid for those too. I wear these mouthguards at night, used to just wear one up top, but I chewed through it like a dog. So now I wear top and bottom."

She continued to talk about the mouthguards, how she put them in the dishwasher once and then her ex-husband paid for replacements, and she hadn't felt silly because the dentist told her the mouthguards were silicon, so why shouldn't you be able to put them in the dishwasher? It seemed to calm her, talking about the teeth, so Vega spaced out a little and tried to remember something from Ashley's file.

"I'm sorry, what does your ex do for a living again?" she said.

"He's a floor manager at a Game On, down in Philly."

"He's done that awhile?"

"Yeah, about ten years I guess."

Vega leaned forward, tried to get deeper into the blackness of Stacy's eyes, searching.

"You have a nice home," she said. "And nice teeth. Does your ex make that much money at Game On—that's sporting goods, I'm guessing?"

"Oh no way," said Stacy, unoffended. "He had this aunt I never heard of, died and left him a wad of cash a couple years ago. And he felt guilty, you know. Only thing that worked out the last four years."

Vega thought of the impalpable entity that was a wire transfer, imaginary money rattling through an imaginary pneumatic tube in the sky. Her phone buzzed and kept buzzing against her ribs as she watched Stacy's mouth moving, showing off the crowns, flawless and counterfeit.

Cap paced, didn't realize he was pacing, alone in Junior's office. He was aware he was talking to himself aloud, but only with words here and there, fragments of thoughts, sometimes his tongue suctioning air off the backboard of his teeth.

Finally, Vega's message came through. He read it once quickly, eyes jumping to the numbers. He tapped the screen to zoom, then realized he had to see the whole thing at once. He went around Junior's desk and pressed the space bar and got a prompt for the log-in and password. Then to the door and stuck his head out, saw Junior at the end of the hall talking to Ralz and called to him.

Junior jogged to him.

"I need your password," said Cap.

"Why?" said Junior, immediately defensive.

Cap stared at him.

"I'd like to download some pornography."

"Mature."

Junior came to the desk, typed in his password, and got out of the way. Cap found the email from Vega and blew it up on the screen.

"Take a look at this," he said.

Junior looked.

"What is this, financial records?"

"Yeah. Sydney McKenna's parents' checking account."

"Don't you need a subpoena for that?"

"You do," said Cap. "I don't."

Cap put his finger on the screen, said, "This is from a year ago, almost a year exactly after Sydney disappeared. Look at that."

"A hundred fifty K," said Junior. "Isn't he a cabdriver?"

"He was. A year ago. Now they run their own car service." Cap scrolled down the page and hit the screen lightly with his fist.

"Look at that," he said slowly. "One week after the wire, forty goes to Lincoln Central in Harrisburg—that's enough for a sedan outright and down payments on what, four or five others?"

He kept scrolling, looking for big numbers. He saw a cluster of them, and he and Junior both leaned in as close as they could without the figures blurring.

"Doctors," said Junior.

"I will bet you my car those are plastic surgeons. He's got new eyes; she's got a new nose. You'll find tanning salons on there too, personal trainers, gyms."

Junior listened to all of it, said, "Your car's a piece of shit." Then he stood up straight, stretched his arms behind his back. "So you think they sold their kid so they could get cars and tans?"

"Not really," said Cap. "But this is something. And they, themselves, it's strange—like they had no problem being here, like they expected to be here."

"Maybe they just want to help."

"Yes, maybe. Or maybe they feel guilty about something. They haven't asked how much longer they'll be here, haven't asked for a lawyer."

"They're still here?" said Junior. "It's almost midnight."

"I know—I was waiting for this from Vega's guy," Cap said, pointing at the screen.

Junior wiped his mouth a number of times.

"So potentially they're just nice Christian folks who happened to experience a windfall, and we're holding them hostage," he said.

"They're not under arrest," said Cap. "And what if that money is related, in some way, to Sydney?"

Cap watched Junior ruminate. The ruminations of Junior, he thought. Alternately abashed and sniffing whatever blood may have leaked into the water.

"You want to talk to them with me?" Cap asked him.

Junior didn't have to think about it anymore.

"Let's go."

Stacy handed the box to Vega at the door, pushed it against her body. Vega took it, and Stacy let it go and stepped back and away slowly like she was in space, floating, hands outstretched with gnarled knuckles, without her realizing it. Then she brought them down to her sides, gripping the skirt of her dress.

"You can bring them back whenever," she said.

"Within the next few days, I promise."

Vega thought she probably hadn't said the words "I promise" since she was a kid, linking pinkies at recess. There was some heaviness to it she hadn't expected as she watched Stacy drift back to her planet of squares and mouthguards.

"Whenever," said Stacy.

They said goodbye, didn't shake hands, and then Stacy shut the door and locked it while Vega stood there. She waited a minute in case Stacy came back out. She didn't, so Vega left, got in the car and dropped the shoebox on the passenger seat, eager to no longer be holding it. She put her hands on the wheel and avoided looking at her own eyes in the rearview because, at this point, the emotions were so varied and numerous she was sure she'd be able to see them as swirling pinwheels in her irises. She was sure it would make her dizzy.

Then her phone buzzed, and she let her breath out, hadn't realized she'd been storing it. Cap was calling; the relief from seeing his name almost made her laugh out loud. She put a bud in her ear and said hello.

"Hey," he said. "Can you talk?"

"Yes," she said, starting the car. "Just leaving Stacy Gibbons."

"You get any breaks?" he asked, breath choppy, like he was walking.

"Nothing with ballet class. But her ex-husband, Ashley's father, inherited a chunk of money from a dead aunt two years ago."

"Really," said Cap.

Vega could tell he had stopped walking.

"That's what he told Stacy. What did my guy get on the McKennas? I didn't have a chance to look."

"A wire transfer—a hundred fifty K, a year ago. They're still here—Junior and I are about to go in."

"We've got to talk to Ashley's father."

"Not now," said Cap. "He's in Philly, and it's late. You should come back. Can your guy track the account the money came from?"

"Probably. I bet the Fed and his boss could too."

"They're dealing with the equipment distributor," said Cap. Then he paused. "What do you think?"

"Doesn't fit," said Vega, speeding on an empty county road. "None of these people strike me as the human trafficking type."

"No," said Cap. "So is it a better or worse story than that?"

"You asking me?"

"If you have the answer, sure."

"I don't have anything," she said, and she could hear how tired she sounded in the words, her voice breaking on the last. "You should get in there. You'll know in a minute if they're hiding something."

"Yes, I think we will," said Cap, sounding distracted. "Look, drive safe but hurry."

Vega nodded to herself in the mirror.

"Yeah, see you soon."

She hung up, pulled out the earbud. She merged with a line of cars heading toward the on-ramp of the state route and thought about the money. A hundred fifty thousand plus probably another hundred fifty thousand makes an even three. No missing-persons situation was less shitty when money was involved. It only meant things were worse, not better. Big big big big big Bad, Vega either thought or said aloud; she wasn't sure. One "big" for every zero.

18

TOBY MCKENNA WAS STANDING WITH HIS BROAD BACK TO THE door at first, hands in his pockets, head down. Erica sat in the chair holding her purse in her lap. Neither of them was doing anything with their phones. When they heard and saw Cap and Junior, Toby turned around and Erica sat up straight. Cap introduced Junior, and they shook hands.

"I'm sorry, you think we might be able to finish this tomorrow?" said Toby, so excruciatingly polite it made Cap a little angry. Why aren't they indignant, vengeful, filled with rage?

"It's getting late," he said, placing a hand on his wife's shoulder.

She blinked in gentle surprise.

"Yes, of course," said Cap. "I apologize for the delay here. Captain Hollows and I just wanted to cover one more base with you and then that's it—we really can't stress enough how helpful you've been."

They smiled. Toby remained standing behind his wife.

"Captain Hollows," Cap said, nodding to him.

"You know, I have to tell you, I've been over the file—your file—a few times," Junior said to them, "and I just didn't recognize you folks."

His regional accent seemed to get thicker as he spoke, and Cap thought he better watch it and not get too hometown PA. People can sense when they're being patronized.

"You both look like a million bucks, honestly," said Junior.

Toby smiled and fiddled with his glasses. Erica looked down, not exactly smiling but like she was thinking about it.

"Why . . ." Junior began, then stopped.

He waited until they both looked at him, second-guessing

themselves—had he already asked the question and we didn't hear it? Asshole had a good strategy, thought Cap.

Then he finished his question: ". . . do you look so good?"

The McKennas' smiles dissipated. They glanced at each other, then at Cap and Junior.

"Pardon?" said Toby, still no trace of impatience.

"You folks have been through arguably the worst thing two people can go through only two years ago, and you look like you just stepped out of an L.L. Bean catalogue."

Junior paused.

"And you didn't used to look like that. I've seen the photos in your file."

Erica wiggled her nose like the witch from the old TV show. But this wasn't a spell; it was a precursor to crying. She touched the corner of one eye with the pad of her manicured ring finger. And that's what put the anger, or at least irritation, in Toby McKenna—his wife upset. He stared at them with his brow lowered, his teeth in an underbite.

"The police have a problem with people improving themselves?" he said.

"No, Mr. McKenna," said Cap. "We just want to know where you got the money for all of it. Cosmetic enhancements and a fleet of luxury sedans."

Cap knew it could play either way—either they break and there are more tears and jumbled confessions, or they're angry, really genuinely angry, and Toby would take off his glasses and blazer and show Cap and Junior what he learned in Ultimate Fitness class.

"It's not anybody's business," said Toby. "How we make money."

"That would be true with the average couple," said Junior. "But you two aren't average, because of what happened to your daughter."

"So together these two un-average things have become a set," Cap picked up. "As things that are possibly connected."

Toby rubbed his chin, then his cheek, wiping off a smudge he couldn't quite locate.

"I don't know what you think is the truth," he said. "But you're wrong."

"Then why don't you tell us the truth," said Cap softly, trying not to sound too desperate. "Please."

Toby shook his head then, but it seemed to be in response to something he was telling himself.

He opened his mouth to speak but Erica cut him off.

"They are connected," she said, as if they were all so dense and she
felt sorry for them. "Just not the way you think."

Vega pulled off for gas at a rest stop. After she filled the tank she parked
in the lot and read the latest emails from the Bastard, along with a pdf
of Colin Cahill's bank statements from the past two years. The Bastard
had circled a number—$150,000 deposited almost two years to the day
since Ashley disappeared.

Vega opened a chat with the Bastard.

"Can you track the accounts that wired the money to Cahill and the
McKennas?" she wrote.

He wrote back: "They're both burner accounts. Like a burner cell.
Use them once then toss."

"So no names," Vega typed back.

"No. Offshore through Panama. Not unusual. I can get into the bank
for current accounts, but not for ones that don't exist anymore."

"No way to tell if both accounts belong to same user?" wrote Vega.

"Not really. Can keep looking."

"Give it thirty more minutes, then drop it."

She signed off, closed her laptop and slid it to the passenger seat,
where it flipped Stacy's shoebox to the floor. The top was off, pictures
and papers fanned out on the black liner mat. Vega sighed and started
the car. Just drive, she thought. Pick them up when you get to Denville.
She squinted at them, could barely make out the images of little girls
twirling pirouettes. She had the uncanny feeling she could not leave
them there.

What do you believe now? she scolded herself. That Ashley Cahill's
soul is in those pictures and you're disrespecting it by leaving images of
her on the floor of a rental car?

She didn't quite say yes, but the answer wasn't no either.

She leaned down sideways, could feel all the muscles in her left hip
stretch as she scooped up the box and pictures, grabbed the last one
left on the floor, the edge under her fingernails, and glanced at it before

dropping it in the box. Ashley at the barre, two other girls behind her, holding it with their left hands, right arms extended, their faces serious and shiny, reflecting the light.

They were in the right side of the frame. In the left, slightly back-grounded, was an upright piano, and the piano player in a three-quarter profile. A fair-haired woman with a strong jawline, delicate long fingers over the keys, concentrating on the sheet music, as if the girls weren't even there.

Vega brought the picture closer to her eyes. It was printed on paper, a thick stock but matte and a little pixelated. Maybe if she had the file on her laptop or her phone she'd be able to see it more clearly, to make out every high-resolution detail of the piano player's face, but she didn't need to. Because she knew who it was, even with the dulled color of whatever secondhand laser printer had produced it; she knew exactly who it was.

Cap felt his phone buzz, over and over on his hip in his pants pocket. He reached for the power button and pushed it with his thumb. His teeth chattered from the sugar, the sweat a cold glaze on his forehead. He didn't feel nervous. But Erica McKenna was about to tell them something, and his body was preparing for it, like pulling the rip cord on a toy race car.

"This is the truth," Erica said.

She removed her glasses and set them in her lap, tapped the bridge of her nose.

"That year, the year after Sydney—"

She paused, stretched her neck and closed her eyes, like she was working out a crick. Then she continued quickly, as if she'd thought about it many times, "Was the worst year any person could have. If you told us we'd have to go through it again, we'd say we want death instead. And we'd pick the worst kind of death too—whatever they do in the Middle East where they bury you and throw rocks at your head? We'd take that over living through that first year again. Do you understand?" she said to Cap.

He nodded.

"So a year ago, a hundred fifty thousand dollars shows up in our checking account. Toby says it must be a bank mistake; we should go down to our branch and tell them. But I said, let's wait a couple of days. You know why I said that?"

She was pleased about asking them, like a teacher who can't wait to tell the kids the answer to a question that seems difficult but is really very obvious. She knows they'll all slap their foreheads and make googly eyes. How could we have missed that?

"Because the night before I had a talk with God. And I was real angry about things. I told Him I was done with Him and done with Toby and the kids and done with this whole . . ."

She sneered as she searched for the words.

"Stupid little life, and He could fucking have it back."

She took a breath, her mouth relaxing.

"And next morning, I wake up, Toby tells me about the money. And I think, maybe that's all He could do right now to make it up to us, but it's a decent start."

She rested a second, folded the glasses in her lap. She was crying, that is, tears were leaking from her eyes, but she was making no sounds. She didn't even seem to be breathing.

"I'm not dumb," she said firmly. "I know God didn't send the wire from heaven. He just pulled some strings is all."

"No one thinks you're dumb," said Cap. "But I have to ask—did you consider that whoever sent this money could have something to do with Sydney?"

"Yeah. Sure we considered it. Then we un-considered it. Who gives a reverse ransom?" she said, aggravated.

"Who knows," said Cap. "We have to ask these questions, even if they don't make sense."

"So you didn't feel any responsibility at all to report the money to anyone?" said Junior, a little too harshly.

"Hey—" Erica said, pointing at him, ready for a fight.

Toby reached over and took his wife's hand, held it.

"Listen," he said, quieter than anyone had been so far. "We have two other kids. Our boy just now stopped having night terrors. He has regular nightmares, but at least he doesn't get out of his bed and scream. Our daughter still draws Sydney in family pictures."

Now he removed his glasses, pulled out a tail of his shirt and wiped the lenses.

"When we got the money, we said, Okay, a little justice after nothing. We're still looking for Syd," he said. "We still take the tips; once a week we talk to the police and the FBI agent who ran the case. But we have other kids. We have to keep living. It's like you can still survive without an arm, right, or a lung? And that's what we're doing; it'll never be as good as it was, but we have to keep going because we don't want to lose anything else."

He was crying now, tears rushing to the tip of his nose and dripping off the edge until he pinched it.

"Are we in trouble?"

"We didn't steal that money, Toby," Erica snapped. Then to herself, "We didn't do anything wrong."

Toby brought the heels of his hands to his eyes and sobbed into them. Erica stared at Cap and Junior disgustedly. Like a teacher again, except the one who keeps you after school, pissed and disappointed.

Just look at what you did.

Vega was five miles from Denville. She gave up trying to get Cap on the phone, figured she was going to see him soon enough. At every stoplight, she sent emails to the Bastard, opened up tab after tab on the Internet, reading. Professional biographies, a wedding announcement. LinkedIn, Facebook, the *Patriot-News*, the *Philadelphia Inquirer*. Houses bought and sold.

The Bastard was churning out social media intel as fast as he could type and double-click, but the next layer—the bank statements, the credit reports, the property deeds—would take him some time, an hour or two, which might as well have been days to Vega's mind.

Houses bought and sold.

She pulled over and searched her Recents on her phone, pressed a contact, let it ring. Maggie Shambley picked up after four.

"Hello? Miss Vega?" she said, her voice heavy with sleep. "What's happening?"

"Hi, sorry to wake you, nothing new yet, but do you know if there's a kind of master list of residential properties, who buys and sells, like a chain of custody? Is that public information?"

"Um," said Maggie, gathering thoughts. Vega pictured her sitting up in bed, putting on a pair of glasses. "Well, when someone applies for a license to alter a property, or a place is up for foreclosure, usually anyone could access that information. But just buying, selling, no; you have to be a licensed broker or representative of the buyer/seller to be able to search a guide like that."

"But there is a database like that, with houses bought and sold and the owners' names?" Vega said, watching her breath form short, cold puffs.

"Sure, hon, there's quite a few."

"Can you search by the buyer's name?"

"Yeah, you can search by name, city, whatever you want. Miss Vega, does this have something to do with the girls?" Maggie said.

"I think it does, ma'am," said Vega. "Can you look up a name for me right now?"

Maggie said yes, put Vega on mute while she started up her laptop and logged in to her account.

"Okay. What's the name?"

Vega told her.

She listened to Maggie type, the definitive tap of the Enter key. She stopped typing as she read.

"Looks like they really like to buy and sell houses," she said finally. "Three in seven years."

Vega thanked her and hung up, put the car in Drive as her thoughts spun thread after thread. Then she pulled out and punched the gas, houses blurring past, all their garage and porch lights on and their million tragedies inside.

Cap walked out with Junior at a quarter after two, leaving the skeleton crew behind, Em in charge, pounding Red Bulls and watching video footage from the strip mall. Traynor and the Fed and the Fed's boss had gone to their home and hotel to sleep. Only five news vans were still outside, reporters leaning against the doors and in camping chairs, cameramen half-asleep with their gear propped on their shoulders.

"Hey Cap, any news?" one of them called.

"Captain Hollows, how about an update?"

"Nothing now, guys," said Junior, waving like a politician. "Just getting a couple hours' sleep."

They fired off a few more questions, to which Junior said, "Tomorrow, guys, tomorrow."

"What time you coming in?" said Cap as they reached the lot.

Junior looked at his watch, yawning.

"Seven, I guess. We got the Feds on the burner account. In the morning we can go have a chat with Ashley Cahill's father."

Cap nodded and they said good night, and Cap was starting to walk away when he heard Junior call his name. Cap turned, saw that the captain wore a queer expression, like he had drunk a beer too fast and was trying not to burp.

"You're really fucking good at this," Junior said to him.

It was earnest and humbled, the burp face. Cap put that in his mental photo album of Junior's unreadable facial expressions. Cap thought of a million gay jokes he could make. Actually just a couple, along the lines of Hey, you want to buy me a drink since you're getting so emotional, you know, the way gay guys do?

But he didn't. Instead he said, "So are you, Junior."

Junior nodded, and then they both got in their cars and took off, and Cap headed for home. He was a block away when he realized he hadn't turned his phone back on since talking to the McKennas. He said, "Shit," pulled his phone out and pressed the power button, sorted through the mess of his thoughts while the white apple glowed.

Erica McKenna was right, ultimately; who the hell would give a reverse ransom? If not an outright payment for a human being's life, which Cap was sure it wasn't, then why else? A sociopath would never pay out money as retribution. He would feel like he deserved those girls.

So maybe the person who took Ashley Cahill and Sydney McKenna, and maybe the person who still had Kylie, the moneyman, maybe he knew he had done the wrong thing and felt bad about it. The only thing stronger than love or hate or fear was guilt.

His phone vibrated repeatedly, and Cap watched while the screen filled with texts and missed calls, all from Vega. The texts were all the same message: "Call me."

He tapped the phone icon next to her name and then the speaker, and Vega picked up before the first ring went through.

"Where are you?" she said, her lips brushing the mike of her earpiece.

"Just left the station," said Cap. "What's going on?"

"Pull over."

"What? Why?"

"Pull over. Let me talk," she said, urgent.

Cap pulled over.

"Okay, I'm parked. What is it?"

"There's a picture Stacy Gibbons gave me. Ashley in ballet class. The piano player."

Vega paused her telegram-speak.

"What, Vega? What about the piano player?"

Vega let out a small, cool breath.

"I think it's Lindsay Linsom. Cole Linsom's mother," she said.

"What? Really? From Tuesday?"

"Yes. And I just had Maggie Shambley search a database of home buyers and sellers—the Linsoms have moved three times in the past seven years. Two years ago they lived in Harrisburg. Two years before that—"

"Lebanon," said Cap.

"Yes," said Vega. "You need to call the McKennas and ask if they remember the piano player from Sydney's class."

"Okay," said Cap. He pressed his hand to his forehead, felt like he'd been hit in the face. "What's the narrative here, Vega?"

"Somehow the Linsoms meet Evan Marsh, pay him to lure Kylie, he gets cold feet . . ."

Cap continued: "One or both of them go to his apartment. They argue." Cap paused. "They kill him."

"Yes. Also they moved into their current house two years ago after selling their house in Hershey, which is halfway between—"

"Harrisburg and Lebanon," said Cap.

"Linsom is a partner at a law firm in Harrisburg. So he makes money."

"He could be the moneyman," said Cap.

He looked at his face in the rearview, tired and ghoulishly white. A fun house spook.

"So Lindsay Linsom plays piano for ballet classes, finds the girls, they kidnap them . . . where are they?" Cap said. "I mean, physically. Where are they? Where is Kylie?"

Vega didn't answer. In the silence Cap stared at the empty street, the stout houses and shops with skeletal trees lining the streets, firmly stuck in winter. Across the street a Domino's Pizza, Fine Wine & Spirits. He stared at the Wine & Spirits sign. Wine.

He remembered the billboard for the Sherwood Forest subdivision—jacuzzis, wine cellars, outdoor grill islands. He heard Junior's voice saying, "Lawyer got the jury to agree that the wine cellar didn't count as immediate."

"Wine cellar," he said, starting the car. "Or basement, garage."

"Yeah, maybe," said Vega. "What about the other two?"

"I don't know. Where are you?"

"Rockland, I think."

"Follow 54 west—you'll see the signs to their subdivision. Meet me at the entrance."

He started to drive, started to speed.

"Do you want to call Traynor?" Vega said, strangely tentative. "To get some backup?"

Cap recognized this was a rare kind of attention from her, that this was her being gracious.

"No," said Cap, immediate and certain. "We call Traynor, the Feds, Junior, we risk the media circus."

"Cap?" she said, almost whispering. "What if we're off?"

Cap held the wheel tight, imagined he was gripping the wiry starfish that were Vega's hands.

"Let's find out," he said. "If we're crazy, then we say sorry and leave and get some sleep and talk to Ashley Cahill's father in the morning. But Vega?"

"Yeah?"

"We're not," he said softly into the air.

He thought he could hear her catch her breath before she hung up.

Cap tapped Erica McKenna's number and apologized for the hour when she picked up.

"It's fine, Mr. Caplan. We're still on the road," she said, sounding only a little resentful since it was he who put her on the road so late to begin with.

"Right. Look, I have just one more question, and then I'll let you go, I promise. I know this is reaching back and sounds pretty random. Was there a piano player in Sydney's ballet class, do you happen to remember?"

Erica paused. Cap heard the white static of the road.

"Piano player," she repeated. "Usually they used an old CD player, except you know, now that I think about it, they did have someone for recitals and the rehearsals leading up to them. Do you remember that, Toby?"

Cap couldn't hear Toby's muffled response.

"Yeah, you're right," she answered her husband. "It was a woman, real thin and pretty. Looked like she could be a dancer herself."

"The name," said Cap, trying not to rush the natural momentum of Erica's memory. "Do you remember her name?"

"God, what was it?" said Erica, reflective. "I know this sounds weird, but I keep thinking of some kind of oil. Like grapeseed, linseed, something like that."

"Linsom," said Cap, running his hand hard down the back of his neck. "Was it Linsom?"

"Yeah, that's it!" said Erica, pleased. "Miss Linsom. And her first name was an 'L' too, right? Like Lily Linsom or something?"

"Lindsay," said Cap, his foot coming off the brake. "Lindsay Linsom."

Erica said a few more things and asked a few more questions, but Cap couldn't really hear her. He said thank you and that he would call her back tomorrow with any news. Then tapped the red button.

He sped up even more, to fifty-five, sixty. He didn't know what they would do when they got to the Linsoms'. His heart rate climbed, and he thought of the Chutes and Ladders game, one bad move and you slide back down to the start.

He knew that somewhere close by Alice Vega had cried with his voice right in her ear. And he knew as soon as he saw her face he would know what to do.

19

VEGA PRESSED HER SLEEVE AGAINST ONE EYE WHILE SHE KEPT THE other on the road. She was still crying and didn't know why anymore; she'd stopped beating the shit out of herself trying to find out because it took too much time. So she drove with blurry eyes and damp sleeves on the streets buckled from the old coal mine where she saw an old mattress on the sidewalk, and then to the neighborhood where there were nail salons and a cheese shop, and then to an undeveloped stretch of land where there was a green-and-brown field that didn't appear to belong to anyone, no houses there, and then she came to the Sherwood Forest subdivision, the monument sign marking the entrance made of staggered bricks, or more likely foam core boards cut to look like staggered bricks, and there was Cap under a tree, leaning against his car.

He waved two fingers at her, and she U-turned and parked next to him. She wiped her eyes one more time and got out.

"Hey," said Cap. "You okay?"

"Yeah," said Vega. "What do you want to do?"

Cap looked toward the houses in the cul-de-sac.

"Walk."

He started to walk, and Vega didn't move. She grabbed the cuff of his jacket sleeve, and he stopped and looked at her, surprised. He didn't pull away.

"Stacy Gibbons reminded me of my mother," she said. "It made me upset."

Cap listened, nodded.

She also nodded, agreeing with herself. She let go of his sleeve and patted the skin under her eyes.

"You have more than ten rounds in that piece-of-shit antique under your belt?"

Cap smiled.

"Twenty."

They began to walk, and it began to snow. Not the real stuff that people had to dig out with shovels but little twirling flurries—Snow Lite. It was spinning around them and landed on Vega's hands and face, but she didn't feel it, exactly. That is to say, she knew it was supposed to be cold, but she didn't feel the cold when it hit her skin. Maybe because it dissolved so quickly, and maybe because she was just a little bit outside of her body just then. And she didn't look at Cap but saw him peripherally, and he was with her. They were, both of them, ready and not ready. She felt like she had already done what they were about to do, one hundred times. Had she? She had to think about it. She had to focus. This was the house. They were right in front of it. All they had to do was go up the narrow path to the door.

"What should we do?" she asked Cap.

He didn't turn to face her. He blinked against the snow. He nodded his head.

"Ring the doorbell," he said.

She looked at his profile, chin out, nearing something like pride or courage, as if he knew exactly what they were about to find. Vega knew he didn't know a thing, no more than she did, but she realized his being proud or brave, even if it was a trick, was enough for her.

And that thought hadn't even rounded itself out in her mind before he started up the path to the Linsom house, the lawn still cut even if not yet green, terra-cotta pots lining the walkway with fresh soil and care tags stuck inside, ready to produce flowers for the season. She followed, running a bit behind him. Sensor lights came on at their feet as they stepped, ending with the one above the leaded glass door.

Cap pressed the bell. Vega held her breath; glittery flecks crowded her eyes. When no one came, Cap pressed it again. They waited, looked at each other. Then a figure, hazy behind the glass of the door, approached. Cap and Vega stood up straighter.

Lindsay Linsom opened the door. She wore a black silk bathrobe and loosely fitting black pajama pants underneath.

"Mr. Caplan, Miss Vega," she said, unsurprised. "You'd like to come in."

It was an odd way to open, thought Vega. Telling them what they'd like, and it being the exact truth.

"Yes, Mrs. Linsom," said Cap. "We would."

She held her arm out, presenting the living room, and Cap and Vega walked in. Vega glanced around quickly—everything appeared to be the same as it had been the other day—the white couches, carpets, the glass deer centerpiece, the upright piano with the table clock on top, ticking away.

"You didn't wake me," she said, as if they'd asked her. "I don't sleep anymore, to be truthful. Just rest my eyes now and then."

She sat on one of the couches.

"Would you like to sit?"

"I don't think so," said Cap. "Were you expecting us, ma'am?"

"Expecting someone," she said. "You or police, or the FBI. Someone. I thought it might be you. I guessed, actually," she said, holding a finger to her lips, pleased with herself. "I kept telling Press we didn't have to worry about you, but I had a feeling about it. I get feelings about things, and I've learned to trust them."

She looked up at them, taking them in, nodding to herself, like they were dresses on a pair of mannequins.

"And why . . . were you expecting us?" said Cap.

Vega's neck tightened; she bent her arm like a wing so she'd be able to pull the Springfield more quickly.

"You found Bailey this morning," said Mrs. Linsom. "I knew it wouldn't be long. That's what happens, unfortunately, when too many people are involved. Too many chiefs and not enough Indians."

Vega made herself breathe now, in and out through the nose. She knew there was something very wrong here, in this house, with this woman. Even someone who had resigned herself to being caught would not be as relaxed, confident. When Mrs. Linsom looked at Cap, Vega peered out of the corner of her eye, trying to see around the room as best she could without turning her head.

"Mrs. Linsom," said Cap, keeping it quiet and civil. "You seem to want to tell us something. Why don't you get that off your chest."

"That's kind of you to offer," she said, sincere. "There's a lot to say, though, and none of us has a lot of time."

What does that mean? thought Vega. Why don't we have time?

"So," she said, rubbing one palm against the other like she was sanding something. "I knew the girls kept those notebooks in that tree. I'd watched them from the window in the kitchen a dozen times."

Vega imagined Kylie and Cole in the backyard, writing in pink and purple pens. She looked over Kylie's shoulder, saw her circling Evan Marsh's name, his real name.

"I'd taken out the page before you came. That's really how it all started," said Mrs. Linsom. "Kylie had written Evan's name down."

She seemed lost in a dream, and then she looked at Cap and Vega and must have seen their bewilderment.

"She wasn't what we were looking for, you understand?" she said. "She's . . . heartier than Cole, bigger. A mature girl, like a teenager."

"Ma'am?" said Cap. "I'm sorry, you're going to have to back up for us. We're not sure what you mean."

"I know what she means," said Vega. "Kylie didn't look enough like Cole. Ashley Cahill, Sydney McKenna—they both did. Blond, slight, petite. Young for their ages."

"Yes," said Mrs. Linsom. She nodded to Vega, like she was proud of her. "Yes, that's right. But the opportunity presented itself with Evan Marsh. It felt fated to me—that was the feeling I had. A boy she had met by coincidence happened to have a tragic story and was desperate for money. Although not so rare in this town."

"So you tracked him down," said Vega.

"Yes," said Mrs. Linsom. "Not difficult. I found him at the supermarket."

Vega saw them, by the loading dock where she'd talked to Marsh. They go for a walk. Evan looks at her like she's crazy.

"He wasn't interested at first . . . then he thought about it. He wasn't stupid."

Vega thought of his face changing, softening as he considered the money, the possibility of finding his brother.

"He had a need too, you understand. Also, of course, a conscience."

She shook her head, disappointed.

"That was really my mistake. I should have known."

"Did you kill him, ma'am?" said Cap.

"No," she said, shifting where she sat, smoothing her robe underneath her. "Evan called and said he needed to talk to us. I could tell from his voice, he wanted to go to the police. So Press went to see him."

"So your husband killed him?" said Cap.

Mrs. Linsom appeared taken aback by the question.

"Yes, Mr. Caplan, he did. He has two guns."

Why is she telling us that? thought Vega.

"None of this was planned," she said, her eyes on some distant point. "Well, that's not entirely true. It was planned; I only mean that when we started we didn't plan on all this damage."

"Do you mean death?" said Cap, sounding just a little bit impatient. "Is that what you mean when you say 'damage'?"

"Yes, I suppose. Death . . . damage."

"So why don't you tell us where Kylie is, ma'am, and then we can talk about what you did and didn't plan on?" said Cap.

Vega heard anxiety in his voice. Mrs. Linsom focused on him and smiled rather kindly.

"Of course. First, though, Mr. Caplan, you should really speak to my husband. He's not as levelheaded as I am. Maybe you can reach him. Man-to-man. Father-to-father."

Vega thought there must be a window open or a busted air conditioner unit blasting cold air on her neck. She felt she was about to discover the source of a recurring wound, that thing that you did over and over again without realizing you were hurting yourself in the same spot.

Mrs. Linsom tilted her head, reminded Vega of a raccoon about to hiss, guarding the garbage cans. There's no question these belong to me.

"I had a feeling about both of you after you left the other day," she said. "You're both famous. You have a lovely daughter, Mr. Caplan."

Vega didn't move, didn't want to call attention to the bluff. She knew he was too smart to flinch, but she could see his posture change, head up, shoulders back, hands near the belt, ready to pull the gun.

"She said such sweet things about you on Facebook," Mrs. Linsom said, without a single note of sarcasm. "It's like she's your friend, but she respects you also. It's extraordinary. People write parenting books on how to do that using positive discipline—I've read them all."

Vega felt a trickle of liquid on her brow. She wanted badly to touch it, to see if the cut had started bleeding again. Don't do it, she told herself. This is not your body.

"They put everything online, teenagers," Mrs. Linsom said, shaking her head. "I'm not planning on letting Cole have her own social media accounts unless I create all her passwords so I can monitor what she posts. It's just not safe."

She shook her head again, eyes momentarily fearful.

"Where's your husband, Mrs. Linsom?" said Vega.

Vega put one hand on the grip of the Springfield, no longer attempting to hide it, pushing back the flap of her jacket so Mrs. Linsom could see it.

Mrs. Linsom saw it but seemed just a little concerned, her light eyebrows barely creased.

"You know, he's not always like that, how he was when you met him the other day. Only when he's under a lot of stress and not able to relieve it."

"Where is he right now?" said Vega again, placing her hand on the grip.

"He went to find you, Mr. Caplan," said Mrs. Linsom. "To talk man-to-man. Father to father. He's been at your adorable house on Pixley Road for a couple of hours now."

Vega drew the Springfield, pointed it at Mrs. Linsom's left eye as Cap stumbled back two or three steps, losing his balance.

"Pick up your phone, call your husband," said Vega, steady. "You can tell him I will shoot you in the head if he touches her. If he has already touched her, I'll shoot you anyway. The only way you won't end up getting shot is if he hasn't touched her yet. So you'd best hope for that."

Vega angled her chin in Cap's direction.

"Caplan, move. Go."

She didn't turn but watched the shape of him run from the room, heard the door slam, his steps on the path outside.

Mrs. Linsom kept her eyes on Vega, not the gun, which was rare. People tended to stare at the barrel when it was pointed at them. Mrs. Linsom seemed mostly indifferent toward it.

"You can't shoot me," she said plainly. "You want to know what's happened to Kylie, don't you? You can't know that if I'm dead."

Vega took three steps closer, keeping the Springfield aimed at her eye socket. Now Mrs. Linsom watched the gun.

"Not real concerned about it," said Vega. "Call your husband."

Mrs. Linsom blinked slowly and brought her gaze back up to Vega's.

"Even if I called, Press wouldn't pick up right now," she said.

Focus, said Perry in her head. If Nell's dead she's already dead. She's not the body you're supposed to bring home. One thing and then another.

"So tell me where Kylie is, and we can get this over with," said Vega, very quiet.

Mrs. Linsom rolled her shoulders back.

"It's not as if I can run away from you, Miss Vega; you don't have to keep the gun on me."

"I'd prefer to," said Vega.

She was so close she could see the light glint off the small diamond studs in Mrs. Linsom's ears.

"Well, then," she said, lifting her chin, looking just above the gun, like she was peering over a hedge. "Like I said, none of this was planned. The first time was an accident, really. I'd been married to Press for five years before he told me. I remember the day too—it was when we got home from the twenty-week sonogram, when we found out Cole was a girl."

She looked drunk with the joy of the memory, smiling broadly. Then, suddenly, the smile evaporated, and she continued.

"When we got home, he told me that sometimes he had these feelings, urges he was ashamed of. And he was afraid that eventually he might not be able to control them, now that he knew we were having a girl."

Vega started to feel the sweat between her fingers, on her palms. She didn't move, didn't want to give the impression the gun could slip.

"I told him he was the strongest man I'd ever met, and together, he and I could beat this," said Mrs. Linsom, looking proud and weathered by her suffering. "Then, when Cole was five—we lived in Hershey then—one night Press came to me and broke down. Said he didn't know what to do. He didn't think he could fight it anymore. He wept in my lap. Can you imagine?" she said to Vega. "Can you imagine what it took for him to admit that? A man like that?" she said, awe in her voice.

Vega didn't answer. Kept the gun steady on the left eye.

"I told him we'd figure something out, but, honestly, I didn't know what I was going to do. And then, this is where fate came in," she said, excited to share her story, like they were two girls chatting over lattes. "The very next day we were on our way back from the pool, and there was Ashley in the parking lot. I guess she'd gone to the vending machines and gotten turned around. She knew us from ballet class, and I was like a celebrity to those girls, the piano player, Mrs. L, they called me. And she . . ."

She paused, touched her finger to her lips, eyes distant.

"She asked to come over. She asked," said Mrs. Linsom in disbelief. "So she came with us. At home she and Cole played for a while, and then they both fell asleep. By then Ashley's parents were calling everyone they knew. They hadn't called the police yet. No one had seen her get into my car. And I thought—can it be this easy?"

She gave Vega a shy smile.

"Yes. It can be."

She seemed to be elsewhere while she recited the rest, channeling the events like a medium in a trance.

"We kept her for two days. At first we thought we'd give her back. We knew that would be the end for us, but then I thought, What if we can have a normal life after all? What if Press can live without having to go through the burden that has been placed on him—what if this got it out of his system, like an antibiotic? My husband and my daughter could be fine . . . forever. And all I had to do was kill a little girl."

Vega started breathing faster. Stared into Mrs. Linsom's clear eyes.

"Of course, as you know, it wasn't forever. Two years later he came to me again. Cole had stopped taking ballet, so I volunteered at a different studio, where I met Sydney. I planned a bit more, rented a car, put my hair up under a cap. Some people are not as careful with their children as they should be. An eight-year-old, walking home by herself."

She shook her head and sighed.

"And now, Kylie."

Vega straightened her arm, fought the twitches in the tendons.

"You can think whatever you want of me," said Mrs. Linsom. "But I opened those accounts and paid those people anonymously because I did feel bad. I do feel bad. I'm a mother too. And none of them seemed to have a problem with that, the money. Even if they didn't exactly realize what it was for."

Vega started to shake. She knew something would have to happen soon—she would have to either drop the gun or shoot.

"You don't have kids, Miss Vega, so I don't expect you to understand this," said Mrs. Linsom. "But if someone tells you: Either your child gets hurt or my child gets hurt. Your child is raped or my child is raped. Your child dies or my child dies. You will *always* pick the other child to die. Always. If you ever become a mother, you'll find that out."

Vega's mouth was dry as bread but she spoke anyway: "Lady, you're a fucking psycho."

She came forward and grabbed Mrs. Linsom by the hair with one hand, pressed the nose of the gun into her eye socket. Mrs. Linsom gave a grunt of surprise, raised her hands instinctually to protect the rest of her face, as if that might help her.

Vega took deep breaths and imagined the pull and release. The recoil would push her back, maybe knock her to the floor since her arm was so shaky. Mrs. Linsom had a small skull—the round would blast the back of it open easily and leave the muddy cavity that would have been her eye.

She tried to imagine how she would feel. She wasn't thinking about Cap and Nell, Jamie Brandt, her mother, the world. She'd never had to kill anyone before. All her years working with Perry and freelancing she'd done a lot of injuring, hit arms and knees like she did with Dena Macht, broken fingers and smashed knuckles, bitten ears and slammed the grip of her gun into cheeks and jaws and temples.

Mrs. Linsom's hair was feathery soft and a blend of blond shades so exact they seemed to run in a perfect pattern across her scalp—light, lighter, lightest.

Vega yanked Mrs. Linsom's head closer to her, Mrs. Linsom's hands flying up to Vega's, digging into her skin, but she wasn't as strong as Vega—no amount of Pilates could level the field. Vega jammed the Springfield into the hollow of her eye so it hurt. It was not nestled; there was no nestling. Mrs. Linsom cried out at the shock of it.

"2545!" she yelled.

"What?" said Vega, annoyed.

"2545," she gasped. "The code to the wine cellar downstairs. 2545."

She had drawn some blood with her scrapes on the skin of Vega's hand.

"2545," she said again. "You can check—I can come with you. I'm not lying."

Vega didn't move or speak.

"I gave her baby Valium . . . to make everything easier," said Mrs. Linsom. "I wanted to be kind. . . ."

This was her begging, thought Vega, but she didn't enjoy it.

"You're not coming with me," said Vega.

She could feel her shudder, and then she heard the dribble of urine on the carpet, running down Mrs. Linsom's elegant pajama pants onto the floor. Like a puppy.

Vega took the gun out of her eye and let go of her hair. She squatted to talk to her. Mrs. Linsom's eyes were wide and bloodshot.

"I'm not going to kill you," said Vega. "I just wanted you to pee on yourself."

Vega took the double restraints from her inside pocket. She grabbed Mrs. Linsom's wrist and pulled her to stand, which she did unstably, then led her to the piano.

"Sit," said Vega, bringing her hand down on Mrs. Linsom's shoulder.

Mrs. Linsom's legs folded underneath her. Vega wrapped one cuff around Mrs. Linsom's wrist and pulled the strap, which clicked as she tightened it. Then she looped the other cuff around the piano leg and locked the strap, Mrs. Linsom's body lurching forward.

"How do I get downstairs?" said Vega, standing up.

Mrs. Linsom looked very small on the floor, her legs crisscrossed awkwardly.

"Through the kitchen," she said, her voice low. "The white door to the right of the refrigerator."

Vega left her and went to the kitchen, hit the lights with her palm and saw the white door. She walked to it and pressed the silver lever handle down and pulled it open. There was a staircase, well lit with wall sconces, and Vega stepped down, felt the air become cooler.

At the bottom was a door, made of a knotty unfinished wood. It was arched at the top and had a black iron handle, weather-sealed jambs in the frame. Something new made to look old.

Vega pushed the numbers into the keypad on the wall, and she heard the mechanism of the lock ticking and snapping. She opened the door.

The first thing that hit her was the smell.

Cap raced through stoplights and signs down dark roads, one hand on the wheel, the other scrolling and dialing—Traynor, Junior, his neighbor Bosch. It would take too long to explain to 911 dispatch, who would send the fire department first. He left frantic short messages for them all and then he remembered—Em was at the station, fifteen minutes from Cap's house if you obeyed traffic laws.

"Cap?" said Em, picking up right away.

"Em," said Cap, swinging around a turn. "The man who took Kylie Brandt is at my house with Nell and he's armed. I can't explain—I'm five minutes out. Get some backup and meet me there."

He couldn't control his breathing or the register of his voice, felt like the words were being choked from his throat.

"I'm coming," said Em, panting, running. And then, "She's gonna be fine, Cap. Let's get her. Drive."

Em hung up, and Cap drove, finally reaching his neighborhood, past the playground where he'd taken Nell after being up all night on third shift. Higher, higher, higher, she'd say on the big-girl swing, legs pumping to spike the velocity. His arms would seize every time she went up, as he imagined her hands losing hold of the chains and her falling to the ground, smashing her nose and breaking bones, her screams echoing through his ears though they hadn't even happened.

Then he heard Jules's criticism: "Just push her higher, Max. She's not glass."

No, he thought now. More fragile than glass. Skin thin as newsprint.

He slowed on his block and parked across the street from his house. He got out of the car and ran to his lawn. There were no lights on inside, but the front door was open, not wide. As he approached he saw the broken frame, splintered. He drew the Sig from his belt and went around to his office entrance.

He unlocked the door and stepped inside. Closed the door quietly and slid his shoes off. He padded through his office, the street light coming through the blinds, making fat stripes across the floor and furniture. The door connecting his office to the rest of his house was open, the way he'd left it.

He came into the living room, dark, quiet, the strip over the dishwasher the only light.

Likeliest scenario, thought Cap. Linsom breaks the front doorframe, maybe muffles the nose of the gun and shoots the lock to keep it quiet. Nell doesn't hear it anyway because of the headphones she wears to fall asleep, listening to the rat-a-tat of snare drumlines because she said it got the more difficult cadences into her subconscious. So Linsom finds her in her room asleep and what? She's too old for his taste in terms of sexual assault, but would that stop him?

Would he just kill her?

No, said Vega in Cap's head. Too much still to lose.

He went up the stairs, skipping over the creaky step. Then he was in the hallway, and he heard Nell's voice, hushed, talking.

He covered his mouth so as not to gasp audibly with relief. He couldn't make out the words and couldn't guess at the situation—did Linsom have the gun on her? Was he restraining her? There was no way to know.

All Cap had was surprise. The only thing he could do was come in fast and keep his aim steady.

He put his back against the wall and moved sideways, Sig pointed toward Nell's open door. He knew he just had to do it—swing around and if the shot was clear, take it.

"So should we try that, Press?" he heard Nell say.

Cap pivoted into the room, leading with the Sig, arms straight. There was Nell in her desk chair, not tied up or visibly injured, and Press Linsom, standing, hovering close to her, a .45 in his right hand, hanging at his side until he saw Cap.

"Dad!" yelled Nell.

Linsom jumped and put his arm around Nell's neck, stuck the .45 against her cheek.

Cap felt every nerve ending in his body catch fire as he huffed breath through his nose. Linsom looked tired and shocked, his hands shaking.

Nell's eyes were huge as they hunted Cap's, trying to tell him things. She gripped the arms of the chair; her lips curled as she spoke.

"It's okay, Dad," she said, her voice eerily calm. "Press and I have been talking. Right, Press?"

Linsom didn't answer her, kept staring at Cap.

"He doesn't want to hurt me," said Nell, her voice cracking only a little. "He just wants to make sure his family's okay."

Cap kept the Sig pointed at Linsom's chest. Could he take the shot?

"That's good," said Cap. "Mr. Linsom, if you put the gun down right now, I can help you and your family. If you don't, I can't. It's just as plain as that."

It was difficult to tell if Linsom heard him. His hand still shook, the nose of the gun slipping around on Nell's cheek. Nell watched Cap but didn't flinch. Cap could not look at her. If he looked at her, he would make a bad decision.

"Why don't you tell him, Press," said Nell, sounding like a proud parent at the science fair. "Tell my dad how far you and I came in two hours, all the stuff we talked about."

Linsom shook his head quickly.

"You tell him," he whispered.

"Okay," said Nell, swallowing air. "Okay, well, Press came in pretty upset when he woke me up, but then we got to talking. We all want the same thing. . . ."

She trailed off. Cap had to look at her. There were the streams of tears, one from each eye, following the bell shape of her cheekbones. Her eyes remained open and fierce, staring at Cap with a strangely familiar insistence. Don't fuck this up, Dad.

"To feel safe," she said, like the air had been pulled out of her. "Not to *be* safe," she added. "To feel safe."

Cap could not begin to think of how a sixteen-year-old had talked a psychopath out of killing her, but then again, this was Nell. And suddenly the true loss of them all—Ashley Cahill, Sydney McKenna, Kylie Brandt—hit him with the force of all the anthracite stuck underneath the foundation of his house. They would never get to be like Nell. They would never get to thrill and amaze and undo every stereotype of Teenage Girl for their parents. Or they would never get to torture and exhaust them, break curfew and drive drunk. But it didn't matter—both outcomes were the tragedy.

Cap felt the tears load up in his eyes but he didn't dare blink. And then he didn't think he moved but he must have, his elbow must have bent, the Sig must have moved an inch left or right, because Linsom saw it, his face lit up with panic as he took the gun off Nell and fired at Cap, a wild pitch.

Nell screamed; Cap heard the round sail past his ears, cut into the wall behind him, and Linsom came toward him, waving the gun. Cap fired and got his shoulder. Linsom reared back, in shock.

"Dad! Dad!" screamed Nell, out of the chair, kneeling on the floor.

Cap was falling backward; he was losing his grip on the Sig, but why? He looked at his hand and tried to squeeze the grip and the trigger and actually thought, Why can't you hold on to it? And then he felt the side of his head wet and cold and saw the blood, his blood, sprayed onto the old uneven panels of the wooden floor and realized he'd been hit.

Linsom ran, shoved Cap out of the way, against the back wall of the hallway, and then he kept going, slowed and disoriented by the shot in his shoulder, hurtling down the stairs.

Cap struggled to stand, and then Nell came to him and held his face in her hands.

"It's just your ear, Dad—he just got your ear, that's all," she said.

As soon as she said it, Cap felt the blood surge to his ear, the whole thing humming like a harp.

"Come on," she said, putting the Sig firmly into Cap's hand. "We have to stop him."

Nell threaded her arms through his and pulled him up to stand, and once he locked his legs he felt like he could walk, step-by-step, and they headed for the stairs, slow and then fast. Cap heard one siren at first and then another and another, stacked on top of one another like a symphony.

"Are you okay?" Cap said, the words muted in his ears.

"I'm fine," said Nell. "Don't worry."

They watched Linsom stagger out the front door, and Cap almost fell down the last three stairs, but Nell held him up. They made it to the door and then the porch, and they saw Linsom on the lawn. And there was Em, getting out of his car with his gun drawn, aimed at Linsom, as the sirens grew louder and closer.

"Drop your weapon! Hands in the air!" shouted Em, advancing across the lawn.

Linsom didn't react, perhaps didn't hear him. Four cruisers and two unmarked cars came from both the cross streets, lights spinning and sirens shrieking.

"Drop your weapon, hands in the air!" Em yelled again.

Linsom raised his gun, and Em fired. Linsom stumbled back, hand on his side, dropped the gun, fell backward. Cap watched his eyes blinking once, twice. Then stop.

Nell pushed her face into Cap's shirt. He hugged her with one arm and set the Sig on the railing, caught Em's eye and pointed at him. You. Em pointed back, his face filled with a roiling energy. No, you.

Cars and vans kept coming. The street filled with every cop in town, newsmen and their cameras, and one ambulance.

Baby powder.

The overwhelming perfume of it. Vega had no emotional response to baby powder but knew other people did. It reminded them of babies. These same people talked about babies' cheeks and thighs and their respective degrees of thickness, how these were marks of a healthy baby. The smell reminded them of this—fat little bodies rolling around in the artificial dust of baby powder, healthy and not sick. Safe.

The wine cellar was not a big room, five by fifteen, the long wall consisting of a floor-to-ceiling rack for the red next to a refrigerator for the white. Both were empty. The air was moist, a small black humidifier whirring quietly next to the door. Pucks mounted across the ceiling cast faint spotlights.

Then, in the corner, a toddler's bed—Vega recognized the size. She remembered visiting her brother a few years back, seeing her three-year-old niece in one just like it.

But on this one lay Kylie Brandt, too big for it, curled up on top of the blankets in a white nightgown. She was either dead or sleeping.

Vega approached the bed and leaned down. The light was dim, but she saw it—the rise and fall of Kylie's chest.

Her mouth was open half an inch. Her breath was stale, but her skin smelled sweet and floral.

"Kylie," said Vega, not too loudly.

She didn't move or wake up.

"Kylie."

Still she slept. Wasn't it *Sleeping Beauty*, Vega tried to remember, where the whole kingdom falls asleep with her? All of them drugged, frozen where they stood, the bakers kneading dough, the cobblers hammering shoes, everyone. Not Denville, thought Vega. All of us are fucking wide-awake forever.

She placed her hand on Kylie's arm and said once more, "Kylie."

As soon as Vega touched her, she woke up with a sharp intake of air and jumped like a flea to the farthest corner of the bed. Her face looked like it did in the pictures, like the video in the ice cream shop, but was also now transformed into a strange sculpture that was not her, full of fear and drugs and trauma, stoned but aware.

"It's okay," said Vega, regretting it instantly, knowing that was exactly what Press and Lindsay Linsom told her. "Your mom, Jamie, sent me here to get you."

Kylie shook her head.

"She's dead. Mr. Linsom says she's dead. Her and Bailey," said Kylie quickly, her voice raw, the information by now rote.

Vega bit her cheeks, so paralyzed by anger she had to remind herself to speak.

"They lied. Your mom and Bailey are fine. They're waiting for you."

She watched Kylie take this in, her eyes rushing around the room and back to Vega's.

"If you come with me, I'll take you to them," said Vega.

Kylie shook her head violently now and cried, "No, no, no, no!"

She began to sob, but it was different from other sobbing Vega had witnessed, because Kylie made no effort to cover her contorting face as the tears came out, making noises like she was suffocating.

Vega was reticent to touch her again but had to bring her out somehow.

"Kylie, Kylie, listen. Just listen," she said.

Kylie quieted to a long whimper.

"I'm here to protect you. They can't hurt you anymore."

"But Mrs. Linsom said . . ." Kylie began, then stopped.

"What did she say?" said Vega. "Tell me."

"She said I was helping Cole. That he was gonna get Cole if I wasn't here."

Vega stood up straight now.

"He's not going to get Cole. Or you. Or anyone."

"But he has a gun," Kylie cried.

Vega pulled back her jacket.

"So do I."

Kylie stopped crying then and just blinked, a tremor still in her lungs as she breathed in and out.

"Let's go," said Vega.

She backed up to give the girl some room. Kylie straightened out her legs; now Vega could see how ridiculously small the toddler bed was for her. She was almost two sizes too long for it. Then she stood up and wobbled, uneasy on her feet. Vega held her by the shoulders.

"Okay?" she said. "Can you walk?"

Kylie nodded. She was only a few inches shorter than Vega. The white nightgown was too small also, the empire waist across Kylie's chest, the hem above her knees. Vega thought it was probably one of Cole's.

Kylie looked toward the open door, uncertain. Vega went to it, nodded. Kylie came to her, slowly, learning to walk. Together they stepped outside the wine cellar to the foot of the stairs. They both looked up, toward the rectangle of light at the top.

Vega put her arm around Kylie's shoulders but didn't touch her, and they began to walk up, Kylie keeping pace with Vega on each step, arms at her sides. They reached the top of the stairs and were in the kitchen, and Kylie squinted at the light.

"It's nighttime?" she asked.

"Yes," said Vega. "Almost four in the morning."

Vega led her out of the kitchen and toward the front door. She was not planning on involving Mrs. Linsom in their exit.

"Kylie!" Mrs. Linsom called from the living room.

Kylie's whole body jerked when she heard her name. Vega shook her head slowly, mostly to herself.

"Let's go," she said to Kylie.

But Kylie peered around Vega, through the entryway, like someone trying to see how far ahead the traffic accident was. Then she stepped away from Vega, hands still at her sides limply, and moved forward, around the oak table with the full flower arrangement, into the living room.

Do not let the skip run the show, Perry said in her head. You let the skip make any decisions, you are cooked cabbage.

But Kylie wasn't a skip. She was a girl looking to settle up, and for all Vega knew, the next time Kylie and Mrs. Linsom would see each other would be in a courtroom. This might be the last time.

So Vega followed her. Mrs. Linsom was right where Vega had left her, crouched on the floor against the piano. Kylie was walking toward her.

"Kylie," said Mrs. Linsom weakly, her skin a washed-out yellow. "Kylie, I'm sorry you had to go through that. But you did the right thing."

Vega gripped her thumbs in her palms. Her imagination expanded with what she could do to Lindsay Linsom. Tell Kylie to wait in the car. Pick up the glass deer centerpiece and crush Mrs. Linsom's forehead, smash the jaw, crack the delicate bridge of the nose. When her free hand goes to her face to protect it, smash each finger one by one on the piano keys. Then make her play something.

Then Kylie took the last couple of steps so she was right over Mrs. Linsom. She leaned down and screamed.

The sound was so shrill, so harrowing, Vega had to slap her hands over her ears. Mrs. Linsom could cover only one with her free hand, her eyes squeezing shut.

Kylie had an enormous amount of air in her lungs, like she'd been accruing it for the past seven days. Even though time in general was working a strange game on Vega, stretching and shrinking, the scream lasted and lasted.

Her voice turned hoarse, and finally she stopped. Beads of tears had sprouted on her lashes from the release. She stood up straight and backed away. Mrs. Linsom stared at her, stunned.

Kylie turned around to face Vega, her eyes vacant. Vega removed her jacket and held it out to her.

"Come on. It's cold," she said.

Kylie wandered slowly to her, slid the jacket on, the sleeves long on her arms by an inch or two.

"Mommy?"

It was Cole calling from upstairs. They could not see her from where they stood.

"Mommy, what was that?"

Mrs. Linsom leaned as far as she could away from the piano, trying to stretch the cuffs.

"Nothing, sweetie. Go back to bed. Everything's okay," she called in a chirpy singsong.

Vega led Kylie to the entryway. Cole stood at the top of the stairs.

"Kylie?" she said, half-asleep.

Kylie lifted her hand and waved, her face blank.

Cole waved back, the confusion just beginning to cloud her eyes.

Vega put her hand on Kylie's back and guided her to the front door. She turned back to Cole.

"Call 911. Everything's not okay."

Cole started to open her mouth to ask more questions, looking like a little lost tourist, but Kylie was already out the front door, and Vega was right behind.

Then they were out in the air, colder than when Vega had entered the house, flurries still twirling, dissolving on Vega's bare arms. Kylie was in a sort of sleepwalk, legs marching. Her eyes were open; she watched the ground a few feet ahead.

"That's my car," said Vega, when they were close, pressing her key, unlocking the doors.

As they walked, Vega pulled out her phone and texted Jamie: "I have Kylie. She is fine. Be there soon." She skipped over texts and messages from Caplan, Junior, the Bastard.

They opened the doors and got in. Kylie buckled her seat belt without having to be told and stared straight ahead. Alive but dead, Vega thought. It was too soon to tell if she was like Christy Poloñez. She won't be when she sees Jamie. Then she'll wake up, Vega found herself hoping.

Vega started the car and drove out of the subdivision, past the field. She cranked the heat.

"Tell me if you're too hot," she said to Kylie.

Kylie didn't respond. Her hands were in her lap.

Vega didn't need the GPS to find Jamie's parents' house anymore. She recognized the county road, and the U.S. route, and then the side streets. The stores and the liquor distributor, the strip malls and the post office.

"What's your name?" said Kylie.

"Vega."

"Vega?"

"V-E-G-A," said Vega. "It's my last name."

"What's your first name?"

"Alice."

Vega glanced at Kylie, who was thinking about it.

"There's a girl named Alice in my class," she said.

"Yeah," said Vega, thinking it would be good to keep Kylie talking. The more engaged she was now, the less likely it would be for her to reside in the shock state. "It's becoming popular now. When I was a kid, I was the only Alice in my school."

"I'm not the only Kylie in my school. There's three of them. Of us."

"But you're the only Kylie Brandt," said Vega.

Kylie was quiet, looking out the window.

She was unsure of the point she was trying to make to the girl. You're special? Vega thought she would see right through that line of bullshit right away. She thought, after the last seven days, Kylie would see through everything, the world now robbed of virtue and, worse, the potential of virtue. The swell of possibility gone.

They were two blocks from Jamie's parents' house. Vega lingered at a stop sign, and a news van sped by them. Vega switched the hazards on.

"Hey," she said. "Are you listening right now?"

Kylie nodded, still gazing out the window.

"You're going to have a nice life. All this shit that's happened to you is over. It's not going to happen again. Your mom really loves you, and she's a good person. You're going to grow up and have a nice life. Get married and have kids and dogs if you want. Any time you get sore about what happened to you, just think about that. And take this."

Vega leaned to the glove compartment and popped it open, held out a card to Kylie.

Kylie regarded it skeptically and then took it from her.

"That's me," said Vega. "Anyone bother you, or your sister or your mom, send me a note. I will get on a plane and come here and put them in the fucking earth. Sound good?"

Kylie read the card start to finish, then turned to Vega and nodded.

"Good," said Vega.

She turned off the hazards and pulled out. As soon as she turned the corner on Jamie's parents' block, she saw the throng of media, the vans with satellites and full camera crews, the street lit up like it was the middle of the day. Kylie peered through the windshield, nibbled her bottom lip.

"I'm going to park as close as I can, and then we'll walk fast. They all know your name and will ask you questions, but don't talk to them and stay close to me, okay?"

"Okay."

Vega slowed. No one saw them yet. She parked halfway down the block and cut the engine, unbuckled her seat belt.

"You ready?" she said to Kylie.

Kylie nodded.

"Ready."

Vega got out and shut the door on her side, and one reporter, a blond woman in a parka, turned her head and saw them.

"It's them!" she announced, giddy.

Vega went around to Kylie's side and opened her door as the crowd rushed to them.

"Don't worry. I'm here," Vega said to her, but Kylie may or may not have heard because of the noise.

You've seen the rest. You saw the footage running for thirty-six hours straight on CNN, or you were forwarded a YouTube video, or your friend or your mom put a link on Facebook. You watched; you clicked: Vega walks Kylie down the sidewalk with her arm around her, people and cameras and mikes in their faces. Vega tilts her head to whisper in Kylie's ear. Kylie blinks a little at the lights but keeps her eyes ahead. The questions keep coming and are variations on the same: Did he hurt you? Where did they keep you? Were you tortured? Are you okay?

The last is really an afterthought.

Then you've seen the paint-by-numbers courtroom drawings of Lindsay Linsom on the stand, the tearful prison interview in which she describes how she crushed the Valium into glasses of orange juice for Ashley Cahill and Sydney McKenna before smothering them with pillows. And then the bodies were placed in heavy-duty garbage bags and buried in the woods on the Linsoms' property in Hershey. The tabloids dub her "Ice Queen."

You've seen the program *Mind of a Monster*, the story of Preston Linsom's sordid childhood, during which he was likely repeatedly molested by a business associate of his father's.

You've heard the whole story, but it's confusing: how Evan Marsh looked like a movie star and John McKie looked like an old man's dead son, how Lindsay Linsom kidnapped three girls and dressed them up to look like her own daughter—all of them stand-ins for someone else.

You've seen the long-awaited funerals of Ashley Cahill and Sydney McKenna, their parents burying the decomposed remains in small white coffins. You notice the mothers, one young and stunning in the way of a high school homecoming queen, the other old and spectral with white hair and a dowdy black dress.

You've seen the speeches made by Chief Traynor, praising his police, the FBI, the ingenuity of the private investigator team. You've seen him take many questions and answer only a few, saying the investigation is ongoing. We'll let you know when we have further information.

You've seen the profile of Max Caplan and seen his professional comeback celebrated, if for no other reason than his tousled charm.

The only thing you remember about Alice Vega is the image of her in a short-sleeved shirt, holster with gun crossing her back, her face bruised and bandaged as she steers Kylie up the path. Then Jamie Brandt, probably meaning to watch at the window until they come inside but when she sees her daughter can't control herself, bursts through the front door and runs, in a cropped football pajama top and shorts, barefoot. Kylie sees her and runs too, both of them toward each other so fast you think they will collide and knock each other unconscious.

But they don't. They know what to do. Kylie jumps into Jamie's arms, even though she is nearly as tall as her mother, and Jamie is frail but doesn't budge under the weight. You can just barely see Jamie's face, because the cameras aren't allowed on the property; they have to stay at the curb. Her eyes are closed; she is crying. They go inside, and Alice Vega follows.

It is all familiar to you by now.

20

THE DOCTOR WAS A WOMAN, IN HER FIFTIES, HAIR DYED AUBURN with gray roots. She was short and a little overweight and had small padded hands like a baby. Cap watched them while she picked up and put down various tools to examine the stitches on his ear, which the ER doctor had sewn. Nell stood in the corner of the room by the door.

Cap was not in pain; they'd given him acetaminophen with codeine and it was working. He didn't feel his ear, but he was also fighting to keep his neck straight and his eyes open.

"The good news is there's no damage to the ear canal or any of the vasculature of the outer ear," said the doctor, facing him, still holding the otoscope. "Bad news is he shot off part of the helix. This," she said, running her finger along the top curve of her ear. "So you've lost about half an inch off the top. Which, if you like, you can reconstruct surgically after the stitches are removed from the laceration."

"Thanks, Doc," said Cap, hoping the words came out fully formed. "What do you think about me going home? I've been here a long time."

"I have to talk to Dr. Muncy, who did your stitches, and then I'll discharge you. No more than an hour. You have someone to drive you home?" she said, turning to Nell in the corner.

Nell said they would figure it out, and they all said thank you, and the doctor left.

"How you doing, Bug," said Cap.

She came up to him and put her arms around his neck.

"Okay," she whispered into his hair. "They said I should go to an ENT for the ringing."

"Good," said Cap. "We can go together."

"And to a psychiatrist for this."

She stepped back from him and held her arm and hand out straight. Her hand trembled, a miniature diving board.

"We can go together to that too," said Cap.

They stood there for a while, with Nell leaning her head on his, Cap listening to the sound of her breathing. He let his eyes close and pictured a soft foamy tide rolling up on the sand. Sun, seagulls, the whole thing.

"Let's go, Nell."

He opened his eyes, and there was Jules in the doorway. He hadn't seen her in a year or so, Nell traveling back and forth between them unaccompanied. She had let her hair grow long, Cap noticed, and was coloring it too, her natural deep brown almost black. He realized how much Nell looked more and more like her as she grew—the cheeks, the eyes, the dark, expressive eyebrows. Gorgeous elegant creatures, both of them. Brunette giraffes.

"Come on, Nell," she said quietly. "Let's go get some sleep."

Nell pulled away from Cap and looked him in the eyes.

"Let's try a week without physical injury, deal?" she said.

Cap smiled.

"Deal."

He hugged her once more and kissed her hair. She walked toward her mother, and Jules came forward to say something to Cap.

She wore a long wool sweater, jeans and boots, and hadn't slept, eyes heavy, arms tightly crossed in front of her as if to prop herself up.

"Are you okay?" she said.

She wasn't looking at him, staring at his lap.

"Yeah, Jules, I'm fine."

Now she looked at him and pursed her lips, trying not to cry. She stepped closer, up to his face.

"I'm so *so* pissed at you right now," she whispered. "But I'm glad you're okay."

Then she kissed him on the forehead. It was so quick he wasn't sure it had really happened afterward. He saw Nell grinning in the doorway.

"Let's go, Professor," she said to her mother.

Jules turned quickly and went to Nell.

"Text if you need anything, Dad," she said.

"Yeah," said Cap.

Then they were gone. Cap glanced at his phone, which was almost out of juice and overrun with texts and voice mails. He didn't have nearly enough energy to navigate them, so he turned his phone off and leaned back on the pillows. He shut his eyes, and his mind sailed along in drugged exhaustion. Again with the small beach and the soft tide. He couldn't recall ever seeing such a beach—maybe near his parents' in Florida? Except that they had to be Gulf waves; the Atlantic would push you over if you got in past your knees. Still it would be nice to try that water—warm if not clear, lying on your back letting the salt push you up.

Then he had a feeling he wasn't alone. He opened his eyes, and Vega was there now, at the foot of his bed, watching him.

"Are you really there?" he asked, genuinely unsure.

"I think so," she said.

Cap sat up and forced himself to wiggle his big toes and make fists, all the old tricks he used to do on a long shift to keep himself awake.

"How's your ear?" said Vega.

"It's fine," he said. "I mean, my career as an ear model is over, but my hearing's fine."

Vega nodded, the littlest squiggle of a smile on her lips.

"How are you?" he said.

"I'm fine," she said. "I'm here to give you a ride."

"That would be great, thanks," he said.

Her hands were clasped in front of her, one wrapped around two fingers of the other, and it made her look very small and young to him suddenly. He felt like he could finally picture her as a kid. For the past week she had seemed to him one of those people who was born as a thirty-year-old.

"Then I have to get going," she said. "Back to California. I have another job."

"What? That's it?" he said.

He felt short of breath, blood rushing out of his head.

"Traynor and the Feds are going to need us for postmortem, for paperwork," he said quickly.

"I can do it all online," she said.

"Have you told them that?"

"No," she said. "They're busy."

"What about media?"

"I never do media."

Cap swung his legs over the side of the bed and prepared to stand. He wiped his eyes.

"So that's it?" he said again.

She stepped closer to him.

"I'll be back soon," she said. "Dena Macht's father wants to press charges against me. So does this guy I hit in the face with a wrench the other day."

"Then you can't leave," said Cap. "You'll be a skip."

Vega rolled her shoulders.

"I'm not worried about it. They can extradite me if they want. Or send me an invoice, whatever."

Cap pressed his tongue against the roof of his mouth, the thousand and four things he wanted to say to her, foremost among them: Please don't leave; let's have dinner; could I just run two fingers along the line of your hip; we are bound together by what has happened here. Please don't leave.

She came closer to him.

"I'll be back soon," she said quietly.

She wasn't looking at him. He liked to think she couldn't, that it would be too overwhelmingly emotional for her, but really he didn't know. What he did know: he knew she liked to break down service rifles to relax and that she liked tea instead of coffee. Her mother died when she was young, and her mentor died a few years back and that seemed to follow her around. She had a high tolerance for pain and a low tolerance for bullshit. She moved her hands and fingers when she was trying not to assault someone. She was the kind of beautiful that snuck up on you. Once she kissed a man she just met in the woods on a warm spring morning.

"That's it," he said for the last time. "You're gone. Like a traveling circus."

That made her smile, and then something caught her eye against the wall. It was a lunch order that had been delivered to Cap's examination room by mistake. She reached over to it and grabbed the bread roll, the applesauce cup, and the small pack of cookies. She held all three in her hands and looked at them thoughtfully, mouthing numbers.

And then Alice Vega started to juggle the items successfully, her eyes following each one as it ascended, her mouth in an open grin now, and Max Caplan laughed and laughed and wondered just how long she could go without dropping them.

Jamie Brandt had the dream again.

She couldn't see anything—either it was dark or she was blind. She was looking for the girls but they were babies, and she could hear them crying, the two-year-old toddler wail and the quivering scream of a newborn. Then Jamie was on her knees, clawing around in the dirt or sand, looking for them like a set of car keys. She must have dropped them; they must be here.

She woke up in her bed and realized it was she who was screaming, yet she couldn't stop herself.

Bailey came running in and jumped onto the bed. Kylie followed behind her slowly in a trazodone daze, which was the only way she would sleep at all since she got back.

"Mama!" yelled Bailey, holding Jamie's face in her hands. "Mama, stop, wake up."

Jamie stopped.

"Breathe, Mama," said Bailey. "Take deep breaths."

Jamie breathed.

"You just had a bad dream."

Jamie nodded. Bailey's face was like a flashlight in the room. Kylie slipped into bed next to Jamie and was already on her way back to sleep while Bailey spoke the words.

"We're here. We're right here."

ACKNOWLEDGMENTS

There are many people who made it possible for me to write this book and get it out. I am grateful and moved by their belief in my work:

Mark Falkin—you saw something in this story when no one else did and found the perfect home for it in record time. You also tend to keep a cool head when I flip out, which I really appreciate.

Rob Bloom—you have made this book what it is. Your editorial instincts are flawless, your guidance invaluable.

Bill Thomas, Sarah Engelmann, Mark Lee, Lauren Hesse, John Fontana, and all the good folks at Doubleday—thank you for your work, your commitment, your enthusiasm.

Lieutenant Mark Rather—thanks for your patience in answering all my dumbass questions; and thanks to all of the extraordinary women in your house: Jessie, Emily, Lillia, and Mirabelle Rather.

Connie Pelzek and Willie Duldulao; Kay and Kurt Frederick; Paul and Susan Pelzek; Danny, Stephanie, Tyler, and Caleb Pelzek—thank you for your love and support for so many years.

Rebecca Sands Coutts—thanks to you and your family for all the PA intel and support.

Mayhill C. Fowler, Craig Love, Ryan Mensing, Tim Marshall, Laura Kang, Britt Reichborn-Kjennerud, Jon Beck—you guys have never given up on me.

Perry Meisel, Elissa Schappell, and Dave Yoo—thank you for reading my work over the years and encouraging me when I needed it the most.

Argiro Rizopoulou, Keisha Peters, Joshua Pyne—thank you for being my cubemates, having my back, and putting up with my nonsense.

Sandra and Norm Luna—you have read every word I've ever writ-

ACKNOWLEDGMENTS

ten, told me to keep writing when I couldn't lift my head off the ground, insisted that I was good when I tried to tell you otherwise. "Thanks" isn't a big enough word for what I want to say to you, but it's all I have, so I'll say it again and again.

Zach Luna—no one has been more unflaggingly optimistic about my career than you, and for that I can never repay you and can't express my gratitude enough. Thank you for being such a good reader. Thanks also to your gorgeous family: Shelley Kommers, Beau and Cal Luna.

Finally, JP and Florie—I love you more than a sea of Selkies, a galaxy of moons (or space stations), a factory of Wonka Bars, a fleet of invisible jets. Without you I am just a weirdo who can't remember why she enters a room. Every word every day is for you two.